THE LAST GIRL LEFT

OTHER TITLES BY A.M. STRONG AND SONYA SARGENT

The Patterson Blake Series

Never Lie to Me

Sister Where Are You

Is She Really Gone

All the Dead Girls

Never Let Her Go

Dark Road from Sunrise

THE LAST GIRL LEFT

A.M. STRONG
SONYA SARGENT

THOMAS & MERCER

This is a work of fiction. Names, characters, organizations, places, events, and incidents are either products of the author's imagination or are used fictitiously. Otherwise, any resemblance to actual persons, living or dead, is purely coincidental.

Published by Thomas & Mercer, Seattle

www.apub.com

ISBN-13: 9781662518263 (paperback)
ISBN-13: 9781662518270 (digital)

Cover design by Faceout Studio, Spencer Fuller
Cover image: © Mike Hill / Getty Images; © Kindra Clineff / Getty Images; © Cyndi Monaghan / Getty Images; © Skylines / Shutterstock; © Krasovski Dmitri / Shutterstock; © rolfo / Stocksy

Printed in the United States of America

For Tiki and Gidget, who are never far away.
Also for Izzie and Hayden, who remind us that love is unconditional (and afternoon walks are mandatory).

PROLOGUE

Theresa Chamberlain lay in the darkness under her bed and held her breath.

She could hear him moving through the house on the floor below, going from room to room. The screaming had stopped several minutes ago, and for that she was thankful, even though she knew what the sudden silence meant.

Her friends were dead.

She choked back a sob, expelling, along with it, the pent-up air she had been holding captive in her lungs. The rush of breath sounded too loud. She wondered if he could hear it all the way downstairs. But that was crazy. There was no way the young man in the black polo shirt and ripped jeans could have perceived such a brief exhalation. If she was lucky, he had given up. Forgotten about her. Maybe he didn't even remember her. They had all been pretty drunk the night before, and he might not recall if there were three girls or four.

Except he hadn't been drunk when they'd met him the day before at Sunset Cove.

Courtney spotted the young man first, walking along the water's edge, shirt tied around his waist, tanned body glistening in the sun.

"Look at that." She pointed, jumping up. "Hey, over here."

"What are you doing?" Theresa flushed with embarrassment. This was typical of her brash friend: dive in without a thought.

"Getting the party started," Courtney replied with a mischievous grin. She waved her arms above her head, hoping to draw the man's attention. "Hey, shirtless guy. Come over here."

He'd turned, eyebrows raised in surprise, and motioned toward himself. *Me?*

"Yes, you." Courtney had beckoned. "Come here."

"What can I do for you girls?" The man came bounding over, full of confidence.

Three hours later, they were back at the beach-house rental, sitting around the firepit on the deck overlooking the cove and downing light beers, wedges of sour lime pushed into the bottles. By the time he left, promising to come back and see them again, Theresa's head was buzzing, and there was an enormous pile of empties, thanks to the combined efforts of the four friends and the man who said his name was Patrick.

She had stumbled to her upstairs bedroom, flopped down on the mattress, and fallen asleep still wearing the same white bikini she'd worn on the beach that day.

That had been five hours ago.

She thought back, trying to remember if there was anything she should have noticed regarding their newfound friend, a clue that might have alerted them to his true nature. Had he been disappointed when they didn't ask him to stay the night? Was he hoping to sleep with one of them—or all of them?

Patrick's words echoed in her head, his promise to come back again. Well, he'd done that, all right. And now he was skulking through the house, not bothering to be quiet anymore because there was no point. She heard him cross the floor. Heard the refrigerator door open. There was a clink of glass. She recognized the sound. A beer bottle. *Oh God. He's helping himself to a drink.* After everything he'd done to her friends, the way he'd made them scream and beg, he was drinking a beer, calm as could be.

Maybe he really didn't know she was there, listening to his every move. She might actually make it out of this alive. She strained to hear him, hoping he was sated, praying he would leave.

Only he didn't.

Instead, he crossed the living room, passing by the expansive ground-floor bedroom complete with an en suite bathroom—the same bedroom Courtney had called dibs on the day they'd arrived—and started up the stairs.

Theresa's throat tightened. He hadn't forgotten about her. He'd known she was there all along. He also knew he could take his time, let her cower and listen to all the dreadful things he was doing to her friends, because there would be no calls for help. Her cell phone, mere feet away on the three-drawer dresser, was useless. Cassadaga Island had lousy reception, almost nonexistent. She had lost service on the ferry connecting the Maine coast to the low hump of land that sat like a granite sentinel in Callaghan Bay and had bemoaned as much the evening before. Patrick had merely smiled and said that was the way of things. There were too few residents on the island to warrant the expense of a cell tower, especially in the winter, when the tourists and summer residents had all gone home and half the town was shuttered, and that was fine by him. It made for a more relaxed atmosphere, which might be true in most cases, but not when there was a homicidal maniac in the house.

Her heart raced.

He was drawing closer. His footsteps were louder now. He was on the landing. She scooted back as far as she could under the bed, her eyes fixed on the bed skirt. The limp curtain of pastel-blue fabric that hung almost to the floor was her last and only defense.

A door opened, creaking on tired hinges. She recognized it as the one from the bathroom. There was a swoosh as he drew the shower curtain back.

The footsteps started again.

She whimpered, a single tear pushing from the corner of her eye and running down her cheek. There were only three rooms on this floor, not counting the locked walk-in attic-storage area, and he already knew she wasn't hiding in the old clawfoot tub. But which room would he go to next?

She stared into the darkness and listened, expecting to hear his heavy footsteps outside the bedroom door, but the house was silent now.

Where was he?

She didn't dare think he had given up, yet she could not help feeling hopeful. Maybe she would survive this awful night, after all.

And then the bedroom door eased back, spilling a sliver of light from the hallway across the floor that inched under the bed skirt toward her.

Her lungs burned, but she didn't dare breathe. And even though she couldn't see him, she knew Patrick was in the room, relishing her fear—but not for long.

Too soon, she felt him shift, felt the floorboards give. Dust motes floated up, disturbed by the movement. The bed skirt moved. Patrick's face appeared in the gap between the bed frame and the floor. A smile, too innocent for the situation, pushed his cheeks higher.

"Hello, Theresa," he said in a soft voice before reaching an arm into her hiding place. "I saved the best for last."

And then it was her turn to scream.

1

Five Years Later

The session started, like they all did, with the same request.

"Tell me about that night."

Tessa looked down at her hands, fingers twisting the fabric of her T-shirt into a tight knot. She remained silent.

"Please?"

"I'm sorry. I can't. I don't want to think about it. I don't want to remember." If Tessa could have shrunk farther back in her chair, she would have. She wished it would swallow her, save her from this line of questioning.

"And yet you think about it all the time." Dr. Claire Lewiston jiggled her pen between thumb and forefinger so that it tapped against the arm of her chair in a staccato drumbeat.

"I know."

"Then what's the harm in telling me?"

Silence.

"It's been five years." Lewiston clicked the pen closed, placed it on the desk. "And you've been through at least six therapists."

"Because it hasn't helped." Tessa wondered how a person who had never gone through such an ordeal could ever know how she felt, let alone give her the means to find acceptance when she couldn't even help herself. "None of you know how to fix me. I don't know how to fix me."

"Which is why you stopped your sessions for so long."

Tessa looked back up. "I'm only here now because Melissa insisted."

"That's your sister?"

Tessa nodded. "I live with her."

"She obviously cares a great deal for you."

"She asked me to come here, even though I told her it was a waste of time. This is my fourth session, and you don't have any more answers than the others."

"The answers have to come from within you, Theresa."

"I've told you before—don't call me that. It's Tessa now. Tessa Montgomery. Has been for a long time."

"I know."

"So why use my old name? To upset me?"

"Because changing your name isn't the solution. Becoming a different person won't make everything magically better."

"It's not so different. Tessa is derived from Theresa, and I never liked Theresa anyway. Montgomery was my mother's maiden name."

"Okay. Fine. I'll call you Tessa. But I still don't see how that benefits you."

"I thought it would keep the reporters and TV news crews off my back. The first few months after I got out of the hospital, when I lived with my parents, they were snooping around all the time, wanting to interview me. Photograph me. *The woman who survived the Sunset Cove Massacre.* They were relentless. Banging on our door at all hours. There was even this editor from some big-time publisher. He wanted me to write a book about what happened. Some grisly tell-all. Said I could make a lot of money. Can you believe that?"

"Surely all that has died down by now. News cycles move on. People forget."

"I know. By the time I moved in with my sister, the reporters had mostly given up. But the damage was done. I felt so vulnerable. Scared they would track me down again. I thought changing my name would help with that."

"Fair enough. But aside from keeping reporters off your back—reporters who even you admit had already lost interest—has the name change made you feel any better?"

"No," Tessa admitted. The name change had been as much because she didn't want to be *that person* anymore—the girl who couldn't save her friends—as it was about hiding from the external world. She had walled off her old identity, just like her mind had walled off the most painful memories of that night and pushed them deep into her subconscious. But switching identities hadn't changed who she was at the core. Theresa or Tessa, her friends were still dead. "I thought it would, but it hasn't."

"That's because it doesn't matter what name you hide behind. You can't move on until you face what happened." Lewiston sighed. "Consign it to the past and look toward the future."

"I'm not sure I can."

"You have nothing to fear from Patrick Moyer. Not anymore."

There was a moment of silence.

"He still comes to me." Tessa picked at her fingernails. She avoided the doctor's gaze. "At night."

"Patrick Moyer is dead." Lewiston let the statement hang in the air for a few seconds. "You must accept that and let him go."

"And what if I can't?" Tessa looked up. "What if that bastard haunts me forever?"

"That's why you're here. To make sure he doesn't."

Tessa raised her hand, touched the puckered line of skin that ran from below her chin to the top of her right ear. Even now, all this time later, she could feel the knife. His knife. The way it sliced her beauty away. "He made sure I'd never forget him."

"He didn't think you'd be around long enough to think about him at all." Lewiston leaned forward, rested her elbows on her knees, and observed Tessa. "That you survived is a testament to your strength. You need to harness that same resolve now to move forward with your life."

"I only survived because Patrick Moyer made a mistake."

"He'd still be out there if it wasn't for you," Lewiston said. "Think about how many other young women would have died—how much more suffering he would have inflicted—if you hadn't found the will to live. That's something to be proud of."

"I don't feel proud." Tessa looked down at the floor. "I couldn't help the people that mattered."

"Your friends."

Tessa nodded. A whimper escaped her throat. She wiped her eyes with the back of her hand.

"There was nothing you could do for them." Lewiston picked up the pen, scribbled notes on a pad. The ballpoint scratched across the paper's surface.

"I didn't even try." Tessa played with her hair, tugged at the honey-colored strands that fell past her shoulders. Hair that helped cover the ghastly scar.

"You did what any normal person would do."

"I cowered under a bed." Tessa looked up, finally. "I lay there and waited for him to come for me."

Dr. Lewiston settled back in her chair and studied Tessa. For a while, the only sound was the steady tick, tick, tick of the wall clock near the door. When she spoke again, the words carried an air of gravity. "I'm afraid for you, Tessa. I'm afraid that if you don't face these fears soon, you may never defeat them. What happened was horrific, but there comes a time when you have to stand up and say, *I won't let Patrick Moyer dictate the terms of my existence for another hour, not even another minute.* It's your move." Lewiston folded her arms. "Now, why don't you tell me about that night."

Tessa bit her lip. A cold sweat broke across her forehead, as it always did when she remembered. She found it hard to breathe. It was like Patrick Moyer's hands were at her throat all over again. Squeezing. Crushing. After that had come the knife . . .

She jumped up, chair scraping the hardwood floor. "I can't do this. Not today."

"Yes, Tessa, you can."

"No." Tessa backed up. "I have to go."

"You still have twenty minutes left."

"I'm sorry. This is a waste of time." Tessa turned and pulled at the office door. She fumbled with the handle, got it open, and stepped through.

The receptionist glanced up, surprised by Tessa's sudden appearance. She started to ask if everything was all right, but Tessa hurried past, out into the hallway toward the elevators. It wasn't until she was on the street, far from the psychiatrist's office, that Tessa could finally breathe again.

2

Tessa reclined in the bathtub, foamy bubbles lapping around her shoulders. The room was lit by a row of flameless candles on a shelf and a wedge of illumination that spilled past the open door leading to the bedroom. Too much darkness was a bad thing. A gloaming half-light was about as black as it ever got in Tessa's world. Even when she slept, an assortment of night-lights kept the shadows at bay.

She sipped a glass of red wine—her second. It was self-medication, she knew, but it worked. Without it, Patrick Moyer would stay in her head, tormenting her for the rest of the night.

Soft music filtered in from the Echo on her nightstand in the adjacent room. Jazz. Right now, it was John Coltrane.

She settled back into the tub, closed her eyes.

Coltrane reached a crescendo. Lightning-fast arpeggios—vertical harmonies that almost seemed to merge from the saxophone's single notes into complex chords—filled the room. And woven into them, another, more urgent sound. At first, Tessa thought it was part of the track, but then she realized the new sound was coming from elsewhere. A siren.

She opened her eyes and glanced toward the door in time to see a flicker of emergency lights bounce over the walls. A police car or maybe an ambulance passing by on the road outside her bedroom window. The siren grew louder, reached its own crescendo, then started on the downward slide, losing pitch and volume, almost in harmony with the music.

Tessa was overcome by a sense of familiarity. A frisson of déjà vu that overpowered her senses. She tried to think. Tried to give the strange sensation a home on the timeline of her life. And in doing so, she dislodged something buried within her subconscious. A memory that raced to the surface like a speeding train, obliterating the reality of her surroundings and dropping her five years into the past.

◆ ◆ ◆

Blue and red lights dance across a vast nothingness.

People are talking, but she cannot see them. They sound muted and far away. One voice rises above the others. "There's another victim in here. That makes four."

Theresa tries to move. Can't.

Footsteps.

"Holy shit, she's still breathing." The voice is closer now. Right above her. "We have a live one."

More footsteps. Urgent. Getting louder.

Hazy forms cluster around her. It feels like she's watching them from the end of a long tunnel. She tries to talk, but all that comes out is a rasping gurgle.

"She's conscious."

There is a flurry of activity.

"Stay with us, sweetie, okay?"

She does her best, but the darkness is closing in. Everything hurts.

"Vitals fluctuating." The voice sounds panicked. "We're losing her . . . We're losing her."

◆ ◆ ◆

A sudden crash startled Tessa back to the present.

She jolted and almost spilled her wine into the bathtub. Her heart pounded against her ribs. She sat still and listened, ears straining to pick up any aberrant sound, but it had fallen quiet again now. Only the faint music from the Echo drifted in from the bedroom. She wanted to make it stop, but that would require a voice command, which would reveal her presence to an intruder. The hairs on the back of her neck stood up. Just because she couldn't hear anyone didn't mean she was alone.

Tessa gripped the sides of the bathtub and pushed herself up, trying not to splash. She picked up her robe and slipped it on. Pulling it closed, she padded toward the door. A baseball bat leaned against the wall. This was another concession she made for her own peace of mind. Whenever she was at home, the bat was within reach. Her sister, Melissa, with whom she shared the renovated fisherman's cottage in Gloucester, Massachusetts, had told her time and again that she was safe. There was no need to carry it from room to room. Tessa kept it close anyway.

Now she took it and stood at the door, peering through the gap into the bedroom. She could see nothing amiss. The door leading to the rest of the house was still closed and locked. Shortly after moving in, Tessa had installed a swing bar lock—the type used in hotels—to secure her bedroom. The latch was still closed. No one had entered that way. That left the window, which she could not see from her vantage point.

Tessa inched the door open wider. More of the room came into view. She didn't want to leave the safety of the bathroom but knew she had no choice. She couldn't hide in there forever. Besides, hiding hadn't worked out too well last time.

Tessa gripped the bat with both hands and used her foot to nudge the door wide enough to pass through. Then she stepped into the bedroom.

Empty.

The familiarity of her surroundings did little to ease her fears. She glanced toward the bed and the dark space beneath. There was no bed skirt. There would never be a bed skirt ever again. She could not see all the way under. An intruder could conceal themselves there if they were small enough. She gave the bed a wide berth and moved farther into the room. She crossed to the window and checked that it was locked. The curtains were only partly drawn, giving her a narrow view of the world beyond.

A streetlamp burned outside, casting a pool of yellow light upon a parked car. An old woman walked a dog along the sidewalk—a small breed. The woman clutched a poop bag in her hand. As she entered the streetlamp's glow, Tessa saw that the animal was a Yorkie. It trotted next to the woman, stopping occasionally to sniff some interesting patch of ground. The woman glanced toward her and then looked away again before hurrying off with the dog in tow. Tessa drew the curtains closed and turned back toward the bedroom.

She still hadn't discovered the source of the sound. Maybe it hadn't been in the bedroom, after all. Melissa was home, probably watching TV in the living room. Maybe that was where the noise had come from. Or maybe not. There was still one place to look. Under the bed. She had left this until last because it was the place that terrified her the most. Now she steadied her nerves and dropped to her hands and knees. She peered into the scant space between the bed frame and floor. Empty. All she saw were dust bunnies and a single discarded sock that lay just out of reach. Tessa stood and tightened the belt holding her robe closed.

The Echo finished one track and moved on to the next.

In the brief interval between, Tessa heard the faint murmur of the television. Just as she thought, Melissa was watching one of her shows, probably about some well-heeled young couple looking for their perfect house, or maybe renovating the one they already owned. As the music started again, Tessa retreated toward the bathroom. Her grip relaxed on the baseball bat. She reached the door and paused, casting one more furtive glance around the bedroom before stepping inside.

She tugged to loosen the robe's belt—about to set the baseball bat aside and shrug the garment off onto the floor—when she caught a blur of motion from the corner of her eye.

The fear lurched back. There was someone in the room with her, after all. Tessa took a faltering step, almost falling over the bathtub. Then she swung the bat with all her might.

3

Tessa screamed.

The bat missed her attacker and smacked into the shelf above the toilet instead. Flameless candles crashed to the floor.

A shape, small and dark, leaped toward her with a screech of alarm. Tessa stumbled away, trying to avoid the sudden assault. She brought the bat up to swing again, but then she stopped when realization dawned. This was no murderer. It was her sister's cat, Corky. The animal landed on the floor at her feet. He let out an angry hiss, then sauntered away, slipping into the bedroom, where he jumped up onto the bed and watched her warily.

Tessa dropped the bat and slumped against the wall, horrified at what might have been.

"Are you all right in there?" Her sister was banging on the bedroom door and rattling the handle in an attempt to enter. "Tessa, what's going on?"

"Hang on." Tessa went to the door, disengaged the dead bolt, and pulled the swing bar back. When she opened it, the cat jumped down and made his escape, skirting its owner and fleeing into the safety of the corridor leading to the living room.

"What happened?" Melissa pushed past Tessa into the bedroom and stood looking around. Her eyes strayed to the bathroom and the discarded baseball bat. Beyond this, one of the flameless candles lay on its side, the batteries that powered it ejected from the compartment in the candle's base. Her attention settled on Tessa. "What did you do?"

"Don't get mad, okay?"

"What did you do?" Melissa repeated, more forcefully this time.

"The cat must have followed me into the bedroom when I came home from therapy." Tessa was shaking now that the adrenaline was wearing off. "I had no idea."

"And?"

"I heard a noise. Thought someone was in the room with me."

Melissa's gaze shifted back to the bat. "What, so you swung at him with your baseball bat?"

"No." Tessa shook her head. "Well, I mean—not on purpose."

Melissa went to the bathroom and surveyed the damage. The shelf now hung at an angle on the wall. Candles lay scattered across the floor. Only one of them was still flickering. "Jesus, Tessa. You could have hurt Corky."

"I know."

"Or worse, killed him."

Tessa could think of nothing to say. What adequate response was there? She hung her head, unwilling to meet her sister's gaze.

"You'd better clean this mess up."

"I will."

"And get rid of that," Melissa said, nudging the baseball bat with her foot. "I don't want it in the house anymore."

"What?" A twist of panic coiled in her gut. "No. I need the bat. It's the only way I feel safe."

"It's been four years since you moved in here. In all that time, has anything bad happened?"

"No," Tessa admitted.

"And it won't. You don't need the bat anymore. The locks on your door are more than adequate to feel safe."

"Mel, don't make me—"

"I want the bat out of here." Melissa glanced toward the soaking tub and the half-empty glass of wine. "You'd better finish your bath before the water gets cold. I'm going to find Corky and make sure he's okay."

"The cat's fine. I missed." Tessa knew it was the wrong thing to say even as the words came out of her mouth.

"Am I supposed to be grateful about that?"

"I'm sorry, okay?"

"I know." Melissa sighed. She started back through the bedroom. When she reached the door, she looked back. "I'll see you in the morning."

"Okay." Tessa watched her sister go. She resisted the urge to chase after her. Pressing the matter would only make Melissa angrier. Instead, she went to the door and closed it, then pulled the swing latch back across.

She returned to the bathroom but had no desire to get back into the soaking tub. She wasn't in the mood anymore. Worse, she'd upset the one person who had stuck with her since the attack.

Tessa went around the room and picked up the candles, replacing the batteries. None of them appeared permanently damaged. The same could not be said for the shelf, which now hung by only a single screw. She placed the candles on the back of the toilet, picked up the wineglass, and drained its contents in one gulp. In the bedroom, she shrugged out of the bathrobe before putting on her nightgown, then retrieved the baseball bat and leaned it against the nightstand. She climbed into bed and turned off the bedside lamp but left the Echo playing because she found the music soothing. It took an hour to fall asleep, and when she did, Patrick Moyer was waiting, despite the wine, as he so often was.

4

When Tessa came out of her bedroom the next morning, Melissa had already gone to work. That was probably for the best. The events of the night before hung over her like a dark storm cloud.

When she entered the kitchen, Corky was sitting on the counter, swishing his tail back and forth and pawing a set of keys. Left to his own devices, he might eventually push them onto the floor, but at her approach, he jumped down, then disappeared into the living room and ran up the stairs. She didn't see him again for the rest of the day.

Her presence offended even the cat.

When Melissa returned home, Tessa was in her bedroom, sitting cross-legged on the bed with her laptop open in front of her. She closed it and went to the bedroom door, then hesitated. Was Melissa still mad at her? Without a doubt. But that didn't change what needed saying. Gathering her courage, Tessa drew back the swing bolt and stepped into the corridor. She found Melissa at the kitchen table with a pizza box. Corky was rubbing against her ankles, purring contentedly.

When she entered, Melissa looked up. "I stopped at Gianelli's on the way home and got pizza. It has eggplant on it."

"I like eggplant." Tessa could tell her sister was still upset. There was a hardness to her voice. She looked down at the pizza, then back up to Melissa. "I'm sorry."

"You already said that." Melissa put two paper plates on the table.

"I mean it."

"Is the baseball bat gone?"

Tessa didn't reply.

"That's what I thought." Melissa opened the pizza box and put a slice on each plate.

"I'm trying," Tessa said.

"That's just it, sis. You're not trying. You're going through the motions to keep me off your back. To keep Mom and Dad off your back. But your heart isn't in it. You've been a closed book ever since that night. Five years of therapy, and you still can't talk about what happened. You won't even talk about it with me. Instead, you hide in your room and carry that baseball bat around whenever you come out."

"I'm not carrying it now."

"Because you know I'd take it away from you and throw it in the trash."

"Don't be like this." Tessa pulled a chair out and sat down.

"Like what? Disappointed? Frustrated?" Melissa shook her head. "I don't mean to be, but you've been struggling with this—we've been struggling with it together—for such a long time. And if something doesn't change, you're never going to get better and have the life you deserve. It's nothing less than a miracle you're still with us, and I feel lucky every day that I didn't lose my sister and best friend that night. My heart still hurts for the families of your friends who were not so fortunate. I let you move in with me because I knew you couldn't be alone. I gave you the downstairs master because you were afraid of sleeping upstairs. I figured that in time, you would get over your fears. But you haven't. You can't hold a job. You haven't even tried to get one in over a year. You don't have any friends. You don't date. When are you going to stop letting Patrick Moyer ruin your life?"

"Now you sound like Claire." Tessa's therapist had said the same thing the day before in their session. She didn't have an answer then and still didn't now.

"Because she's right." Melissa reached across the table and took Tessa's hand. "I get it. What happened to you was beyond horrendous.

I can't imagine what it must have been like. But *you* aren't dead. Patrick Moyer *is*. He can't hurt you anymore. You need to move past this."

"What if I can't?"

"You don't have a choice," Melissa said. "You've lost five years of your life. You were less than twelve months from graduating college. It was within reach. Instead, you dropped out. I remember how you used to tell everyone you were going to write for the *Times* or maybe the *Post*. You were going to make a difference."

"I still could."

"How? Are you going to finish your education? Get a job? Do anything other than hide in your bedroom?"

Tessa didn't answer.

"I rest my case." Melissa fixed her sister with a glowering stare. "It's time to end this, Tessa. Going after Corky with a baseball bat was the last straw."

"I told you already—it was an accident." The old frustration was seeping back in. She wondered why no one understood her. "I would never hurt Corky."

"Not on purpose," Melissa replied. "I can't do this anymore. I've tried to be understanding. Tried to help you. It's all useless if you won't help yourself. This situation clearly isn't working. I think you should find somewhere else to live."

"What?"

"You heard me."

"You can't be serious." Tessa's throat closed in panic. "Melissa, you know I've—"

"No." Melissa held a hand up. "Don't tell me you're trying, because you aren't. I've been thinking about this all day, and it's best for both of us. You'll never move forward if I keep enabling you."

"Please. Don't make me go." Tessa was close to tears. How could this be happening? "I swear I'll change. I just need more time."

"You've had five years."

"I'll do whatever you want. Go back to therapy. Please, Mel?"

"No. This is for your own good." Melissa's eyes were wet, her voice cracking. "I've made up my mind."

"Fine." Anger supplanted the panic. How had things gotten so bad so fast? How could Melissa abandon her so easily? It felt like a betrayal. Tessa scraped the chair back and stood up.

"What are you doing?"

"I'm going, like you asked me to." Tessa was already halfway out of the kitchen. "I'll be in my room looking for somewhere else to live."

"I didn't mean right this second." Melissa threw her arms in the air, exasperation painted on her face. "Come back here and eat. Let's talk it through."

"I'm not hungry," Tessa lied. The last thing she wanted to do was keep talking. Melissa had made her feelings clear. Tessa swallowed a sob; then she turned and fled back toward her bedroom.

5

Tessa closed the bedroom door and leaned with her back against the frame. She felt strangely numb.

How had it come to this?

Five years ago, when she had left to go on that fateful trip with her friends, the future had been a brightly lit pathway. Finish college with a degree in journalism. Get a great job. Take the world by storm. Except instead, Patrick Moyer had taken *her* by storm. The memory of that night, from the time he dragged her out from under the bed, was still a blank all these years later. At least on a conscious level.

She could remember the rest of the day with crystal clear precision. Going down to the cove and sitting on the empty crescent of beach. Their secret paradise. Being surprised when Patrick Moyer appeared from the woodland trail along the shoreline that led to town and strolled along the water. Courtney calling him over. Drinking beer around the firepit as the sun went down. Waking up to the tortured screams of her friends. But of the abuse Patrick Moyer had inflicted upon her after that, there was nothing. Just a bottomless hole in time.

The therapist had called it dissociative amnesia. She had suppressed the memories of her trauma to protect her sanity.

Only it hadn't worked, because she still heard the dying screams of her friends every night when she closed her eyes . . . still saw Patrick Moyer peering into her hiding place with a leering grin on his face. On an intellectual level, she knew what he had done to her after that, because other people had told her. Doctors. Police. Therapists. Hearing about an event in her life from a third-person perspective when she had no recall of it was unsettling. Even worse was the knowledge that those memories, *those actual memories*, could come back at any time. They were all there, held behind a dam of amnesia. And if that dam broke? This was what she feared the most. It would plunge her into a whole new level of hell. Her head was a bomb, and she didn't know how long the fuse was.

Tessa crossed to the bed and flopped down.

Melissa was right. Despite years of therapy, she had made no progress. Tessa was as damaged today as she had been in the aftermath of Patrick Moyer's brutal assault. The only difference was that her wounds were now internal. If she didn't take meaningful action, Tessa would never be free of Moyer. He would win, even in death. But knowing it and being able to change it were two different things.

She didn't want to live like this. She despised the constant terror. A nightmare with no end.

The problem was that nothing she had done to alleviate her fears worked. Ignoring the situation was impossible. That was the first thing she had tried. Medication didn't help. The drugs just made her feel weird and out of it. Her therapy sessions felt more like weekly scheduled arguments than anything else, mostly because of Tessa's inability to open up. Alcohol dulled the pain, banished Moyer for a few hours, but he always came back, and anyway, it was hardly a long-term solution. Now she stood on the precipice of disaster, on the verge of being kicked out of the one place that made her feel safe.

And maybe that was the problem. She could always retreat to her bedroom, lock the door, and feel secure. Or at least as close to secure as Tessa ever could be. Instead of fighting the fear that writhed within her, Tessa was acquiescing to it. Which was how she'd ended up swinging a baseball bat at Corky. And how she had brought the one person who truly cared about her to want her gone.

This was a wake-up call. Sure, she and Melissa had argued before. But something was different this time. Her sister actually meant it. If she didn't defeat her demons now and find a way to change her trajectory, Tessa would lose everything. That thought scared her almost as much as Patrick Moyer. And she had to do more than merely throw away the baseball bat, which would be a symbolic gesture at best because she would just replace it with something else. A knife. A taser. Heaven forbid—a gun.

But what to do?

Claire had told Tessa she needed to face her demons. *Shine a light into the darkness,* she had said more than once, *and you might be surprised to find there's nothing there to harm you anymore.*

That was what Tessa must now do if she ever wanted to escape the cycle of fear. If she wanted to show Melissa that she could beat this.

Shine that metaphorical light into the darkness.

And she knew there was only one way to do that, even though the thought made her chest tighten.

She pulled her laptop close and opened it, then typed three words into Google.

Cassadaga Island rentals.

6

Melissa was in the living room, watching TV, when Tessa emerged thirty minutes later. Corky was sitting next to her on the sofa, eyes half-closed as Melissa rubbed the cat's neck. This time, at least, the animal didn't bolt from the room at the mere sight of her.

"Hey," Tessa said in as cheery a voice as she could muster.

Melissa pointed the remote at the TV and muted the sound.

"Can we talk?"

"Didn't we already do that?"

"Last time was more of a confrontation than a conversation." Tessa sat down and gathered her thoughts. "You're right. I've been floundering around for years, refusing to face what happened to me. I'm terrified of what lies in my subconscious, held back by that wall of amnesia, and what will happen if it crumbles. But that's not good enough. I realize that now. If I don't do something to face my fears, I'll never get any better." She paused, overcome by a swell of emotion. "I don't want to live this way for the rest of my life, sis. I don't want another incident like last night. It scared the hell out of me. I could have hurt Corky."

"I'm glad you recognize that, but it doesn't change anything."

"Which is why I've done something about it. I got a reprieve last night. Thank heavens Corky has nine lives, otherwise . . ."

"Yeah," Melissa said. "I'm trying not to think about that. Are you ditching the bat?"

"Better. I'm going back."

"What do you mean?" Melissa looked confused. "Going back where?"

"Cassadaga Island."

"You mean, like for a day trip? A weekend?"

"Not quite." Tessa's nerve was failing. This was harder than she had imagined. But she was in too deep to change course now. "The month of November."

There was a moment of stunned silence before Melissa spoke again. "You're kidding, right?"

"No." Tessa couldn't imagine why Melissa thought she would ever kid about the place where her innocence was so brutally stolen. "This isn't some sick joke."

"You want to spend a whole month in the house where a sadistic maniac murdered three of your friends and almost killed you?"

"Claire said I should face my fears. You did too. I can't think of a better way to do it."

"I can't think of a worse way. That isn't what either of us meant. Going back to that island won't fix you. All it will do is leave you more traumatized than ever."

"You told me less than two hours ago that I need to make an effort. Get my shit together. Well, this is me getting my shit together."

"I didn't say it quite like that. You should wait and discuss it with Claire."

"Claire isn't working out. She's no better than any of the others. I'm not going back to her."

"Tessa, this is crazy. Stop and think about it."

"I already did, and I've made up my mind. Besides, I've reserved the house now, and there are no refunds." Tessa hesitated. "I booked the beach house."

"Wait." Melissa stopped petting the cat and leaned forward. "Please tell me you don't mean *the actual* beach house?"

"There wouldn't be much point if I wasn't staying where it happened," Tessa said, ignoring the flurry of apprehension that made her wonder if she really could do it. "I'm trying to face my fears, after all."

"You can face your fears here. That's what therapy is for. Claire would say the same thing. You need to go back to her, Tessa."

"I'm done with therapy. Claire hasn't helped me. She has no clue what I'm going through or how I feel. In almost five years of sessions with who knows how many therapists, nothing has changed. I'm still the same now as I was then."

Melissa rubbed her temples. "This is a bad idea, Tessa. A terrible, awful idea."

"It's either that or I spend the rest of my life cowering in a locked room and having nightmares about Patrick Moyer."

"Okay, let's assume you're right. Why go for so long? A month? That sounds more like torture than therapy. Not to mention how cold it's going to be. What if there's a nor'easter? It's early, but it could happen."

"It'll be fine." Tessa wasn't so sure about that but wasn't going to admit it.

"Or you'll spend four weeks cowering in the corner like a nervous wreck," Melissa said, voicing what they were both thinking.

"If it gets to be too much, I can always leave early. And anyway, I'm doing this as much for you as me. I've been living here far too long. You've never complained, but I realize how hard it's been. You won't even bring your boyfriend home because you don't want him to meet your crazy sister."

"That's not the reason, and you know it. I was being considerate. I figured you wouldn't want a man in the house after what happened."

"I know, and that's my point. This crippling fear isn't just wrecking my life. It's ruining yours too. If this works, you'll be free of me."

"I don't want to be free of you. You're my sister. But I do want you to put this trauma behind you and live your life."

"Which is exactly what I'm trying to do by going back there," Tessa said. "I've made up my mind, so you might as well accept it. And anyway, while I'm gone you can have Josh over here and live a normal life for once."

"I appreciate your concern for me and Josh, but this is too much. I can't condone you going back to that island." Melissa shook her head.

"You're not going. I'm your big sister, and I say no. Mom and Dad will agree with me. You watch."

"That isn't your call."

"Isn't it? How are you paying for this trip? That rental house can't be cheap, even in November."

"I put it on my credit card."

"You mean you put it on *my* credit card."

"You gave it to me."

"To buy groceries and toiletries. Pay your cell phone bill. Not rent the house where you almost died. I'm not paying for a single cent of it. You want to go? Find the money elsewhere."

"Mel—"

"I mean it. How much was this rental, anyway?"

"Twelve fifty a week."

Melissa's eyes flew open wide. "That's five thousand dollars."

"I'll repay every penny. I promise. When I get back from the island, I'll get a job." Tessa had hesitated before booking the house, wavered over the cost, but then she reasoned that it was a small price to pay for a resolution to the issues that had plagued her for five years. She had briefly considered talking to Melissa about it first, but somewhere deep down, she knew what would happen. Her sister would say no and force her to keep on with the useless therapy. So she'd gritted her teeth and paid. How did the expression go? *Better to ask for forgiveness . . .* ? "I'll do whatever it takes."

"No. You'll cancel it right now. I have a mortgage. A car payment. Bills. Real-life issues you wouldn't understand because you've never had to."

"I do understand."

"Really? Then why would you do this to me? I don't have that kind of money laying around, and I sure as hell don't want it on my credit card. Cancel the rental."

Tessa swallowed. She hadn't told Melissa the worst part yet. But there was no choice. "I can't. The booking is nonrefundable. One hundred percent cancellation fee."

"Oh, this just keeps getting worse." Melissa rolled her eyes. "I'm calling the credit card company in the morning and reporting the transaction as fraud; then I'm canceling your card."

"No. Don't do that," Tessa begged, sensing her last chance to heal slipping away. "There's two weeks before I leave. I'll get the money. I swear."

"How?" Melissa stared at her in disbelief. "You can't find five grand in fourteen days. That would be hard for anyone, let alone you."

"I'll find the money. Just don't cancel the card. Give me a chance."

"Okay. I'll call your bluff. You have until next Tuesday. A week. If you don't have the money by then, I'm making that call to the credit card company."

7

Back in her bedroom, Tessa sat on the edge of the bed and reflected upon her situation. *Five thousand dollars.* It was an insurmountable obstacle.

Seven days from now, Melissa would cancel her credit card and report Tessa's booking as fraud. That would end her hope of going back to Cassadaga Island. And maybe that wasn't a bad thing. Could she really have spent an entire month in that murder house all alone? Now she would never know. She would also never know if facing her fears in the place where her ordeal began would set her on the road to recovery. Tessa was back where she started, with no hope of moving past the event that had paralyzed her for the better part of half a decade. And Melissa had not recanted her threat to throw Tessa out.

Tessa buried her head in her hands. The situation had gone from bad to worse with head-spinning rapidity. She could think of no way to salvage her plan or repair the rift that threatened to ruin her relationship with Melissa. Unless . . .

A sudden thought popped into Tessa's head. For years, she had avoided publicity and shunned the media. Over that time, the journalists and TV shows had turned to fresher fields, probably because she refused to interact with them. Now, though, she had an idea.

Tessa went to the desk and rummaged through the drawer until she found what she was looking for—a business card with a name, email address, and phone number on it. The company name and logo were embossed in green lettering above: Olive Publishing Group. It was an imprint of one of the biggest publishers in the world, and the man who had given her the card, Thomas Milner, was one of their editors. He had pursued her with dogged determination for six months after she got out of the hospital, despite Tessa's insistence that she wanted nothing to do with him. Now, he might be her best hope of repaying Melissa before she canceled the credit card.

Assuming he was still with the company.

Tessa went to the bed, where she had left her laptop. She typed his name and details into the web browser, quickly finding a LinkedIn profile. He was still with Olive Publishing, but as a senior editor. Tessa wondered if the phone number on his business card still worked, but it was too late to find out now. Tessa set the card down on her nightstand, propping it against the bedside lamp. Eager as she was, the call would have to wait.

8

Tessa called the number on the Olive Publishing Group business card first thing the next morning. She wondered if the number was Thomas Milner's direct line or even his cell phone, but instead it connected to a receptionist. When she asked for Milner, the woman took her details and asked Tessa to wait before putting her on hold.

Fifteen minutes later, just when she thought no one was ever going to pick up, the hold music ended and was replaced by a baritone male voice who introduced himself as Thomas Milner.

Tessa drew in a quick breath and swallowed hard. She had a hard time talking to men, even if they were hundreds of miles away on the other end of a telephone. But she *had* to do this. For Melissa. For herself. She hoped her nervousness didn't come across in her voice. "My name's Tessa Montgomery. You wanted to work with me on a project several years ago. I'm the sole survivor of a triple murder. My friends and I were renting a beach house on Cassadaga Island in Maine. A man broke in during the night. He killed my friends and left me for dead."

"Ah, yes. My senior editor thought it would be a good fit for our true crime imprint. But I don't recall a Tessa Montgomery."

"That's because I didn't go by Tessa Montgomery back then. My birth name is Theresa Chamberlain."

"Wow. Didn't think I'd ever hear from you again," Milner said, sounding genuinely surprised. "I wanted that book so bad, but you slammed the figurative door in my face. Which begs the question, why are you calling me now, all this time later?"

"Because I'm ready to talk. You want a book? I'll give you one. I'll tell you what it was like that night, listening to my friends scream and die. Whatever you want."

"Just like that?"

"Uh-huh."

Milner was silent on the other end of the line for so long that Tessa wondered if he'd hung up. Then he spoke in a measured voice. "I appreciate the offer, but I needed it five years ago. Sorry."

"What?" Tessa shook her head in disbelief. She fought back an urge to tell the man to go screw himself. "After all the months you hounded me, you're saying no?"

"That's exactly what I'm saying. Timing is everything. Back then, people were interested—the girl who survived the Cassadaga Island Ripper. If we'd put that book out right away and capitalized on the hype, well . . . let's just say it would have made everyone involved a pile of cash. We publish now, we'll be lucky to sell fifty copies. No one cares or remembers."

"I do."

"Great. That's one of the fifty copies sold."

"It took a lot of courage for me to pick up the phone and call you today," Tessa said angrily. "More than you'll ever know. And by the way, I'm not just offering you a retelling of what happened five years ago. I'm offering to write about the demons I'm facing now."

"Look, no offense, but no one wants to read about your therapy sessions."

"I'm not talking about therapy. I'm talking about going back to that island and spending a month living in the house where I almost died."

There was another long pause.

This time, Tessa knew the editor hadn't ended the call.

"You serious about this?"

"I've already booked the house. I'm going in November, regardless."

"That's pretty gutsy. It's also a great angle."

"Does that mean you've changed your mind?"

"You've piqued my interest," Milner said. "Tell you what. Get a proposal over to me and I'll pitch it at the next editorial meeting. If they like the idea, we'll set you up with a ghostwriter and get this thing going."

"No ghostwriter." Tessa had no intention of letting someone else write her story. If she was going back to hell, she wanted to write about it herself. "I'll do it."

"Not going to happen."

"Why not? The book will sell better if the words come straight from me."

"I don't even know if you can write."

"I studied journalism in college."

"That doesn't mean you can write a book."

"I'm writing the book," Tessa said. "That's the offer. Take it or leave it."

Milner sighed. "How about this. The editorial meeting is on Friday. Send me a five-page sample of your writing and the proposal. We'll see where it goes from there."

"Friday? That's the day after tomorrow."

"Hey, you're the one who wants to write this thing. Better get used to deadlines." Tessa heard a door open on Milner's end. There was a muted conversation, which meant he'd cupped a hand over the phone. When he came back on, he said, "I have to go. My nine-thirty appointment is waiting."

"Okay," said Tessa, then realized she'd missed the most important part of the deal. "Wait. We didn't talk about money."

"That's because we don't have a deal yet."

"But I—"

"I really have to go." Milner sounded impatient. "Goodbye, Tessa."

Before she could say anything else, the line went dead.

9

Tessa spent the next two days working on the sample pages and book proposal. At first, none of it was easy, and she scrapped the first three drafts, but eventually, the words flowed. By the time she gathered everything together on Thursday evening and sent it off in an email to Thomas Milner, Tessa was riding high on a wave of hopefulness mixed with more than a dash of trepidation. What if it wasn't good enough? What if the editor hated it? What if the publisher decided to pass? Those and a thousand other what-ifs flashed through her mind in a never-ending carousel of self-doubt.

But she needn't have worried. Her phone rang at four o'clock on Friday afternoon, just when she was beginning to accept that she had blown her chance.

It was Thomas Milner.

She answered on the second ring.

"Tessa. Sorry for the late call. You must've been worrying that I'd forgotten about you."

You have no idea, Tessa thought. She realized she was shaking and took a long, measured breath. "Did they like the proposal? The people in your meeting?"

"They loved it. Even better, my boss loved it. Called it immediate. Started throwing around words like *visceral.* The victim, paralyzed by fear, faces her demons at the scene of the crime. People will lap it up. You get this right and we'll have a bestseller on our hands."

"Wow. You really think so?"

"I wouldn't say it if I didn't believe it."

"That's fantastic. Do you have a contract for me to sign?" *And a check,* Tessa thought. That was the important thing. Money.

"Whoa. Slow down. There are conditions."

"What conditions? I already told you I have to write the book. I don't want somebody else doing it."

"I agree. Your writing was passable. Not great, but good enough. As long as the rest of the manuscript lives up to that standard, our editorial team will take it to the next level, and we'll all come away from this deal with smiles on our faces. But we want to see fresh pages every few days, at least at first. If things get off track, we'll need to correct course."

"I won't get off track."

"With all due respect, we don't know that. You're an unknown quantity, and we're taking a huge gamble. Which is why we want to keep a tight rein. Is that acceptable?"

"Yes."

"Also, the first draft needs to be written at the beach house. Nowhere else. That's what you pitched, and that's what we want. It's a marketing slam dunk. There's a specific clause in the contract stipulating as much. Can you handle that?"

"Yes." Tessa wasn't sure if he meant the pace of writing or an entire month at the beach house. Either way, she had no intention of scuttling the deal now. "I can handle it."

"Excellent. There's one more thing. Your compensation. I discussed a suitable advance with my editorial director, and he agreed to my number. I think you'll like it."

"How much?" This was it. The moment she would find out if she could pay her sister back—if she was really going to Cassadaga Island.

Milner paused, as if milking the moment. "Sixty-five thousand."

"Seriously?" Tessa almost collapsed with shock. She hadn't even dreamed about such a huge amount. It was incredible. "That's so much money."

"Which means you'll be incentivized to do a good job, and we'll be incentivized to make sure the book sells." Milner took a breath. "You also need to understand that we're buying more than a manuscript. We're paying for exclusive access to your story. That's why the advance is so much. You can't talk to anyone else. Give any interviews. Only us. That goes for TV and movie studios too. They want a slice of the pie, they come to me. Do you understand?"

"Yes." Tessa didn't even hesitate.

"Now, you won't get all the money at once, of course. We'll pay thirty-five percent when you sign the contract, another thirty percent when the final manuscript is accepted, and the rest on publication. I'll send a contract to your email within the hour. Read it. Make sure you understand what you're signing. If you have any questions, reach out. There's also a direct-deposit form attached. Once I get the signed contract back, we'll transfer the first advance payment into your bank account."

"I don't know what to say." She did some quick arithmetic in her head. More than $20,000. And that was just the first payment.

"I'll take a thank-you. How about that?"

"Of course." Tessa couldn't help but grin. "Thank you."

"You're welcome." Milner said his goodbyes and hung up.

Tessa put the phone down and lay back on her bed. She had done it. Found a way to pay her sister back every penny. Even better, she would have more than enough to set herself up for the future. It was beyond anything she could have hoped. A surge of excitement welled inside her. She was doing this. Taking back her life. Going back to Cassadaga Island. Until now, it hadn't felt truly real. And then that thought sank in, and the excitement morphed into dread.

She was going back to Cassadaga Island.

10

The weekend practically crawled by. Tessa didn't want to tell her sister about the book deal and associated advance until the money was actually in her bank account, but keeping the secret was almost more than she could stand. By the time Monday rolled around, she was climbing the walls. But when she checked her account, the deposit was there: $22,750 that had the potential to change her life.

The first thing she did was write a check for $5,000 payable to her sister. In the memo field, she wrote, *Told you!* before deciding it might be taken the wrong way and adding a smiley face.

Yet it didn't feel like enough. Tessa wanted to do something else for her sister, who had let her live in the downstairs bedroom for years and only pay rent sporadically on the few occasions that she held a job for more than a few weeks. Now she had the money to show her gratitude.

After Melissa left for work, Tessa went to the drawer in the kitchen where her sister kept the bills. She rummaged through it, pulling paperwork and receipts out until she found what she was looking for. The statement for her sister's car loan.

Melissa still owed $11,000 on the two-year-old VW she had bought six months earlier when her old car gave up the ghost. It was a lot of money, but nothing compared to her sister's generosity. It took less than fifteen minutes to make a phone call and pay off the balance. Then she found a Sharpie and wrote a single word in large black lettering across the statement: *Paid.* Next, she went to the grocery store and bought a bunch of flowers, which she arranged in a vase and set on the kitchen table, then propped the statement and check against it.

When Melissa returned home at six o'clock, Tessa hurried into the kitchen to find her looking at the flowers with a puzzled expression on her face. She picked up the check. "Five thousand dollars?"

"Told you I'd pay it back."

"And what's this?" Melissa set the check down and unfolded the loan statement, her eyes widening when she saw what Tessa had written on it.

"I wanted to thank you for all you've done for me," Tessa said before Melissa could say anything else, "so I paid off your car."

"Is this a joke?" Melissa lowered the statement. "You don't have enough money to pay me back for the beach-house rental, let alone pay off my car."

"I do now." Tessa pulled a chair out and sat down.

"How?"

"I earned it. Or at least, I will."

"What's going on?" Melissa's eyes glinted with concern. "You haven't left the house since your therapy session. How could you possibly have earned so much money?"

"I agreed to write a book about what happened to me. I've already signed the deal."

"What? Who with?" Now it was Melissa's turn to sit down.

"Olive Publishing. I called one of their editors and ran the idea past him. He wanted me to do the book five years ago, but I said no. I found his number and told him I changed my mind."

"And he just handed you a pile of cash on the promise you would write a book."

"Pretty much. It's an advance."

"How much was this advance?" Melissa looked dazed.

"Sixty-five thousand. But they only paid thirty-five percent up front. I don't get the rest until the book is done."

"Holy cow. That's a lot of money. A lot of responsibility. Are you sure you're up to this?"

"Please don't make this hard." Tessa didn't want to get into another argument with her sister, and regardless of what Melissa said, the deal was already done, and she had now spent more than two-thirds of the preliminary advance. There was no going back. "I can handle it."

Melissa was silent for a moment; then she nodded. "Great. Then you can cancel this harebrained trip of yours now that you've found another way to work through your trauma."

"No. I already told you . . . the beach house is nonrefundable," Tessa said. "I can't cancel, regardless. The book is about going back to Cassadaga Island. That was the only way the publisher would agree to it."

"Crap." The edge was back in Melissa's voice. "You should have talked to me before you signed anything."

Tessa reached across the table and gripped her sister's hand. Gave it a reassuring squeeze. "I'm an adult. I can make my own decisions."

Melissa appeared to think about this for a few moments. "You're right. I'm sorry. It must've taken a lot of guts to make that call."

"It wasn't easy."

"Just answer me one question: Is this what you really want to do?"

"Yes. You're always saying I've done nothing with my life since Patrick Moyer, and you're right. I've let what happened eat me up inside. I'm frozen in a never-ending spiral of misery, and I'm sick of it. This is my way out. I can face my fears and do something productive at the same time. The editor said the book could be a bestseller. If that's true, I won't have to rely on you anymore."

"I don't mind you relying on me. I'm your big sister. That's what I'm here for." Melissa glanced back down at the statement. "You really paid it off? The entire loan?"

"Yep. All of it. The car is yours."

"Tessa, it's too much."

"No. It's nowhere near enough." Tessa grinned. She felt better than she had in months. Years, even. "Besides, it's already done."

Melissa looked down at the check. "I never thought in a million years you would actually come through."

"I know. I wasn't so sure myself."

"But you did," Melissa said. "Wow. This is going to take time to process. I'm not used to you being so independent."

"I'd hardly call myself independent. Every time I think about going back to the island, I feel like throwing up. But I'm excited too. It's like, for the first time, I can see the rest of my life ahead of me instead of constantly looking backward. This book is a good thing. I want you to know that."

"I do know." Melissa stood and hugged Tessa. "And I'll be the first in line to buy it."

11

Tessa departed before dawn on a misty Tuesday morning the following week. She left Gloucester and drove to Route 1, then followed it up through Newburyport and over the border into Maine. At Old Orchard Beach, she stopped for a quick breakfast at a café overlooking Saco Bay, then continued on through Portland and up the coast past Boothbay before arriving at the ferry terminal, which was really nothing more than a drive-up dock, in plenty of time to catch the noon crossing. Before boarding the ferry, which also doubled as the mail boat, she checked her phone one last time to discover a text message from Melissa.

Be safe, sis. Don't stay a minute longer than necessary.

Missing you already.

Hugs, Mel

Tessa fired off a quick reply, then turned her attention back to the ferry. There were only three cars ahead of her waiting to board. In the summer, it would be ten times as many, and that was with the ferry running twice a day. Some of them would be tourists heading to the small town of Seaview Point to stroll the art galleries and eat fresh-off-the-boat lobster rolls. Others would stay awhile, especially on hot week-ends when the Massholes—as the locals referred to the inhabitants of their neighboring state—drove up the coast in search of relief from the city. The rest would be summer residents coming and going from their second homes. Now, though, Tessa's car sat apart from the few other vehicles on the ferry, which was actually nothing more than a big floating barge with a wheelhouse at one end and a couple of metal ramps.

Tessa exited her vehicle as the crew untied the mooring lines and lifted the ramp; then she stood at the rail and watched the shore recede as the ferry made its way out into Callaghan Bay. Away from land, a chilly breeze whipped up that tugged her hair and wormed its way beneath the folds of her coat. She shivered and hugged herself for warmth. The last time she'd made this crossing, it was the height of summer, and her friends were still alive. She remembered it as if it had happened only yesterday. Courtney, always the flirt, found a group of frat boys from UMass, and they'd spent the forty-five minutes between the mainland and Cassadaga Island joking and laughing. The two groups exchanged numbers before parting ways, not yet aware that their phones would be useless on the island. If the phones had worked, maybe her three friends would still be alive because they would have spent that day with the guys from UMass instead of bringing a killer back to their house. Patrick Moyer would have kept going and perhaps unleashed his twisted urges on some other unfortunate group of young women while Tessa and her friends would have gone about their lives without ever knowing how close they had come to an encounter with true evil.

That wasn't what happened.

So now Tessa stood on the ferry's frigid deck alone and contemplated a return to the place where her life had changed forever. She wiped a tear from her eye and looked out over the heaving water.

Above her, a gull circled, riding a thermal as it flew in ever-widening spirals, perhaps hoping the boat's wake would stir up some tasty morsel. The island sat like a crouching beast near the horizon, the low hump of land dark and dreary beneath scudding gray clouds. Tessa had the strange feeling it was waiting for her, anticipating the return of a soul it never meant to let escape.

"Breathtaking, isn't it?" a voice said over her shoulder.

Tessa turned to see a woman in her fifties approaching the rail. "I was thinking more like bleak."

The woman laughed. "It presents better in the summer, that's for sure." She leaned on the railing next to Tessa. "I must say, we don't get many out-of-state visitors to the island at this time of year."

"How do you know I'm—"

"Massachusetts plates. I saw you drive onto the ferry."

"Ah." Tessa stiffened. Was this woman watching her? Did she recognize her from back then? She had to know. "Do you live on the island?"

"Sort of. Summer place. Although I've rented it out the last few years. I'm heading over to close down and winterize. Don't want any burst pipes when the temperatures plummet. I should have done it a month ago after the last renter left, but things have been hectic . . . I'm Cindy, by the way."

"Tessa." It didn't sound like the woman recognized her. She relaxed.

"It's been nice chatting with you, Tessa," Cindy said, glancing toward the front of the boat. "A couple more minutes and we'll be there."

As if on cue, a shift in the boat's engine tone reverberated through the deck. Tessa followed Cindy's gaze. The ferry dock was in sight now and, surrounding it, the small town of Seaview Point.

Shingle-clad houses with wraparound front porches rose with the swell of land behind the waterfront. Lobster boats and pleasure craft bobbed in a fishing harbor surrounded by dockside warehouses built up on stilts over the water or sitting on massive blocks of granite, cut and placed one atop the other to create a long seawall. The thin ribbon of Seaview Point's Main Street was visible, lined with local art galleries, a pair of quaint hotels with views of the bay, and summer eateries that would surely be closed for the season by now.

"Guess I'd better go back to my car," Tessa said, happy for an excuse to escape.

Cindy nodded. "Maybe we'll run into each other again."

"Maybe," Tessa agreed as the dark spit of land that was Cassadaga Island loomed large ahead of them. A shiver ran up her spine. For better or worse, she was back in the place where her nightmare had begun.

12

It took another fifteen minutes for the ferry to dock. Tessa gripped the steering wheel and watched the activity on deck with a mixture of pride that she hadn't lost her nerve and stayed in Gloucester and apprehension about what waited for her on the island.

She saw Cindy still standing at the rail. The woman stared out over the ocean for a few minutes more, then wandered toward the front of the boat and joined a small gaggle of passengers waiting near the ramp to disembark on foot.

A pair of crew members lowered the boarding ramp and secured the ferry. The cars ahead of Tessa inched forward. She started her engine and followed, exiting the boat.

The foot passengers were gone by the time Tessa drove off the pier, but when she turned onto Main Street, she saw Cindy walking at a brisk pace with a backpack slung over one shoulder and a fabric grocery bag over the other. Her head was bowed against the biting wind that whipped off the water.

A brief moment of indecision enveloped Tessa. Should she stop and offer the woman a ride? It was the polite thing to do, but Tessa was in no mood for more idle conversation. Her arrival on the island had brought with it a sense of foreboding that sat like a lead weight in her stomach. She just wanted to reach the rental house and get that first glimpse of the place where she nearly died over and done with—because she dreaded that moment more than anything. And then there was the ever-present baseline anxiety. Her new normal for the last five years. Tessa was uncomfortable with strangers at the best of times, which this was most certainly not.

But she had returned to the island to face her fears . . . all of them. And besides, Cindy might be a good resource for the book. As a part-time resident, she obviously knew the island.

Tessa made up her mind. She eased to the side of the road ten feet ahead of the woman and lowered the passenger window.

"Can I give you a ride?" she asked as Cindy drew level with the car.

"Oh. Thank you. That would be wonderful." Cindy pulled the door open and climbed in. She put the bags on the floor between her feet and pulled the seat belt across her chest, clicking it. "You're a lifesaver. I don't usually mind walking, but that wind is brutal today."

"Where can I take you?" Tessa asked as she started forward again, hoping it would be close by.

"Sunset Cove. It's about as far as you can drive—a couple of miles outside of town."

Tessa's heart sank. "I know where it is. I'm renting a cottage there."

"Oh. That must be the Frasier property. It's the only other home overlooking the cove." A troubled look flashed across Cindy's face; then it was gone. "You must really like your solitude. That end of the island is pretty isolated."

"Not too isolated, apparently." Tessa hadn't noticed any nearby houses the last time she was on the island. Not that she had been paying any attention.

Cindy chuckled. "You needn't worry. This isn't the city. Our houses are a good distance apart."

"Right." Tessa was curious. "You live so far out of town. How come you didn't bring a car?"

"I prefer not to drive on the island, especially at this time of year. When that fog rolls in off the ocean . . . well, let's just say that pea soup has nothing on it, and my eyesight isn't as good as it used to be."

"So you were going to walk there?"

Cindy nodded. "I don't mind. Keeps me fit."

"That must be inconvenient when you need something in town."

"Not really. I keep a bicycle at the house, and the young man who works at the grocery store is more than happy to deliver if I don't feel like making the trip." Cindy fell silent for a moment. "If you don't mind me asking, why did you book the Frasier place?"

Tessa kept her gaze fixed on the road ahead and tried to sound casual. "No particular reason. It was available for the month."

"That long?" There was another pregnant pause. Cindy looked like she wanted to impart some piece of dire knowledge, no doubt regarding the history of Tessa's rental house, but then her face softened. "Well, I'm sure you'll find the island very peaceful."

"I hope so." They had left Seaview Point behind and were now traversing a road surrounded by woodland that offered brief glimpses of the ocean whenever it meandered close to one of the many coves and inlets dotting the rocky shoreline.

Here and there, they passed homes sitting on wooded lots overlooking the ocean, until finally, as they came around a bend, Cindy spoke again. "Sunset Cove is dead ahead. I'm on the left after the next curve."

Tessa couldn't have been more relieved.

She pulled off the road in front of a two-story Cape-style home with two dormers jutting from the second floor's sloping roofline that overlooked a sweeping, rugged cove. Farther away, beyond a stand of birch trees, stood another dwelling.

After Cindy thanked her and climbed out from the car, Tessa sat there awhile, peering through the windshield, past the trees, at a house she never thought she would see again but that lived on in her nightmares. The house where Patrick Moyer had torn away her innocence in a frenzied bloodlust.

13

The caretaker was already waiting when Tessa pulled up in front of the house. Since the owners didn't live locally, they employed a woman from town to look after the place in their absence. Tessa parked next to an older-model Jeep Cherokee with fat tires and killed the engine.

"You must be the brave person who thought a vacation in November was a good idea," the woman said cheerfully when Tessa opened her car door and got out.

"That would be me," Tessa replied, approaching the house.

"And staying a whole month too. I don't think we've ever had anyone rent all the way into December before. We're normally shut down and winterized by now." She waited for Tessa to join her on the front porch and then held out a hand sheathed in a fingerless red mitten. "I'm Lillian."

"Tessa."

"Pleased to meet you, Tessa." Lillian was in her sixties, with a wild tangle of graying hair and the hardy complexion of a person who lived in a place that spent half the year enduring frigid temperatures and gale-force winds. "Would you like help bringing your bags inside?"

"It's fine. I only have one bag and my laptop, and I'll bring them in later." Tessa wondered if Lillian had been waiting in this same spot the last time she was here. The woman didn't look familiar, but then again, it was so long ago, and Tessa had been distracted back then by thoughts of summer sun, beer, and adventures with her friends.

Lillian didn't appear to recognize Tessa either. "Let's get you inside, shall we? It's a mite nippy out here. And that windchill . . ." She typed a code into a keypad on the door and opened it. "We don't use keys anymore. The owners installed this electronic thingy a few years ago. There's another one just like it on the back door in the kitchen. I wasn't so sure about it at first, but I have to admit, it's made my life easier. One less key to carry around. I wish all the people I watch homes for had this."

"How many homes do you manage?" Tessa asked, following the caretaker inside.

"In the summer, I manage twelve short-term rentals. In the winter, when the seasonal residents leave, I caretake upwards of fifty. More than half the island are summer residents at this point."

"Wow." Tessa looked around, uneasy. They were standing in an open-plan living and dining room combo with a kitchen beyond. On the far side of the house, a short corridor led to three downstairs bedrooms, including the master within which a set of sliding doors led directly to the rear deck. This was where Patrick Moyer had entered when he returned. Either they'd forgotten to lock it after their evening of drinking, or he simply busted the door open. It was hardly Fort Knox. To their right, a set of stairs climbed to an open landing and more rooms beyond, including the bedroom Tessa had stayed in five years ago. It all looked the same, yet different. She wondered if the owners had redecorated after the gruesome slayings.

Lillian typed a code into a keypad on the wall. There were two short beeps, and a green light came on. "This is the alarm system. It's easy to operate. Just type in the code and hit hash to arm or disarm it. You have one minute once you enter the home. If you're inside the house and want added security, use Home Mode. Press the button with the home symbol and enter the code. That will arm the window and door sensors to alert you if anyone tries to enter, but not the interior motion sensors." She pointed to a button at the bottom of the box. "Remember to shut off Home Mode or put the alarm system on standby before you open any doors or windows."

"I will."

"The door and alarm code are the same. 1-0-6-5-4-7. It's easier that way. Less to remember."

Tessa made a note of the code in her phone. She was glad there was an alarm system. Maybe if it had been there the last time she was in this house, her friends would not be dead.

"Are you okay, my dear?" Lillian asked.

"Yes. I'm fine." Tessa forced a smile. "It's been a long drive up from Massachusetts, that's all."

"I won't take much more of your time, then. The kitchen has everything you'll need. One of those fancy coffee makers that does cappuccino and latte. Toaster oven. Air fryer. There's even a bread maker if you feel so inclined."

Tessa found that strangely comforting. Her sister made bread all the time back in Gloucester. The heavenly scent of bread baking might ease her trepidation, help her feel less alone.

Lillian pointed to a stack of flyers and restaurant menus on a narrow table next to the front door. "There are only a handful of restaurants in town, and most of them are closed already, but the Harbor Diner stays open year-round, and Acadia Pizza is open Friday and Saturday evenings until nine. If you're looking for activities while you're on the island, take a look through these. There are fishing charters, whale-watching trips, and there's a local history museum. It's out of season, so I can't guarantee what will be running, but you never know. We also have the Halloween Ghost Tram. It's a ninety-minute tour, if you're into that sort of stuff. The tour runs until at least mid-November. It's a hoot. We've got a lot of spirits on the island, one way or another."

"I'll keep that in mind," Tessa said politely, even though she had no intention of going on such a tour.

"You should. This house is the last stop." Lillian turned and pointed to a framed newspaper hanging above the table. The headline screamed "Tourists Slain in Horrific Mass Killing." A smaller subhead underneath read "Statewide Manhunt Underway for Unknown Killer." "Those killings took place right here. Four young women, college students on vacation, brutally murdered. Our very own Chief White caught the killer, a local fisherman by the name of Patrick Moyer. Shot him dead at his cottage on the other side of town. Ever since, there have been tales of weird stuff happening here. Items moved of their own accord. Strange sounds in the middle of the night. Ghostly cries for help. Some guests have even claimed to see the tortured spirits of the four murder victims, still trapped in the place where they died."

"Three."

"I beg your pardon?"

"Three people were killed, not four. One of them survived."

"Oh, I don't think so," Lillian replied with a shake of her head. "Are you sure?"

"I'm absolutely sure."

"Well, whatever. Either way, it was a nasty business. The owners of this house couldn't rent it for love or money after those murders. They even tried to sell the place at one point, but no one would pay what they were asking, even after they slashed the price, pardon the pun. In the end, they came up with the idea of renting the place out to folks like you."

"I'm sorry . . . like me?"

"Murder junkies. Ghost hunters. People obsessed with soaking up the atmosphere of dark and dangerous places. They've been running ads on true crime and paranormal websites and in magazines ever since. If it weren't for the morbid curiosity of those like yourself, the house would be abandoned by now, I'm sure."

"I'm not one of *those* people," Tessa said, horrified. "I didn't come here out of some sick obsession."

"Really? I just assumed—"

"You assumed wrong." Tessa didn't bother hiding her displeasure. "If you don't mind, I'd really like to settle in now. Unless there's anything else I should know."

"Well now, I don't believe that there is." The caretaker looked uncomfortable. "My address and phone number are on a dry-erase board on the fridge along with any other emergency numbers you might need. Police department—which is pretty much just Chief White at this point. Water company. Electric. There's a phone on the kitchen wall next to the refrigerator, but I doubt you'll need it. Don't know why the owners bother to keep it connected. Even I've ditched my landline at this point. My cell phone is so much easier."

"There's cell service on the island now?" Tessa asked, surprised.

"Oh yes." Lillian nodded. "There's been a cell tower for a couple of years. It's a godsend. Before that, we were cut off whenever there was even the smallest winter storm. Internet would go down too."

Tessa took her phone out and checked it. Four bars of service. Her anxiety dropped. "I'm so relieved. I didn't think my phone would work out here."

"Wonders of modern technology," Lillian said. "Speaking of the internet, the username and password are on the dry-erase board too, along with the door and alarm codes in case you forget. I change both codes between bookings so no one else will have access."

"Got it."

"All right, then," Lillian said. "Don't forget about the alarm system. If you use it, remember to type the code in when you come home. Otherwise, it'll blast your ears off."

"I will."

"Okey dokey." Lillian nodded, then turned and descended the veranda steps. "I'll get out of your hair."

Tessa watched her climb into the Jeep and drive off. Once Lillian was out of sight, she went straight to the newspaper hanging in its frame and took it down, then placed it on the floor, leaning inward against the wall so she wouldn't have to look at that dreadful headline every time she came and went. She turned and surveyed her surroundings, and for a moment, she actually *could* imagine that the ghosts of her friends were there with her, watching from the shadows.

14

Tessa brought her travel bag and computer in from the car and dropped them near the foot of the stairs. She went around the downstairs, consumed by memories of the past. There was a strange familiarity about the house, as if she knew it from another life. In the master bedroom, she stood rigid, overcome with a sense of guilt. This was where Courtney died, murdered by Patrick Moyer while she cowered upstairs and did nothing.

Tessa stared at the bed. Had the homeowners changed the furniture since the slayings, or was this the mattress her friend had died on? But it couldn't be. That bed would have been ruined. Tessa hadn't seen the aftermath of Moyer's spree—had avoided looking at the crime scene photos that some insensitive asshole had posted on the web—but she knew there must have been a lot of blood. You didn't stab a person eight times without making a mess. This was not the same furniture for sure, which made her feel better. Even so, she cried. Wept until all the emotion had drained away, then she went to the sliding doors that led out onto the deck. She opened them and stepped out, thankful for the fresh air.

The house stood two miles from town on a rise of land that gave it commanding views across Sunset Cove. A set of wooden steps led from the deck down to a paved area with a circular stone firepit and four brightly colored Adirondack chairs surrounded by jagged granite outcrops. Beyond this was another set of wooden steps to a pebble-strewn beach hemmed in on three sides by balsam fir and white pine interspersed with huge boulders. To her left, visible through the trees, was the only other house in the cove. Cindy's house.

It all looked the same—and also different. Five years ago, Madison had squealed with delight when they slid the patio doors back and stepped out into the bright sunshine on that deck with the firepit and the beach beyond. Saw those Adirondack chairs.

◆ ◆ ◆

"I declare this place our personal paradise. It's perfect!" Madison flings her arms wide and spins in a circle before she collapses into a sea-blue Adirondack chair and props her feet up on the firepit. Theresa and Shelby can't wait to join her. Theresa picks a lime-green chair because green is her favorite color.

"I'm surprised you decided to come on this trip. I was sure you'd beg off this year," Shelby says to Madison.

Madison tilts her head and furrows her brow. "Why are you surprised? We always vacation together."

"Well . . . I just thought that you'd be spending the summer with Adam. You know, since you guys are all kinds of serious." Shelby looks sheepish, like she regrets bringing up her friend's relationship.

Theresa understands why. Madison's newfound romance has clearly put a wedge between the besties. They've been growing apart for months.

When Theresa met Madison and Shelby, they were roommates and best friends. Everywhere Madison went, Shelby was by her side. Whether it was the lunchroom or an off-campus party, it didn't matter—the girls were inseparable. When Madison started dating Neil, it all changed. She started spending all her free time with him. *He had a single dorm room, and it wasn't long before she started spending the night, leaving Shelby feeling left out.*

"Of course I wouldn't miss this, silly. I love our girl time. I'll be seeing enough of Neil come fall. I think he can last a week without me." Madison

reaches out and takes Shelby's hand, squeezing it. The friends smile at each other, and the tense moment passes.

Theresa thinks this is exactly what her friends need to reconnect. A guy-free week in the sun.

◆ ◆ ◆

Tessa pulled her gaze away from the green chair and looked out over the ocean.

Other islands lay close to the horizon, strips of black land that sat low in the dull-gray water. Someone had pulled a rowboat up onto the beach above the tide line and turned it upside down, leaving the weathered planks of its outer hull exposed to the elements. She wondered if it belonged to the owners of the house, or if it was just some relic that had washed ashore during one of the many storms that ravaged the island during winter.

Somewhere out in the bay, the low and doleful moan of a foghorn carried on the stirring breeze, even though she could see no fog.

Tessa shuddered and stepped back inside, locked the slider, then returned to the front of the house. At the bottom of the stairs, she stood and looked up with trepidation. Exploring the downstairs had been dreadful. Seeing where her friends had died, knowing she was right there, made her feel sick. But the second floor . . . that was dreadful compounded by ten. It was where Patrick Moyer had dragged Tessa from her hiding place under the bed and done unspeakable things. Raped and beat her. And as if his degrading and painful assault hadn't been enough, he carved a line with his knife from under her chin all the way to her ear. Then he discarded the knife and squeezed her throat before leaving her for dead. She had never understood why he chose to strangle her after stabbing the others. It was the only reason she had survived.

Tessa lingered with one foot on the bottom step, hesitant. She willed herself to go up, even though she had no intention of sleeping in the second-floor bedroom where Moyer had assaulted her.

Just do it, she encouraged herself. *Get it over with.*

The sharp ring of her cell phone made the choice for her.

She took it out and looked at the screen. The caller ID read *Maybe Thomas Milner*.

It was the New York editor. What did he want? She'd gotten here less than ninety minutes ago. Tessa stepped away from the stairs and answered.

Milner's baritone voice boomed in her ear. "Miss Montgomery, I'm calling to see if you arrived on the island yet."

"Barely. Just took a look around the house." *As much as I could manage, anyway,* Tessa thought.

"How does it feel to be back there?"

"Weird," Tessa admitted. "Like a half-remembered dream from long ago. But not in a good way. It's unsettling."

"That's a good description. Write it down. Use it," Milner said. "Get those first impressions on the page while they're fresh. Don't wait or you'll forget."

"You mean, like right now? I haven't even unpacked yet." Tessa wondered what she had gotten herself into.

"No, no. Take some time to settle in, of course. But maybe tonight."

I have a whole month to write this thing, Tessa thought. But all she said was, "Sure. Tonight."

"Wonderful. This is exciting. Can't wait to see those pages." Milner cleared his throat. "Look, I have an important call coming in. This is my cell. Put it in your phone and reach out if you need anything. We're in this together, okay?"

"Okay." Tessa hung up. They weren't in it together. Not by a long shot. Milner was over four hundred miles away in a comfy Manhattan office suite, while she was alone on the island. Which was *her* idea, she reminded herself. Tessa looked at the stairs and suppressed a shudder. In that moment, she decided. The upper floor could wait. There were more important things to do. Like buy groceries so she wouldn't starve.

Tessa went to the front door, scooped up her car keys, and stepped outside. Moments later, she was on her way back toward Seaview Point.

15

The establishment that passed as a supermarket in the town of Seaview Point would, in most places on the mainland, have been categorized as more of a convenience store. It occupied a squat and not particularly charming building in the center of town wedged between an art gallery with a sign in the window that read Closed for the Season and an ice-cream parlor with darkened windows. Across the street, fishing boats bobbed in the bay, anchored like miniature islands. Stacks of lobster traps lined the piers. A guesthouse that looked like it had been cobbled together from at least three previously separate structures pushed out over the colorless water, supported on thick wooden stilts. Its windows were dark. A sign hanging in one window read See You in April.

Tessa parked and made her way toward the store, collecting a shopping cart from a bay in the entrance lobby. When she entered, an older gray-haired gentleman wearing a green apron with the name Walt embroidered on it looked up from a magazine he was reading behind the counter. The only other person in the store was a younger man about her own age, or maybe a few years older, filling bins in the produce section.

"Afternoon," said Walt, adjusting a pair of spectacles on the bridge of his nose. "You let me know if you can't find anything, you hear?"

"I will, thank you." Tessa turned down the first aisle and all at once was hit with a sense of déjà vu. She had been here before, in this exact spot. She stopped, clenching her fingers around the cart handle just as the past rushed back to meet her.

◆ ◆ ◆

"What are we doing here?" Courtney asks with a scowl. "This isn't the alcohol aisle."

"We need more than booze," Theresa replies. They've only been on the island a few hours, and already her friend is in party mode. She wishes someone else had come to the store with her. Anyone else. If Courtney has her way, they'll drive back to the beach house with the entire contents of the liquor aisle in their trunk and not much else. She is, in a word, infuriating. "We have to eat too."

"Meh."

"You may not care about groceries, but the rest of us do."

"No one's going to be cooking. There's a pizza place down the road. I saw it on the way here. I'm sure they deliver. Problem solved."

"I'm not eating greasy pizza for an entire week."

"Fine. You get the boring stuff. I'll handle the rest." Courtney starts down the aisle. When she reaches the end, she stops and looks back. "This is going to be so awesome."

"Please don't overdo the booze," Theresa pleads. "We can always come back for more."

"Yes, Mother," Courtney shoots back. "Don't worry. I'm going to make sure you never forget this vacation." Then she vanishes around the corner.

◆ ◆ ◆

"Miss? Are you all right?" Walt rose to his feet, starting around the counter.

"Yes." Tessa's voice trembled when she spoke. The sudden memory had been so vivid and unexpected. She could almost believe Courtney would come rushing back around the corner, a couple of six-packs of beer in her arms and an excited grin on her face. Almost.

"You sure now?" The clerk came to a halt.

"I'm fine. Honestly." Tessa avoided making eye contact and hurried away, aware of his gaze on her back.

She moved quickly along the aisles and filled her cart, eager to leave the store. When she reached the produce section, the young man was finishing up his chores. He glanced her way and nodded a silent greeting.

"Hello," Tessa said, noting how his gaze lingered on her just a little longer than it should.

"Hey." The word came out as a barely audible grunt; then he turned away and wheeled a cart piled with empty produce boxes toward a pair of double doors marked EMPLOYEES ONLY at the rear of the store.

Tessa collected the last of her items. On her way back to the register, she grabbed three bottles of wine.

Walt's nose was back in his magazine. He glanced up and closed it at her approach. "Find everything you were looking for?"

"Yes. Mostly," Tessa replied, unloading the cart.

Walt scratched his chin. "What couldn't you find?"

"Dry yeast," Tessa replied. "To make bread."

"Bread, huh?" Walt smiled. "I sure do like the smell of fresh-baked bread." Walt nodded toward the back of the store. "The yeast will be in the baking section."

"I looked. It's not. The shelf is empty."

"Well, that won't do. Not at all. Tell you what, we had a delivery today. There's more in the stockroom. I'll have Noah fetch it." Walt glanced toward the produce section, his face creasing into a scowl. "Where has that dang boy gone now?"

"He went out back." Tessa motioned toward the double doors marked EMPLOYEES ONLY. "I don't think he came back."

"Figures. He probably snuck outside for a smoke. He's a nice enough lad but doesn't have much in the way of get-up-and-go, if you know what I mean."

"Is he your son?" Tessa wondered what life must be like for Noah in such a remote and inaccessible place. Cut off from the rest of the world by geography and the elements. It occurred to her that they shared something in common. Cassadaga Island was the cause of her own isolation these past five years, although for a different reason.

"Goodness, no." Walt shook his head. "I'd have whipped that boy into shape by now if he were. If you'll excuse me, I'll go find him."

"No need," Tessa said. "I won't be making bread today, anyway. I'll pick it up another time."

"If you're sure." Walt shot another glance toward the stockroom, clearly annoyed that Noah hadn't yet returned.

"I am." Tessa grabbed a sliced loaf from a wire rack near the first aisle and handed it to Walt. "I'll take this in the meantime."

"Okay, then." Walt scanned the loaf of bread. "If you don't mind making the trip back into town. I hope you're not too far out. Not that anyone on the island really is."

"I'm staying at the last beach house near the southern tip. I rented it for a month."

"The last house?" Walt's face changed. "I suppose you know the history of that place."

"I'm familiar with it," Tessa replied without elaborating.

"A whole month, huh?" Walt packed her groceries into brown paper bags. "Guess you don't scare easily, then?"

"I wouldn't go that far." Tessa paid for the groceries. "It's been nice chatting with you. Take care, Walt."

"You too, young lady." Walt's glasses had slipped down his nose again. He pushed them back up with one finger. "When you come back in, I'll have that yeast waiting."

"Thank you." Tessa moved toward the door and pushed the cart out into the parking lot. She loaded the groceries into her trunk and then returned the cart. When she turned to walk back to the car, she noticed Noah standing near the corner of the building, at the entrance to a narrow alleyway that ran between the supermarket and the ice-cream parlor. He watched her, a cigarette dangling from his fingers.

She climbed into the car and started the engine. When she glanced back, he was still standing there, leaning against the side of the building.

A knot twisted in Tessa's stomach. She could feel the weight of his gaze. It made her uncomfortable. Finally, she raised a hand and waved a hesitant greeting, but he didn't reciprocate. Instead, he turned and retreated into the alley. Tessa watched him leave; then, when he was out of sight, she pulled back out onto the road and headed toward the beach house and her first night back under the same roof where Patrick Moyer had killed her friends.

16

Tessa drove back to the beach house as the sun slipped low on the horizon and disappeared behind a dense forest of pine and fir trees that lined the road beyond the scattering of condos and summer homes. Here and there, she caught snatches of rugged boulder-strewn coves and inlets pounded by a somber ocean. She hated the northern winters with their short, frigid days. But not as much as she hated the long and even colder nights. The worst was when it snowed. Thankfully, there had been none so far this year and probably wouldn't be until well into December or maybe even January.

By the time she pulled up in front of the house, the fiery-red and burnt-orange hues of sunset had faded to a dense bluish black, with only the barest hint of color left. She hauled the groceries out of the trunk and transferred them to the porch in two trips, wishing she had possessed the forethought to turn on the outside lights.

The darkness pressed in, thick and heavy.

Tessa glanced around, half expecting to see Patrick Moyer lurching out of the gloom, knife held high. But that wasn't going to happen. Moyer was long in his grave. Still, the sense of unease remained, which was why she returned to the car a third time for one more item—the baseball bat that had been her constant companion the last five years.

She slammed the trunk lid and hurried up the porch steps into the house, where she leaned the bat against the wall and flipped the lights on, thankful for the sudden illumination.

She enabled the security system's Home Mode, then hauled her groceries to the kitchen and unpacked them.

There was a pine wine rack sitting on the counter. She slipped two wine bottles into the rack and almost opened the third but then decided against it. It was her first night on the island, and she wanted to remain sober and alert. She slid the last bottle into the rack, then went into the living room and lit a fire. After retreating to the couch, she took out her phone and called Melissa.

Her sister answered on the third ring.

"Hello?" Melissa sounded distracted.

"Hey, Mel. It's me."

"Tessa." The distraction melted from Melissa's voice, to be replaced by delight. "I thought there was no cell service on the island."

"There wasn't last time I was here, but they have a cell tower now, so I thought I'd call and let you know I got here in one piece."

"That's fantastic. I've been thinking about you all day. I wish you'd come on home."

"You know I can't. The book, remember?" *And the healing,* thought Tessa. That was important too, no matter how uncomfortable she was. "How's Corky?"

"Fine. He's gone into your bedroom twice looking for you. I think he's gotten used to someone being in the house all the time."

"He's a sweetie." Hearing her sister's voice and thinking about the stupid cat made her wish, just momentarily, that she'd stayed in Gloucester. At least there she wouldn't be sitting alone in a cold and unfamiliar house facing a bleak, windswept cove. "Give Corky a scratch on the neck for me," she said, shrugging the feeling off.

"Consider it done." Melissa fell silent for a moment, then spoke again. "Are you going to be all right on your own tonight?"

"I'll be fine," Tessa said, not sure if she meant it. What if it really was too much to bear? The ferry only ran once a week. If spending the night in the house where her friends had been murdered proved intolerable, she would have no option but to wait it out that long. Maybe it would have been better to come in the summer, when the ferry ran daily and she could leave at a moment's notice. Except there was the book. She had signed a contract, which meant she had no choice but to stay and face her fears regardless of how often the ferry ran. "Baptism by fire. I'll either come out of this stronger or a gibbering wreck."

"Let's hope it's the former. Besides, I'll be enough of a wreck for both of us thinking of you all alone on that island."

"No, you won't," Tessa laughed. "You'll spend the entire time with that boyfriend of yours having fun and living it up because I won't be there to cramp your style."

"You don't cramp my style."

"Yes, I do, and we both know it. You're living in a ten-by-twelve bedroom upstairs because I stole the master suite. And don't say your love life hasn't been impacted, because we both know it has."

"Okay. I'm not saying it's been easy," Melissa admitted. "But you're my sister, and I love you."

"I know, and I appreciate everything you've done for me. Which is why I'm going to stick it out here and do something for you this one time."

"Just put Patrick Moyer's ghost to rest. That's all I want."

"That's the plan. What are you doing tonight? Something fun, I hope."

"Josh is picking me up in a few minutes. We're seeing a movie."

"I knew it," Tessa said, unable to suppress a grin. "You aren't missing me one bit."

"That's not true! I miss you tons. It's not the same around here without you."

"That much I believe."

"Stop it. You know what I mean." From the other end of the phone line, the doorbell rang. "That'll be Josh now. I can ask him to wait. I'm sure we can catch a later movie."

"Don't be silly," Tessa said. "Go out and have fun. I'll be fine. I was only calling to let you know I got here."

"And I'm super happy to hear your voice." Melissa was at the door, letting Josh in. Tess heard a brief conversation between them, and she spoke into the phone again. "Okay. I'm going to run. Love you lots."

"Love you too," Tessa replied, moments before her sister hung up.

Alone again, Tessa stared into the fire for a while; then she pulled her laptop close. Thomas Milner had told her to dive right in. Get her first impressions on the page. Now was as good a time to start as any.

17

Tessa struggled to write for two hours, but the words would not come. She deleted three attempts, each worse than the last, before frustration overwhelmed her and she slammed the laptop closed. Wallowing in misery, she put another log on the fire, then sat transfixed by the flames as they danced and licked at the dry wood.

The house felt like a tomb holding the memories from her previous visit.

The last time Tessa had been at this beach house, it was nothing but fun and laughter, at least until that dreadful night. There had been long days on Sunset Cove's pebble beach and evenings spent around the firepit, where the girls drank beer and talked about their plans for the future.

Courtney had been heading for California after college to try her hand at acting. Tessa had no idea if she would have succeeded, but her friend was brash, confident, and always loved to be in the spotlight. If anyone could have conquered Tinseltown, it was Courtney. Even if she hadn't ended up in the movies, the LA lifestyle would have suited the sun-loving young woman, who liked nothing more than to stroll the beach in a skimpy bikini and turn heads.

The others were less ambitious in their plans.

Shelby wanted to be an artist but had ended up getting a degree in human resources and had readily admitted that it was probably a more stable career choice.

Madison had taken some of the same courses as Tessa and would have graduated with a degree in journalism and media. There had been a competition raging between the pair, each trying to outdo the other's grades, and that would have undoubtedly carried on after they left college. But it was a friendly rivalry, and they had talked about starting their own blog or even a podcast. Something to pad their résumés.

None of those plans had come to fruition, thanks to a chance encounter with a handsome guy on the beach and one terrifying night that had left three of them dead and Tessa so psychologically scarred that she had put her life on hold ever since.

She wished they'd never set foot on Cassadaga Island. Of all the places in the world to visit, what cruel force had steered them to this particular location and into the path of Patrick Moyer? It was a question she'd asked herself so many times. Everything would have been different if only they'd chosen Pensacola instead of coming up here. Florida was Madison's idea. She'd been to spring break there the year before and claimed that it was super rocking, even if she couldn't remember much about it, thanks to an unhealthy number of rum cocktails. But Maine was cheaper because they didn't need flights or a rental car, and they were all broke.

Tessa pushed the maudlin thoughts from her mind. She had returned here to heal, not to wallow in self-pity. Besides, dwelling on the past would do nothing to help her get through the night. She went to her travel bag and found her Kindle tucked into the front pocket. She opened it and read for the next hour, but she was distracted and barely comprehended the words on the page. In the end, she set the e-reader aside and focused on the issue that had been in the back of her mind ever since getting to the house.

Where was she going to sleep?

The upstairs bedroom was out of the question. Totally, unequivocally out of the question. She hadn't even mustered the courage to climb the stairs and reacquaint herself with the second floor yet. There was no way she was sleeping in that bedroom where she had cowered under the bed and listened to her friends die. Where Patrick Moyer had so brutally assaulted her.

Then there were the three bedrooms on this level. The master was the obvious choice, with its en suite bathroom and king-size bed, but Courtney had died in there. The other two bedrooms were no better. Shelby had died in one, and Madison in the other.

That only left one place. Tessa rose and went to the master bedroom, grabbed a pillow and blankets, then returned to the living room and settled down on the sofa with the baseball bat tucked next to her and a single lamp battling the darkness. She didn't think sleep would come, but soon her eyelids drooped, and she fell into a light and fitful slumber.

18

The sound jolted Tessa from her sleep.

A bump, hard and quick.

Loud.

It was still dark. The middle of the night. The only illumination came from the lamp on the sofa's side table and the glowing red embers in the hearth.

She sat up and sucked in a sharp breath, even as her dream dissipated like the silvery strands of a spider's web snatched by the breeze. In it, she had been sitting around the firepit with her friends, drinking beer. While, in the darkness beyond the deck, an ominous figure lurked, unwilling to step into the light and reveal themselves.

She let the nightmare fade and strained to listen.

The house was quiet now.

The baseball bat was still next to her on the sofa. She grabbed it and stood up, gaze sweeping the room. Nothing was out of place. The living room was still. The house beyond lay in darkness.

Padding softly to the foot of the stairs, Tessa peered up into the gloom. Had the noise come from the second floor? She didn't think so. One thing was for sure: She wasn't going up there to check. Not before daylight.

She turned away from the stairs and hurried through the living room to the kitchen, switching on the light. Nothing. That left the three ground-floor bedrooms. She poked her head into each in turn, clutching the bat with both hands, ready to swing it at the slightest movement, but the bedrooms were empty. In the master, she crossed to the sliding doors. Wedging the bat between her legs, she cupped her hands to the glass and peered out. She might as well have been staring into an endless void.

She flipped the switch that controlled the outside lights. Bright halogen floods illuminated the empty deck and firepit. In the cove beyond, the ocean crashed ashore, leaving behind a thin line of foam and tangled seaweed. The foghorn was a distant rumble, barely audible over the sound of the waves.

Tessa went back to the living room, letting the bat hang at her side. She glanced toward the side window next to the fireplace. Through a gap in the curtains, she saw a faint light in the direction of Cindy's house. Was the woman still up, or had she just left a light burning?

Tessa went to the window and reached out to pull the curtains back and get a better look.

Then she heard a creak, soon followed by another.

They came from the front of the house.

She stopped, hand outstretched. It sounded like—God, she didn't even want to think it—footsteps on the front porch.

Her chest tightened. Someone was outside, skulking around. She half expected to see a face pressed against the front door's small square accent window, peering in.

Another creak.

A whimper rose in her throat.

"It's nothing," she chided herself in a barely audible whisper. "Just a raccoon or some other critter looking for food." Maybe it was a bear. Did they have bears on Cassadaga Island? She didn't know.

Tessa did know one thing. She had to look.

You can do this, she silently encouraged herself, not sure if she believed her own words.

She crossed to the front window and inched the curtain back just enough to peek out.

The faint outline of porch railings filtered through the darkness. Beyond them was nothing but the ghostly impression of her car and barely perceptible trees beneath a starless black sky.

She released the curtain and went to the front door, reaching out to snap the porch light on. Before she could flick the switch, there was another creak.

Floorboards shifted under her feet.

Tessa froze. Her skin crawled as if a thousand tiny ants were marching across it.

Someone was outside, standing close by with only the front door between them. She was sure of it.

A minute passed, then another. She heard nothing else. Were they still there, listening on the other side of the door, waiting silently for her to make the next move?

Tessa's arms ached from holding the bat up for so long.

Another minute passed, and she began to wonder if she had imagined the entire incident. She lowered the bat, stood on tiptoe, and peered through the accent window in the door.

All she saw beyond was blackness.

She fumbled for the porch light switch, unwilling to drag her gaze from the window, and turned it on, then closed her eyes momentarily against the sudden glare.

When she opened them again, the porch was empty. No one was there.

Maybe it really was just a critter sniffing around, curious about the newcomer in its midst. A fox or some other creature that had checked her out, then slunk away quietly into the night.

Tessa wanted to believe that so badly, but those noises sounded too much like footsteps.

She went to the fireplace and threw another log on, then sat on the couch with the bat cradled on her lap. The silence pressed in around her. She stayed like that, wide-awake and listening for any further sounds, until the first rays of dawn crept across the floor and filled the house with welcome sunlight.

19

It was ten in the morning, and Tessa was restless. She had been on the island less than twenty-four hours and had already ended up spooking herself. It was disappointing.

Her thoughts kept returning to the strange sounds that had woken her up in the dead of night. At the time, she had been convinced someone was skulking around on her porch. It sounded so much like footsteps. But now, in the light of day, she wasn't so sure. Old houses made sounds. They shifted and settled. Wood contracted as the temperature fell and expanded when it warmed up. Maybe building a fire and heating the place had caused the creaks. That had to be it. Nothing more than the building adjusting to her presence.

Now she felt foolish. All that fuss over nothing. Scaring herself so badly that she stayed up half the night.

Redemption was in order.

Her eyes roamed toward the stairs and the still-unexplored second floor beyond. Now was as good a time as any to face that particular fear. A small victory would bolster her resolve.

But not without the baseball bat.

She went to the couch and scooped it up, then hurried to the bottom of the stairs.

Her heart thudded as she climbed. At the top, she paused and glanced around. The landing was full of shadows. There was a switch next to the stairs. She clicked it on, breathing easier when the light came on and banished the gloom.

She went to the closest door—the bathroom—and stepped inside. Everything was how she remembered. Toilet. Porcelain pedestal sink. Shower complete with a pink floral curtain pulled across.

A chill ran through her.

Patrick Moyer had come in here when he was prowling through the house looking for her. Pulled the curtain back. The swooshing sound it made and the clink of metal shower rings would be forever etched in her memory. Was this the same curtain? There was no reason to think otherwise.

Tessa stared at it, imagining his hands on that curtain. Then she imagined something worse. There could be someone hiding behind that curtain right now.

Don't be so silly, she scolded herself silently. *There's nothing but an empty tub behind that curtain.*

But her mind would not let the thought go. It blossomed and grew until she was sure some interloper with evil intentions lurked on the other side. Which meant she would have to pull it back and look.

Her heart pounded in her chest.

She reached out with a shaking hand and gripped the curtain, then yanked it aside, quick as she could, before jumping back. Her racing heart slowed. Nothing but an empty bathtub.

Tessa breathed a sigh of relief and hurried from the bathroom, then made her way along the landing.

There were only three more doors. One was a bedroom—her bedroom on that fateful night. The other was a cramped space hardly bigger than a walk-in closet that the owners had set up as an office. Back when the house was built, before indoor plumbing was common, the office and bathroom had probably been one larger bedroom, which explained its now tight dimensions. Not big enough for a bed. The farthest door at the end of the landing was narrower than the others and made of flat boards, differing from the more ornate four-panel craftsman-style doors in the rest of the house. She didn't know what was beyond it because the door had been locked the last time she was here.

Her old bedroom could wait. Saving the worst for last.

Tessa went to the office, pushed the door open, and stepped inside. The floor was wood planks like the rest of the upstairs. A dusty-looking rug reached almost to the baseboards. Light entered from a narrow window. A desk and chair stood against one wall. There was a bookcase against the opposite one. She examined the books sitting on the shelves, curious to see what the owners of this summer home liked to read. It was a mix of fiction and nonfiction, mostly romance and cookbooks. There were also local history books from small presses. She turned from the bookshelf and made her way to the window, peering out toward Cindy's house and the road that led to town weaving through the woods. She spotted a lone cyclist, appearing in the gaps between the trees before moving out of sight again. Was it Cindy coming back from an early-morning trip into Seaview Point? She couldn't tell.

Tessa stepped away from the window and returned to the landing, then went to the plain door at the end of the hallway. A sign declared the space beyond to be private. She tried the handle anyway, expecting the door to be locked, as it had been on her previous visit to the house five years before—she distinctly remembered being nosy back then—but to her surprise, it opened. The space beyond was swathed in darkness except for one lone spear of sunlight slanting down from a small grimy window at the rear of the space.

Tessa reached inside and found a light switch mounted on the wall. She turned it on and discovered an unfinished walk-in attic area with sloped walls sitting under the rear third of the building's roof. Rough floorboards covered the joists below bare trusses. Over the years, an assortment of items had made their way into the storage space, including an old secretary desk caked in decades of dust, an iron bed frame and headboard, and cardboard boxes of various sizes and shapes stacked at the rear. Tessa pulled her head back out of the opening and closed the door, wishing she could lock it. There was a dead bolt on the door with a key slot on the corridor side so the owners of the house could lock it to keep renters out. She decided to call and ask the caretaker if there was a key. It would allow her to sleep easier. The attic was beyond creepy, and the last thing she needed was her overactive imagination using the dark space as fodder for her fears.

After giving the door a final tug to make sure it was firmly closed, she retreated along the landing to the bedroom.

Tessa had been dreading this moment since she decided to return to Cassadaga Island and the house where her friends died. She paused, overcome with a sudden desire to flee and put as much distance between herself and this dreadful place as possible. Beyond this door, Patrick Moyer had done unspeakable things to her. Things her mind had blocked out because they were too painful to remember. But she had come here to face her demons, not surrender to them, and that was what she intended to do.

With a shaking hand, Tessa turned the knob and pushed. The door swung inward on unoiled hinges, and she came face-to-face with the spot where her five-year-long ordeal had begun.

20

Five years melted away in the blink of an eye. The breath caught in Tessa's throat as she surveyed her surroundings. There was the queen-size bed under which she hid when Patrick Moyer started his killing spree. The bed skirt was still there too, covering the dark space beneath. Against the opposite wall stood the dresser where her phone had rested on that fateful night, useless because the island had no reception back then. The walls were the same pale mustard yellow. She was sure the drapes hadn't been changed either. This room was a time capsule of bad memories.

Except for one thing.

The rug was different. She knew this, not because she remembered the original floor coverings in any great detail—she couldn't recall what Patrick Moyer had done to her, let alone the pattern on the rug—but because this was where his assault had taken place. *This exact spot.* He had carved a line across her face right there before strangling her and leaving her for dead. Hours later, she had been found on that rug, naked and unresponsive. Her blood would have soaked through the fibers, and no amount of cleaning could have gotten that out. Besides, Forensics undoubtedly took the original. Not that Moyer ever made it to trial. The Seaview Point police chief saw to that, shooting Moyer dead in his own home when he resisted arrest after Tessa ID'd him from her hospital bed. And good riddance. The chief's bullet had saved her from testifying in court, which would surely have left her even more traumatized.

She crossed to the bed and sat down, then closed her eyes. She could almost hear her friends' terrified screams, the way they begged for their lives. The beach house wasn't haunted. She knew that. But the ghosts of the past were there anyway, inside her head. She lay back on the bed and opened her eyes, staring up at the ceiling. She wished it were possible to bridge the years between then and now and send a warning back to her past self. A message to avoid Patrick Moyer at all costs. A lump formed in her throat. And then she cried for the second time since returning to the beach house. The tears fell hot and wet down her cheeks. She wiped them away with the back of her hand. She hated this room. Loathed it more than any other place on the face of the planet. Swinging her legs off the bed, she stood up and turned toward the door. She hadn't even taken a step when the memory slammed into her like an avalanche—a fragment of lost time that swam up from the inky void of her subconscious and hijacked her senses.

She is lying on the floor, exposed. Vulnerable.

The coarse weave of the bedroom rug under her bare skin is uncomfortable. The bikini she hadn't bothered to change out of earlier that evening is gone. Ripped off and discarded on the floor near the bed.

She struggles against her attacker, but Patrick Moyer is strong. Too strong. He forces her arms above her head, holds her wrists in a powerful grip. He snarls at her to lie still. It will be easier that way, he says. Then he leans forward, straddling her nakedness with a leering grin.

She bucks and screams, but there is no one to hear.

Everyone else in the house is already dead . . .

The vision shattered as quickly as it came. Tessa stumbled back and sank onto the bed, sitting on the edge. She sucked in a trembling breath and looked down at the rug in front of her—not the same rug but close enough—and the tears flowed anew. The flashback, short as it was, had been potent. Visceral. Maybe if she had discussed returning here with her former therapist, she would have been better prepared for something like this, but she hadn't. Claire would likely have tried to talk her out of it anyway, and Tessa didn't feel like she had any other option but to go through with the trip. She had crossed a line when she swung a bat at Corky—worn out her welcome—and maybe this was her punishment. A self-imposed hell she could not escape.

Tessa leaned forward with her head in her hands and wiped the tears away. She didn't trust her legs to hold her. She sat on the bed for ten minutes, unable to move, as the disjointed memory sank back down like a wave receding from the shore. Finally, her breathing normalized, and she sensed her strength returning. She stood up and ran. Fled onto the landing, slamming the bedroom door behind her, and raced downstairs. She stopped at the bottom and paused, then turned and looked back up at the second floor.

A pang of disappointment pushed through the terror.

This trip had been about healing and coming to terms with her ordeal. Instead, she had awakened a horrific memory and allowed her fear to get the upper hand. That was not a good sign so early in her trip. She was desperate to prove Melissa wrong and show her that it wasn't a mistake coming back to this house. Now Tessa wondered if it was.

Maybe there was somewhere less stressful she could explore and achieve at least a minor victory over the dread that followed her for so long. Somewhere that wouldn't trigger another memory.

The only other part of the house she hadn't yet explored was the basement. She walked to the narrow door tucked under the stairs. There was a heavy-duty cast-iron barrel bolt mounted near the top. She leaned the baseball bat against the wall, then reached up and lifted the finger knob. The bolt was tight in its sleeve, but a little jiggling worked it free, and she was able to open the door.

She fumbled for the light switch and clicked it on.

A rough wooden staircase revealed itself. There were thick cobwebs in the corners around the frame on the basement side. A fat black spider lurked in a crevice where the plaster had chipped away to reveal the lath beneath. The arachnid scuttled farther into the crack, realizing it was no longer alone.

A shudder wormed up Tessa's spine.

She peered down into the dark space beneath the house and placed a foot on the top step. The bare bulb hanging from a cord in the stairwell did little to illuminate the gloomy space below. Tessa hoped there would be another light switch at the foot of the stairs. She took a step forward, careful to avoid a large cobweb that hung down. But before she descended more than a few steps, her attention was drawn by three short, sharp knocks. Someone was at the front door.

21

Tessa froze on the stairs. She struggled to tame the familiar flood of anxiety that occurred whenever she was alone in a house and confronted by an unexpected visitor. The flashback was still fresh in her mind. A leering Patrick Moyer straddling her with wicked intent.

Her heartbeat quickened.

She retreated from the basement and quietly closed the door, drawing the bolt back across, then lingered out of sight in the space under the stairs near the hallway leading to the downstairs bedrooms. She considered staying there and waiting for the unknown caller to leave. After all, there was no reason for anyone to be at the beach house. She had no friends on the island and wasn't expecting anybody. Unless it was the caretaker returning. If so, she had the door code and would soon let herself inside if there was no reply. The thought of a stranger entering the house unannounced was worse than the prospect of just answering the door.

Tessa picked up the bat and stepped out from her hiding place. When she reached the front door, she hesitated. Instead of opening it, she went to the window and pulled the curtain back to look out. There was a figure standing on the front porch. A person she recognized. But it was not the caretaker. It was Noah, the guy from the supermarket.

When he noticed her peering out, he lifted an arm. In his hand was a bottle of dry yeast.

Tessa let the curtain fall back into place and went to the door. She disarmed the security system, attached the security chain, then answered the door.

"Hello," she said through the narrow gap permitted by the taut chain.

"Hiya." The word came out as an extended drawl. "Walt said you were looking for yeast. I unpacked yesterday's delivery from the mainland and thought I'd bring it out to you. Save you the trouble of going back into town."

"That's nice of you," Tessa said.

"Don't mention it." Noah tried to insert the yeast into the gap between the door and the frame, but it wouldn't fit. "Oops. Won't go through."

"I have the chain on," Tessa replied, caught between a desire not to be rude and her fear of opening the door any wider to this man she didn't know.

"It's all good," Noah said. "I can just leave it right out here on the porch. Don't want to scare you or nothing."

"No, don't be silly." Tessa swallowed her fear and drew the chain back. Keeping the bat out of sight, she widened the gap enough for him to pass the yeast through but braced the door with her foot lest he try to enter.

"I only brought one." Noah handed her the yeast. "I can go back and get more if you need it. It'd be no trouble."

"One will be fine, I'm sure." She couldn't help but notice his eyes. They were colorless. A light gray that lacked warmth. *As if he were already dead,* she thought. Tessa shuddered and pushed the strange notion from her mind. "Thank you for bringing this to me. I appreciate it."

"Happy to be of help," Noah said. He glanced around casually. "Strange time of year to visit the island, don't ya think? Most folk come over in summer, when it's nice and warm."

"I don't mind the cold. I'm not here on vacation."

"Why *are* you here, then?" Noah asked.

"You might call it a spiritual retreat," Tessa replied without elaborating further.

"You're here alone?"

"What makes you say that?"

"No reason." Noah shrugged. "You were by yourself in the store yesterday, and a spiritual retreat sounds like the kind of thing a person does on their own."

"I'm here with my boyfriend," Tessa lied. "He stayed behind to unpack while I drove into Seaview Point yesterday."

"Uh-huh. Makes sense." Noah's gaze strayed briefly past Tessa and into the house, then back to her. "He's a lucky man."

"I'm sorry?"

"I shouldn't have said that. Thinking out loud, is all. I do that sometimes." Noah's brow furrowed. "I just meant you seem like a nice person."

"Oh. I see."

"I've taken up enough of your time. I should get going. Have to be at work soon. Walt hates it if I'm late. He says tardiness is a sign of laziness." Noah took a step back. "It was nice meeting you again."

"You too." Tessa resisted the urge to slip the chain back on.

"I'm Noah, by the way."

"I know. Walt told me yesterday. My name's Tessa."

Noah nodded. "And your boyfriend?"

"What?"

"Your boyfriend. What's his name?"

"Oh. Of course." Tessa's mind was blank, caught in the lie. She struggled to come up with a name that sounded plausible. After a short pause that felt like forever and a day, she said the only one she could think of. Her sister's boyfriend. "Josh. His name is Josh."

"Ah." Noah smiled. "Well, say hello to Josh for me. Hope I meet him soon."

"Me too," Tessa said, breathing a sigh of relief.

Noah lingered a moment longer, as if he were waiting for Josh to appear; then he backed up, his grin widening. "See you around, Tessa."

"Yes." Tessa watched him. "I'm sure you will."

Noah's gaze drifted back to the interior of the house before he turned, descended the steps, and disappeared behind a tall bush growing near the porch railing. He reappeared wheeling a bicycle, which he mounted before giving her a quick wave, then cycled off past Tessa's car and down the road toward Seaview Point.

Tessa placed the bat on the table inside the door—the one with all the flyers—and stepped out onto the porch. It hadn't been Cindy she'd seen from the upstairs window. She leaned on the railing and watched until Noah and his bike disappeared from view behind the other cottages lining the road. She went back inside and placed the jar of yeast on the kitchen counter, then returned to the basement door and reached up to draw the bolt back again. But then stopped. The caretaker's comments echoed through her head . . . that the house was haunted by the spirits of those who perished within. Were her friends still there, unseen and watching, trapped by the violence of their own demise?

The walls pressed in around her. The air was thick and heavy.

Tessa drew her hand back, overcome by a sudden urge to escape, if only for a few hours.

Turning away from the basement door, she hurried to the front of the house and grabbed her coat. A minute later, she was outside and striding across the back deck toward the blustering cove beyond.

22

A chilly wind whipped off the ocean. Tessa pulled her coat tight around her slender frame and shivered, brushing a wayward strand of hair from her forehead.

She made her way down toward the water and the line that formed the high-tide boundary. A piece of driftwood had become tangled within the seaweed and been dragged ashore. Barnacles encrusted one side, while on the other were three rusty nails. She wondered if it was part of a ship's hull. It looked old and had clearly been in the water for a long time.

She stopped briefly to examine it, then stepped away and approached the upturned rowboat, climbing onto its keel. She stayed there for several minutes, sitting atop the sun-bleached hull, and watched waves lap against the shore before climbing down and continuing along the shoreline toward the edge of the cove and a narrow rocky path winding up over the bluff.

Tessa's house was the last one on this end of the island and one of only two overlooking Sunset Cove. The other belonged to Cindy, the woman she had met the previous day. The next nearest house was a good quarter mile away on the other side of the bluff. As she clambered down over the rocks and started past it through a smaller, sheltered inlet, faint cries drew her attention. She glanced sideways and saw a family at the rear of the house. Two parents, an older boy, who looked to be in his late teens, and a younger girl, who ran back and forth off the deck and onto the pebbles before jumping up onto the deck again with excited whoops. The father raised a hand in greeting.

Tessa returned the gesture and kept walking toward a path that wound up from the inlet to a rocky high point covered in trees. When she was at the top of the path, she turned and glanced back. The girl was still jumping up and down off the deck, but the parents had disappeared back inside. The teenage boy, however, was standing with his arms folded, watching her progress.

Tessa turned and quickened her step until the teenager and his sister were out of sight. She followed the path as it wound through the trees, then dropped back down around another cove with jutting headlands on each side before rising again.

She followed the coastal path for half an hour before the land flattened out, the trees thinned, and she found herself at the start of town. There were more summer homes here looking over the ocean. One- and two-story buildings that sat close together with large windows facing Callaghan Bay. Storm shutters protected pretty much every structure facing the ocean, the residents having departed back to the mainland. She guessed that many of these condos had been empty since Labor Day when summer on Cassadaga Island officially ended and most of the stores and restaurants either closed for the offseason or switched to winter hours. In other areas of New England, the demise of summer meant the beginning of a new batch of tourists flooding in to see the leaves change from green to fiery reds and brilliant yellows. There would be hot apple cider, often spiced with cinnamon, and cozy nights gathered around the hearth.

But not out on the island.

Winter came early here, thanks to its exposed location far out in the bay. And even if the locals wanted a fall season, the trees would not cooperate. Balsam fir and white pine—both evergreens—covered the land. The deciduous trees that did turn were spread so thinly that it wasn't worth riding the ferry or braving the bitter cold to see them. Other than year-round locals, the few hardy people that stayed into

November were either seeking solitude or taking advantage of the seasonal lull in rental activity to perform yearly maintenance and winterize their properties before temperatures plummeted and the snow came.

Tessa made her way past the summer homes, turned away from the ocean, and climbed a set of wooden steps that led to the road through town. She strolled down Main Street. Most of the art galleries, shops, and restaurants were shuttered and dark, but one building caught her eye.

The Harbor Diner.

A wide deck overlooking the bay and moored fishing boats had been cleared, the chairs and tables stacked to one side. But the lights were on, and an illuminated Open sign hung in the window. A sandwich board announcing lunchtime specials stood near the restaurant's entrance.

Tessa realized she was hungry. She hadn't eaten anything, and now her stomach growled. She hurried toward the restaurant and entered.

She saw a long counter with stools and a kitchen beyond. Tables filled the rest of the room. The restaurant was empty except for a pair of men in the far corner huddled in hushed conversation over mugs of coffee and sandwiches. A fire cracked in a wide hearth opposite the counter. Rows of weathered oars, hanging one above the other, adorned the stone chimney stack. Vintage photos, probably depicting Seaview Point in its early days, hung on both sides of the fireplace. Spotlights lit the room, attached to exposed beams beneath a vaulted ceiling.

Tessa closed the door against the November chill and unbuttoned her coat, happy to be in the warmth. She approached the counter and slid onto a stool before taking her coat off and hanging it on a hook under the counter. When she looked up again, a woman about her own age was breezing toward her, menu in one hand and a coffeepot in the other.

23

The server approached Tessa with a smile and placed a laminated menu on the counter in front of her. “A new face.”

Tessa nodded. “I came over on the ferry yesterday.”

“Let me see.” The server stared intently at Tessa. “You don’t look like a laborer come over to fix up someone’s summer house before the snow. I know you don’t own property on the island because everyone knows everyone else around here. I’m pretty sure you didn’t come just to take that stupid ghost tour because no one ever does.” She rubbed her chin. “I bet you’re either a masochist punishing yourself, or you’re on the run and think an island in the middle of nowhere is a great place to lay low until the heat dies down.”

“Actually, it’s neither of those things,” Tessa said, bemused by the server’s quirky sense of humor. “But I can assure you, I have no intention of taking the ghost tour. The caretaker at the house I’m renting already tried to sign me up for that.”

“Good. The ghost tour is super lame. Most of it isn’t even real. They just make it all up so they can sell tickets to people that don’t know better.”

“So, pretty much like all ghost tours, then.”

“Ah, so you’re a connoisseur of the supernatural arts.”

“No. I just don’t believe in ghosts.”

“Me either.” The server grinned. “I’m Roxanne, by the way.”

“Tessa.”

"Cute. Nice name. You want a mug of coffee to warm your bones while you look at the menu?"

"Sure."

Roxanne took a mug from under the counter and filled it.

The aroma of strong black coffee wafted toward Tessa. She picked up the menu. "You got any recommendations?"

"Eggs Benedict isn't half-bad." Roxanne leaned on the counter. "You can't go wrong with pancakes. Our maple syrup is local. The owner of this place has a friend with a sugar shack over on the mainland. All small-batch organic."

"They both sound good," Tessa said.

"Don't they? The only thing I wouldn't recommend is the corned beef hash. Frank's the only person I know who can burn potatoes on a hot plate."

A voice, presumably Frank, wafted through the serving hatch leading to the kitchen. "I heard that, young lady."

"You were meant to. I had your hash last week after my shift ended, and it was like eating jerky."

"Yeah, yeah." Frank did not sound amused. "Just keep your opinion to yourself and take the woman's order. She's probably hungry."

"What gave it away?" Roxanne retorted, looking over her shoulder toward the hatch. "The fact that she's in a diner?"

There was no response from the kitchen except a clattering of pans.

"You'll have to excuse Frank," Roxanne said, turning back to Tessa. "He's always cranky after a busy season. You wouldn't know it to look at this place now, but a few months ago we were rushed off our feet. Packed dawn till dusk."

"No worries," Tessa said, looking around. "I like this place. It feels homey."

"That's only because you don't work here." Roxanne grimaced. "Sorry, I shouldn't say that. I'm supposed to be polite to the customers."

Tessa smiled.

From behind her came a scrape of chairs. The two men who were eating when she came in had finished and were walking toward the counter. Tessa glanced sideways toward them. They were approaching middle age but looked like they worked out. The shorter of the two noticed her watching them and said hello. She thought she detected a southern drawl to his accent. She said hello back and then quickly turned her attention to the menu.

Roxanne took their payment and made change, which they left on the counter as a tip before heading toward the door.

"See you later, Rox," the taller of the two said as they departed.

"Later, Adam." Roxanne watched them leave, then scooped up the money and slipped it inside her apron pocket before turning her attention back to Tessa. "If it wasn't for those guys and their colleagues, I wouldn't be able to make rent in the offseason."

"They work on the island?" Tessa asked.

"Nah. They work at some government facility on Stadler Island up off the north tip. Technically, it's the next island over from Cassadaga, but it's only separated by a narrow channel with a causeway that's dry most of the time. It only floods at high tide. The workers come over if they get fed up with the food in their cafeteria, which is pretty often. That's the only reason we stay open through winter."

"What do they do over there?" Tessa asked, her curiosity piqued.

"Who knows?" Roxanne shook her head. "They play it pretty tight to the vest. My guess is they're talking to nuclear submarines or downloading data from spy satellites. All I know is that there's a big gate blocking off the causeway, and they're pretty strict about making sure people don't go over there uninvited."

"How far is it to the other end of the island?" Tessa realized she had no clue how large Cassadaga Island actually was.

"About ten miles. The entire island is only eighteen miles tip to tip and half that at its widest. There are some neat coves on the southern end of the island where most of the summer homes and rental properties are. The northern end is pretty much all woodland and rocky coastline with sheer drops. The only other thing out there is an old lighthouse, but it hasn't worked in years. They built a new lighthouse out in the bay on Snake Island back in the forties. They put a foghorn out there too. Runs all the time because the weather can change on a dime. At least, that's what the town says, but I think it's just broken. When the wind is in the right direction, you can hear it."

Tessa nodded. She glanced around the empty diner. "It must get lonely living here year-round."

"Not really. You get used to it." Roxanne nodded toward the menu. "You know what you want yet?"

Tessa nodded. "The pancakes. You sold me on them with the local maple syrup."

"A solid choice." Roxanne looked pleased. "You won't regret it."

"I'm sure I won't," said Tessa. She could imagine many things she might come to regret about returning to Cassadaga Island, but pancakes were not among them.

24

By the time Tessa left the diner and started back toward the beach house, the weather had turned. A damp drizzle hung in the air, and the temperature had dropped by several degrees. She retraced her route back along the coastal path toward the rental home, walking faster now.

The melancholy drone of the foghorn out on Snake Island echoed across the slate-gray ocean, the sound distant and unmoored. But this time, it served a purpose. A slow rolling bank of wispy nothingness had obliterated the smaller islands out on the horizon and reduced everything beyond the shore to a featureless expanse with no indication where the water ended and the sky began.

Tessa climbed a bluff and followed a meandering woodland path until it dipped back down toward the shore. The teenage boy and his sister were gone when she passed their house. She was glad. The teenager's gaze had lingered a little too long when she walked by earlier. Or maybe it was just her paranoia. Ever since that awful night in the beach house five years before, she had overanalyzed every sideways glance or curious look. One lingering stare was all it took to send her rushing for the safety of her sister's house, where she could hide behind the locks and bolts on her bedroom door.

Climbing another bluff, she soon came upon Sunset Cove and hurried up the beach toward the rental house. And in the nick of time. The fog was coming in fast and hard. It devoured the shoreline and sent wispy tendrils over and around the upturned rowboat until it was nothing more than a ghostly outline.

Tessa ascended the steps to the deck and hurried inside, slamming the back door against the elements. She switched the alarm to Home Mode and stood a moment, listening. When she didn't hear anything untoward, she moved farther inside and made a quick circuit around the property, peeking into every room even though the alarm had been set and it was unlikely anyone had gotten in. But it was the only way to quiet the low-level anxiety that always bubbled beneath the surface.

Satisfied, she went to the living room and lit a fire, then sat in front of the computer. Her attempt to write the previous evening had been nothing but a frustrating waste of time. Now she tried again. But just like before, the blank page with its blinking cursor taunted her.

A moment of panic gripped her. What if the words never came? What if she couldn't transfer the emotions and fears that had consumed her these past five years into a cohesive narrative? Thomas Milner would want to see the first batch of pages in a few short days, and if she had nothing to show him, it would just prove his suspicion that she wasn't up to the task. And then what? Would he bring in a ghostwriter? Pull the plug on the entire project and ask her to return the advance money? She couldn't do that, because a big chunk of it was already spent.

"Come on, you can do this," she whispered to herself. "Get a grip."

But the more she stared at the page, the more stuck she became. It wasn't so much that she didn't know what to write—after all, the book was about her return to Cassadaga Island and her struggle to confront the past—but more that she didn't know where to start the story.

The obvious starting point was her arrival on the island, but that felt expected. Dull. She wanted something better. Something that would leave Thomas Milner wowed and prove that he hadn't wasted his time with her. She just didn't know what.

Then, while she was still contemplating this and staring at the computer screen in frustration, there was a knock at the door for the second time that day.

25

It was Cindy.

She stood on the doorstep with a cardboard box cradled in her arms. "I come bearing gifts."

Tessa looked at the box and the words *Cindy's Books* scrawled across the side in permanent marker. "You brought me a box of books?"

"Goodness, no. This box has been lying around for years. I must have used it to bring stuff to the house when I moved in. It's the contents of my kitchen cupboards and freezer that won't last until next summer. Thought it might save you a trip to the grocery store since you're here for a month."

"Ah." Tessa moved aside to let Cindy into the house. "That's very thoughtful of you."

"You're welcome." Cindy sidestepped Tessa and made her way to the kitchen. "It's nothing terribly exciting, so don't get your hopes up. There are some cans of soup. A frozen pizza. Turkey burgers. Stuff like that. Feel free to toss anything you don't want."

"I'm sure it will all get used," Tessa said, following behind. "I hope you didn't leave yourself short."

"I kept enough back to feed myself while I'm here. Don't worry about that. When I leave, you can have anything else I didn't get through. I can't take it with me—no car—and no point in wasting it."

"How's it going over there?"

"Pretty good." Cindy placed the box on the counter. "I'm tackling a few odd jobs that need to be done before the season next year. Some painting and a leaky tap. Nothing major. It won't take me more than a day or two. Then I have to drain the pipes and winterize before I head back to the mainland." Cindy looked around, her gaze drifting toward the living room and the bedrooms beyond. "More to the point, how are you getting on in this drafty old place all alone?"

Tessa knew what the older woman was thinking. This was the infamous murder house. Scene of the Sunset Cove Massacre. Cindy must surely have owned the property next door back then. Was Cindy over there, just a stone's throw away, when Tessa lay broken and dying in that upstairs bedroom five years ago? For a moment, she was tempted to ask. If nothing else, it might trigger her creativity, and heaven knew, she needed that. But she couldn't quite bring herself to do it. Instead, Tessa turned to the box and opened it to put the frozen food away, then answered with a vague assurance that she was doing fine.

"I'm pleased to hear that." Cindy laid a gentle hand on Tessa's arm. "But if you get lonely, I'm only a short walk away around the cove. At least until the house is done and I leave."

"Thank you. I'll keep that in mind." Tessa got the impression that Cindy was saying this as much to ease her own loneliness as to assuage hers. She briefly considered asking if Cindy wanted to stay for a cup of coffee or maybe a glass of wine, but at the same time, the thought of entertaining this woman who she barely knew made Tessa's stomach clench. She had gotten used to being alone over the last five years and had already used her allotment of bravery for the week by visiting the diner earlier that day and even engaging in light conversation.

Cindy wasn't so hesitant. "If you're not doing anything this evening, I was planning to open a bottle of wine and watch the fog roll off the ocean. The island is so atmospheric at this time of year. It's like a different place. Come on around. I'd love the company."

"Thanks for the invite, but I have work to do," Tessa said, glancing through the kitchen door toward the laptop sitting on the living room coffee table. It wasn't exactly the truth—she hadn't written a single page worth keeping yet—but it wasn't a total lie either.

"That's a shame." Cindy stepped out of the kitchen and made her way across the living room. At the front door, she paused. "The offer's there if you change your mind."

Tessa forced a smile. Friendliness wasn't her forte. Not since Patrick Moyer. "Thank you."

"I'd better let you get back to your work, then." Cindy opened the front door and stepped onto the porch.

Tessa nodded. It was late afternoon, but already the light was fading. She was surprised to find the fog had not completed its advance. Aside from a few vague wisps that curled around the house, the front yard and road beyond were clear.

Cindy hesitated, as if expecting Tessa to say something more, then turned and descended the steps.

Tessa waited for her to disappear around the side of the house, then went back inside, locking the door and pulling the front curtains.

The laptop taunted her from the coffee table. It dared her to try again. To face the blank page. She could sense the metaphorical clock of Thomas Milner's deadline ticking away.

I want to see pages every few days.

Shit. What had she gotten herself into? Being back at this place was bad enough, let alone having to write about it when she had no clue where to begin.

Then she remembered something else Milner had said only the previous day when he called to check that she had arrived on the island.

Reach out if you need anything. We're in this together.

Tessa still wasn't so sure about that last part, but his offer felt like a lifeline. Better to face the situation head-on and ask for help than be forced to explain why she had nothing written when the first pages came due. She slipped the phone out of her pocket, found the editor's number, and called.

26

Thomas Milner answered on the first ring. "Tessa, I wasn't expecting to hear from you again so soon."

"I know. And I'm sorry to disturb you, but you said I could call if I needed anything."

"And I meant it. What's up?"

Tessa hesitated. Calling the editor had seemed like a good idea a few moments ago, but now that he was on the other end of the line, she wondered what he would think about her being stuck before she even began. But her reason for calling was still valid. If she didn't have something to show for her efforts soon, he might start to think that taking a gamble on the book was a mistake. That taking a gamble on *her* was a mistake. Her mouth was dry. Her throat was scratchy like sandpaper. She tried to speak, but all that came out was a small croak.

"Tessa, are you all right?"

"Yes." Tessa cleared her throat. She focused her thoughts. "I need your advice."

"That's what I'm here for. Shoot."

"I'm struggling with the book. I mean, the first pages. I don't know how to begin." Tessa felt stupid. Inadequate. "I know you put a lot of trust in me, but—"

"Hey, slow down. It's okay. Have you got anything written? Anything at all?"

"No," she admitted, her face burning. Then she told him about her failed attempts to write. How she had discarded page after page because they simply weren't good. She had written an opening chapter about the incident with Melissa's cat. Another about her arrival on the island. She even tried to start the book back when she was in the hospital after Patrick Moyer's attack. But whatever she wrote wound up sounding dull and flat. In short, she lacked direction.

When she finished, Milner was silent for a while. "Maybe you're focusing too much on the internal struggle and not enough on the wider story."

"I don't understand."

"Look, you gave me a great pitch: the girl who survived, facing her fears in the place where she almost died. But it doesn't sound like that's what you're doing. I'm not a psychiatrist, but it seems to me that just living in that house for a month with the memories of your dead friends isn't going to help you move past what happened and heal. You need to do more. Confront the past head-on. Incidentally, that's also what your book needs."

"Okay. That makes sense, I guess." Tessa hadn't actually given much thought to how the process of facing her demons on Cassadaga Island would actually work. She had been so caught up in the wider idea that she hadn't bothered to consider the details. Far from making her feel better, Thomas Milner's words had plunged her into a deeper pit of frustration than before. She could feel the hope slipping away. "Where would I even begin?"

"Well, why not start with the person who put you in this situation. Patrick Moyer. It's him you need to confront if you're ever going to live a normal life."

"Patrick Moyer is dead."

"He is. But that hasn't stopped him from terrorizing you all these years. He's the only reason you're there in the first place."

"I suppose."

"What do you even know about the man? I mean, besides the obvious fact that he was a killer."

"Nothing," Tessa admitted. "I've actively tried to avoid reading about him and what happened back then."

"Maybe you should take a different approach. He grew up on the island. Still came back every summer. Start your book there, digging deeper into Patrick Moyer's background. What did he do on the island? Where did he live? How friendly was he with the locals? Why did no one see the monster that lurked inside him?"

"I don't know . . ." The last thing Tessa wanted was to know more about the man who almost killed her. But at the same time, Thomas Milner had a point. Avoiding the truth of what happened that night and hiding behind a wall of ignorance and insomnia would sabotage any hope of conquering her fears. "You really think I can do this?"

"The only person who can answer that is you." Milner took a breath. "But I know one thing. It will give your book the opening you've been struggling to find. Think you can handle it?"

"I'll give it a go." Tessa's mouth was dry again. A thousand butterflies swarmed inside her stomach.

"Wonderful. Glad I could be of help." Milner bade her goodbye, saying he had another call coming in, and hung up.

Tessa stared at the phone for a long minute, wondering if she really could handle it. A weight of silence pressed in around her, thick like mud. The house was holding its breath. And at that moment, she could almost hear the whispering voices of her friends. Sense the lingering reverberations of their long-extinguished screams.

A chill ran through her.

Tessa shook the feeling off and turned toward the kitchen, intending to take a bottle of wine from the rack. But as she did so, her eyes wandered toward the window next to the fireplace and across the wild expanse to the house next door. Cindy's house. A light burned on the back porch; the glow diffused by a creeping blanket of mist that lay close to the ground.

Cindy was in a rocking chair, wineglass in hand, staring beyond the bluff and out to the restless ocean with a blanket wrapped around her shoulders.

Faced with drinking alone while thoughts of Patrick Moyer rattled through her head, socializing with Cindy didn't seem quite so bad. It would also be a minor victory that she could build on to gather the courage for what she had to do next.

Baby steps, she muttered to herself. *You really can do this.*

Then she pulled on a sweater, left through the back door, and hurried across the deck toward her neighbor's house before she thought about it some more and changed her mind.

27

Tessa spent a second night on the couch. Her phone call with Thomas Milner and uncharacteristically brave social interaction with Cindy had still not left her ready to face any of the bedrooms. She had returned from her neighbor's porch buzzed and pleased with herself, but once she stepped inside the rental house, the old anxieties returned. She briefly considered starting her search for Patrick Moyer's past right there and then, even opened her laptop to see what she could find, but then thought better of it and closed the lid. Instead, she lit a fire and curled up on the couch, falling asleep to the distant moan of the Snake Island foghorn.

She woke sometime after dawn and sat up, almost knocking over the baseball bat she had leaned against the couch. She stretched, feeling the knots in her back twist in protest. A few more nights of this and she would really be feeling it.

After getting dressed, she went to the kitchen and made coffee, then walked outside and settled on one of the Adirondack chairs near the firepit and stared across the ocean.

The fog had vanished. A boat was moving across the bay, far out near one of the other islands that dotted the horizon, and leaving a frothy wake as it went. Tessa guessed it was a lobsterman heading out to the fishing grounds in the Gulf of Maine. She watched until the vessel slipped out of sight, then let her gaze wander back over the pebble beach to the deck.

Five years ago, her friends had sat in this exact spot. She could picture the four of them sitting around the firepit each evening, drinking bottles of light beer and laughing, blissfully unaware of the horror that lurked in their future. She could see Patrick Moyer in her mind's eye as he strolled along the beach toward the far side of the cove that last afternoon while they sunbathed. She wondered if their encounter was purely circumstantial or if he'd spotted the girls previously and was already anticipating his gruesome fun.

They had been on the island for several days when he crossed their path. Sunset Cove was one of many inlets and small tucked-away beaches on the island. It was remote and quiet. But even so, he could have wandered past at some point earlier in the week and identified the girls as suitable targets. Isolated and helpless.

This thought made her blood run cold.

Were they his only victims, she wondered, or had he killed before?

Moyer had been cool and calculated. Calm. He drank beer with them and flirted as if he were just another regular Joe enjoying the company of four attractive college girls. He even used his real name, which had always surprised her. Of course, he didn't anticipate any of his victims living long enough to identify him. This was not a crime of circumstance. It was planned. He laughed and joked around that firepit, knowing full well that he was going to come back later and commit murder.

She sucked in a deep breath. What would she find when she dug into Patrick Moyer's past? Were the inhabitants of Seaview Point really oblivious to the monster who walked among them, or had they suspected a devil lurked within the handsome man with pale-blue eyes even before he paid a deadly visit to Tessa and her friends?

She was still contemplating this when a voice rose over the breeze, calling her name.

Tessa opened her eyes and glanced around, saw a lone figure on the beach looking in her direction. It was the server from the diner,

Roxanne. She wore high boots, jeans, and a tight sweater with a red beanie hat pulled down over her head.

She waved a hand and started up the beach toward the house.

Tessa's throat constricted. She looked around desperately for an escape but saw none.

"Hey." Roxanne appeared oblivious to Tessa's discomfort. She stepped off the beach. "I wasn't expecting to see you again so soon, especially out at this end of the island. I figured you'd be renting a condo in town."

"Nope. This is home for the next month."

Roxanne's eyes strayed past Tessa toward the house. "It's big. You're not staying here all by yourself, are you?"

Tessa opened her mouth to answer, but then closed it again. She didn't want to admit to a virtual stranger that she was all alone in the beach house.

"Sorry. That was intrusive," Roxanne said quickly.

"No, it's fine." Tessa's mug was empty. She stood up. "I'm getting myself another coffee. Would you like one?"

"Sure. I usually keep walking until the trail splits at Bartle Cove about a mile from here and then take the woodland path in a loop back around to the road, but what the hell. I can walk anytime. Coffee sounds great."

"Take a seat." Tessa nodded toward an Adirondack chair and picked up her mug. She went back into the kitchen. When she returned to the firepit with two fresh mugs of coffee in hand, her visitor was sitting, studying the house.

When Tessa approached, she smiled. "This is nice. I'm not used to someone fetching coffee for me."

Tessa laughed. "Just make sure you leave a decent tip."

"I already gave you a good tip. I told you not to eat the corned beef hash at the diner." Roxanne's eyes sparkled with mischief. "That's worth way more than money."

"You really don't like the hash at that place, do you?" Tessa said.

"Try it one time and you'll see why." Roxanne sipped her coffee. "This is much better than walking. I should stop by here every morning."

"I'll be here. It's not like there's much else to do on the island."

"Tell me about it. You think it's bad now, wait until the dead of winter. Even the diner closes in January and February when we're knee-deep in snow and the nor'easters blow through."

"Have you always lived on the island?"

"Pretty much. I thought about leaving a few times but never got around to it. My parents have a house they rent to me at a rate that makes it hard to go somewhere else. They moved to Florida a few years ago. My mother has arthritis and couldn't take the cold anymore."

"That must be tough."

"She gets by," Roxanne said. "They still come up here in the summer, and then I really wish I lived somewhere else. The place isn't big enough for all of us, at least that's how it feels to me now. It's only a two-bedroom fisherman's cottage. What about you?"

"I live with my sister in Gloucester. It's a long story."

"And one you don't want to share, judging by the tone of your voice." Roxanne's eyes strayed toward the house yet again. "I assume you know the history of this place?"

"It would be hard for me not to," Tessa said. "I mean, there's a framed newspaper in the front hallway with a headline about the murders. I couldn't stand seeing it every time I went to the door, so I took it down the day I got here."

"Don't blame you. I would too." Roxanne set her coffee mug down. "What happened here was horrific. It shook the entire town. We didn't feel safe in our beds for months. Even after the chief took care of the killer, we were still nervous. Before that, people used to leave their doors unlocked. It wasn't like in the city. Crime was practically nonexistent. But after Patrick Moyer, everyone bought dead bolts and chains."

"I would too," Tessa said, thinking of the locks she'd installed on her bedroom door back in Gloucester. Of course, she had much more reason to be afraid. "Did you know him?"

"Who?"

"Patrick Moyer."

Roxanne hesitated, as if gathering her thoughts. Tessa thought she saw a dark shadow pass behind her eyes. "He was a few years older than me, but I knew him in passing. It's a tight-knit community, and everyone knows everyone else."

Tessa said nothing. She sensed the tension in the air and wasn't sure if it was coming from her or from Roxanne. Maybe it was coming from both of them.

Roxanne leaned forward. "Patrick grew up on the island, but he was pretty much a seasonal resident by the time of the murders. He worked as a guide on the whale-watching boats. Who knows where he went in the winter, but it was probably a good thing he wasn't here year-round. There was talk that perhaps the killings in this house weren't his first."

"Seriously?" A chill ran up Tessa's spine.

Roxanne nodded. "Those were the rumors. Maybe it was just small-town gossip. There was never any hard proof. I'm not sure they even investigated after he got shot."

"I wonder why?" Tessa said.

"Beats me." Roxanne shrugged. "I don't know if anyone off the island ever looked into his past, but around here, people were just glad he was gone. I know I slept easier."

"I get that," Tessa said, suppressing a shudder.

"Strange thing was, he didn't come across as a psycho. He was always outgoing and friendly. Good-looking too. He had these piercing pale-blue eyes. Kinda neat-looking."

"I remember," Tessa said. A sudden image of Patrick Moyer peering into her hiding place under the bed forced its way into her mind. She would never forget those eyes as long as she lived. She must have made a sound, because when the real world snapped back into focus, Roxanne was staring at her with a perplexed expression. She shook the moment off and quickly added, "From the news coverage, I mean."

"Ah. There was a lot of that. Town was practically overrun with reporters after the murders. Especially over on Seabreeze Avenue after the chief shot him."

"Is that where he lived?"

Roxanne nodded. "It's on the outskirts of town. The yellow cottage with the blue door and white picket fence."

"You make it sound so quaint."

"It is, except for the sick monster who lived there." Roxanne glanced at her watch, then downed the last of her coffee. "I've taken up enough of your time. I should probably get going."

"You don't have to rush off." Despite herself, Tessa was enjoying the company. "I can get you a second cup of coffee."

"It's tempting, but I really should go. Lots to do today. It was nice chatting, though. We'll have to hang out again sometime."

"I'd like that. As you probably guessed, I'm all alone here," she admitted.

"I figured as much." Roxanne stood up. She rubbed her hands together for warmth. "Don't freak yourself out in that house, okay?"

"I'll do my best," Tessa said with a smile.

"Later." Roxanne stepped off the deck onto the beach and made her way toward the coastal path climbing over the bluff and out of the cove. She turned and waved.

Tessa waved back, then gathered up the coffee cups and went inside with thoughts of Patrick Moyer's cute coastal cottage still fresh in her mind.

28

Tessa stood in the middle of the living room and stared at the framed newspaper facing inward on the floor next to the front door. Thomas Milner had suggested she jump-start her writing by confronting her fears. Learning more about Patrick Moyer and what drove him to murder. Her conversation with Roxanne had been a beginning, but it wasn't enough. Not by a long shot. If she was going to write anything worthwhile, she had to give herself a jolt—and fast.

She crossed the room and lifted the frame, then carried it to the couch where she placed it face up on the coffee table and sat in front of it.

The headline screamed at her, igniting a flurry of conflicting emotions. She almost stood and put the frame back where she found it. After all, this newspaper was printed right after the murders, before anyone knew the killer's identity. But she didn't—because even if she couldn't glean any information about Patrick Moyer from the paper, it would hopefully contain other information she would find useful for the book.

Tessa had avoided reading newspaper accounts of the crime or watching news reports back then. Her only perspective on what happened came from her limited viewpoint as she hid under the bed upstairs. How could she write about a crime she knew practically nothing about except the fact that her friends had screamed in terror before they died?

Tessa leaned forward and examined the framed front page, ignoring the coiling snake in her gut. But aside from the sensational headline and a photo of the house with cop cars outside, there was little else visible. The article itself was cut off behind a cream-colored matte board.

She turned the frame over and pulled at the tabs holding the back on, then lifted it out. The single newspaper page was folded in half and stuck onto the matting by a single yellowed piece of brittle tape that came away when she plucked at it with the nail of her index finger. Now the page came free. She lifted it gently and unfolded the sheet on the coffee table to reveal several column inches of the article and another photo of two paramedics bringing a victim out of the house on a gurney. She couldn't tell which of her friends it was because there was a sheet covering the body. The accompanying article was light on detail, recounting the number of victims, that there was a survivor, and that the unidentified perpetrator was still at large. There was a brief statement by the Seaview Point chief of police, asking residents to stay in their homes and lock their doors. He also promised to bring the killer to justice. A line at the bottom of the column read *Continued on page 5.*

There was no page five. Just the front page. And when she looked on the back, a full-page ad for a car dealership in Biddeford. Tessa put the newspaper back in the frame and returned it to the wall near the door, facing inward. She felt a rush of satisfaction. A small demon faced. But it hadn't given her any new information.

Going back to the couch, Tessa opened her laptop. Maybe the newspaper had an online archive. There might be more articles. Some of them about Patrick Moyer. But then she stopped, fingers poised above the keyboard. Those articles would also be full of details. Horrific details she wasn't sure she was ready to absorb. Not yet.

She closed the laptop again and pushed it away, then stood up. The house pressed in on all sides. It was as if the oxygen had been sucked from the room. She needed to get out. Get away from this place, if only for a few hours. Then she could return refreshed and ready to face whatever the newspaper archives had in store.

Maybe it was time to explore the island. After all, it was the setting for her book, and she had seen none of it except the grocery store, the diner, and Sunset Cove. Making up her mind, Tessa went to the front of the house, grabbed her keys from the table next to the door, and hurried outside.

◆ ◆ ◆

She drove south first, but the road ended abruptly a mile past the beach house. Beyond this was nothing but a walking trail and endless woodland. She turned around and headed back in the other direction, following the coast road until she arrived in Seaview Point.

The town was pretty much deserted. The parking lot in front of the supermarket contained two cars, one of which Tessa figured must belong to Walt. She continued on, noting the number of businesses that were closed for the season. There were two more restaurants in town aside from the diner in which she'd eaten the day before and the ice-cream parlor next to the supermarket. Acadia Pizza, which was only open limited hours in the winter, and a shuttered and dark seafood shack. She did, however, notice a bar on the north side of town with a red neon OPEN sign flashing in its blacked-out window. A sign hanging above the door announced the saloon's name: THE SHIP TO SHORE TAVERN. There were a couple of cars and a motorcycle parked out front. It looked like one of those places that had been around for decades and probably catered more to locals than tourists.

On the edge of town, Main Street took a gradual curve and meandered up a low hill. A small white church with a square spire clad in decorative shingles came into view, and beyond that, a narrow side street. As Tessa drew closer, she noticed the road name: Seabreeze Avenue—the location of Patrick Moyer's house. It was such a pretty name. Innocent. Quaint. And yet that unassuming road had sheltered a monster.

Tessa's curiosity was roused.

She slowed and turned, then drove along at a crawl, looking left and right for the yellow house with the blue door. She passed a cute white Cape-style with three dormers. The house on the opposite side of the street was just as picturesque, with a wraparound front porch and a widow's walk. A name plaque near the front door identified it as Oceanview House. The glimpses of rippling water between the trees and heaving boulders beyond the dwelling made the name's origin obvious.

She continued on, passing three more gorgeous homes on large wooded lots, and wondered if she had made a mistake. The Patrick Moyer in her head didn't fit in here. He was an incongruous detail in an otherwise tranquil setting. Maybe there was another similarly named road in less pleasant surroundings.

But there wasn't, because she saw it now, tucked back at the end of the street behind a leaning picket fence. The house was shedding its paint in scaly yellow flakes. The asphalt roof tiles were lifting, and some had come off altogether, giving the roof a patchy, uneven appearance. The windows were dark, soulless voids obscuring what lay within. A separate one-car garage was in a similar state of disrepair. A huge stack of lobster traps, fifty or more, stood next to the garage, with weeds growing up through their wire frames. Coils of old rope, hundreds of feet of it, had been dumped nearby. The property stood in stark contrast to its neighbors, giving off an air of decrepit abandonment. And if there was any doubt regarding the previous occupant, it was dispelled by the fading name painted on the dinged and rusting mailbox: MOYER.

Tessa's heart leaped into her throat. She brought the car to a halt and climbed out, then stood and stared at the house. This was where evil had lived. Behind that faded-blue door had lurked a true monster—at least until Seaview Point's chief of police ended him there. She took her phone out and snapped a photo, ignoring the creeping sensation of horror the house instilled in her. This moment would be in her book—of that she was sure—and she didn't want to forget that first flicker of revulsion. She looked down at the screen, about to raise the phone for a second picture, when a voice rang out.

"Hey. What do you think you're doing?"

Tessa looked up to find the blue door standing open and a man striding toward her, his face creased in anger. And in that moment, she almost collapsed from shock because she recognized those dusty-blue eyes, that dark wavy hair, and that chiseled jaw.

It was a face she would never forget.

It was Patrick Moyer.

29

Tessa screamed.

She stumbled backward, never taking her eyes off Moyer, until the car blocked her retreat. A thousand panicked thoughts washed through her mind in a tsunami of confusion and terror. But one thought rose above all others. How could the man who had abused and almost killed her still be alive? Chief White had shot Moyer dead in this very house. That was what everyone had said. The newspapers. News channels. The caretaker. Even Roxanne earlier that day. Yet here he was, coming down the path toward her with a simmering rage glinting in his eyes.

It was impossible, but what she was seeing didn't lie.

Patrick Moyer was right there in front of her, as real as the day she and her friends first met him at Sunset Cove.

But once the initial shock ebbed and she looked closer, a more reasonable explanation presented itself. The man resembled Moyer, but there were subtle differences. His eyes were darker. His jaw was not so straight. And he was at least a couple of inches shorter, too, she thought.

"Why are you photographing my house?" he asked, coming to a stop at the end of his path. "Didn't you see the signs?"

Tessa's gaze flicked briefly to the fence, and now she saw them. Two weathered planks of wood screwed to the slats, bearing commands in sloppy hand-painted black lettering. One simply read Go Away. The other bore a more pointed message—No Photos. She flushed with shame. "I'm so sorry . . . I didn't realize . . ." She fumbled to unlock her phone. "I'll delete them."

"Damn right, you will." The man placed his hands on the closed gate, as if he thought she might attempt to encroach upon his property. "People like you make me sick."

Tessa's heart was racing. All she wanted to do was jump back in her car and slam the door closed. Put a barrier between herself and this man. But she was afraid to move—to take her eyes off him even for an instant—in case he pounced. "I don't understand."

"Murder groupies. People who don't come to the island for the lobster rolls or the puffin tour, but to get a cheap thrill from what happened five years ago. That is why you're here, right? Because my dumb brother killed a bunch of people."

Brother. That was why he looked so much like Patrick Moyer. But it didn't put her at ease. Insanity could run in families—couldn't it? "I'm not one of those people. I just . . ." Tessa swallowed. "That isn't why I'm here."

"Sure. Which is why you're so interested in my house. Standing out here like some slack-jawed tourist. Honestly, I've had enough. People been coming around here harassing me for five years. If I could cut my losses and get the hell off this godforsaken island, I would, but no one wants anything to do with the house where the Cassadaga Island Ripper lived and died. But hey, you're here taking photos. You must like the place. Want to buy it off me?"

Tessa shook her head. The cold, hard metal of the car's trunk pressed against her lower back.

"No? Didn't think so." Patrick Moyer's brother snorted. "Figures."

"I'm sorry. I didn't mean to offend you." Tessa edged along the car toward the driver-side door.

"Yeah." Now it was the brother's turn to shake his head. He leaned on the gate and watched as Tessa fumbled for the door handle without turning her back on him.

She had the uncomfortable sensation that he was staring straight at the puckered scar curving up her jawline and beneath her hair. A scar that might as well be a flashing neon sign that proclaimed I'M THE VICTIM YOUR BROTHER DIDN'T QUITE KILL.

Had he recognized her?

Tessa's fingers finally found the door handle. She tugged at it with a profound sense of relief and scrambled into the driver's seat, slamming the door behind her and starting the car with trembling hands. She pulled away with a squeal of tires, pressing the accelerator much too hard and fast, and kept going until she reached Main Street, never daring to look in her rearview mirror for fear that Patrick Moyer's brother would still be there, watching.

30

Tessa's heart was racing. The man who currently occupied the yellow cottage with the blue door looked so much like Patrick Moyer . . . It felt like the past and the present had come crashing together to occupy the same moment in time. Worse, she was sure he was looking at her scar. Studying it. If he realized who she was, then he might also wonder what she was doing back here. Might try to find out. That thought made Tessa squirm in her seat. Was she in any danger from Moyer's brother?

That was a hard question to answer, but she knew one thing. She wasn't ready to return to the beach house and sit in terrified isolation as that thought rattled through her mind. So instead, she turned right onto Main Street and drove in the opposite direction from town, continuing toward the north end of the island until it picked up the coast road again.

Roxanne was right. There wasn't much on this end of the island except trees and immense granite ledges where the bedrock lay exposed to the elements. She drove by a cluster of small inlets and a couple of larger coves before the road took a turn inland through dense woodland with only sporadic signs of habitation. A dilapidated cottage with busted-out windows. A barn with a sagging roof. An old double-wide with plywood over the windows and scorch marks creeping up the sides, sitting in a small overgrown clearing next to a rusting car with no hood. It had obviously caught fire at some point in the past and had been abandoned.

And that was how this end of the island felt. Abandoned. As if no one dared to live in the wilds beyond Seaview Point.

Then, as if to confirm her suspicion, the road curved back toward the ocean, and she glimpsed another abandoned building rising over the trees on a jetting headland. It was the lighthouse Roxanne had told her about. The tower still stood, and Tessa could see the faint outline of alternate black and white stripes even though the wind had long ago scoured most of the paint away. But the lightkeeper's dwelling was nothing but a chimney stack and broken foundation scattered with loose bricks. Weeds grew up and around it as if they were trying to reclaim the structure for nature.

She pulled off the road onto a graveled area to the side of the structure and climbed out of the car, then strolled closer to the base of the lighthouse and craned her neck to look up toward the lantern room at the top of the tower. She could make out the railings on the gantry circling the top and, beyond them, the lantern room's glass panels, some of which were cracked. Others were completely gone. Within that room would be the long-dead beacon itself and the Fresnel lens that sent the light out over the open ocean in a tight beam. She felt a pang of sadness for this long-forgotten relic that would never be put to work again.

It was like her. Lonely and broken.

She turned back to the car. And that was when she saw the vehicle parked on the road fifty feet distant. It was an older-model sedan with faded-blue paint. The interior lay in shadow, and all she could see of the occupant was an unidentifiable dark shape hunched over the steering wheel—as if watching her.

Tessa drew in a quick breath.

Was it Patrick Moyer's brother? Had he followed her here? She couldn't remember seeing a car after she drove away from the house on Seabreeze Avenue, but maybe he'd hung back. Stayed out of view until she stopped at this lonely place. Then she remembered something else. The first night and the sounds she had thought were footsteps on her porch. Maybe it wasn't Moyer's brother. He seemed more interested in getting rid of her than following her. Could she have attracted the attention of someone else? It didn't seem likely. Yet . . .

The car was still there, engine idling. A faint plume of white smoke curled from the vehicle's exhaust and dissipated on the breeze.

Tessa was sure the person behind the wheel was staring at her—could almost feel their gaze like a heavy weight, full of menace. She stood frozen, unsure what to do. The vehicle was parked such that she would be forced to drive past it to escape.

Her thoughts turned to the baseball bat, which she hadn't brought with her because she never carried it in public. Absent that meager protection, she was defenseless. Except for the cell phone, which sat snug in her hip pocket. She reached for it and was dismayed to see the words *No service* on the screen. Apparently, the cell tower's range didn't extend this far north on the island.

Tessa stepped toward her car, reached out to open the door.

The sedan's engine revved. It inched forward.

Tessa yanked the car door open and jumped inside, heart pounding. She tried to slip the key into the ignition without dropping her gaze from the blue sedan but failed. She swore and looked down, just for an instant. When she lifted her head again, the other car was making a slow turn on the gravel lot, tires crunching. It passed by her—the driver still nothing but a dark shape—and swung back toward the road.

Tessa watched it go, thumb and index finger still on the key, until the sedan disappeared back toward Seaview Point. It was only then that she realized her hand was shaking.

31

Tessa returned to town, driving as fast as she dared. Her encounter with Patrick Moyer's brother and then the creepy car out at the lighthouse had left her more than a little uneasy, even though she had tried to reason it all away on the drive back to Seaview Point. Just because Patrick Moyer was a depraved killer didn't mean his brother was. And as for the car . . . It was probably just some other bored individual out for a drive. But she wasn't sure how much of that she believed. Which was why she dreaded going back to the beach house and sitting there all alone as the sky grew dark and the fog crept off the ocean. Instead, she found herself overcome by a rare desire for company. A friendly face. And she knew where to find it.

The Harbor Diner.

Except Roxanne wasn't there when she entered. Instead, a plump woman of more advanced years with wiry gray hair and ruby-red cheeks occupied the spot behind the counter. There were more customers in the diner today too. A younger couple sitting at a table near the hearth, warming themselves in front of the crackling fire. A group of older men with white beards and faces wrinkled like roadmaps—probably commercial fishermen fresh off a boat—occupied a corner. She almost left, but didn't. She had wanted companionship, and even if Roxanne was not around, this was progress. Besides, she was hungry.

Taking a stool at the counter, she gave the menu a quick look before ordering the Thursday special: chicken pot pie. She hoped Frank was better with pies than Roxanne said he was with hash. She also ordered a hot tea, which she drank quickly before signaling for a refill.

She took her phone out and checked her email while she waited, then browsed the web, mostly to occupy herself with something other than thoughts of the yellow house on Seabreeze Avenue and the man who dwelt within.

She was still staring at her phone when a voice cut through her concentration.

"Did you make the bread yet?"

Tessa looked around and was dismayed to find Noah loitering a few feet away, hands pushed into his pockets. "I'm sorry?"

"You wanted dry yeast so you could make bread. I wondered if you made it yet?" Noah's face was expressionless, his eyes a pair of shiny marbles with dark centers that observed her, unblinking.

"No, I haven't made bread yet." Tessa squirmed on the stool, trying to tame the unease that always accompanied unexpected social interaction, especially with those of the opposite sex. Now she wished she had driven on by and returned to the cottage.

"I bet it will be real good. I like fresh bread. My ma used to make it all the time, but she died when I was still a kid."

"I'm sorry to hear that." Tessa squirmed on her seat. Why was he was telling a complete stranger such a thing? She wondered again if he was lonely. Looking for attention.

"It's okay. Happened a long time ago. She fell down the basement stairs. Snapped her neck. She went pretty quick."

"That must've been awful for you." Tessa tried to sound sympathetic. Thought she did a pretty good job under the circumstances.

"I was in the house with her when it happened. My pa was at work. I found her laying there all broken." Noah gave a small exhalation that sounded like a cross between a sigh and a cough. "It was an accident."

"I'm sure it was." Tessa motioned toward the phone. "If you don't mind, I have work to do."

"Looked like you were playing on the web to me." Noah sniffed. "Have you met Roxanne yet?"

"Yes. I came here yesterday, and she was working." Tessa didn't mention that they'd also shared coffee that morning at the beach house. She didn't want to engage Noah any more than necessary, even though she knew he was probably just trying to be friendly in his own weird way. Over the years, various therapists had talked about the need for Tessa to grasp the difference between a genuine threat and an imaginary one. Most people did not harbor hidden agendas, at least not violent ones, and were merely being sociable. Tessa had been urged to work through the emotions that came to the surface whenever she found herself in such a situation. This was easy when it was someone like Roxanne, whom she did not view as a threat. She actually felt safe around other women. Men were an entirely different matter, and after her encounter with Moyer's brother—even if he was an innocent victim of Patrick's reputation—her nerves were raw.

Noah didn't appear to sense her discomfort.

"You shouldn't get too close to Roxanne," he said.

"Really? Why is that?" Tessa asked, surprised by Noah's forthrightness.

"No particular reason." Noah shrugged. "I've known her a long time, and I'm offering some friendly advice. She's not what she seems, that's all."

"I'll keep that in mind. If there's nothing else, my food will be here soon."

"Ah. I'm intruding on your peace." A thin smile broke across Noah's face. "I'll leave you to get back to your . . . work. Think about what I said, okay?"

"I will," Tessa said, although all she could think about at that moment was getting rid of Noah.

"Okay, then." Noah took a step toward the door before looking back over his shoulder. "Oh, I almost forgot. If you need any more groceries and don't want to drive into town, just give Walt a call at the supermarket and tell him what you want. I'd be more than happy to bring them out to you. I deliver to a lot of the homes hereabouts, especially in winter. Some folk can't get about when the weather turns bad."

"That's a very kind offer," Tessa said. "But I'll be fine. It's good to get out of the house once in a while."

"Offer's there if you need it," Noah said with a shrug, then stepped through the door and was lost from sight.

Tessa sat for a while watching the empty doorway, then turned back to her phone. She wasn't sure what to make of the encounter with Noah. He scared her. Then again, every man she'd met in the past five years scared her. Her compass on normality was so far off she wasn't sure what to think. Tessa reached up and touched the puckered scar under her chin where Patrick Moyer's knife had sliced her. Why had Noah warned her about Roxanne? As far as he knew, Tessa had only spoken to the woman briefly the previous day in the diner. Tessa resolved to ask her about Noah the next time they saw each other. There was clearly an issue between the pair, and Tessa would need to decide if one—or both of them—should be avoided.

She looked down at her phone but didn't feel much like clicking around the internet now. She slipped the phone back into her pocket and sat leaning on the counter. Less than a minute later, the food arrived.

32

After she finished eating, Tessa left the diner and drove home. The chicken pot pie was good. A hearty portion that left her overstuffed. She figured she wouldn't need to eat for the rest of the day.

As she drove, the sun dropped below the horizon, and by the time she arrived at the house, it was already dark. She hadn't intended to stop and eat in town and so had left no lights on. She climbed out of the car and hurried indoors, only feeling safe once the dead bolt was engaged and she had gone through the house and turned on all the ground-floor lights. The house was cold. Actually, more like frigid. She considered checking the boiler to see if it was working—but nixed that idea. There was no way she was going to venture into the basement at night. A basement she hadn't even explored yet. It could wait until morning. Or she could just call the caretaker and ask her to deal with it. Instead, she lit a fire and settled on the couch.

She pulled the laptop close and opened it. An idea had formed while she was driving back to the house. A way to start the book with a bang. Thomas Milner had been right. She needed to get out, explore Patrick Moyer's past, even if it had resulted in an uncomfortable encounter with his brother. But maybe it was worth the brief terror of seeing someone who bore such an uncanny resemblance to the demon who had haunted her these past five years, because she finally knew what to say and how to say it.

Consumed by inspiration, she hunched over the keyboard and started to write:

◆ ◆ ◆

The house stands on a quiet backstreet near the edge of town, next to the ocean. It would look like its neighbors—quaint and picturesque—except for the peeling paint and unkempt yard. An air of abandonment wafts from the two-floor shingle-style home like a bad smell. And something else too. The stench of evil. Because this is not an ordinary house. Not anymore. A killer made this place his lair. Patrick Moyer. The man who ripped away the lives of my friends five years ago and almost did the same to me. Almost!

And now, as I stand on the street outside this monument to the perverse urges of a sick mind and survey its decaying facade, I wonder what drew me back here—to the place where I almost died. To the island where I encountered a devil in human skin. And the answer comes quickly. To survive. To put the demons that haunt me to rest. Face my past in order to save my future . . .

Tessa paused and looked over the words on the screen. She smiled, the anxiety melting away. She could do this. She really could. Eager to keep going, she went back to work.

At ten o'clock, after pounding away at the keyboard for hours and producing ten pages of what she considered good writing, Tessa closed the laptop, mentally exhausted, and turned the TV on. She watched until midnight with a blanket wrapped around her, trying not to think about the impending decision of where to sleep.

She had spent the last two nights on the couch and knew it wasn't a viable long-term solution. The knots in her back were still there and would only get worse the longer she avoided the bedrooms. She rose and wandered into the master, gazing longingly at the king-size bed and the crisp, clean sheets. It looked so inviting. It would also take more nerves than she currently possessed to sleep in there. Not going to happen. Not tonight.

She went to leave, but then, out of the blue, a memory rose out of her subconscious. She stopped. Turned back. Could almost see her friends right there in that room.

◆ ◆ ◆

She rushes through the house with Madison on her heels. She's going to pick the best bedroom first, but Madison figures out what she's up to and is hot on her trail. Theresa opens the first door in the hallway and sees a quaint room with a blue-floral coverlet and a full-size bed. Not the best room, *she thinks as she quickly moves on to the next door. This room reveals a queen-size bed with a sunny-yellow coverlet. The room is a bit bigger, but Theresa has seen the pictures of the place online, and she knows that there is still a better room. The next door is the jackpot. A large master bedroom with its own bathroom and large sliding glass doors looking out over a beautiful beach, the clear blue water sparkling from the rays of the sun.*

"Aha, caught you," laughs Madison as she grabs Theresa by the belt loop of her shorts and tugs her back from the doorway.

"I'm here first, fair and square," Theresa says, reaching out and grasping the doorframe while Madison tries unsuccessfully to drag her out of the room. The girls look at each other and break out in a fit of giggles as they both dive for the bed, each making a claim for the master bedroom.

At that moment, Courtney walks in, suitcase rolling behind her. "Out of my room, girls. The first one with a suitcase gets dibs, and that's me." She smirks as she depresses the handle and opens a dresser drawer.

"That's not how it works."

"It is now." Courtney makes a shooing motion toward them. "My room. Out."

◆ ◆ ◆

The unexpected memory left Tessa shaken. If it wasn't for Courtney's overbearing personality, it would have been her lying dead in that bedroom while someone else cowered upstairs. She owed her life to that stupid suitcase and her friend's made-up rules. Tessa turned and hurried back into the living room, where she sat for several minutes, thinking about her friends and wondering why death had decided to pay them a visit and not some other house. But if there was an answer to that question, it remained elusive.

Enough was enough. She wiped away a tear and changed into her flannel pajamas. Then, with the television playing and the lamp next to the sofa on the lowest of its three brightness settings, she climbed under the blanket and closed her eyes.

33

"Theresa."

The voice floated over the landscape of Tessa's dream as nothing more than a gentle whisper. It weaved itself into the fabric of the false world her mind had conjured. A place where she ran along an endless beach while bloodred waves lapped against the shore and a teenage boy leered at her from the back deck of a house that she could never reach.

"Hello, Theresa. I saved the best for last."

The voice spoke again, sibilant and menacing.

Tessa stopped on the beach and looked around—first one way, then the other.

The boy on the deck raised an arm, pointing along the shoreline toward a figure walking near the water. A man backlit against a pale winter sun that hovered near the horizon. Even though she could not make out his features, she knew instinctively who the man was.

Patrick Moyer.

The breath caught in her throat. She gave a strangled cry and turned to run, but her legs were heavy, like they were made of lead.

Moyer had no such limitations. He gained ground with every step, and now she saw his face—skeletal in death—and the rictus grin that split it.

"No!" she cried out, battling the terror that clawed within her like a trapped beast. "Stay away from me."

The boy on the deck whooped with glee. He clapped his hands together and jumped up and down, unable to contain his excitement.

Tessa stumbled along, desperate to reach the safety of the beach house where she could lock the doors and hide. But the house grew more distant with each footfall, as if it were trying to elude Tessa in the same manner that she was frantic to evade Patrick Moyer.

"Leave me alone." Tessa's voice sounded thin and hollow. Any moment now, he would catch up with her. Throw her to the ground.

She dreaded the feel of his hands upon her neck. The weight of his body as he pressed down on top of her and did unspeakable things. Painful things. And even though she realized this was only a dream, a nightmare conjured from her own subconscious, it made no difference.

Awake or asleep, the terror was the same.

"Theresa . . ." There was that voice again, but it wasn't Moyer who spoke. Nor was it the boy on the deck. It swirled around her, coming from every direction at the same time.

The voice spoke again, more forcefully now. "Wake up!"

The beach fractured and fell apart, splitting into a million shards that tumbled into blackness just as Patrick Moyer reached out with grasping hands, intent upon completing what he'd left unfinished five years before.

Tessa's eyes flew open. It was the early hours of the morning. The room was dark except for the yellow glow of a lamp sitting on the side table next to the couch and the flickering television screen. A presenter, who looked like he'd spent too much time in a tanning bed, was talking too fast, hawking garish costume jewelry on some late-night infomercial. There were only eighteen minutes left to purchase the Deal of the Day. An ugly brooch with an obviously fake glass ruby sitting at its center.

For a moment, the infomercial held her attention as she wondered who would wear such a thing—apparently lots of people if you believed the ticker at the bottom of the screen.

The presenter moved on to another item—a necklace made from chunky teal slab beads of turquoise—and the sales pitch began anew.

Tessa lay still, listening, hardly daring to move. The voice in her dream had sounded so real. Almost like—a thousand pinpricks ran up her spine—it had come not from within the dream but outside of it.

The presenter was still talking. Only ten minutes left to snag the turquoise necklace, and then the chance would be lost forever.

A minute passed, then another.

People were *actually* buying the gaudy jewelry. The ticker claimed it was almost sold out.

Another minute.

The anxiety started to fade. The voice had been in her dream, after all.

She reached for the TV remote. The infomercial was inane. Mind numbing. There had to be something better on. But as her fingers touched the cool, hard plastic, there was a faint noise from somewhere above on the upper floor, like a shuffle of stealthy feet. Tessa's ears pricked up. She prayed there would be nothing else. But then, a moment later, the sound of a door quietly clicking closed.

Tessa's hand dropped to the side of the couch, groping for the baseball bat, but it wasn't there. She looked down to find it lying on the floor. The bat must have fallen while she was sleeping. Tessa swung her legs off the couch, picked up the bat, and stood. Beyond the window next to the fireplace, she could see the vague silhouette of another house through the trees, backlit by moonlight. Cindy's house. The windows were dark.

Her eyes flicked to the TV. The necklace had sold out. She turned it off, then stood and listened, straining to pick up any aberrant sound from the rooms above. Another skulking footfall. A brief exhalation of breath. Anything. But only silence greeted her ears.

Intruders could be silent. That was kind of their thing.

She didn't want to go up there. Hated the thought of climbing those stairs. Knew it would be impossible to relax until she was sure—*absolutely 100 percent sure*—that she was alone in the house.

Gathering her nerve, Tessa went to the stairs, turned on the hall light, and started up toward the second floor.

At the top, she stopped and studied her surroundings. Satisfied all was in order, she padded along the landing, checking the bathroom and the office first.

So far, so good.

She went to the narrow door leading into the unfinished attic area and opened it, sticking her head inside briefly before withdrawing and shutting the door again. Heart thumping, she crossed to the last door. The room where Patrick Moyer had tried to take her life. She gripped the doorknob and turned it—pushed the door open. Darkness consumed the room beyond. Only a thin sliver of pale moonlight intruded, casting a faint outline of the window on the floor. A blast of frigid air rushed past her as she swung the door wide and stepped inside, reaching for the light switch.

Then, without warning, the floor-length curtain on one side of the window moved.

Tessa stifled a scream and backed up, bumping into the doorframe. But then the curtain dropped back into place before billowing out again, and she realized it was just moving in the breeze.

Tessa slumped with relief. She turned the light on, then crossed to the window. It was open a crack, allowing a stir of frigid air into the room. She pulled the window closed with a grunt and latched it, then looked outside. The sloping porch roof lay a few feet below. It would be easy enough for a person to gain access by clambering onto that roof, assuming it would hold their weight. Likewise, an intruder could slip back out the same way.

But that wasn't possible. The alarm system, set in Home Mode, would have sounded if the window was opened. Tessa looked up at the small oblong box attached to the window frame. There was another screwed to the surround.

A contact sensor.

She unlatched the window and opened it again.

The alarm didn't respond. The system was supposed to go off when the sensor's connection was broken. It obviously didn't work. The window might have been unlatched the whole time she was here.

Tessa closed and secured the window again. As she did so, her gaze drifted beyond the glass to the dark landscape outside. And that was when she saw the car, shrouded in fog.

It was loitering a little way up the road almost beyond her field of vision. The car's headlights were off, rendering it nearly imperceptible against the backdrop of the woods. She pressed her face against the glass to get a better view.

The headlights snapped on, spearing the mist with twin shafts of brightness that reflected and bounced back. The car eased forward and rolled past the house at a crawl.

Tessa caught a better glimpse of the vehicle as it cruised by, and she was sure it was the same one that had been out at the lighthouse earlier that day. Who were they, and what did they want? More to the point, would they try and get inside the house—or had they already been inside? Alarmed at this thought and feeling suddenly vulnerable, Tessa backed away quickly from the window, turned, and raced toward the stairs.

34

Tessa's footfalls thudded on the steps as she flew downstairs, baseball bat swinging at her side. At the bottom, she rushed to the front of the house and peered out through the window, terrified of what she might see. Would the car be sitting there, the unknown occupant staring up at the house with ominous intent?

She needn't have worried. The car was gone, leaving only the dark, empty roadway and shifting fog. Tessa was alone. But what about before? The strange voice that had invaded her dreams. *Hello, Theresa. I saved the best for last.* Had she really just dreamed that or . . . Tessa didn't want to think about the alternative. The upstairs window hadn't been locked. Anyone could have shimmied up onto the porch roof, climbed in, and stood there watching her sleep. She imagined that same intruder leaning close as she lay on the couch. Imagined him whispering in her ear. A whisper that her sleeping mind had twisted into that of Patrick Moyer. Then, in the brief moment of panic after she awoke, they retreated quietly back upstairs and out the same way, only to sit in their car. Watching. Waiting.

She shuddered and moved away from the window, letting the curtain fall back in place.

Her phone was on the end table next to the couch.

Tessa ran to it and fumbled to enter the unlock code since facial recognition wouldn't work in the half-light. The number for the local police department was on the fridge. But before she started toward the kitchen, Tessa paused. What exactly could she say? That an upstairs window wasn't properly latched and a car drove by the house? She could imagine how that conversation would go.

Do you have any evidence of a break-in?

No.

Did the occupant of the car threaten you in any way?

No.

Did he even get out of the car?

No.

Did you actually see anyone inside the house?

No.

Ma'am, you had a bad dream and spooked yourself. Anyone could have left that window unlatched. It's a rental house. And even you admit that the sensor must be faulty. As for the car . . . Well, it's a public road. That's what cars do on public roads.

It didn't sound convincing, even to her. Then there was the other issue. According to the caretaker, Seaview Point's police department consisted of a single officer—Chief White—who would undoubtedly come out. Then there would be a man inside her house in the small hours, which was more than she could handle.

Tessa's shoulders slumped. She turned away from the kitchen and looked down at the phone. So, no police. But that didn't mean she couldn't call someone else. Like her sister. This time, she almost went through with it. Her finger hovered over the number. But instead, she went back to the couch and laid the phone on the side table again. A crazy-sounding call in the middle of the night would only convince Melissa that her coming to the island had been a terrible idea. At best, Tessa's credibility would be shot, and at worst, it would leave her sister fraught with worry for Tessa's state of mind. Frustrated, she put the phone down and turned the TV back on, then sat with the bat cradled in her lap and waited for dawn.

35

Even though she was determined not to sleep, Tessa must have dozed off, because the last thing she remembered, it was still dark, and now sunlight streamed through the windows.

Thankfully, the nightmare had not returned, nor the whispering voice. When she went to the window, there were no cars outside except her own. As often happened in the calm light of day, she began to wonder if she had overreacted yet again.

But there was still the matter of the upstairs window and the broken sensor.

It was too early to call the caretaker, so instead she made a pot of coffee and poured herself a cup. Grabbing a coat, she went out onto the back deck and sat, looking across the beach toward the ocean. She was still sitting there when a familiar figure came into view, strolling near the water's edge.

It was Roxanne. She waved and started up the beach toward the house.

Tessa placed her coffee cup on the deck and descended the steps to meet her new friend halfway.

"Fancy some company?" Tessa asked as she drew close. "Unless you'd rather hang out on the deck and have a coffee?"

"Already had my fill of caffeine for the day." Roxanne pushed a stray hair from her face. "But I'd love some company. I can never convince anyone else to walk with me in winter."

"It is kind of nippy out here," Tessa said, pulling her coat tight and zipping it up.

Roxanne laughed. "You're one to talk. You were sitting outside drinking coffee when I came along."

"I guess that makes me as crazy as you," Tessa said, walking alongside Roxanne. They crossed the beach, walking parallel to the water before climbing up a steep trail that ran toward the south tip of the island. Boulders and trees pressed in on both sides of them. The view across the bay was stunning from their high vantage point, but Tessa was in no mood to enjoy it.

Roxanne must have sensed her unease. "You still getting on okay at the beach house?"

"You mean, have I gotten myself freaked out yet?"

"Yeah. Have you?"

"A couple of times," Tessa admitted. She looked away so Roxanne wouldn't see the fear in her eyes. When she had gotten her emotions under control, she spoke again. "It's worst at night."

"I bet." Roxanne shuddered visibly. "I wouldn't spend the night in that place on my own. Not in a million years. How do you get any sleep?"

"It's not easy." Tessa stopped near a rocky outcrop and stared out across the ocean. She could see a small boat moving across the water, leaving a wake in its trail. "You want to hear something weird?"

"Sure." Roxanne turned back toward her.

"I was watching TV last night and fell asleep on the couch." Tessa didn't bother to mention that she was actually sleeping on the couch because she hadn't yet gathered the nerve to use a bedroom. "I don't know how long I was asleep, but I woke up to someone calling my name. I mean, not loud. More like a whisper."

"Ooh. That's too creepy."

"It gets worse. I could have sworn someone was standing right there behind the sofa, watching me."

"Oh my God. Stop. You're giving me goose bumps." Roxanne rubbed her arms.

"Sorry. We don't have to talk about this."

"Are you kidding? If you don't tell me what happened, I'll never sleep again. What did you do?"

"What do you think? I jumped up and looked. No one was there. But the thing is, I could have sworn the shadows moved like someone was right there, looming over me."

"Wow. That's intense." Roxanne glanced sideways toward Tessa. "It's no surprise you're imagining things. You rented a murder house, after all. And not just any old murder house. One where a triple homicide took place. The Sunset Cove Massacre. You must have been so scared."

"Terrified. I knew I'd never be able to sleep after that, so I grabbed my baseball bat and searched the entire house."

"You brought a baseball bat with you?"

"I'm staying in a strange place all by myself," Tessa said, figuring this answer was mostly true. "It makes me feel safe."

"Oh. I assume you didn't find anyone in the house?"

"Obviously not." Tessa hoped she didn't sound too crazy. "I did find a window open upstairs. It must have a broken alarm sensor."

"You should get that fixed."

"I'll call the caretaker when I get back to the house," Tessa said. "But it gets worse. There was a car sitting outside on the road. Like someone was watching the house. I'm sure I saw the same car earlier in the day too. Out at the abandoned lighthouse when I was exploring the island. At least, it looked the same in the darkness."

"I hope you called Chief White."

"The car was gone by the time I got back downstairs, and I had no proof of anything. I figured he wouldn't believe me." *And I didn't want a man in the house,* Tessa thought. *Any man, especially so late at night, even if he was a cop.*

"Still . . ." Roxanne frowned. "I hate to think of you all alone out here."

"I'm not totally alone. There's Cindy in the house next door. I met her coming over on the ferry. She's closing up for the winter. Even brought a box of food around for me."

"I don't think I know her." Roxanne's brow furrowed.

Tessa shrugged. "She's owned the house for years, apparently. She's older, but I like her."

"It's just her?"

Tessa nodded. "She's divorced. Kept the house when they split up." When she saw the quizzical look on Roxanne's face, Tessa added, "She invited me over a few nights ago. We sat on her porch and drank wine while the fog rolled in."

"Guess I'm not your only friend on the island."

"I guess not."

"Good. I'm glad you have someone close by." Roxanne looked at her watch. "Goodness. We should turn around. I have to be at work soon."

"Sure." Tessa nodded.

They started back, retracing their steps toward Sunset Cove. When they reached the rental house, Roxanne walked her to the door and then stepped into the kitchen.

"Will you be okay on your own here today?" she asked, lingering near the door.

"Do I have a choice?"

"Right." Roxanne looked like she was about to leave but then turned to Tessa. "Look, I'm going out for drinks with a friend tomorrow night at the Ship to Shore. You should come."

"I don't know." Tessa balked at the thought of going to a bar and hanging out in public.

"Come on. What else have you got to do? Drink wine on an old woman's porch in the fog?"

"Well . . ." Tessa wavered. She loathed social situations, but it was also an excuse to get away from the house. "When you put it like that . . ."

"Then it's settled. You're coming. Meet us in the bar at seven." Roxanne stepped onto the deck. The wind grabbed her hair and tugged at it, the dark strands blowing across her face until she flicked it back. She looked at Tessa.

Tessa threw her arms up and conceded defeat. "Fine. I'll be there."

"Wonderful." She turned and skipped down the steps onto the beach, then looked back with a grin. "You'll have fun. I promise. And in the meantime, try not to get too spooked. Remember, there's nothing that can hurt you in that house." She took another couple of steps, then called back over her shoulder. "And don't forget to call about that broken sensor. Better safe than sorry."

36

Tessa called the caretaker right away. Lillian answered with a cheery hello and promised to come out later that afternoon.

"Can't have you worrying yourself silly out there," she said. "That won't do at all."

Relieved, Tessa thanked her and hung up.

But what to do until then? If she didn't occupy her mind, she would sit there stewing over the previous night and the strange events that led her to discover the broken sensor. The solution was obvious. Write more pages. She had flown through her writing the previous evening, caught up in a frenzy of inspiration fueled by her visit to Patrick Moyer's old house. Now she could feel that same inspiration swirling around her again, just waiting to be tapped.

She went to the couch, sat down, and opened her laptop. The machine sprang to life, her word processor filling the screen. Except instead of what she expected to see, there was only a blank page.

Huh. She stared in confusion at the page for a moment before realizing that the laptop must have updated itself and restarted. That was it. No biggie. But when she browsed to her writing folder, the file wasn't there either.

Tessa drew in a sharp breath.

She had saved her work before packing it in for the night. She remembered doing it. Maybe she'd put the file in the wrong folder by accident? It was easy to do. But when she searched the hard drive, nothing came up. Even when she searched by file extension or arranged by newest date, she got no results. In fact, according to the computer, there were no files created the previous evening. Nada. Zip. It was like she had done no work at all.

This was ridiculous because she knew otherwise, and when she went to the Open Recent tab in her word processor, she could see the file name right there: Island-Chapter 1.

But when she clicked on it, all she got was a File Not Found error. Which was, of course, impossible. For the file name to be listed, she must have saved it, and *she* sure as hell hadn't moved or deleted it.

So where was the file?

Tessa checked the Trash folder, praying the file would be there—which it wasn't—and made another search of the laptop's hard drive, even though she knew it was pointless. If the file had still been on the computer, she would have found it the first time.

"Shit." She pushed the laptop away in frustration. This was unbelievable. After all that hard work, her pages were gone. Just vanished, like they had never even been there.

But then she remembered something. A flicker of hope broke through the frustration because there was one more place she could look. Somewhere she should have tried at the beginning.

The cloud.

All her files were backed up to an online cloud storage as standard. It was something she had set up when the computer was new but rarely thought about because it ran in the background. Now it might be a lifesaver. She opened a web browser and accessed the cloud service, but as expected, the file was not there. At least, not where it should be if it wasn't deleted. But there was another option. A button in the bottom-right corner of the screen that read Recently Deleted. And there it was—Island-Chapter 1.

Tessa breathed a sigh of relief and clicked Restore.

A moment later, the file appeared, back where it should have been all along. She opened it and confirmed that it was correct, then sat back and took a moment to compose herself.

Tragedy averted.

But the question still remained: What had caused the file to vanish in the first place? She was certain she hadn't accidentally deleted it, and there had been no one else in the house to even touch her computer, let alone trash a file.

So how had it gotten deleted?

The logical answer was that the laptop had glitched and wiped the file. It wasn't unheard of. Melissa had lost a whole folder full of work documents a few years ago because her hard drive was failing. She had backed everything else up to an external drive before the computer went completely, but it proved that files could disappear. Tessa hoped her own hard drive wasn't on the fritz. But it was unlikely. The laptop was only ten months old—a Christmas present from Melissa—and it had a solid-state flash drive. That left human error. Maybe she really had deleted it by mistake. Except . . . Tessa's mind flew back to the strange incidents the night before. Could there really have been someone in the house with her? Someone who crept past her while she was sleeping and deleted the file? It sounded far-fetched. Yet the thought of an intruder being right there, inches from her while she slept . . . It made her skin crawl. But then another thought struck her. Had someone entered the house while she was walking with Roxanne? Somehow that felt better and worse, both at the same time.

Screw it, Tessa thought. She didn't want to think about either of those scenarios. Better to tell herself it was a glitch—or a mistake on her part. The file was back, so no harm done. She forced her attention away from the nagging feeling of uncertainty, turned her attention to the screen, and started to write.

37

Tessa was reading back through the pages she had written when Lillian arrived to fix the window sensor. She closed the laptop and went to the door, checking it was the caretaker before answering.

"How are you liking the place so far?" Lillian asked when Tessa opened the door.

"It's fine," Tessa said with little enthusiasm, letting the caretaker inside.

Lillian unzipped her coat. Her smile waned as she picked up on Tessa's mood. She glanced at the framed newspaper Tessa had taken down and leaned inward against the wall on the day she arrived. "Too much for you, huh?"

"Little bit." Even though Tessa had taken it out of the frame and studied it, she could not understand why anyone would want to look at it every time they came and went. The homeowners using tragedy as a marketing ploy struck her as crass. How many morbidly curious travelers had stayed here to soak up the negative energy contained within? Tessa shuddered. "I'll hang it back up before I leave—I promise."

"It's fine. I'm sure you're not the first person to take that dreadful newspaper down off the wall," Lillian said. "If it were up to me, I'd get rid of it, but what do I know? I only look after the place."

"I understand." Tessa wondered if she would be so easily offended by the tasteless marketing ploy if she were not a victim of Patrick

Moyer's deadly crime. Although, she certainly understood the difficulties faced by the owners. How many potential renters had been put off by the home's blood-soaked history? She guessed it was a lot.

"Enough of this glum talk." Lillian's smile was back now. A mask of congeniality, no doubt honed through years of dealing with guests. "You asked me here to fix the alarm system. Why don't you show me that broken sensor, and we'll get it taken care of?"

"It's in the second-floor bedroom," Tessa said, leading Lillian upstairs. "The window was open a crack too."

"Really? That's not like me. I always check the house before new people arrive. I must have missed it."

"No worries." Tessa led Lillian into the bedroom and over to the window.

"Let's see what we have here." The caretaker unlatched the window and opened it, then closed it again. There was no telltale beep from the alarm system's control box on the first floor to indicate that anything was amiss. Lillian looked at Tessa with a furrowed brow. "You're right. This sensor isn't working."

"I know that already."

"I bet the battery's dead. They don't last so long when it gets cold." Lillian reached up and pried open the small plastic box affixed to the window frame that made up one-half of the sensor. Inside was a single AA battery. Lillian frowned. "That's odd."

"What is?"

"The battery is in backwards. No wonder it doesn't work."

"How could that happen?" Tessa asked, concerned.

"I probably wasn't paying attention when I changed it." Lillian pulled the battery out and turned it the other way, then pushed it in and put the sensor back together. "There. That should do the trick."

"Thank you." Tessa watched Lillian unlatch the window and test the sensor. This time, there was a gratifying beep from the unit.

"Is there anything else?" Lillian turned away from the window.

"There is one thing." Tessa led her back out to the open landing. She pointed to the small half-size door under the sloped ceiling that followed the roofline. "I don't suppose you have a key for that?"

"I can't let you in there, I'm afraid. The owners use that space for storage when they're not here. It's the only part of the house not included in the rental."

"No." Tessa shook her head. "I don't want to get inside. It's already open. I want it locked."

"It's unlocked?" Lillian went to the door and turned the handle. It opened. "Huh. The property owners have the key, but they gave me a spare when the alarm system was installed because we had to run wires through the attic. I don't have it with me. To tell the truth, I'm not even sure where it is at this point. I have no need to go inside."

"Could you find it?" Tessa pleaded. "I know it sounds silly, but I'll sleep easier at night knowing this door is secure."

"Of course, my dear." Lillian gave her a strange look. "It won't be today, though. I have errands to run after I leave here."

"That's fine," Tessa said, hiding her disappointment.

Lillian closed the door. "You needn't worry. It's just an attic-storage space. There's no access from the outside."

"I know."

"If there's nothing else, I'll be on my way."

"I almost forgot. The boiler."

"What about it?"

"I don't think it works. The house is freezing."

"Ah." Lillian looked uncomfortable. "I turned it on before you arrived, but between you and me, it's broken down a couple of times recently. The homeowners haven't done anything about it because we don't usually get renters after Labor Day. I did tell them this might happen."

"Can it be fixed?"

"I'm sure it can. How about I go down and take a peek?" Lillian started for the stairs. "Don't want you freezing to death."

"That would be awesome." Tessa cast a glance over her shoulder toward the still-unlocked door, then followed the caretaker back down to the first floor.

When they reached the basement door, Lillian drew back the bolt, opened it, and flicked a switch. The stairs were bathed in pale-yellow light. "This won't take but a minute."

Tessa stared down into the gloom beyond the basement stairs. "I'll stay up here if it's all the same with you."

"By all means." Lillian started down and vanished into the basement.

Tessa lingered in the doorway. A chilly draft wafted up from below the house. And something else. A faint odor of mildew. She stepped away from the door and went back to the living room, where a fire still burned in the hearth.

A few minutes later, Lillian reappeared.

"I've done my best with the old girl," she said. "She's working again for now and should start to warm you up in here. But I don't know how long that will last. The boiler's on her last legs. She'll need a proper repair, and it's more than I can do. I'll call Ronnie's Oil and Heat. That's who we always use. They'll be coming from the mainland, so it won't be until the next ferry at the earliest. Maybe even the week after. They get busy this time of year. I'll let you know when I have a date. Okay?"

"I guess it will have to be," Tessa said, not bothering to hide her frustration.

"I know it's inconvenient." Lillian shot her a sympathetic smile. "But you have plenty of firewood, and there are nice heavy blankets on the beds. Maybe I can even drop off a couple of space heaters. I'll see what I can find."

"That would be great."

"I would offer you alternate accommodations, but everything else on the island is closed for the season. Of course, if you would prefer to leave—"

"No. I'll make do until you fix the heat." There was no way Tessa could leave. She had too much riding on this. And not just facing her past. There was the book deal.

"In that case, I'll be off." Lillian turned toward the door. Her gaze fell to the framed newspaper with its grisly front page, sitting on the floor and facing the wall. "Are you sure you want to stay here? You don't seem comfortable in this house, and I don't think it's just the boiler. Maybe you should have found a less . . ." She paused as if searching for a suitable word. ". . . storied accommodation."

"Perhaps. But I'm here, and I'm going to stay."

"You're not a quitter. I'll give you that much." Lillian opened the front door and stepped out onto the veranda. She turned back to Tessa. "If you need anything else, I'm just a phone call away."

"Thank you." Tessa stood in the doorway with one hand on the door. Lillian lingered a moment as if she wanted to say something else but didn't. Instead, she pulled her coat tight and hurried down the steps to her Jeep, then turned back and said goodbye before she climbed in.

Tessa watched the Jeep swing around and start back toward town; then she went inside and closed the door behind her.

Looking up, Tessa studied the landing at the top of the stairs. The attic door was still unlocked, at least until Lillian came back with the key. She didn't know why, but it made her nervous. Attics and basements. Two places she had never liked, even as a child. Maybe it was because they were spaces inside a home not meant to be lived in. Dark voids where people stored the crap they didn't want anymore but couldn't part with. Where memories gathered dust in cardboard boxes. Old VHS tapes of family gatherings. Christmases and birthdays shot on eight-millimeter film by long-dead relatives. Childhood toys, moth-eaten and well-worn, that no child would ever play with again. Or maybe it was because attics and basements were where the monsters of her childhood lurked, and somewhere deep down, she worried they still did.

Regardless of the reason for her disquiet, the unlocked door left her uneasy. But there was nothing she could do about it. Better to occupy her mind elsewhere. Like the book she should be writing instead of fretting over stuff she couldn't control. Tessa went to the couch, reclined with the laptop on her knees, and started to write. But even as the words flowed onto the page, that attic door was there, in the back of her mind, and so were the monsters that dwelled beyond.

38

Tessa spent the rest of the afternoon and most of the evening writing, then went through the pages before sending them off to Thomas Milner with a swell of pride. She also fired off a quick email to her sister and promised to call in the next few days. She did not, however, mention the whispering voice that had called her name and roused her from sleep, the strange car, or her run-in with Patrick Moyer's brother. The purpose of this trip was to exorcise the demons that haunted her, not to give Melissa the impression she was more batshit crazy than before. She finished the email by telling her sister to give Corky a scratch behind the ear from her. Then she turned to a task she had been dreading. Other than visiting Patrick Moyer's house and looking at the framed newspaper clipping, she still hadn't done any research into his background—or the crime she had lived through but avoided reading about. Her knowledge of the killings was solely based on her own experience, most of which was trapped behind a wall of amnesia. If she wanted the book to ring true, she would have to step outside of her comfort zone. That meant doing the unthinkable. Seeking those facts that were still missing from her memory, and those she couldn't know because she was cowering upstairs under a bed.

Tessa lingered a moment with her fingers poised over the keyboard; then she typed *Patrick Moyer killings* into the search bar of her browser. The first page of matches hit her like a slap in the face.

Cassadaga Island Ripper Raped and Tortured Victims Before Stabbing Them

Police Chief Says Crime Scene Drenched in Blood, Vows to Catch Killer

Survivor of Cassadaga Island Ripper IDs Killer from Hospital Bed

Tessa read the headlines with a mixture of curiosity and revulsion. She stared at the words as if they might somehow cease to be true if she wished it hard enough. But that would never be the case. She was one of those victims raped and tortured by the Cassadaga Island Ripper. And she had seen enough . . . at least for one night.

Tessa slammed the laptop closed and put it down on the coffee table. She was shaking. Maybe she could face the truth behind those headlines tomorrow, or the next day. Maybe next week. But not right now. Not so soon after her encounter with Moyer's brother.

She reached for the remote and turned the TV on, mostly to distract herself from the awful thoughts tumbling through her mind. She sat there for two hours, barely watching. The baseball bat leaned against the couch next to her. Like an old friend, ready to leap to her defense.

At eleven, exhausted, she prepared for bed. The still-unused bedrooms called to her from beyond the couch. Curling up on the king-size bed in the master and pulling the blankets up against the cold sounded divine. But just as she had before, Tessa lost her nerve. She changed into her pj's and wriggled down under the blanket on the sofa instead. She knew it was not a long-term solution. She still had more than three weeks to go at the house, and her back could not take too many more nights of sleeping like this. Tomorrow, she promised herself, she would use the master bedroom even if she had to get stinking drunk first.

Her eyelids grew heavy. She yawned and pushed a hand under her pillow, relishing the cool, soft fabric against her skin. A few minutes later, Tessa was asleep . . . only to be snapped back awake sometime later by a frantic scream that pierced the cold, dark night like a knife.

39

Tessa almost fell off the couch in alarm. She jumped up, grabbed the baseball bat, and swung it around wildly, still groggy and convinced someone was in the room with her.

But there was no one.

The scream still rang in her ears. But where had it come from? It wasn't inside the house. She was sure of that now. It sounded more distant . . . somewhere outside, perhaps.

She ran to the front window, pulled the curtains aside, and peered out into the night. The road beyond the house was empty and quiet. Maybe it had come from the direction of the cove. She went to the back of the house and stared out across the deck but saw nothing there either. That left only one place to look.

Sunset Cove's only other residence.

Cindy's house.

Tessa ran to the side window near the fireplace and looked out across the swath of rugged boulder-strewn land and past the trees toward her neighbor.

A downstairs light burned in Cindy's house, the yellow glow visible even through the drawn curtains that prevented Tessa from seeing inside. There was no outward sign anything was amiss. No car parked out front. Nobody skulking around the home's perimeter, at least as far as she could tell. She didn't have Cindy's phone number—which now seemed like a stupid oversight—so she couldn't call to confirm that her neighbor was all right. Which meant going over there in person and knocking on the door, something Tessa was loath to do, especially at such a late hour.

But what choice did she have? Cindy might have fallen and hurt herself. Even now, she could be lying at the bottom of the stairs, unable to move. Or it might be something else. Something more sinister. Tessa wavered, trying to reel in her thoughts and focus.

A shadow fell across the window. A dark shape silhouetted against the curtains that appeared to stumble before disappearing out of sight on the other side.

Tessa stood transfixed, heart pounding.

Another distant scream, shrill and full of terror, drifted across the gulf between the houses. It rose in pitch, then abruptly cut off.

Tessa's heart leaped into her throat.

She turned and snatched her phone from the table next to the couch and fled to the kitchen. The local police department's number was on the dry-erase board. She dropped the baseball bat and dialed, praying someone would pick up.

After two rings, a groggy voice answered. "Chief White."

"Yes, hello. My name is Tessa Montgomery. I'm renting a cottage on the island—46 Ocean Way. It's a couple of miles out of town toward—"

"I know where it is." The chief sounded more awake now. He also sounded vexed. "It's the last house out on the southern tip."

"Yes," Tessa said.

"What seems to be the problem, Miss Montgomery?" The chief was moving around. Tessa could hear rustling. Was he getting dressed while they spoke?

"I think something bad happened to my neighbor, Cindy. She was screaming."

"Just now?"

"Yes."

"Is she still screaming?"

"No." Tessa's voice cracked. She fought back a sob. "It stopped all of a sudden. It was like . . ." Tessa didn't even want to say it. "It sounded like someone was murdering her."

"All right. Take it easy. Let's not jump to conclusions. I'll drive on out and take a look around."

"Thank you."

"Do you have your doors and windows locked?"

"Everything's locked tight."

"Good. Make sure you keep it that way. Stay inside and wait for me. Don't go over there on your own. You understand?"

"I understand." Tessa had no intention of going outside. She cast a nervous glance over her shoulder toward the side window. "Please hurry."

"I'll be there in fifteen minutes. If anything happens in the meantime, call me back."

"Don't go," Tessa said, panicked. "I don't want to be alone."

"Ma'am, the longer I'm talking to you on the phone, the more time it'll take me to get there. You'll be fine. Keep the doors locked, and don't let anyone in until I get there. Can you do that?"

"Yes."

"Good. One more thing . . . do you have a gun in the house?"

"God, no."

"That's fine. Just checking. You sound kind of jumpy, and I'd hate for you to shoot me out of panic when I arrive. I'll be with you soon. Just sit tight."

"I'll try." Tessa heard a door slam and the distinctive rustle of wind hitting the phone.

The chief was outside, no doubt walking to his car. "Fifteen minutes, okay?"

"Okay."

There was a moment of silence before the line went dead. The chief had hung up. Tessa walked back through the living room and stared out the side window toward Cindy's house. It was in darkness now. Someone had extinguished the light.

40

The Seaview Point chief of police showed up as promised, exactly fifteen minutes after he hung up the phone. She watched through the front window as his shiny, black police department SUV pulled up behind her car. He climbed out and hitched his pants up, adjusting the gun sitting in a holster on his hip, then climbed the steps up to the porch. Chief White was a large man in his early fifties. He must have once been muscular, but the years had turned his physique to flab, and now his gut hung over his belt as if it were trying to escape. He carried a wide-brimmed hat in one hand but made no attempt to put it on and cover his thinning hair, which had turned a silver shade of gray.

"Tessa Montgomery?" he asked when she opened the door.

Tessa nodded.

The chief deposited the hat on his head and glanced toward Cindy's house. "You hear or see anything else over there since we spoke?"

"No. Well, yes. Sort of. There was a light on downstairs, but after I hung up the phone, the light was off. I kept watching but didn't see anything else." Tessa had spent the entire time glued to the window, standing far enough back to remain out of sight if anyone was staring at her from the opposite direction. There had been no more screams. No movement behind the curtains. Nothing.

"Good. I'm going to take a quick look around." The chief's hand rested on the butt of his gun. "Close and lock the door until I come back, okay?"

"Sure." Tessa had no problem with that. If someone had murdered Cindy, they might still be around. She waited for the chief to descend the porch steps and start toward the other house before closing the door and engaging the dead bolt, then went to the side window where she could see him approaching Cindy's place.

As he drew near, the chief pulled a flashlight from his belt and swung it in a wide arc, the powerful beam playing over the ground and steps leading to Cindy's porch and front door. He climbed up and stood there a moment, looking around.

"Hello?" The chief shouted out, his voice carrying faintly across the distance between the houses. He knocked on the door. "It's Chief White. Anybody home?"

When there was no answer, he went to the window and peered in, cupping his hand against the glass, then repeated the process with the window on the other side of the door.

Retracing his path, the chief descended the porch steps; then he turned and vanished around the side of the house. Tessa could see the beam of his flashlight splashing across the ground for a few moments, but soon even that faded.

She stood at the window, holding her breath. What if something happened over there and Chief White didn't come back? What would she do then?

Five more minutes ticked by, then ten.

The landscape around the house remained swathed in impenetrable darkness. There was no sign of the chief or his flashlight.

Fifteen minutes.

An image of Chief White sprawled helpless and bloody on the ground while Patrick Moyer loomed over him ran through her mind.

Moyer is gone, she told herself. Whatever happened over there, it wasn't him.

That didn't make her feel better. Something or *someone* had caused Cindy to scream like that, and now she wasn't answering the door.

An errant thought popped into Tessa's head. *Because she can't. Cindy is dead.*

She pushed the thought from her mind. The chief would be back soon. He had to be because the alternative was too frightening to contemplate.

Twenty minutes.

This was taking too long. Tessa glanced toward her phone. The police department number must have been forwarded to Chief White's cell. That was why he picked up groggy and half-asleep. Maybe she should call him again. Ask what was happening. But what if Cindy's murderer was still over there? The ringing phone would alert them to the chief's presence, assuming they didn't already know.

She wavered. Reached for the phone in her pocket. Drew her hand away again. At that moment, a flashlight beam sliced through the darkness. Chief White appeared around the other side of Cindy's house.

Tessa rushed to the door and flung it open when he climbed onto the porch. "Well?"

"You heard a scream, all right," Chief White said, turning the flashlight off and pushing it back into his belt. He looked past her into the house. "Mind if I come inside and we'll talk about it?"

41

As soon as Chief White stepped across the threshold and closed the door, he turned to her. "Bobcat."

"I'm sorry, what?" Tessa shook her head.

"You heard a bobcat. There's a pretty big population on the island. They're attracted by the deer, and there's a lot of those too."

"No. It was a woman screaming for her life. I'm sure of it." Tessa knew the difference between a woman's frantic shriek and an animal.

"Miss Montgomery, it was a bobcat—I promise you. They breed in winter and wail like the devil to attract a mate. That call sounds just like a scream. I've only heard it a few times over the years, but it's bloodcurdling. I can see why you thought someone was being murdered over there."

"Are you sure?"

"A hundred percent. I checked the house, and it's locked up tighter than a drum. There's no sign of an intruder, and your neighbor doesn't appear to be there. Honestly, it doesn't look like anyone has been at that house in a while. It's probably a summer rental, and yourself aside, we don't get renters this late in the year."

"No. Cindy is there. There was a light on, and I saw a shadow in the window right around the time of the second scream."

"Lots of people leave lights on, especially now with all those smart switches and bulbs you can control from your phone. It's likely on a timer. As for the shadow, it was probably just the curtains moving. That house is old, and I'm sure it's drafty."

"Did you go inside?"

"No. That's not within my power, unless there's an indication something is wrong."

"Like a scream," Tessa said.

"Ma'am. I saw the bobcat with my very own eyes on the other side of the house. It was a big one too. Probably a male. I would have snapped a photo with my phone to show you, but it slunk back into the woods before I got the chance." The chief sighed. "Look, that house is a summer rental. There shouldn't be anyone over there right now. Season's over. There isn't even a car, so . . ."

"Cindy doesn't drive on the island. Bad eyesight. She's there shutting the place down and winterizing. She came over on the ferry. I gave her a ride out here a few days ago."

"Well, she's not there now." The chief folded his arms. "It only takes a day to drain the pipes and winterize. Two at most. She probably did what she needed and went back to the mainland."

"The ferry only runs once a week in the winter."

"You just told me she didn't have a car. That's your answer. The ferry might only run once a week, and if you have a vehicle, it's your only option, but there are plenty of fishermen willing to make the run. People do it all the time. A few extra bucks can come in handy this time of year. She probably hired someone to take her across the bay."

"She hasn't gone back."

"And how do you know that?"

"I . . ." Tessa was stumped, but then she remembered the box her neighbor had brought over. The one with *Cindy's Books* written on it. She had cut the tape to flatten it and put the box next to the recycling bin in the kitchen. "Wait. I can prove there was someone at that house."

Tessa turned and hurried into the kitchen with the chief striding behind. But when she went to the recycling bin, the box wasn't there.

"Miss Montgomery?" The chief stood, leaning against the kitchen doorframe with folded arms.

"Give me a minute." Tessa looked around, frantic. The island had no trash or recycling pickup. Everything had to be dropped off at the local waste transfer station on the other side of town. She hadn't accumulated enough trash to make that trip yet, so the box could not have been thrown away. Yet it was not in the kitchen either. She pulled the recycling bin out, then pushed it back and looked behind the trash can, even though she could already see there was no box tucked behind it. "I don't understand. It must be here."

"Mind telling me what you're looking for?"

"A box Cindy brought over with groceries she didn't want. It had her name on it." Tessa whirled around to face the chief. "It was here, and now it's not."

"Or maybe you got confused?"

"No. I'm not making this up." Tessa glared at the chief.

"I never said that you were. But you seem on edge. Look, this is a small community—tight-knit—and I've never met anyone named Cindy."

"She rents the house out and doesn't come to the island very often. She told me."

The chief raised an eyebrow.

"I didn't imagine her." Tessa might be a lot of things, but delusional wasn't one of them.

The chief nodded. "Look, I'll ask around the next few days and see if any of the local fishermen remember taking a woman back to the mainland recently, all right? Best I can do. In the meantime, you needn't worry. Nobody has been murdered. You heard a big ol' bobcat out looking for a mate, that's all."

"If you say so." Tessa realized there was no use in arguing. The chief was adamant, and she had no good counter to his claim that it was an animal, especially since the one piece of proof she possessed had gone missing.

"All right, then. If you need me again, I'm just a phone call away." The chief sauntered back through the living room to the front door, where he paused with his hand on the handle. He glanced up toward the second floor, then back to Tessa. "Look, I get it. This place is creepy. How could it not be after what happened? You're jumpy, and you've freaked yourself out with that bobcat. But try not to let the house get to you. What went on here was a tragedy, but it's in the past. There are no murderers roaming this island either, at your neighbor's place or anywhere else."

"I'll keep that in mind," Tessa said glumly.

"Good. You take care now." Chief White opened the front door and stepped outside, then turned back to her. "If you were a daughter of mine, I wouldn't want you out here all alone and vulnerable. I'll tell you that for nothing. If it gets too much, you might want to think about following your neighbor back to the mainland."

"I've booked the house for a month, and I've only been here a few days," Tessa said. "But thank you for your concern."

"Just a suggestion." White's gaze lingered on her a few seconds more. "Before I go, I have to ask . . . You look familiar. Have we met before?"

"I don't think so." Tessa wondered if the chief had been at the house on the night her friends were murdered. The same night she had almost died. She guessed he must have been, but it wasn't surprising that he didn't recognize her now. Severely beaten and strangled, her face sliced open by an assailant's knife, covered in blood, Tessa would have looked entirely different. Afterward, when she arrived at the hospital in Portland where she had been airlifted, hovering between life and death, a detective was waiting. He tried to interview her as she fell in and out of consciousness. As they wheeled her into surgery, Tessa had mumbled two words. "Patrick Moyer." That was what led the man now standing before her to Moyer's cottage, where he shot and killed him during a confrontation. Her gaze dropped to the gun at his hip. Was this the same weapon that meted out a death sentence to the man who changed her life forever? She supposed it must be. How many times did cops replace their guns, anyway?

The chief gave a small cough. "Ma'am?"

"Sorry." Tessa lifted her eyes from the gun. "I'm positive we haven't met before."

"You're probably right." The chief shrugged, then descended the steps toward his car and climbed in. A moment later, the engine roared to life.

Tessa closed the door and retreated back into the house. She returned to the window and stared over at her neighbor's property. She wanted to believe the screams were nothing more than a bobcat looking for a mate and that Cindy really had gone back to the mainland, but it didn't make sense. Her neighbor hadn't mentioned going back before the next ferry, and she didn't think for one second that the light was controlled by a timer or that the silhouetted figure was only a trick of the light caused by the curtains moving.

Maybe the chief was right and she should pack up and get the hell out. There was no shame in admitting defeat. Then an image of Corky leaping away in fright as she swung the baseball bat toward him entered Tessa's head. If she went back to Gloucester now, nothing would change. She would just go right back to hiding in her bedroom behind a locked door and attending pointless therapy sessions once a week. And even if she wanted to leave, there was the book she had agreed to write and taken a sizable advance for, most of which was already spent. Then there was the ferry, which only ran once a week and wouldn't be back for days. Screams in the night or not, Tessa was stuck on Cassadaga Island.

42

Tessa sat on the sofa cradling the baseball bat until the sun crept up over the horizon and cast the darkness away. There was no way in hell she was going to get any sleep with those screams still fresh in her ears. Which meant there was lots of time to think, and in doing so, she had come to an inevitable conclusion. She needed to go over and see for herself if Cindy was still around . . . just as soon as it got to be light.

Which was why, with the early-morning sun slanting through the trees, she found herself crossing over the expanse of rocky woodland toward her neighbor's house.

"Cindy, are you there?" she called, knocking on the front door and then stepping back, baseball bat at the ready in case it wasn't Cindy who answered. Instead, no one answered.

Tessa tried again and waited. Then, just as the chief had done earlier, she went to the window beside the door and cupped her hand to peer inside.

The curtains at the front of the house were not drawn, but the interior was dark and full of shadows. She was looking at a living room with a sofa and love seat forming an L around a coffee table made from an old steamer chest. Beyond that was a TV hanging on the wall and a half-closed door that led deeper into the house. The room was unoccupied.

She went to the other window. This was a dining room with a craftsman-style table and chairs underneath a hanging brass chandelier. Empty, just like the living room.

She returned to the front door and knocked again, less hopeful this time. When there was no answer, she descended the porch steps and followed the police chief's route around the side of the house.

Here the land fell away to a rocky cliff that bounded the edge of Sunset Cove. She could see the path Roxanne took when she walked from town, which was really nothing more than a narrow dirt trail that weaved between trees and enormous granite boulders. She turned back to the house and picked her way toward the rear, where a back porch overlooked the ocean. The same porch where she had sat with Cindy days before and drank red wine. The windows were too high to see in there. She stepped around a weathered cellar bulkhead mired in weeds and kept going, then mounted the porch. The back door was locked too. When she looked in through the windows, all she saw was an empty kitchen.

Tessa stepped back off the porch.

This was a waste of time. She was obsessing, as usual. If the police chief—a trained law enforcement professional—thought Cindy had gone back to the mainland, and the screams were just the mating call of a wild animal, then who was she to argue with that? Chief White would surely drive back out later that day and tell her he'd found the fisherman who took Cindy across the bay, and then she would feel foolish for thinking her neighbor had met with foul play.

It was a bobcat. Nothing more. If she kept telling herself that, maybe she would believe it.

Tessa glanced around one more time, then circled to the front again and started back toward the rental house. She was tired and cold. Actually, she was exhausted.

Back inside, she engaged the dead bolt and put the alarm system in Home Mode, then went to the sofa, kicked her shoes off, and lay down without bothering to get undressed. She pulled the blanket up over herself, leaned the baseball bat against the coffee table, and closed her eyes.

She was fast asleep within minutes.

43

Tessa woke to the sound of hammering on the front door. She jumped up and grabbed the baseball bat, then rushed to the window and looked out.

Roxanne was standing on the porch clutching a brown paper bag.

"Hey, let me in. It's freezing out here," Roxanne called out, seeing Tessa's face at the window. "I brought lunch."

Tessa's heart fell. She had intended to hide at the house all day so she could avoid going to the bar that evening. Now her plan was foiled. Unless Roxanne had forgotten about it, which seemed unlikely. Why else would she have shown up?

Roxanne hopped from foot to foot. "Hello? Are you waiting till I turn into a Popsicle?"

"Sorry. Coming!" Tessa shouted. She put the baseball bat aside and went to the door, unlocking it.

Roxanne pushed past her without waiting to be invited. She turned and stared at Tessa. "Holy crap. You look worse than yesterday. You don't so much have bags under your eyes as boulders."

"Yeah. I had a terrible night."

"Clearly." Roxanne's gaze dropped. "You thinking of getting dressed at some point today?"

"What?"

"You're still wearing your pj's. Were you sleeping when I came to the door?"

"Little bit." Tessa flushed.

Roxanne's gaze settled on the couch and the crumpled blankets. The pillow. "Out here?"

"I fell asleep in front of the TV last night," Tessa said, which wasn't really a lie. She just omitted that it was deliberate. "What time is it, anyway?"

"Two in the afternoon." Roxanne held up the brown bag. "That's why I brought lunch."

"That late?"

"Uh-huh."

"Shouldn't you be working?"

"Just finished. Had Frank whip up a couple of BLTs before I left. You like bacon, right?"

"Duh." Tessa's dismay at Roxanne's unannounced appearance faded. The previous night's events still rattled her, and she was glad not to be alone. Also, she was starving, and a BLT sounded great. "Who doesn't?"

"Only crazy people." Roxanne walked into the living room, then made a beeline for the kitchen. She placed the sandwich bag on the table by the window. "You have wine?"

"Right now?"

"Sure. I'm done for the day."

"There's a bottle of merlot in the rack on the counter," Tessa said. She found two glasses and handed Roxanne the corkscrew. "You might as well pour me one too."

"Awesome. Then you can tell me about your terrible night." Roxanne pulled the cork from the wine with a pop.

"I don't know. It's probably nothing." Tessa went to the table and sat down.

"Hold that thought." Roxanne poured them two large glasses and put the wine bottle on the table before taking a seat opposite Tessa. She opened the bag and took out two sandwiches wrapped in waxed paper, then pushed one across the table. "Here."

Tessa took the sandwich and unwrapped it. She had to admit it looked good, and she was starving. She took a bite, then rolled her eyes. “I’m getting one of these the next time I come into the diner. It’s delicious.”

“Right? Frank’s lousy at some things, but he does make a mean BLT. Sources his meats locally. The bacon is divine. Tomatoes are from around here too. He’s a stickler. Only Maine farms.”

“It shows.” Tessa took another bite, relishing the smoky meat flavor and juicy tomato. “Holy wow.”

“Guess we’ve got ourselves a convert.” Roxanne smiled and leaned on the table. “Now, tell me all about last night.”

Tessa’s sandwich-induced excitement faded. She could almost hear that scream, still ringing in her ears. “You’ll probably think I’m crazy, but I was sure something bad happened to the woman in the house across the way.”

“The woman you had wine with on the porch? Why would you think that?”

“I heard the most god-awful scream from the direction of her house. Thought I saw someone in her window, just for a second. Scared the crap out of me. The chief looked around and didn’t find anything.”

“You woke Chief White?” Roxanne chuckled. “What time was it?”

“About three in the morning.”

“Ouch. Bet he was grumpy. The man likes his beauty sleep. Between you and me, it’s not working. He looks a bit like a mangy old grizzly bear wearing a cop uniform.”

“Yeah.” Tessa smiled at that image despite herself. “He was kind of short-tempered. Didn’t seem inclined to take me seriously. Said that no one was over there. That Cindy must have finished shutting the house down and went back to the mainland. That she paid a fisherman to take her over. He said there was a bobcat prowling around over there, and that was what I heard.”

Roxanne was quiet, her brow furrowed.

“Well?”

Roxanne drew in a long breath. “I think the most obvious explanation is usually the right one.”

"Then you agree with the chief?"

"I've heard bobcats around here before. Not often, but once in a while. And holy crap, do they send a shiver up your spine when they make that call. I mean, they really do sound like someone being murdered. My money is on the bobcat."

"And what about Cindy? She isn't answering her door."

"Because she went back to the mainland, like the chief said. It's obvious."

"I saw a light on over there. A shadow in the window."

"The light was probably on a timer."

"That's what the chief said too."

"And as for the shadow . . . you were half-asleep."

"I don't know. What if something really did happen to her?"

"It didn't. Stop worrying." Roxanne waved an arm around. "Look where you're staying. A freaking murder house. It's no wonder you're jumpy. You need to get out of this place before it drives you completely nuts. Good thing we're going to the Ship to Shore tonight."

Tessa groaned. "I'm not sure I'm in the mood to go out."

"Don't be silly. You're coming with us to the bar, and I won't take no for an answer."

"Roxanne . . ." Tessa tried to think of a good reason why she couldn't go but failed to come up with one, so she resorted to a feeble "Maybe we can do it next week."

"Nuh-uh. Tonight. What else are you going to do? Sit around in this drafty old house and stare at the walls while you listen to bobcats and scare yourself into thinking there's a murderer prowling around?"

"All right. Fine. I'll go to the stupid bar with you." Maybe it would do her good to get out of the house, after all. "Happy now?"

"Ecstatic," Roxanne replied. "Now finish your sandwich. We have a bottle of wine to drink. It'll get us in the mood, and I have a couple of hours before I need to go home and get ready." Roxanne lifted her glass. "Cheers."

Tessa's shoulders slumped in defeat. She picked up her own glass and tipped it. "Cheers."

44

The Ship to Shore Tavern occupied a weathered two-story clapboard building that sat between a gift shop-cum-art gallery, which was closed for the season, like most of the other such businesses in Seaview Point, and the town library.

Tessa pulled down a street at the side of the building and parked in a small lot at the rear. She exited the vehicle and stood for a moment, looking at the tavern and gathering the courage to enter.

Her phone vibrated.

Tessa took it out, expecting to find a text message from Roxanne asking where she was, but it was Lillian.

Found the attic key. Will drop it round next time I'm out that way.

Tessa shot off a quick reply thanking her, then turned her attention back to the bar.

The tavern's rear door opened. A couple stepped out with their arms wrapped around each other. Along with them came a blast of music and raucous conversation until the door swung closed again, reducing it to a dull murmur. She almost turned around and got back in the car at that moment. This was more than she could handle. The few occasions a therapist had convinced her to venture out socially had ended in disaster, with Tessa all but fleeing back to the safety of her bedroom with its locks on the door and her baseball bat within easy reach. Why would this be any different? But at the same time, she couldn't stop thinking about Cindy and those dreadful screams. Did she really want to spend another night alone?

Tessa wavered. But then the old anxiety got the better of her, as it always did. Alone and afraid was preferable to this.

She swiveled, keys in hand, ready to climb back into her car, and almost collided with Roxanne, who was coming up behind her flanked by another woman Tessa didn't recognize.

"Where do you think you're going?" Roxanne blocked her path.

"I can't do this," Tessa said. "I thought I could, but I can't."

"Nonsense. You came this far, right? You're coming inside with me and Kyla, and that's all there is to it."

"Hi." Kyla, standing next to Roxanne, raised a hand in greeting and smiled. "I don't bite. Promise."

"You don't understand . . ." Tessa glanced wistfully toward her car. The knot of apprehension in her gut tightened into a ball of fear.

"What is there to understand?" Roxanne reached out and hooked an arm around Tessa's, pulling her toward the door. "It's just a girls' night out. You'll be fine. Unless you're saying you'd rather hide out alone in that ghastly house you rented and hope you don't get another visit from that bobcat."

"It's not that." After what happened the previous evening, Tessa had no desire to spend the night alone at the house. What if it wasn't a bobcat and someone really had killed Cindy? Tessa was caught between conflicting emotions. She had no desire to be alone tonight, but she was terrified of walking into that bar and facing the unknown. In the end, she decided on a compromise. "I'll come in for one drink. If I'm not feeling it, I'll leave. How's that?"

"Good enough." Roxanne pulled the door open and ushered Tessa inside, then waited for Kyla to enter before following behind.

The bar's interior was dimly lit. A faint woody odor hung in the air, overlaid by a medley of meaty aromas that wafted from the direction of the kitchen. Roxanne led them through a smattering of locals, the number of which would have constituted a slow Saturday night for a bar in Boston but was probably a good weekend crowd for the Ship to Shore Tavern.

They claimed a spot at the bar and hopped up onto three stools. Roxanne waved toward the bartender, a woman not much older than herself with a round pimply face and bobbed hair. After they ordered, the trio sat in silence for a few moments, sipping their drinks. Roxanne and Kyla had opted for a local brew. A beer with the dubiously commercial name of Fish Gut IPA. Tessa stuck to red wine. A smoky cab that tasted better than the bottles she'd purchased at the store.

A two-piece band was playing on a small platform at the back of the bar. A guitarist and singer. She vaguely recognized the song but couldn't place it. Not surprising given her hermit lifestyle over the past five years.

The low ceiling, complete with exposed wood beams, made the space feel small and intimate. Neon signs advertising regional beers hung on the walls between paintings of lobster boats, schooners with white sails, and rough seas. People sat on stools around tables made from old oak barrels, their flat tops worn and dinged from decades of glasses being placed upon them. No one paid any attention to Tessa, and the anxiety ebbed away.

Until she spotted the figure walking in their direction, glass in hand. Someone Tessa recognized with a sinking feeling.

It was Noah.

He was making tracks directly for them, weaving through the small crowd that filled the middle of the bar. A goofy smile spread across his face as he drew close. His eyes twinkled, reflecting the glow of lights hanging over the bar. His gaze fixed upon her with unwavering intensity.

Tessa shrank back, hoping that by some miracle he would veer off, but he didn't. He reached the three girls and came to a halt before downing the last dregs of his beer.

"Hello, Tessa," he said. "Good to see you again."

45

"What do you want, Noah?" Roxanne asked, glaring at him over her drink.

"Need another beer. Seemed like a good time to come over and say hello." The smile faltered, then fell from Noah's face. His gaze shifted to Roxanne. "You're not the only one who likes to be friendly."

"Well, you said hello. Now you can leave," Kyla said. "Go on, scoot."

"I wasn't talking to you." Noah's eyes darted briefly to Kyla and then drifted back to Tessa. "Was the yeast okay?"

"It was fine," Tessa replied.

"You made bread, then?" Noah reached between the girls, just a little too close, and set his glass down on the bar. "I bet it tasted real good."

"Well . . . I . . ." Tessa didn't want to admit that she hadn't baked any bread yet, but she also didn't want to tell an outright lie.

"How did Josh like it?"

"Josh?" Tessa looked at him, perplexed.

"Your boyfriend. You said he was staying with you at the house."

"Oh . . . that's right." Tessa had forgotten about telling Noah that she wasn't alone at the house. The irony that she was trying to avoid lying about baking bread when she'd already laid a much bigger trap wasn't lost on her.

"Where is he tonight?" Noah's gaze never strayed from Tessa.

"He didn't feel like coming out," Tessa said, ignoring the confused look from Roxanne. "Tired."

"Shame. He wasn't in the diner the other day either." Noah made a tutting sound. "I would've liked to meet him. I guess he must be really shy, huh?"

"Something like that." Tessa wished the ground would open up and swallow her.

"Still, it's good that you're not staying in the house alone." The smile returned to Noah's face—only this time, Tessa thought it looked more like a smirk. "After what happened there and all. I don't know how anyone can get a wink of sleep in that place. It would send me screaming for the door, and that's for sure."

Tessa's stomach flipped.

Roxanne glared at him. "Cut it out, right now."

"If you say so." Noah shrugged.

"Isn't there somewhere else you need to be?" Roxanne raised an eyebrow.

"Not until I get a beer."

"Let me help you with that." Roxanne raised a hand and called to the bartender. "Hey, Erin. Over here."

Erin sauntered over, wiping her hands on a dishcloth.

"Noah." Roxanne pointed at the empty glass. "He'll have another of whatever he's drinking. Put it on my tab."

"Well now, that's a gracious gesture." Noah watched Erin fill a fresh glass.

"A small price to pay for you to go away."

"Seems like a fair trade." Noah reached between Roxanne and Tessa to retrieve his drink. As he withdrew, beer in hand, his arm grazed Tessa's.

She jerked away and looked at him. "Have a nice evening, Noah."

"Right back at you. Don't let this pair tell you any lies about me."

Roxanne snorted. "Like we'd need to."

"Don't forget. I know all sorts of stuff about you too," Noah said, turning toward her. "Maybe I should stay and reminisce awhile."

"And maybe I should get that drink taken off my tab."

"Touché." Noah turned his attention back to Tessa. "Don't mind our banter. It's a small town, and we grew up together."

"I see." Tessa's discomfort was reaching a breaking point. She didn't enjoy talking to men at the best of times, but there was something decidedly unpleasant about Noah. Maybe it was the way he looked at her with those steely gray eyes, or maybe it was how he talked, quiet and slow, like he was weighing every word.

Noah took a sip of his beer and nodded in appreciation. He looked at each of the girls before his gaze settled back on Tessa. "Stay safe now."

Tessa wasn't sure how to respond to that. But she didn't need to, because Noah turned and strode back across the bar, weaving between the tables and stopping at a high top, where he stood alone and stared down into his pint.

"That was uncomfortable," Kyla said.

"What is that guy's deal, anyway?" Tessa asked, tearing her eyes away from Noah and turning back toward her companions.

Roxanne shrugged. "He's just a creeper that never made it off the island. Went straight from school into a dead-end job at the grocery store."

"Loser," Kyla snorted.

"I see." Tessa didn't point out the hypocrisy of Roxanne's comment, given that she herself had grown up on the island and now worked as a server in the diner. It might not be stocking shelves, but it was hardly a high-flying career.

"Tell me about Josh," Roxanne said with a wicked grin.

"Oh my God, don't." Tessa groaned. "It was just a stupid thing I said because I didn't want him to know I was alone in the house."

"Seriously? You just made up a fake boyfriend?" Roxanne giggled. "That's awesome."

"He's not totally made up. Josh is my sister's boyfriend."

"That's okay. I once made up a fake boyfriend to get rid of some guy who was pestering me in high school." Roxanne looked at Kyla. "Todd Burgess. You remember?"

"I remember," Kyla said with enthusiasm. "He was such a pain in the ass. After he gave up on you, he started asking me out. Wanted to take me to prom. Not a chance. Still, when I think back, we were so mean to that guy."

"He deserved it." Roxanne turned back to Tessa. "What does this Josh—the fake but not really fake boyfriend—look like?"

Tessa hesitated. "I don't know. I've never . . ." She was cornered. "I've never met him."

"How is that possible? Didn't you say you live with your sister?"

"It's a long story." And one Tessa didn't want to share at that moment. She looked down at the bar and her empty wineglass. Then, mostly to change the subject, she said, "Who wants another drink?"

46

Tessa had intended to leave after one drink, but two hours and as many glasses of wine later, she was still inside the Ship to Shore Tavern, feeling surprisingly relaxed despite the previous night's scare and her encounter with Noah.

When Kyla excused herself to visit the restroom, Roxanne focused on Tessa. "I've been meaning to ask you something."

"What?" Tessa watched Kyla weave through the Saturday-evening crowd inside the bar, which had waxed and waned as the night wore on.

"Why are you here?" Roxanne asked, leaning close to Tessa. "Staying on the island for so long at this time of year . . . and in that freaking house, of all places."

"Why not?" Tessa countered, watching Roxanne's reaction and wondering if this was a test. Did the friendly waitress already know who she was? After all, it wouldn't take much digging on the internet to discover her past. Her photo had been published in the *Bangor Daily Telegraph*, the *Portland Herald*, and who knew how many other local and national newspapers within a day of the murders. She still remembered the *Telegraph* headline because some inconsiderate jerk left the paper lying around for her to see in the hospital. "Sole Survivor in Horrific Island Slaying Clings to Life." And beneath the blaring headline, a picture lifted from her high school yearbook. But if she knew more than she was saying, Roxanne didn't show it. "I wanted to get away from Gloucester and needed a place to lay my head. The beach house was available."

Roxanne didn't reply. Instead, she picked up her beer and took a long swig.

"The place was cheap enough too," Tessa said, justifying her answer in the wake of Roxanne's silence. "It's not like I'm filthy rich or anything."

"Makes sense." Roxanne smiled, but there was concern in her eyes. "I bet you would have thought twice if you'd known what happened in that house before you booked, right?"

Tessa didn't have a good answer for this. She didn't want to lie to Roxanne—heaven only knew, she didn't want to dig more holes for herself—but the only other choice was admitting she was in Seaview Point specifically because of that house. She struggled to find a suitable answer, but then she was saved.

"Hey." Kyla reappeared at Roxanne's shoulder. "You guys weren't talking about me while I was gone, were you?"

"You should be so lucky." Roxanne moved aside to let Kyla climb onto her barstool. She downed the dregs of her beer. "My round."

Tessa knew she should object. It was getting late. But the thought of going back to that house alone was worse. What harm could one more glass of wine do? It would bolster her courage to face the overnight hours. She drained her glass and placed it on the bar. "Let's do this."

"Screw it." Kyla let loose with a whoop. "Now we're having a party."

"Oh yeah." Roxanne flagged down the bartender.

While they waited for their drinks to come, Tessa hopped off her stool. "Gotta pee."

"Wait. We should immortalize this night." Kyla jumped down. She pulled her phone out and handed it to Erin, then pulled Tessa and Roxanne toward her with arms draped over their shoulders and heads together. "We need a photo."

"Really? I hate having my photo taken." Tessa squirmed, but it was no use. Kyla held firm. Realizing she was caught, Tessa quickly flicked her hair to the side and turned her face slightly to the left, making sure her scar was covered and away from the camera.

Erin clicked off several pics. Then the bartender motioned for the girls to pose awhile longer and took down a Polaroid camera from a shelf behind the bar.

"For the memory board," she said, the camera clicking as she took another photo.

"What's that?" Tessa asked.

"You'll see." Kyla took her phone back and browsed the pics. "These are awesome. We look so hot."

"I doubt it," Tessa said. "We probably look drunk off our asses."

"Nah. Give me your phone number. I'll text them to you."

"If you must." Tessa rolled her eyes but gave Kyla her number. "Now can I pee?"

Kyla nodded.

"Great." Tessa started toward the back of the bar and the door labeled RESTROOMS. Beyond it was a short corridor with aluminum beer kegs and plastic crates full of empty bottles stacked at one end near an emergency-exit door. The restroom doors were on the right. And then she saw what the bartender was talking about. A giant corkboard packed full of Polaroid photographs held in place by pushpins. They were layered over one another like some haphazard photographic collage. An impromptu record of many boozy evenings spent at the Ship to Shore. Some were taken at Christmas or New Year's—the decorations in the background and festive outfits giving them away—but others documented random nights. The oldest photographs were yellowed and fading, peeking out in gaps between the more recent ones. She guessed that some of them must go back decades, judging by the fashions on display. Her hunch was confirmed when she saw a banner hanging above the bar in one photograph: HAPPY NEW YEAR AND A NEW MILLENNIUM. SEE YOU ON THE OTHER SIDE!

Tessa smiled. She was only a kid back then—too young to remember it—but her parents had told her about the hullabaloo when people thought the computers would go crazy and start World War III or melt down the stock markets and plunge the world back to the Middle Ages, all because the programmers of the time used a two-digit date instead of four.

Lost in nostalgia, she continued poking through the photos until a nasty thought rolled through her head. She pulled her hand away. Was Patrick Moyer smiling at the lens in one of these old images? He'd lived on the island, and the photos went back far enough—so why not? Her smile faded and she stepped away, then hurried into the bathroom.

A few minutes later, she rejoined her companions at the bar and took her seat.

"You all right?" Roxanne asked, her brow furrowing.

"Yes." Tessa nodded. But she couldn't shake the strange feeling that she was walking in the footsteps of the man who had killed her friends, abused her body, and left her for dead. She forced a weak smile. "I'm fine."

"You look like you saw a ghost." The concern in Roxanne's voice was hard to miss.

"Really. I'm okay." Tessa picked up her drink and sucked back a large gulp. She swallowed, then took another swig, chugging back the wine like it was soda. "Let's get another round. I'm buying."

Roxanne shot her a strange look but didn't press the matter further. "You sure? It's getting kinda late."

"The girl wants to buy us a round. Who are we to stand in her way?" Kyla slapped her palm on the bar. "Lighten up."

"Whatever. I don't have to be up in the morning." Roxanne finished her beer and placed the empty glass back on the bar. When the refills came, she picked up her drink, studied Tessa for a moment longer—as if trying to decide if she really was okay—then hoisted her pint in the air with a flourish. "Cheers."

47

Another drink and an hour later, Tessa stood in the parking lot and tried to decide if it was her head spinning or the world around her. She clutched her car keys in one hand and her purse in the other. Back inside the bar, she had assured Roxanne and Kyla that she was fine, but now that she was outside in the crisp night air, she wasn't so sure.

"I might need to stand here awhile before I drive," she said.

"Yeah, you're not driving." Roxanne plucked the car keys from Tessa's hand and shoved them into her pocket. "Not tonight. You'll end up going off the road and into the ocean."

"Well, someone has to drive." Tessa wondered if her speech was slurred. Decided it wasn't.

"No one is driving. Kyla and I walked here."

"We live in town," Kyla added. "My place is like five minutes away. Roxanne's isn't much farther."

"Which is why you're coming home with me," Roxanne said.

"I am?"

"You are." Roxanne hitched an arm around Tessa's and steered her away from the car. "This isn't up for debate. You can have your keys back in the morning."

"I don't want to put you out." Tessa allowed Roxanne to lead her down the side of the bar toward the road. "I'll take a taxi back to the beach house."

"Good luck with that around here at this time of year." Kyla snorted.

"Or any time of year," Roxanne said with a chuckle. "Old Man Gibby used to ferry tourists around in a clapped-out old Chevy during the summer months, but he went down to some retirement community in Florida a couple of years ago."

"Probably a good thing too," Kyla said. "He was half-blind and had more speeding tickets than the rest of Maine put together."

"In other words, no taxi." Roxanne led them through town, past the diner and the fishing pier. A light fog coiled off the ocean, drifting like smoke between the buildings and muting the landscape. Soon they reached a narrow side road that meandered off into the darkness.

Kyla stopped. "This is where we go our separate ways." She nodded toward a bait-and-tackle shop on the other side of the street. "I rent an apartment on the second floor."

"It's not an apartment," Roxanne said. "It's one room with a sofa bed and a hot plate."

"Two," Kyla corrected her. "I have a bathroom."

"My bad."

"You guys want to come up for a quick drink before heading off?" Kyla asked. "There's a six-pack of beer from that new brewery that opened over on the mainland in Ellsworth."

"I think we've had enough," Roxanne said.

"Definitely." The thought of more alcohol made Tessa's stomach lurch. "Maybe another time?"

"Lightweights." Kyla shook her head before crossing the road. When she reached the steps leading up to her apartment, she turned and blew them a kiss before starting up.

Tessa watched until she was safely inside, then followed Roxanne.

The side street climbed steadily upward away from the shore. There were no streetlamps here. As they walked, the sea fog looked as though it had cleared, but when Tessa glanced over her shoulder, it was still there, cloaking the town below them in a haze of silvery nothingness.

Soon they arrived at a ranch-style house with a detached two-car garage that looked like it might have been a barn at one time.

Roxanne fumbled with her keys for a few seconds, then opened the front door and stepped aside to let Tessa enter.

"You can sleep in the back bedroom," Roxanne said. "It's only a twin bed. I use it when my parents visit since they own the place and want the master. The room's cramped but comfortable enough."

"Honestly, I don't care what size it is. I'm sure the bed will be heavenly." Tessa was looking forward to a real mattress. The couch back at the rental house grew more uncomfortable each night. She made a pact with herself to sleep in the big bedroom with the king-size bed the following night. But first, she would enjoy a night at Roxanne's, away from the haunting and lonely beach house. "Want to show me the bedroom?"

"Sure." Roxanne nodded, then she let out a small, excited sound. "You know what? We should make cocoa first. I haven't done that in ages. You like cocoa?"

"Who doesn't?"

"Awesome." Roxanne took Tessa's hand and led her into the kitchen, where she went about making the cocoa.

Tessa crossed to the kitchen island and perched on a stool. "How long has your family lived here?"

"Longer than they probably should have. My great-grandfather built this house when he came here to work the lobster boats."

"Wow. That's incredible."

"There's a lot of history in this place, for sure. I love it here. I'm not sure how much longer I'll get to stay, though."

"Why?"

"The town is shrinking. It's hard to make a living, at least in the winter. Half the houses in Seaview Point are summer homes owned by out-of-towners. Some of them come from as far away as Florida and even California. They still catch lobster here but not like they used to. Fewer people want to work on the boats, and tighter fishing regulations have decimated the industry. Now that my parents have moved out of state, it's only a matter of time before they decide to sell. And I don't blame them. Some rich stockbroker or banker from Boston will snap this place up and pay twice what a local could afford."

"You think they'll do that?"

"I don't know. Probably." Roxanne shrugged. "It's not like I can pay much rent, and they don't come back here as much as they used to."

"That's too bad."

"It's life. It might be good to move somewhere else and make a fresh start. Heaven knows, I'm going nowhere fast here." Roxanne poured hot cocoa into a pair of mugs. "Besides, the town isn't what it used to be. People would leave their doors unlocked, even at night. Now they don't."

"Because of the murders?"

"Partly. But with tourism comes transience. I can see it happening. Each summer, I recognize fewer of the faces who come into the diner. The old-timers are selling and cashing in. The events in that house you're renting didn't help. We get our fair share of what you might call dark tourists. People looking to get a thrill out of the pain attached to that place."

"Did you think I was one of those people?"

"It crossed my mind when I first met you."

"And now?"

"I think you have your reasons for staying there. I also think you haven't told me the whole truth about those reasons."

"You're right. I haven't." Tessa looked down into her cocoa. She yearned to come clean with Roxanne. They were becoming fast friends, and it wasn't fair to keep lying. But she was afraid of what would happen if she did. Would Roxanne still want to know her? Would she end up even more alone at that house than she already was?

Maybe it was alcohol-fueled courage, but Tessa decided she wouldn't hide behind half-truths and lies of omission anymore. "If you want to know why I came to the island, then I'll tell you. But you have to promise not to be mad."

"Tessa, it's fine. You can open up to me." Roxanne reached across the counter and took Tessa's hand. "How bad can it be?"

"It's not good." Tessa wished she had another glass of wine instead of cocoa. Her resolve was faltering. But she kept going because if she stopped, she might lose her nerve. "There were four girls at that beach house five years ago. Patrick Moyer murdered three of them. He thought he'd killed all four . . ." Tessa trailed off. A tear pushed at the corner of her eye.

"It's okay . . ." Roxanne squeezed Tessa's hand. "Let it out."

"But one girl didn't die." Tessa fought back a flood of emotion. "I survived . . . I'm Patrick Moyer's fourth victim."

Roxanne met her gaze. A moment passed. Then she said, "I know."

48

"You know already?" Of all the things Roxanne might have said, Tessa wasn't expecting that.

"Don't look so surprised," Roxanne said. "Those murders were the biggest thing to happen on this island in fifty years. The *Bangor Daily Telegraph* ran it on their front page for a week. Your face was everywhere. And it was all over the local news. When you came into the diner that first day, I thought you looked familiar. Plus, you have that scar."

Tessa's hand flew to her face.

"Sorry, I didn't mean to embarrass you."

"You didn't."

"Good. Because it really isn't so bad. Hardly noticeable."

Yeah, right, thought Tessa. *Try seeing it in the mirror every day.*

Roxanne continued. "Anyway, I did some snooping on the internet. It took all of about a minute to find a photo of you from after you left the hospital."

"Oh." Tessa remembered the reporters waiting the day she was discharged. They pushed forward, almost suffocating her as they jostled for position, shouting questions and snapping photographs. That experience was pretty high in her rotation of nightmares—right behind Patrick Moyer and his knife. Nothing topped him.

"You changed your name."

"Wouldn't you?"

"Probably." Roxanne paused. "I like Tessa better than Theresa. Less old-fashioned."

"Thanks. Me too."

Roxanne looked into Tessa's eyes. "You must have known people would recognize you, coming back here like this."

"The thought crossed my mind," Tessa admitted. "But after five years, I figured everyone would have forgotten, and like you said, I changed my name."

"This isn't New York or Boston." Roxanne gave Tessa's hand one more squeeze and then withdrew it. "Things move slower, and people have long memories."

"God. I feel like such an idiot." Tessa wiped tears from her cheeks. "You must think I'm awful for hiding my identity."

"I would have done the same thing—trust me. I can't imagine what it's like to go through such a dreadful ordeal. To lose your friends like that and be forced to carry those memories for the rest of your life."

"I've spent the last half a decade afraid of everything." Tessa sipped her cocoa, mostly to relieve her suddenly dry throat. "I feel so vulnerable all the time. I'm a wreck."

"Is that the real reason you came back?"

Tessa nodded. "It was that or run from the ghost of Patrick Moyer until my dying day . . . Plus, I almost killed my sister's cat with a baseball bat."

"Holy crap. Really?"

"Yeah. She was not amused." Tessa cringed at the memory. "She gave me an ultimatum. Straighten up my life or get the hell out of her house."

"That's harsh."

"Okay, she didn't quite say it like that, but she was right. I've spent too long cowering behind locked doors. Therapy hasn't helped. Drugs didn't do anything but make we feel wonky. Nothing worked. That's why I booked the house for the month and came back here. I don't want to lose my sister. She's been so good to me." Tessa paused. "I didn't want to lose *myself*."

"Weren't you afraid it would do more harm than good, coming back here? Dredge up memories you aren't equipped to cope with?"

"I live with the memory of this place no matter where I am. Patrick Moyer is always with me." Tessa's hand went to her face and the scar Moyer had left there, like some macabre signature carved into her skin. "I'm reminded of him every time I look in the mirror."

"You're too hard on yourself. You're beautiful. You should look at the scar as a symbol of your own will to live . . . your strength . . . not a reminder of what Patrick Moyer took from you."

"Easier said than done."

"Except you are doing it. It must have taken a boatload of courage to come back here. If the roles were reversed, I'm not sure I would do the same. How on earth are you sticking it out in that house all on your own?"

"I don't have a choice."

"You always have a choice."

"No. I mean it. I signed a contract with a New York publisher. I'm contractually obligated to stay for the entire month and write a book about it."

"Are you serious?"

Tessa nodded. "They paid me a lot of money up front, and I've already spent most of it."

"I see." Roxanne didn't pry further. She looked concerned. "Book aside, how are you coping?"

"Not well. I haven't even slept in the bedroom yet. I can't bring myself to do it because that's where the attacks . . ." Tessa's throat tightened. The tears threatened to flow again. "That's where Patrick Moyer did all those awful things to my friends."

"Goodness. No wonder you always look so tired. Where *have* you been sleeping?"

"You remember when I told you I fell asleep on the couch watching TV?"

"Sure."

"I didn't doze off watching TV. I've been sleeping in the living room with the lights on and the TV playing." Tessa took a quivering breath. "I sound like a nutjob, don't I?"

"You sound like a traumatized woman trying to reach an acceptance of something no one should ever have to deal with," Roxanne said. "I have nothing but respect for you."

"Really?" The tension drained away. "This doesn't change anything?"

"Of course not, silly. If I didn't want to hang out with you, I would have steered clear of that house."

"What about Kyla? Does she know?"

"I might have mentioned it." Roxanne looked sheepish. Before Tessa could answer, she jumped right back in. "But only because I didn't want her to say something out of place when we were at the bar tonight. She can be blunt sometimes. And I swore her to secrecy. She won't tell another soul."

"It's fine," Tessa said. "It's not like I'm trying to hide my identity. I'm just not shouting it from the rooftops. This trip—coming here to the island—is about me facing my fears and putting the past back where it belongs. Part of accepting what happened is being able to deal with people knowing who I am."

"I'm happy to hear you say that." Roxanne smiled. "For what it's worth, I haven't heard a single soul talk about you at the diner. I don't think anyone else in town knows."

Tessa nodded. "I don't think the caretaker who let me in on the first day has a clue. She even corrected me about the number of murders as if she knew more about them than I do and suggested I take the ghost tour because it stops at the beach house. If it weren't so horrific, it would be hysterical."

"I wouldn't read too much into that. Lillian can be scatterbrained." Roxanne tipped her mug back and drained the last of the cocoa, then licked whipped cream from her upper lip. "What about Chief White?"

"I don't think he recognized me either. At least, if he did, he didn't say so."

"That's surprising," Roxanne said.

"I figured he deals with a lot of cases. It must be hard to remember every name and face. And the only time he saw me was right after the attack. I would have been pretty much unrecognizable, given the circumstances."

"What about afterward?"

"He never came to see me in the hospital. They sent a detective from Portland to interview me." Tessa finished the last of her cocoa. "And, of course, there was no trial because the chief shot and killed Moyer trying to arrest him."

"And a good thing too. Saved you from having to go on the stand and relive that nightmare all over again."

"That's how I felt back then. But now I'm not so sure. I wonder if a trial would have been better. At least then I'd know why he did it."

"He did it because he was a sick and twisted individual. End of story. The chief's bullet did everyone a favor." Roxanne stood and gathered up the mugs, then put them in the sink. She glanced at the clock on the stove. "Crap. I've kept you up talking way too long. It's two in the morning."

"I'm pretty sure I'm the one who kept *you* up."

"Either way, you haven't gotten a full night of sleep since you arrived on the island." Roxanne motioned for Tessa to follow her and started toward the kitchen door. "Come on. We're going to fix that right now."

49

When Tessa woke up the next morning, she didn't know where she was at first. But then it all came crashing back. The Ship to Shore Tavern. Noah hassling them at the bar. Drinking too many glasses of wine. Going back to Roxanne's place and climbing into bed as the room spun around her. Then she remembered something else. Admitting she was the girl who'd survived Patrick Moyer's knife and Roxanne confessing she already knew.

Tessa groaned.

Would this make things weird between them? Sure, Roxanne had said she didn't care, but was she telling the truth?

There was only one way to find out. Tessa swung her legs off the bed and stood up, pulling down the hem of the rumpled T-shirt Roxanne had loaned her the night before, and stumbled to the bathroom.

Fifteen minutes later, after getting dressed and fixing her morning hair as best she could, she arrived in the kitchen to find Roxanne sitting at the counter, browsing on her phone. Her cheeks were rosy.

"Hey." She looked up as Tessa entered. "You slept late. It's ten 0'clock. I've been up for hours. Even took a walk."

Tessa looked around, hoping there was coffee. She didn't see any. "You went for a walk?"

"Uh-huh. I almost woke you to come with me, but you looked so tired last night I figured I'd let you sleep in. Got back about ten minutes ago."

"Oh." Tessa wasn't sure what to say.

"How are you feeling?"

"How do you think?"

"Right." Roxanne slipped from the stool. "Grab your coat. We're going down to the diner."

"Thanks, but I figured I'd just grab a quick cup of coffee and head back to the beach house." Tessa felt safe at Roxanne's, but she also knew that hiding there was putting off her inevitable return to the house.

"Nope. We're going to the diner. My treat. I get a fifty percent discount. Perk of working there. And so do you since you're eating with me." Roxanne took Tessa's arm and steered her toward the front door. "Come on."

Tessa resisted a moment, then gave in to the inevitable.

Ten minutes later, they walked through the Harbor Diner's front door and found a table near the back overlooking the water. The plump woman who served Tessa the last time she was there came over and poured two coffees, then placed menus on the table and retreated while they decided what to eat.

After they ordered, Roxanne leaned forward, elbows on the table, and fixed Tessa with a deadpan stare. "I've been thinking—you should stay with me awhile longer instead of going back to that horrendous beach house."

Tessa was surprised by Roxanne's offer. "Don't you think that defeats the purpose of facing my fears?"

"Not really." Roxanne spooned sugar into her coffee. "Look. You came here to the island because you want to turn your life around, and that's great. It really is. But staying at that house is just plain crazy. It's too much."

"That's kind of what my sister, Melissa, said," Tessa admitted. "She thought I should talk about it with my therapist first."

"She's right. What if this does more harm than good?" Roxanne stirred her coffee. "You're having a hard time there. You said it yourself. For heaven's sake, you haven't even slept in the bedroom yet."

"I know."

"You thought someone murdered your neighbor."

"So would you if you heard those screams."

"Exactly. It was just a bobcat. Which means you're not facing your fears. You're putting yourself through hell in a place that scares the living daylights out of you."

"At least I'm trying."

"It sounds to me like you're jumping at every shadow and imagining danger around every corner."

"Which is exactly what I'm like back in Gloucester," Tessa said. "I just need to settle in. Get used to my surroundings. It will get better."

"Are you sure about that?"

"Honestly, I'm not sure about anything."

"Then stay with me, at least for another night or two. Go back during the day if you must, but give yourself a break. If you insist on staying at the house, you'll end up having a nervous breakdown."

"That isn't going to happen," Tessa assured her. "I can do this."

"I'm not saying you can't. But do you really need it to be all or nothing?"

"Yes. If I give in to my fears, I'll never defeat them. Everything I've tried for five years has failed. Countless hours of therapy. Forcing myself to go out in public. Pretending there's nothing wrong, even though I just want to hide behind a locked door and curl into a ball. This is my last chance to fix myself. If I fail here, I'm broken for the rest of my life. Besides, if I stay with you another night, I might lose my nerve and never go back. Then I'll be in breach of my contract with the publisher."

"Fine." Roxanne sighed. "I understand. But just so you know, I'm going to drop by every day and check on you. I need to make sure you don't start talking to the walls."

Tessa smiled. "I'm counting on it."

"And on that note, I need the restroom." Roxanne pushed her chair back and stood up.

She headed for the front of the restaurant and disappeared down a corridor next to the service counter.

Tessa took out her phone, looked down at it. Checked her messages. When she looked back up, her heart skipped a beat. Patrick Moyer's brother was looming over the table, staring at her.

50

Tessa almost fell off her chair in shock. She pushed it back, legs scraping the floor, and went to stand, a scream rising in her throat.

"No, no. It's okay." Moyer's brother held his hands up, palms out, in a gesture of suppliance. "I'm so sorry. I didn't mean to startle you."

"What do you want?" Tessa sank back into her chair, arms folded across her chest. She wondered how long Roxanne would be gone.

"Look, we got off on the wrong foot the other day. I might have overreacted just a bit." He took a step forward, reached for a chair to sit down.

"Don't come any closer." Tessa tried to ignore the crawling sensation that prickled her skin. "Stay where you are."

"Okay." Moyer's brother dropped his arms to his sides. "I'm Daniel, by the way."

Tessa said nothing.

Daniel Moyer cleared his throat. "I came over to apologize. I shouldn't have blown up at you. It's just that . . . It hasn't been easy the last several years, living in the shadow of what my brother did. You were just taking a photo. Heaven knows, people have done much worse."

"Like what?" Tessa's interest was piqued despite the way her gut twisted when she looked up into that face that so resembled the man who stole her innocence.

Daniel shrugged. "It depends. Some people sneak onto the property, wanting to get a closer look at the place where my brother lived and died. They peer in the windows. One person even pried a shingle off the house to take as a souvenir. I don't know. Maybe they think the house is abandoned."

"That's what I thought," Tessa admitted.

"Yeah. I can see where you'd get that idea." Daniel placed a hand on the back of the chair opposite Tessa. He pulled it out ever so slowly, as if expecting her to leap back in protest. When she didn't, he hesitated a moment, then sat down equally slowly. "I should probably do the place up. I'm sure the neighbors would be happier. But honestly, I can't see the point. Given half a chance, I'd get the hell out of there and leave it to rot. Better yet, douse the place in gasoline and throw a match over my shoulder as I walk away."

"Why don't you?" Tessa swallowed. She clasped and unclasped her hands under the table and tried to ignore the barely tamed panic that made her heart race. She could hardly stand to look at him, to be close enough to detect the faint aroma of his musky aftershave. *Just one more minute,* she told herself. *One minute, and then I'll make him leave. I'll scream if I have to. Scream until the roof comes off the place.* In the meantime, chapter 2 of her book was sitting right in front of her. She couldn't waste the opportunity to give Thomas Milner what he wanted. The backstory on the Cassadaga Island Ripper. She let out a breath she hadn't realized she was holding. "Can't be easy living in the house where your brother died."

"That's an understatement. I would never have come back here if I had any choice."

"You weren't on the island when Chief White . . . ? I mean . . ." Tessa faltered.

A wry smile played across Daniel Moyer's lips. He shook his head. "Maybe my brother wouldn't have killed those girls if I had been. But no, I was off on the mainland, living my life and trying to put this wretched island in my rearview mirror. Couldn't wait to get away the minute Patrick was old enough to look after himself."

"Where were your parents?"

The smile faded. "Good old Dad made his own bid for freedom when I was seventeen and Patrick was fourteen. He had a lobster boat with my uncle Brian. Guess he wanted something else from life. Left one morning as if he was going to work and never came back. Haven't seen him since. A year later, Mom died. After that, I cared for Patrick as best I could and worked the lobster boat with my uncle to make ends meet. When my brother turned eighteen, I escaped. Went down to Portland and got a job as a line cook. It was hard work but better than catching lobsters."

"But you came back."

"Didn't have no choice. Patrick used to help Brian out on the lobster boat in the summers. Even took to guiding whale-watching tours when he wasn't needed. In the winter, he used to pick up work on the mainland wherever he could. Construction. Factory work. Whatever. Brian didn't like lobstering in the winter. It's tough in the summer, but it's intolerable in the winter. Colder than hell, and you have to head out farther to sea too. A lot farther. I was glad to be free of it, truth be told. Patrick always liked being out on the water, though. Then he killed those gals and got himself shot dead. Stupid. By then, I was spinning my wheels in Portland, struggling to keep my head above water. Line cook don't pay much. The house was sitting empty, and Brian needed a body on the boat, so here I am. Trapped just like those damn lobsters with no way out."

"I'm sorry about what happened to you." Tessa hung her head. Despite her revulsion, she actually meant it. "I wasn't trying to be nosy when I stopped outside your house the other day."

"Nah. It's okay. I get it." Daniel waved a hand. His eyes roamed across her face. "Looks like you had some troubles of your own."

"I don't know what you—" The words caught in Tessa's throat, choked off by a swell of emotion. She closed her mouth.

"The scar." Daniel looked sheepish. "I'm making you uncomfortable."

If only you knew, thought Tessa. Then another thought occurred to her. A worse thought. *What if he* does *know?*

Roxanne was coming back from the restroom, hurrying toward them. "Daniel."

"Roxanne." Daniel pushed the chair back and stood. "I'm in your seat."

Roxanne glared at him.

Daniel returned her look. "It's been a long time. Haven't seen you since—"

Roxanne cut him off. "Yeah. Long time. Goodbye, Daniel."

Daniel watched her awhile longer, as if trying to figure out what he'd done wrong; then he turned his attention back to Tessa. "Guess that's my cue to leave. It was nice talking to you. And again, I'm sorry."

"That's all right." Tessa avoided his gaze. She couldn't stand to look into those eyes, even though she knew it wasn't Patrick Moyer looking back at her.

Daniel nodded. He went to leave, but after a couple of steps, he stopped and looked back, his gaze finally catching hers. "I'll see you around."

Tessa was momentarily taken aback. Was he just being friendly? She wasn't sure.

Daniel lingered, as if expecting her to say something else, but when she didn't reply, he turned and made his way toward the service counter. He took a heavy coat off the back of a chair before heading quickly toward the exit.

Roxanne sat down. "You okay?"

"Yes." Tessa pulled herself together. "What just happened between the two of you?"

"Nothing. I just figured you don't need Patrick Moyer's brother hassling you." Roxanne glanced over her shoulder and watched him step out the door. "You've been through enough."

"Why didn't you tell me he was on the island?"

Roxanne shrugged. "I don't know. Didn't occur to me, I guess."

Tessa watched her with narrowed eyes.

"What?" Roxanne threw her arms up. "I'm just looking out for you. I should have mentioned that Daniel was on the island. My bad but—"

"It's fine." Tessa waved her off. She didn't want to argue with her only friend. But yet . . . there *had* been a moment between Daniel and Roxanne. She was sure of it. What she wasn't so sure of was if it meant anything.

51

The beach house felt cold and barren when Tessa walked in, like an empty shell waiting for its soul to return. She stepped across the threshold and whispered to the stirring air, or possibly the lingering spirits of her three dead friends, "I'm back. Did you miss me?"

Her only answer was the shifting weight of silence.

She went to take her coat off, but then changed her mind. Stepping back out onto the porch, she walked to the far end and stared across the gap toward Cindy's house. It looked just like it had the previous day. Descending the porch steps, she crossed the distance between them.

No one answered when she knocked on the door.

That's because Cindy is safely back on the mainland, Tessa thought, but she wasn't sure she believed the words even as they rolled through her head. Stepping off the porch, she craned her neck and peered at the upstairs windows, but they were dark and impenetrable. When she walked around the side of the house, nothing was amiss.

There was no sign of movement beyond the windows.

Tessa wasn't sure if that made her feel better or worse. She started back around the front of the house, and her gaze fell on the space underneath the porch.

She stopped in her tracks.

There, tucked away out of the elements, was a bicycle. Presumably the same one that Cindy said she used to get around the island without a car. Tessa drew closer. The bicycle looked like it hadn't moved in a while. The silky strands of a spiderweb bridged the gap between the handlebars and the support post of the porch. A fat brown spider sat in the middle, waiting for some hapless insect to wander on by and get caught in its trap.

Tessa suppressed a shudder and looked away.

Cindy obviously had not used the bicycle since arriving on the island. But did that mean anything? She clearly didn't mind the walk from her house to Seaview Point because she had been on foot when Tessa picked her up that first day. And she wouldn't take her bike into town to go back over to the mainland because there would be nowhere to leave it.

So *why did* the sight of that bicycle bother her so much?

She stepped back and looked up at the house again, wishing Cindy would appear at the front door and solve the mystery, but the building stared back at her, unwilling to give up its secrets.

Digging her hands into her coat pockets, Tessa walked back to the beach house, shucked her coat off, and hung it on a hook near the door.

She needed something to distract herself, so she built a fire and then went into the kitchen. The bread machine was still sitting on the counter. She gathered the ingredients, including the yeast Noah had brought out to her the second day she was on the island, and followed an Italian-loaf recipe she'd found on the internet.

The bread would take several hours, which gave her time to write. She went to the living room, sat on the couch, and went for her laptop. Then she stopped.

The computer was sitting open on the coffee table, the screen dark.

Had she left it like that?

Tessa didn't think so. She always closed the laptop out of habit because Corky was forever on the lookout for something to break, and an open laptop would be too much for the feline to resist. There was no cat here, so maybe she had left it open, yet . . .

Tessa stared at the machine for a while, trying to remember, but no moment of clarity came to her. In the end, she shook off the vague unease, hunched over the keyboard, and went to work.

◆ ◆ ◆

Four hours later, while she was reading through a productive fifteen pages, there was a ding from the kitchen.

The bread was ready.

Tessa went to the kitchen and removed the loaf from the machine, placing it on the counter. It smelled so good. She reached for the bread knife. But before she could cut a slice, there was a knock at the front door.

Tessa's heart jolted. Maybe it was Cindy. She put the bread knife down and rushed through the living room to the front window, then peeked out onto the porch, but it wasn't her neighbor standing there. It was Chief White.

52

"Miss Montgomery," White said, tipping his hat when she opened the door. "I was passing and thought I'd stop to see how you're getting on."

"I'm fine," Tessa replied. She kept the door partially closed between them.

"Pleased to hear that." The chief flashed a smile that quickly dissolved. He cupped his hands and blew on them. "Cripes. It's freezing out here. Mind if I come in for a minute to warm up?"

"Oh." Tessa was torn between complying with the chief's request and her own insecurities. "Well, I don't think—"

"I won't keep you for long." The chief put a hand on the door, pushed it wider, and stepped past her into the house.

Tessa shrank back. She hadn't let a man into her personal space for five years, and now the chief of police was standing in her hallway for the second time in three days.

After a tense interval of silence, she said the only thing that came to mind. "I was going to make tea. Would you like a cup?"

"Not much of a tea drinker," the chief replied. "Really not my bag. But hey, if you'd consider putting some coffee on instead, my arm could be twisted."

"Coffee it is." Tessa closed the door and scooted past the chief. She hurried through the living room into the kitchen and went about putting on a pot of coffee.

Chief White followed. He removed his hat and leaned on the doorframe, watching her work. His gaze drifted to the loaf of bread. "Something sure smells heavenly."

"I just baked it," Tessa replied. "Would you like a slice?"

"Don't mind if I do. Can't beat fresh-baked bread."

Tessa sliced the heel from the bread, then cut a generous slice, which she buttered and handed to the chief on a plate.

He took a bite and smacked his lips. "My oh my. That is perfection. Yes, sirree. Just heavenly. You have a talent for baking, young lady. Yes, indeed."

"I hardly think so." Tessa wanted to get to the point . . . and get the chief out of her house. "What did you find out about Cindy?"

"Right. The missing neighbor." Chief White shook his head. "Haven't had time to make any inquiries yet."

"Then why are you here?" Tessa struggled to mask her irritation.

"Welfare visit, like I said." The chief polished off the bread, then brushed crumbs from the front of his shirt. He put the plate down. "You were mighty upset the other night."

"Wouldn't you be?"

"Well now, that depends. Maybe if I were staying out here all on my lonesome. Those bobcats can make the hairs on your neck stand up, and that's for sure." The chief nodded toward the bread. "Mind if I cut myself another slice?"

"Go ahead." Tessa wondered how long this man would be invading her space.

"Much appreciated." He picked up the bread knife and carved off a thick slice, which he quickly buttered. "Lillian tells me you're here for a whole month."

"That's right."

The chief whistled. "You must really like your solitude."

"Something like that." Tessa watched coffee drip into the carafe, willed it to brew faster.

"Your employer can't be too happy. That much time off work? Whoa. Can't imagine the town administrator would let me go MIA for so long."

"I'm not working. I mean . . . I am, but I just don't . . ." Tessa stumbled to answer without telling the chief her real reason for being in Seaview Point. She said the only thing she could think of. "I'm self-employed. A writer."

"I see. A writer." The chief nodded. "And what type of writing would that be? Anything I might have read?"

"I can't imagine." *Because nothing has been published yet,* Tessa thought.

"Ah." The chief started into the second slice. "You one of those true crime types? Come here to tell the world all about us?"

"No." Tessa shook her head. This was getting too close to home. "I'm not one of those true crime types."

"Come on, we both know what happened in this house. Four college students on summer break. Cute young things. Went and got themselves murdered. Well, three of them did, anyway. Fourth gal almost didn't make it, but I guess she was more tenacious than the others. Had more fight in her." Chief White strolled across the kitchen to the table. He pulled out a chair, letting the legs scrape across the floor, and sat down. He took another bite of bread. "You telling me you're not here because of those murders?"

"Not exactly," Tessa replied. She couldn't decide if the chief recognized her and was playing dumb so she wouldn't feel awkward or if he truly didn't know who she was. If it was the latter, maybe letting him think she was just some random crime writer was the easiest way out. He already thought she was jumping at shadows. How would he ever take her seriously from here on out?

"That's what I thought." The chief tapped a finger on the table. "But hey, it's no skin off my nose. Frankly, there are folk in town who like the notoriety. Good for business. Brings the tourists. And hell, we need all the tourists we can get ever since the lobster boats started leaving.

Too many fishing regulations. They say tourism is the future of this place. Pretty soon, we'll be like every other quaint little coastal town in Maine. Shops selling smelly candles and art galleries by the dozen. Not that we don't have our share of those already." Chief White cleared his throat. "And why not? I'll be retiring in a few years and handing over the reins to some other poor SOB. Might be fun to open my own little place and make some money off the flatlanders. I do wood carvings, see. Miniature wolves and bears. Been doing it ever since I was a kid. Just a hobby, mind you."

"Really?" Tessa poured a mug of coffee and put it down on the table in front of the chief. "Why are you telling me all this?"

"Just figured you might like a little local color for that book of yours. Maybe I'll buy a copy when it comes out. I'm not usually into that kind of thing, but if it's about Cassadaga Island, well . . . I might just give it a go. Now, my son, he's the opposite of me. Loves all that true crime stuff. Can't get enough of it. Don't know why when his old man's a cop. The stories I could tell . . ." He picked up the coffee, blew on it, then took a sip. "My heavens, that's good. Strong."

"I'm glad you like it." Tessa hadn't mentioned a book, only that she was a writer. She thought about her open laptop and the unshakable feeling that someone was watching her. She hovered near the back door and wondered how long the chief intended to linger, talking about mundane trivia.

As if he'd read her mind, the chief took another gulp of coffee, then said, "Well, I've taken up enough of your time. I'm sure there's a teenager or two smoking weed behind the supermarket or skidding their cars out on the backroads to make tire tracks. Call themselves burners. I call 'em a nuisance. Just begging for me to crack their heads. Can't blame 'em, though, I suppose. Just trying to let off steam. Everything winds down here after Labor Day. By October, there's nothing much to look forward to until Memorial Day rolls around again. Gets mighty boring."

"I'm sure it does," Tessa said, forcing a smile. "I have a lot to do today, but I appreciate the visit."

"Beats chasing those dang burners around." Chief White laughed. He hauled himself up and stretched, cracking his back. Wide-brimmed hat held in one meaty hand, he picked up the coffee cup with the other and drained it before smacking his lips. "You make better coffee than the diner in town."

"That's quite a compliment." Tessa glanced back through the living room toward the front door, willing the chief to use it.

"And better bread too." The chief deposited the hat atop his thinning hair, walked across the kitchen, and put his empty coffee mug in the sink. His gaze fell wistfully to the loaf. "Hard to beat good hometown baking."

Tessa took a step forward. "I'll walk you to the door."

"Well now, I'd appreciate that." The chief followed her through the living room to the front hallway. He pointed to the framed newspaper article sitting on the floor. "Looks like you have a little problem there. You want some help putting that back up?"

"No, thank you."

"Don't like seeing it every day, huh?"

"It's creepy." Tessa reached past the chief and opened the front door.

"I get that." Chief White nodded slowly. "You know, if this house makes you feel so uncomfortable, maybe you should go back to the mainland. I mean, a big place like this, with such a morbid history . . . hardly a place for a nice young woman like yourself."

"I appreciate your concern, but I'll manage."

The chief shrugged. "Just sayin', you could write that book of yours from anywhere. You've soaked up the atmosphere of this place. Why torture yourself?"

"Like I said, I'll be fine."

"Okay, then." The chief studied her for a moment longer, then stepped out onto the porch. "You take care while you're here, Tessa Montgomery."

"I will, thank you." Tessa gripped the doorknob, waiting to close the door as soon as the chief was far enough away.

"And call me if you have any more issues," he called over his shoulder as he descended the porch steps. "You can never be too careful, even on an island like this."

53

At eight o'clock that evening, Tessa was still unnerved by the unexpected visit from the Seaview Point chief of police. She found it hard to believe he had arrived on her doorstep just to see if she was doing okay. Especially since he had made a point to mention the events of five years before. Did he know she was the only survivor of that dreadful evening and had subsequently changed her name from Theresa Chamberlain?

If so, why didn't he just come out and say it? While she didn't want to broadcast her presence in town, she wasn't exactly denying who she was either. Sure, she had neglected to tell Roxanne, at least until their friendship blossomed, but she hadn't actively lied about it. Except by omission.

So what was the deal with the police chief?

She didn't have an answer any more than she had an answer for the other weird events that had occurred since she arrived on the island.

In the end, Tessa retreated into the master bedroom. She pulled the blinds across the sliding doors leading out to the back deck and the firepit beyond, then went to the bathroom and turned on the shower. She might not have gathered the courage to sleep in here yet, but she preferred the downstairs en suite to the shower upstairs, mostly because she still heard Patrick Moyer pulling that curtain back every time she went in there.

She undressed, grabbed a towel from the linen shelf, then stepped under the steaming jet of water and pulled the shower curtain closed.

She lingered in the shower longer than normal, the hot massaging spray playing over her shoulders and back, relieving her tense muscles. Back at home, in the Gloucester house, she would have reclined in the clawfoot tub with a glass of wine. But the downstairs tub at this house had been converted into a cubicle.

Tessa closed her eyes and rubbed shampoo into her hair. When she rinsed off, the heat made her scalp tingle. She stood there a few moments longer, then reached to turn the shower off.

And then she heard it.

A quick bump from somewhere beyond the bathroom.

Tessa froze with her hand over the shower knob. It sounded like a door closing. But how was that possible? She was alone, and the alarm was set. She held her breath and listened but heard nothing else. Maybe it was just a branch falling on the roof. But even as she reasoned the noise away, she didn't believe that any more than she thought the strange noises on the porch a few nights before were raccoons or that the scream was a bobcat.

Tessa bit her lip and wondered what to do next. Her hand still hovered over the shower knob, but she couldn't bring herself to turn the shower off.

A minute passed with no further incident.

The water was losing its heat now.

Tessa decided the noise must have been something hitting the roof outside, after all. Besides, the frigid air that seeped in around the shower curtain was giving her goose bumps. Her hair clung to her shoulders in cold, wet strands. She didn't want to be in the shower anymore.

Her fingers closed over the knob.

Close by, a floorboard creaked.

The breath caught in Tessa's throat. There *was* someone in the house with her.

Another creak.

She stood paralyzed by indecision. She didn't want to step out of the shower into the arms of an intruder, but she had no desire to stay here naked and vulnerable either. Worse, her towel was folded on the sink cabinet, too far away to reach. Why hadn't she hung it on the hook next to the shower? She cursed her stupidity.

Creak.

This one was louder. It sounded like—she didn't want to think it, couldn't help herself—a footstep so close it might be in the same room with her.

A shadow moved on the other side of the shower curtain, as if someone had walked into the bathroom and was blocking the light from the wall sconce.

Tessa stifled a whimper and shrank back against the shower wall. Cold, smooth tiles pressed against her bare skin. She watched the shower curtain, sure an intruder was standing right there on the other side, savoring her fear. She braced, expecting the curtain to swoosh back at any moment to reveal a nightmare figure lunging toward her, knife in hand.

But nothing happened.

The curtain didn't move, and she heard no more sounds except the light patter of water on the shower tray at her feet.

Tessa reached out and gripped the shower curtain, heart pounding so loud she thought they must be able to hear it all the way in Seaview Point.

She steeled herself, counted backward from three, and pulled the curtain back in a swift jerking motion.

The bathroom was empty.

Tessa almost slid to the floor in relief.

She turned the shower off and stepped out, then stood listening to the silence, praying she would not hear more footsteps. Trying to convince herself it was nothing but her overactive imagination. But she couldn't shake the feeling someone was inside the house with her. Watching. Waiting. The atmosphere was suddenly heavy. Oppressive. Worse, her only defense—the baseball bat—was all the way on the far side of the house in the living room next to the couch. It was all she could think about. Her chest tightened. She had to get that bat. She never left it lying around. What was wrong with her?

Tessa grabbed the towel and wrapped it around her body, then pushed the bathroom door open and peered into the master. Still no sign of an intruder. But he could be anywhere. In the closet looking back at her through the door slats. Under the bed. Behind the door.

There was only one thing to do, and she had to do it now or she would lose her nerve. And then where would she be? Cowering in the bathroom, afraid to move until morning, with the bat out of reach and no way to defend herself.

Tessa willed her legs to obey her and sprinted forward.

She raced through the master bedroom, expecting a hand to grab at her or an intruder to lunge from the shadows. But they didn't. She reached the hallway, heart pounding, and sped past the other two bedrooms into the living room.

She lunged for the couch, overcome by a sudden sense that she was not alone, and snatched up the bat with one hand while holding the towel closed with the other. She turned back toward the master bedroom, her gaze sweeping across the hallway. And then she froze because a figure was standing there, staring back at her from the open front door.

Tessa screamed.

54

"Hey, calm down. It's just me," Roxanne said quickly, stepping into the hallway and closing the front door.

Tessa stared at her. She clutched the towel tight to her body with one hand, aware she was dripping on the floor. She gripped the baseball bat with the other. "You scared me half to death. What are you doing here?"

Roxanne held up a bottle of wine. "Thought I'd come and keep you company. I wasn't expecting you to scream like a banshee when you saw me. I almost dropped the bottle out of fright."

"Of course I screamed," Tessa said. "*I wasn't expecting* to see someone standing in my doorway."

"Well, duh. That's obvious, considering you're walking around the house in nothing but a towel," Roxanne said, taking in Tessa's sodden hair, which clung to her neck and shoulders, and the growing puddle of water around her feet. "What's the deal?"

"I thought there was an intruder in the house. I heard footsteps." Tessa's eyes shifted to the front door. "Was it you?"

"No. I just got here. Like two seconds ago."

"You weren't in the bathroom while I was showering?"

"That's a hard no. I'm not some weirdo who likes to watch people in the shower. Maybe you shouldn't leave the front door wide open if you don't want visitors."

"I didn't leave it open." Tessa remembered locking the door after she let the police chief out of the house earlier. She had also set the alarm to Home Mode. One glance at the box told her it was now disarmed. She fought a surge of panic. "The door was locked. The alarm was on."

"Don't know what to say. It was open when I got here. Maybe you forgot to lock the door and set the alarm. It happens."

"Not to me."

"Then maybe it didn't catch properly and blew back open."

"That's a stretch." Tessa shivered. And not just because she was wearing a thin towel in the chilly living room. "Did you see anyone outside? Out on the road?"

"No one." Roxanne went to the coffee table and set the wine bottle down. "You really think someone was in the house with you?"

"I'm sure of it." Tessa wondered if Roxanne was telling the truth. Had she really shown up and found the door open, or was it her walking around the house? But that was crazy. Roxanne had been nothing but wonderful. A true friend. And how would she know the alarm code or door code? Then again, someone did. "If it wasn't you, then who?"

Roxanne shrugged. "Beats me."

A horrible thought occurred to Tessa. "Maybe they're still here."

"One way to find out. Let's search the place."

"You mean together, right?"

"Hell yeah. I've seen enough horror movies to know you don't split up."

"Okay. We'll start with this floor, then check upstairs."

"Um . . . you forgetting something?"

"What?"

Roxanne nodded toward the towel. "Might want to get dressed first."

"Oh. Right." Tessa turned back toward the bedroom and the en suite bathroom beyond. Then she hesitated. "What if someone is hiding in the bedroom?"

"Wouldn't you have seen them already?"

"I don't know."

"Want me to come into the bedroom and keep guard?"

Tessa nodded. "It would make me feel better."

"Do I get the baseball bat?"

Tessa didn't answer.

"Guess that's a no, then." Roxanne went to the fireplace and plucked a poker from a stand next to the grate. "This will work just as well."

Tessa pulled a face. "Sorry. The bat is kind of like my safety blanket."

"No need to explain." Roxanne followed Tessa to the bedroom. She stopped at the bathroom door. "I'll wait here. Don't take too long."

"I won't." Tessa ducked into the bathroom and leaned the bat against the sink console. She patted herself down with the towel, wrung the worst of the water out of her hair, and threw her clothes on.

When she opened the bathroom door, Roxanne hadn't moved.

"You look better, if a little bedraggled."

"Didn't exactly have time to make myself presentable," Tessa replied. "Are we going to search this place or what?"

"Whatever helps you relax," Roxanne said. "If we come across a corkscrew while we're searching, all the better."

"I get the feeling you're not taking this seriously." Tessa went to the built-in closet on the other side of the bedroom and stared at the doors.

"I think you're freaking out because of what happened to you in this house," Roxanne said, joining her. She grabbed the knob and pulled the closet door back, poked her head inside and glanced around. "All good. No bogeymen hiding in here."

"Don't joke. Please?" Tessa was shaking. "I swear, there were footsteps when I was in the shower. Someone was in the bathroom with me. I saw their shadow on the other side of the curtain."

"Then we keep looking, if that's what it takes to make you feel safe." Roxanne went to the bed and dropped onto her knees to look underneath. "All clear down here too. No monsters under the bed." Roxanne stood up. "I declare this room safe."

"I feel better already."

"Good." Roxanne walked to the door. "Let's build on that."

Tessa nodded and followed her. They checked the other two bedrooms on the ground floor with the same results. Empty. They went back to the living room.

As they walked past the basement door, Tessa stopped.

Roxanne turned back to her. "You okay?"

Tessa didn't reply. She stared at the door.

"There's no one in the basement," Roxanne said. "I promise."

"How can you be sure?"

"Because it's locked." Roxanne pointed to the barrel bolt, which was drawn across. "Kinda hard to engage that lock from the other side of the door, don't you think? Unless your phantom visitor is Houdini."

Tessa looked at the bolt, relieved they wouldn't have to descend into the dark unknown beneath the house. "Of course."

"Living room and kitchen look good," Roxanne said, looking around. "One place left."

"The upstairs."

"And then we can open that wine." Roxanne crossed to the foot of the stairs. The landing above was dark. She flicked on the light. "Want me to go first?"

"Yes." Tessa didn't want to go up there at all. She almost suggested they go back to Roxanne's house for the night. The second floor would be easier to deal with in daylight. But it was too late. Roxanne was already halfway up the stairs.

Heart pounding, Tessa followed.

55

By the time Tessa reached the top of the stairs, she could barely breathe. Her eyes flitted nervously down the dark hallway toward the bathroom, where Patrick Moyer had swished back that shower curtain five years before, and the bedroom opposite, where he'd done much worse things.

"Hanging in there?" Roxanne asked. "You look pale as a ghost."

"I'll be okay," Tessa gasped, trying to contain her fear. "Just give me a second."

"Take all the time you need. No hurry." Roxanne turned the hallway light on and waited with her arms at her sides.

After thirty seconds, Tessa took a step forward. She was gripping the bat so hard that her knuckles had turned white. "Let's get this over with."

"If it gets too much, you can go back downstairs. I can do this alone."

"I'm not leaving you up here." The last time Tessa had left her friends alone, they ended up dead. She took a faltering step down the hallway, hesitated, then took another. She stopped at the bathroom door and rested her hand on the knob.

"Going to open that?"

Tessa nodded and turned the handle. She pushed the door. It swung back to reveal the bathroom beyond. A wedge of light spilled from the hallway but did little to banish the shadows farther in.

Roxanne moved past Tess into the bathroom. She found the light switch and turned it on. After giving the room a cursory inspection, she turned and stood, hands on her hips. "See. Nothing to worry about in here."

Tessa stared at the tub and the bunched shower curtain hanging from a tarnished silver rod. The tub was empty.

"Where next?" Roxanne said, hurrying back into the hallway. "One down, three more doors to go, at least if you count that weird half-size opening at the end of the hallway."

"It's a storage area under the eaves."

"Pick one."

"The door on the left." Tessa wasn't ready to face the door opposite the bathroom. Her room from five years ago. "The office."

"Consider it done." Roxanne went to the door and opened it, then stepped inside. After a moment, she reappeared. "That is one small room. Not sure you could even get a bed in there if you wanted to. Guess that's why it's set up as an office." When she saw Tessa looking at her with pleading eyes, her shoulders slumped. "It's also empty."

"Want to check the door at the end next?"

"Uh-huh." Tessa glanced toward her old bedroom. Patrick Moyer's voice rang in her head. The last thing he'd said to her in that room before raping and trying to kill her. *I saved the best for last.* Well, now she was saving the worst for last.

Roxanne went to the door and turned the handle. It didn't open. "Locked."

"What?" Tessa grabbed the handle and tried it. "It wasn't the last time I was up here."

"Well, it is now. What's in there, anyway?"

"An attic-storage area. The caretaker didn't know where the key was. She was going to look for it."

"There's your answer. The caretaker came by and locked it."

"No. She texted when I was in the parking lot for the bar last night to say she'd found the key. She promised to drop it around the next time she was out this way, but she hasn't come by yet."

"Are you sure of that? She probably stopped by while you were out."

"Maybe." Tessa wasn't convinced. She took out her phone. "I'll call her and ask."

Roxanne waited while Tessa found Lillian's number and called. It rang, then went to voicemail. She left a message asking the caretaker to call back, then slipped the phone back into her pocket.

"No answer?"

Tessa shook her head.

"She'll call back, and when she does, I'm sure you'll find it was her who locked the door."

"Maybe."

"No maybe about it." Roxanne started down the hallway to the last door. "Come on. One more room to go."

"That's where Patrick Moyer . . . where he . . ." Tessa struggled to finish the sentence. She held the bat to her chest as if it were some sort of magic shield that would protect her against whatever lay beyond.

"Hey. I'll go in alone. You don't need to—"

"No. It's fine." Tessa reached past Roxanne and pushed the door open. "I came here to face my fears, not cower from them."

"You don't have to put so much pressure on yourself. Take it one day at a time."

"No pressure." Tessa crossed the threshold into the bedroom before she had time to think about it and change her mind. She stood in the center of the room, feeling the familiar prickle when she looked down at the spot where Patrick Moyer had assaulted her.

"This is the place, huh?" Roxanne came up behind her and looked around.

Tessa didn't reply. Her throat was as dry as parchment. She hated this room.

Roxanne went to the bed, dropped onto her knees, and peered underneath. She stood and went to the closet, opening the doors and sticking her head inside. "We're good here. Want to go back downstairs?"

Tessa nodded. She still didn't trust herself to speak. She looked at the window, still securely shut and locked. She let Roxanne steer her toward the door. As she stepped out into the hallway, her gaze fell to the doorframe.

The memory hit Tessa like a wave breaking on the shore. She stumbled. Reached out. Steadied herself against the wall.

◆ ◆ ◆

She is lying on her back. She feels a rug underneath her, the fibers scratchy. Pain dances around the edges of her consciousness. She is vaguely aware of her nakedness.

There are people here. Strangers. They look down at her. Tend to her. Talk to her.

She tries to lift an arm to cover herself, but her body refuses to respond.

"Take it easy, okay?" The voice sounds far away, but she knows it isn't. "We've got you."

Hands are touching her. But not like before. These hands are gentle. Caring. They lift her. Slide her sideways. Place her on . . . a stretcher.

Someone covers her with a warm blanket. A mask drops over her mouth. She sucks in a stream of oxygen.

"We're going to move you now, okay?"

She tries to answer but manages nothing more than an incoherent mumble.

"Don't talk." The voice sounds kind. "Save your strength."

A jolt. The stretcher sways. There is a brief sensation of rising through the air; then she is moving. The ceiling slips by above her.

Her arm falls from under the blanket.

As they carry her into the hallway, her fingers brush against the doorframe. She feels smooth gloss-painted wood under her fingertips.

Then the world goes dark again.

◆ ◆ ◆

"Hey. You okay?" Roxanne's voice sliced through the memory, shattering it.

"What?" Tessa shook her head.

"You spaced out on me for a second there."

"I'm fine." Tessa glanced back into the room. Her heart was racing. The sudden flashback had left her shaken.

"You don't look fine," Roxanne said, moving toward the stairs. "Let's get a glass of wine into you. It'll steady your nerves."

"I'm sorry." Tessa grabbed Roxanne's arm. "You didn't have to humor me and search the house, but I'm grateful you did."

"No worries," Roxanne said in a light voice.

"You must think I'm crazy."

"Hell yes. I think you're a complete lunatic for wanting to come back and spend a month in the house where you almost got murdered. I couldn't do it. But I also admire you for the same reason. It takes guts to face your fears head-on."

"Took me five years to get up the nerve."

"At least you finally did. Some people never face their demons." Roxanne descended the stairs, then waited for Tessa at the bottom before crossing to the coffee table where she had set the bottle of wine down earlier. She sat on the couch. "I think you could use a drink."

"I agree." Tessa went to the kitchen and grabbed two glasses, then rummaged in the cutlery drawer for the corkscrew. She turned to head back into the living room, but before she made it to the kitchen door, the landline phone on the wall gave a shrill ring.

56

Tessa jumped and almost dropped the glasses.

She turned to stare at the phone.

The phone kept ringing.

"You going to answer that?" Roxanne's voice drifted from the living room.

Tessa set down the glasses and corkscrew on the counter, but as she reached for the receiver, the phone fell silent.

She drew her hand away and picked up the corkscrew and glasses again, then returned to the living room. Roxanne had put another log on the fire, and it was crackling fiercely. Tessa set the glasses down on the coffee table.

"Well?" Roxanne took the corkscrew from her and went about opening the bottle, then poured two glasses.

"They hung up. It was probably the caretaker calling back," Tessa said.

"On the old-timey landline?" Roxanne looked skeptical. "Why wouldn't she just call your cell?"

"Beats me. I don't remember if I gave her the number."

"Except you just called her on it."

"Right." Tessa took out her phone and dialed Lillian's number again. It rang a few times, then went to voicemail. "No answer."

"Which means it wasn't the caretaker."

"Then who was it?"

"Maybe it was the bogeyman." Roxanne grinned.

"Stop. I'm jumpy enough already." Tessa scowled.

"Sorry, it was just a joke. Trying to lighten the mood."

"Well, don't." Tessa gave Roxanne a light slap on the arm. "One more quip like that and I'm kicking you out."

"You do and I'm taking the wine with me."

"Try it." Tessa reached across the coffee table and slid the bottle toward her. "You can bring wine into this house, but there's only one way it's leaving."

"Look at you, getting all assertive." Roxanne laughed.

"You'd better believe it." Now it was Tessa's turn to laugh.

Roxanne swished wine around her glass and then took a sip. "That's better. I knew there was a fun-loving woman hiding inside you somewhere."

"That's the alcohol." Tessa downed almost the entire glass. She picked up the bottle and topped off. "Tomorrow I'll be back to my usual maudlin self."

"I like you better when you're jolly."

"Jolly?" Tessa almost snorted wine down her nose. "Who uses the word *jolly*?"

"I do." Roxanne topped off her own glass. "I like it."

"It makes me sound like Santa Claus."

"You're much prettier than Santa Claus," Roxanne said, smiling at her.

"Don't." Tessa's hand went to her neck and the scar that meandered up to her ear.

"Hey. Stop being so self-conscious. I meant it."

"I'm not pretty. Patrick Moyer saw to that."

Roxanne took Tessa's hand and pulled it away from her neck. "There's nothing wrong with you. You're beautiful inside and out. Patrick Moyer could never take that away from you. The quicker you realize that, the faster you'll be able to put him in the past where he belongs."

"Now you sound like my therapist." Tessa shook off Roxanne's hand.

"Maybe that's because your therapist is right."

"Or maybe she doesn't understand me and what I went through in this house." Tessa struggled to keep a hard edge from her voice.

"Okay. Time-out." Roxanne held up her hand. "I don't know how we got sidetracked into this, but it wasn't my intention. Can we reset back to where I called you jolly and forget the rest of this conversation ever happened before we end up in a huge argument?"

"I'd like that." Tessa forced a smile.

"Me too." Roxanne looked at Tessa's glass, then the bottle. "I hope you've got another one of those stashed around here somewhere because I'm not sure this one is going to last long."

"I think that can be arranged," Tessa said before a thought occurred to her. "Don't you have to drive home later?"

"I figured I'd stay here with you tonight if that's okay. After the scare you had this evening, I'm not sure you should be alone."

"I'm not sure I *want* to be alone."

"Then it's settled." Roxanne poured the dregs of the bottle into their glasses. "I'll probably regret this tomorrow."

"Sure you want to open a second one?" Tessa asked.

"We don't have to drink the whole thing . . . Of course, we probably will."

Tessa put her glass down and stood up. She grabbed the empty and made her way into the kitchen where she dropped it into the recycling bin, then took another from the countertop wine rack and turned back toward the living room.

But then she hesitated, thinking back to Roxanne's arrival. The open door still troubled her. There was no way she would have left it like that after Chief White's visit earlier in the day, and there was no way the wind had blown it open. She also remembered setting the alarm. Which meant one of two things. Either someone really had been in the house, or Tessa was losing her mind. She considered calling the police chief again but quickly discounted the idea. She and Roxanne had searched the house and found no sign of an intruder, so what exactly would she say?

Still, the thought of sleeping here after hearing those footsteps and finding the door open terrified her. She was glad Roxanne was staying the night. Unless it was Roxanne who snuck in while Tessa was showering. But she still could not see how that was possible. Roxanne would need to know the door and alarm codes. Which left Tessa right back where she was before. She was either delusional—seeing and hearing things—or she had a stalker who knew how to get in and out of the house unseen. Daniel Moyer's parting words from the diner flashed in her head. *I'll see you around.* Was it him? Maybe. But she would need more than vague suspicions to accuse him, because Patrick Moyer's brother hadn't actually said or done anything that would single him out as a threat. At least in the eyes of someone like Chief White. And she was sure that being related to the Cassadaga Island Ripper wasn't enough on its own.

"Hey." Roxanne's voice drifted from the living room. "Are you coming back or making that wine from scratch?"

"Coming." Tessa took a step toward the living room.

At that moment, the wall phone rang again.

Tessa froze. It was eleven o'clock at night. Who would be calling so late, especially on the landline?

Tessa set the wine bottle down, went to the phone, and lifted the receiver. She put it to her ear with a shaking hand. "Hello?"

Silence.

"Hello?" Tessa stiffened. "Is anyone there?"

More unnerving silence answered her.

Tessa held her breath, strained to hear any sound through the receiver. Maybe it was just a bad line? "Lillian, is that you?"

Still no response.

"Lillian? If you're there, I can't hear anything. It must be a bad line."

Another ten seconds ticked away. She resisted the urge to slam the phone back onto its cradle. Fought the sensation that someone was on the other end, quietly listening.

She turned to look out the kitchen window facing Sunset Cove. She could see nothing but darkness beyond, except for the occasional distant flash from the lighthouse farther out in the bay on Snake Island. The phone had rung both times when she entered the kitchen, and she didn't think it was the caretaker. Was someone standing out there, concealed by the night and watching her?

A shudder slithered up Tessa's spine.

Then the line went dead with an audible click.

57

Tessa placed the receiver back on its cradle and stared at it for a long moment. She tried to shake off the feeling that she was being watched. She stared out into the darkness beyond the window. A wisp of fog curled over the deck.

It's all good, she told herself. *Nobody is out there.*

But the creeping unease remained. She could almost feel the weight of unseen eyes staring back at her.

Screw this. Tessa shuddered and picked up the bottle of wine, then hurried back to the living room.

Roxanne was holding her phone, focusing intently on the screen. When Tessa entered, she let it go dark and put it down. "Another call?"

"Uh-huh." Tessa set the wine bottle down on the coffee table.

Roxanne shrugged. "Probably just a wrong number."

"Maybe." Tessa wasn't convinced. Her gaze wandered to Roxanne's phone. Her friend had been holding it when she came back with the wine. Holding it like she had just made a phone call and hung up. A chill ran through her. Was it possible that Roxanne had made the calls? Both times, she had been in the living room while Tessa was in the kitchen.

"Hey, you all right?"

Tessa shook the feeling off. Mostly. "Sure. I'm good."

"You don't look it."

"Just thinking about those calls."

Roxanne rolled her eyes. "I already told you . . . it was a wrong number. Don't worry about it."

Tessa forced herself to sit down. "Why would they call twice in one night?"

"Who knows . . . Drunk off their ass, maybe?" Roxanne opened the bottle and poured two fresh glasses before handing one to Tessa. "Which is what we'll be pretty soon."

Tessa took the glass but didn't drink. After the odd phone calls, she was having second thoughts about opening another bottle. Maybe it would be better to stay alert. "It's getting late. I think we should put this back."

"What? Why? Neither of us has to be up early in the morning. Come on, don't be so boring. Live a little." Roxanne lifted her glass. "Cheers."

Tessa reluctantly lifted her glass and clinked it against Roxanne's. "Cheers."

An hour later, the second bottle was empty, and Tessa couldn't stop yawning. Her eyes refused to stay open. She reclined on the couch and succumbed to the moment.

"Hey. Not here." Roxanne nudged her in the ribs to make sure she was still awake. "Do you have a spare pillow and blanket anywhere?"

"I have the pillow and blanket I've been using." Tessa opened her eyes and pointed. "You should take the bed in the master. I'll sleep out here on the couch."

"Oh no. That isn't happening. You're sleeping in a real bed tonight. No more couch. We have to get you over this phobia."

"I don't think I can do it." Just the thought of sleeping in the bedroom where Courtney had taken her last breath made Tessa feel sick.

"Don't you have a book to write?"

"I don't see what that has to do with where I go to sleep."

"It has everything to do with it. People don't want to read about how you spent the whole month too scared to sleep in a real bed. That New York editor isn't going to be happy if you don't show some spunk and actually face those demons of yours."

"I know. But this is about more than the book. It's my life too, and I can't help how I feel."

"You're sleeping in that bed tonight. I'll take the couch. You have nothing to worry about. I'll be right here, just one room away."

"Please don't be difficult about this. I'll just sleep on the couch. Maybe tomorrow night I'll try the bedroom."

"We both know that won't happen."

Tessa said nothing because it was true.

Roxanne glanced at the baseball bat. "You can take that in with you. I'll keep the poker."

Tessa shook her head.

"All right, how about we both sleep in the bedroom? That way, you won't be on your own."

Tessa thought about Roxanne's offer. If she was ever going to face the bedroom where her friend had died, this might be her best opportunity. She didn't want to sleep there alone. "You'll stay with me all night?"

"Every second," Roxanne said mischievously. "Even if you snore like a trooper."

"I don't but thank you."

"Does that mean you'll do it?"

"Against my better judgment."

"Hey, you've come this far. This is just the next step on your road to recovery."

"I hope so."

"And it will make a great chapter for the book." Roxanne started toward the bedroom. "Especially because I'll be in it."

"What makes you think I'm writing you into the book?" Tessa asked with a laugh as she picked up the baseball bat and followed Roxanne into the bedroom.

"Ouch. That was harsh."

"You deserved it." Tessa looked at the bed and her stomach flipped. Could she really do this?

"You'll be fine," Roxanne said, reading the look on her face. "And I'll be right beside you all night."

Tessa nodded.

Roxanne closed the bedroom door. "There's just one thing left to decide."

"What's that?"

"Which side of the bed do you want?"

58

Tessa woke to find herself alone in the bed. It was the middle of the night and dark outside. When she had fallen asleep, Roxanne was there with her, curled up on the other side of the bed, wearing a T-shirt Tessa had lent her to sleep in. Now there was no sign of her friend.

Tessa's breath caught in her throat. The bathroom door was open. Roxanne was not in there. She slipped out from under the covers. The baseball bat was leaning against the nightstand. She picked it up and crept toward the bedroom door.

Roxanne's jeans were draped over a chair. She almost walked right past them but then stopped and turned around. A cell phone poked out of the back pocket, only the top inch visible. Roxanne's phone.

Tessa glanced around. She was still alone.

Two phone calls had come in on the landline earlier that evening while Tessa was in the kitchen. The first had stopped ringing before she had time to answer. The second was nothing but an open line, as if someone was on the other end, listening but refusing to speak. She didn't believe for one moment that they were wrong numbers—not after everything else that had happened—and the crazy thought that Roxanne was behind them refused to go away. Now she had a chance to confirm her suspicion. She reached down and plucked Roxanne's phone from the pocket.

The screen lit up, and a message asked for a passcode.

Damn. She should have expected that. Guessing the code would be practically impossible. She couldn't even try something obvious like Roxanne's birthday because she didn't know it. Frustrated, Tessa returned the phone to her jeans' pocket, then continued to the bedroom door.

The corridor and living room beyond were dark and silent. There was no sign of her friend.

Tessa hesitated.

The bedroom was illuminated by night-lights plugged into every available outlet. She had done this before they climbed into bed earlier. When Roxanne had questioned her, Tessa explained she could not sleep in the dark. It would either be the night-lights or they'd leave a bedside lamp burning. Now Tessa didn't want to step beyond the safety of the bedroom into the unlit house beyond. If it had been up to her, the living room light would still be on, but Roxanne had turned all the other lights off before they went to bed, and Tessa didn't want to come across as too nutty, so she hadn't objected. Now she regretted that. She reached for the light switch, then thought better of it. If Roxanne was up to something, turning on the light would alert her to Tessa's presence.

She crossed to the nightstand and picked up her phone, turned on the flashlight and aimed it at the floor, then went back to the door and stepped out into the hallway beyond. The other bedroom doors were closed, and Tessa could see no reason why Roxanne would be inside either of them. She kept going toward the living room.

Roxanne stood motionless near the side window next to the fireplace. She was wearing Tessa's tee, her bare legs pale against the darker window. She held the poker in her hand.

Tessa lifted the phone and aimed the flashlight toward her friend. "What are you doing out here?"

"Thought I heard a noise. It woke me up." Roxanne stepped away from the window and out of the light.

"What kind of a noise?"

"I don't know. Kind of like footsteps. At first, I thought I must have dreamed them, but I lay there listening and heard them again. I got up and checked the house but couldn't find anything amiss. I wondered if the noise was outside, so I went to the window and looked out. That's when you snuck up on me."

"I didn't sneak." Tessa tried to stay calm. She had heard footsteps when she was showering earlier. "Are you sure it was footsteps?"

"That's what it sounded like. But I'm not used to this house. Maybe I was just hearing things."

"If you were, then I've been hearing them too." Tessa turned the overhead lights on. Her anxiety dropped. At least until she saw the wall next to the front door. The framed newspaper article—the same one she had taken down days earlier and placed facing inward so she couldn't see it—was now hanging back up.

She stifled a cry. "Did you do that?"

Roxanne looked confused. "Do what?"

"That." Tessa pointed toward the article. "Did you put it back on the wall?"

Roxanne turned and studied the framed newspaper page and the headline: Tourists Slain in Horrific Mass Killing. She shook her head. "Goodness, no. Why would anyone frame something like that and hang it up? Especially in this house. It's macabre."

"Well, someone put it back on the wall, and it wasn't me." Tessa walked closer. "I took it down when I arrived. I didn't want to look at that awful headline every day."

"I remember you telling me that. I didn't put it back up—I swear. What kind of monster do you think I am to scare you like that?"

Tessa's thoughts strayed back to the phone in Roxanne's jeans pocket. She almost said something but bit her tongue. Now was not the time. "If you didn't do it, then someone else did."

"Maybe the caretaker put it back up when she locked the attic door. You probably just didn't notice."

Tessa thought back over the last few days. She had spent the previous night at Roxanne's house and couldn't remember noticing the framed newspaper one way or the other after she returned home. Had Lillian come to the house while she was gone and hung it back up? Tessa didn't think so, but she couldn't be sure.

Roxanne went to the picture and lifted it off the wall, then placed it back on the ground facing inward. "Better?"

Tessa nodded. "Thank you."

"Want to go back to bed?" Roxanne asked. "I've already checked the front and back doors. Both locked. The alarm is still set to Home Mode. Anyone comes into this house, we'll know it."

"What about up there?" Tessa's gaze lifted to the dark second-floor landing.

"I didn't check, but the doors are locked and alarmed, so I can't imagine anyone is in the house."

Tessa didn't move. "Could the noise have come from outside?"

Roxanne shrugged. "I don't know. Maybe. I know how much you were freaked out the other night by the neighbor's house. Thought I'd see if anything was going on over there."

"And?"

"Nothing. Place is all dark. No sign of anything. Not even a horny bobcat."

"You still don't believe me about those screams."

"I think you heard something, but I promise you—that house is empty. Your neighbor isn't lying dead on the floor over there."

"How can you be so sure?"

"Because it's ridiculous."

"No, it's not." Tessa wondered if Roxanne thought Cindy was safely back on the mainland, just like the chief did.

"Okay. Let's find out. We'll go over there right now and see for ourselves."

"What?" Tessa took a step back. "No. That's insane. It's the middle of the night. And what about that noise you heard?"

"It's gone now, whatever it was. We'll be fine. It was probably just the wind."

"I don't know." Tessa could hardly stand the thought of going outside at such a late hour, let alone going over to the neighbor's house where she heard that dreadful scream. "And anyway, it won't do any good. I've already walked around the entire outside of the house. So has the chief. There's nothing to see."

Roxanne was already on her way back to the bedroom. "That's why we're going to find a way in."

"You can't be serious."

"Wanna bet?" Roxanne grabbed her jeans and pulled them on. "Now hurry up and get dressed."

59

It was freezing outside. Tessa pulled her coat tight and shivered as they crossed the gap between the houses, using the flashlights on their phones to light their way. The bitter November wind whipped around them, tugging at Tessa's hair and sending it flying across her face. The baseball bat was in her free hand. Roxanne clutched the poker.

"Why couldn't this wait until morning?" Tessa asked as they pushed through a stand of trees and maneuvered around a huge slab of granite that had heaved out of the earth as if it were trying to escape the island's clutches.

"Because you'll lose your nerve." Roxanne swung her light back and forth across the ground ahead. "And because if we don't do this now, you won't relax for the rest of the night thinking some murderer is hiding over here waiting until we go back to sleep."

"That's not true."

"Yes, it is." They were at the porch steps now. Roxanne climbed up and tried the front door handle, but the door didn't open. "Worth a try."

"I'm sure Chief White already did that when he was over here."

"Maybe. Maybe not." Roxanne went to the window beside the door and peered inside, then tried to lift the sash. She went to the other window and tried that one too. "Locked."

"Guess we aren't getting in that way."

"It was a long shot." Roxanne looked around the porch until her eyes alighted on a heavy plant pot sitting in the corner. She walked over, leaned the poker against the wall, and lifted it.

"What are you planning to do with that thing, smash a window?" Tessa wasn't sure she wanted to venture inside the house. What if Cindy really was lying dead in there? Or worse, her killer had been using the house to spy on Tessa and was, even now, waiting for them.

"Let's hope it doesn't come to that," Roxanne said, putting the plant pot back down and heading to a similar one in the other corner of the porch. She lifted it and peered underneath, then put that one down as well before turning back to Tessa, who was standing near the front door. "Move away."

"What? Why?"

"Because I want to look under that," Roxanne said, pointing downward.

Tessa looked down at the welcome mat under her feet. She took a step back.

Roxanne lifted it, then dropped the mat back into place and picked up the poker again. "Nothing. We're wasting our time here. Come on. Let's go around the back."

"Or we could just go home and warm up by the fire," Tessa said, following Roxanne down the porch steps.

"Not a chance." Roxanne was several steps in front, moving fast.

They reached the back of the house and stepped up onto a wide deck. Behind them, Sunset Cove was cloaked in darkness. The only signs of its presence were the waves crashing onto the beach.

Roxanne crossed to the back door. She bent down and lifted the mat sitting beneath it, then came up with a small shiny object clutched between her finger and thumb. "Bingo."

Tessa stepped closer. "A key."

"Told you we'd find a way in." Roxanne unlocked the door and pushed it open. "Want to go first?"

"Not a chance."

"Figured as much." Roxanne stepped inside and waited for Tessa to join her before closing the door.

She swung her flashlight around. They were in a kitchen with butcher-block counters and white-painted cabinets.

"Hello?" Roxanne called out. "Anyone here?"

"What are you doing?" Tessa hissed. If there really was someone hiding in the house, Roxanne had just announced their presence.

"Relax. There's no one here."

"Then how do you explain this?" Tessa said, going to the sink, within which sat a knife and fork, two plates, and a drinking glass. She aimed her light down into the sink. The plates were encrusted with dried food. She went to the fridge and opened it to reveal an opened package of deli meat, half a loaf of sliced bread, and a quart of milk. She picked up the milk and looked at the date. "Doesn't expire for another week."

"So?" Roxanne shrugged. "I've bought milk with dates three months out before. And who knows how old the meat and bread are? The last people to rent the place probably left that stuff here."

Tessa went back to the sink and turned on the tap. A gush of water came out and splashed on the plates. The unease that had been simmering below the surface ever since those screams morphed into full-scale panic. Cindy wasn't back home on the mainland. She was sure of it. "The pipes haven't been drained. That's why Cindy was here. She wouldn't have left without winterizing."

"So maybe something came up and she had to go back." Roxanne turned and picked her way through the kitchen and into a narrow hallway that ran alongside a set of stairs. "Stop freaking yourself out. I'm sure there's a logical explanation."

Tessa couldn't shift her gaze from the plates in the sink. How could Roxanne be so calm?

A whispered voice floated from beyond the kitchen door. "Hey, you coming?"

"Yes." Tessa forced herself to move. She hurried through the kitchen, to the hallway.

Ahead of them was an entrance hall and the front door. To their left, the living room Tessa had seen through the front window, and opposite, a small dining room. Both were empty. The basement door was tucked under the stairs.

Roxanne was already climbing to the second floor.

Tessa followed, eager not to be left alone.

There were three bedrooms on the second floor. The first contained a pair of twin-size beds with bare mattresses. The second contained a queen-size bed that had also been stripped down to the mattress. When they reached the third, Tessa stopped in the doorway.

She stared at the king bed that took up most of the floor space. Unlike the others, this one had sheets on it, and they were pushed back and crumpled as if someone had been sleeping there. The pillows were askew, and one had a head-size dent in it. A comforter was half pulled off the bed, the bulk of it bunched on the floor.

"Cindy was sleeping in here," Tessa said.

"You can't possibly know that." Roxanne pushed past her into the bedroom. "You know what I think?"

"What?"

"I think there were renters in this place at the end of the season, and no one has come in to clean up after them yet." She turned to look at Tessa. "I know that you think the owner was here, but maybe you just saw a renter. I work at the diner, and we're a small community. I know pretty much everyone on the island, even most of the summer residents. I have no idea who owns this house, and I certainly don't know anyone named Cindy."

"That's because she doesn't come here much anymore." Tessa thought back to her conversation with Cindy on the porch a few nights before. The older woman had explained that she and her husband purchased the house over a decade before, but they were now divorced. The house went to her, but it wasn't the same coming to the island alone, so she converted it into a short-term rental. "She hasn't come here much the last few years. She rents it out to vacationers."

"Well, if this person named Cindy was here, she's gone now. She probably went back to the mainland on one of the lobster boats, like the chief said."

"No." Tessa was sure. No matter what anyone said, the woman had not just decided to go back to the mainland without finishing the job she came there to do. "I told you already, Cindy was closing the house down. She wouldn't leave plates in the sink or food in the fridge. She wouldn't leave an unmade bed. And she sure as hell wouldn't risk a burst pipe by leaving the water on."

"Hey, calm down. There's a reasonable explanation. She wasn't murdered—I promise. Do you see a dead body anywhere?"

"No."

"Don't you think there would be a body if someone had killed her, or at least some sign of a struggle?"

Tessa didn't answer. Roxanne was right, but even so . . .

"That's what I thought." Roxanne apparently took her silence for agreement. She turned and left the bedroom, then started back to the stairs.

Tessa followed behind, happy to leave the eerily silent upper floor behind. At the bottom of the stairs, she crossed to the living room. There was one more thing she wanted to check.

A floor lamp stood near the window while a smaller lamp sat on an end table next to the sofa. Both were plugged directly into outlets. She couldn't see a timer or smart plug. No smart bulbs. She clicked the switch on the floor lamp. It lit up. She clicked the switch again, and it shut off. She did the same with the table lamp.

"What are you doing?" Roxanne asked, standing in the doorway.

"I saw a light on in this room the night of the scream; then it was off the next time I looked. The chief claimed it must be on an automated schedule, like to make people think someone was here when they weren't."

"So?"

"These lamps aren't turning on and off on their own. Cindy was here. I'm not crazy."

"Well, she's not here now, and we're trespassing. Time to go back. I'm tired."

"There's one place we haven't looked." Tessa's gaze shifted beyond the living room to the cellar door under the stairs.

"Seriously?" Roxanne grimaced. "You want to go down there?"

Tessa nodded. "It's the only place we haven't searched."

"I hate cellars."

"So do I, but . . ."

"Fine, but if I have to go into the dark and creepy cellar, you're coming with me." Roxanne took a step toward the door. She had only made it halfway when the room lit up with flickering blue light.

Tessa hurried to the window and peered out.

Her heart skipped a beat.

The Seaview Point chief of police was driving up the road toward them, flashers silently illuminating the surrounding woodland in a stark and strobing chiaroscuro dance.

60

"Crap. It's Chief White." A swell of panic rose in Tessa's throat. She stepped back from the window as the police cruiser grew closer, praying he hadn't seen her there. "This is bad. We have to get out of here."

"It's the middle of the night." Roxanne stopped and turned toward the window. "What do you think he wants?"

"How would I know?" Tessa hurried across the living room and stepped back into the hallway, grabbing Roxanne's arm and dragging her along. "If he finds us in here, we'll end up sitting in a jail cell. What we did pretty much amounts to breaking and entering."

"We didn't break into anything. We used the key, remember?" Roxanne said breathlessly as they made their way into the kitchen toward the back door. "Besides, he isn't going to find us. Once we're back to your house, we'll be fine."

Tessa wasn't so sure. There must be some reason why Chief White was rolling up the road with his flashers on in the middle of the night. "Maybe Cindy has an alarm and we tripped it."

"Do you see an alarm anywhere?"

Tessa looked around. There was no keypad near the kitchen door. She didn't remember seeing one by the front door when they were in the hallway either. "No, but that doesn't mean—"

"You worry too much." Roxanne pulled the back door open. "If there was an alarm, the chief would've been here before now. We've been wandering around the house for at least twenty minutes."

"He was probably in bed. It took him fifteen minutes to get here last time when I woke him."

"There's no alarm—I promise you." Roxanne stepped out into the frigid night air. "Besides, it doesn't matter. Alarm or not, he's here. Do you want to be standing around on Cindy's back porch with no good explanation when he comes looking for us?"

"No."

"Then shut up and let's focus on getting out of this situation." Roxanne bent down and put the key back where she found it, then straightened up again and made for the porch steps.

They descended the steps and used the flashlights on their phones, keeping the beams low as they hurried across the land between Cindy's home and the rental.

Off to their left, Tessa could see the police cruiser's lights bouncing off the trees more clearly as it drew closer. Another minute and Chief White would be at her door. "We need to hurry."

"I'm going as fast as I can." Roxanne climbed up over a ledge of granite and dropped on the other side with a grunt. "Unless you want me to break a leg out here."

Tessa followed behind, scrambling up and over rocks thrusting out from the ground, then picked up the pace on the relatively flat land beyond. Even so, her foot caught a tree root snaking over the trail. She stumbled, letting out a small cry, and only regained her balance after Roxanne grabbed her by the arm.

They were almost at the beach house now. It loomed out of the darkness, the living room light shining through the side window like a beacon to guide them.

"Turn the light on your phone off," Roxanne said, glancing sideways as they approached the back deck and firepit.

Tessa followed her gaze to see the chief's car almost parallel to them on the road. One glance sideways and he would surely see them. She fumbled to turn her light off. "We have to get inside before he stops."

"You think?" Roxanne climbed onto the deck and hurried across, then waited at the back door for Tessa to type the entry code into the dead bolt's numeric keypad.

A moment later, they were tumbling inside, closing the door behind them.

Tessa discarded her coat on the kitchen floor and sprinted into the living room, then went to the window, expecting to see the police cruiser parked next to her own car and Chief White climbing out. Instead, she watched him move slowly past without paying the house any attention.

Soon, only his taillights were visible in the darkness.

"What's he doing?" Roxanne asked, stepping up next to Tessa and peering out.

"I don't know." Tessa stayed at the window, with the curtains pulled back just enough to allow her to see out without being noticed.

A minute later, the glow of headlights reappeared. The SUV crawled past in the other direction with its light bar now turned off.

"You think someone saw us go over to the house next door and called him?" Roxanne asked.

"There's no one out here on Sunset Cove except us," Tessa replied. "Who is there to call?"

"I don't know."

"He promised to drive by once in a while and keep an eye on things," Tessa said. "Maybe that's what he was doing."

"At this time of night?"

Tessa shrugged. "I don't have anything else."

"Well, he's gone now."

"Yes." Tessa was still standing at the window. She let the curtain fall back into place. "We didn't get to look in the basement."

"I'm not going back over there again." Roxanne kicked out of her shoes. "And anyway, Cindy isn't going to be in the basement."

"How do you know?" It was the only place they hadn't looked. The only place she could be, unless everyone was right and her neighbor had gone back to the mainland without finishing her tasks on Cassadaga Island.

"Because the cellar door was closed. If Cindy had gone down there and something happened, like she fell down the stairs and couldn't get back up, wouldn't the door be open?"

"I don't know." Tessa wasn't convinced.

"Well, I do." Roxanne returned the poker to its cradle near the fireplace, then made her way back toward the bedroom. "There's no one in that house."

Tessa lingered near the window. An image of Cindy lying sprawled at the bottom of the cellar stairs popped into her head. But she had no intention of going back over to that house all on her own.

"Hey." Roxanne turned back to her from the hallway leading to the bedroom. "I'm tired. Are you coming, or do I get the bed to myself?"

"No. I'm coming." Tessa cast one more glance toward the side window and her neighbor's dark house beyond, then hurried to join her friend.

61

Tessa slept late for the second morning in a row. Roxanne was already up and making coffee when she entered the kitchen. "Hey. You didn't wake me."

"We were up so late . . . Thought I'd let you sleep." Roxanne was at the toaster oven.

"What about you?"

"I never sleep in. Wake up early no matter what." Roxanne shrugged. "I guess it's genetic or something."

"Must be nice." Tessa was the exact opposite.

"Meh." Roxanne shrugged again. "I'm making breakfast, but don't get your hopes up. It's nothing fancy. I would have rustled up a more substantial offering, but you don't have much in the house. I could only find one egg."

"I know. I'll go to the store today. I should have gone before, but . . ." Tessa had been avoiding the store because she didn't want to run into Noah again. He made her uncomfortable.

"No need to explain." Roxanne dropped four slices of toast onto a plate, then brought them to the table. She made two more trips, fetching butter and jelly, and lastly, two steaming mugs of coffee. "It's Monday, so I have an afternoon shift at the diner, but I can come back here after that. If you want me to, of course."

"Sure." Tessa sat down at the table and fidgeted in her seat. Something was bothering her. The two mysterious landline calls from the night before. She had tried to reason them away as Lillian returning her call, but that didn't make any more sense now than it had the previous evening. Did Roxanne have something to do with them? After all, both calls came in while Tessa was in the kitchen and Roxanne was in the living room. Coincidence? Maybe. Or did her friend dial the landline? If only she had been able to unlock Roxanne's phone the night before and check it.

But it wasn't just the phone calls. The framed newspaper had ended up back on the wall, and Tessa was sure it hadn't been like that earlier. Roxanne had claimed she heard a noise outside, but what if that was a lie? What if Roxanne had hung the picture back up? And why was she standing near the side window, staring out at Cindy's house like that? Was it because she knew something about the woman? Or worse, did she know what had happened to her? After all, she found the key to get in easily enough. That thought made Tessa feel sick. Tessa wondered how to broach the subject, then decided that being direct was the best course of action. "Can I ask you a question?"

"Anything." Roxanne was slathering a slice of toast with apple jelly. "Shoot."

"I saw your phone in your jeans pocket last night when I got up to find you."

"So?"

Tessa leaned on the table. "Do you know the landline number for this house?"

"That's a weird thing to ask. Why would I?"

"So you don't know it?"

"No. I don't know the landline number for this house." Roxanne put her toast down and stared at Tessa. "What are you trying to say?"

"Nothing." Tessa took a sip of her coffee. Her bravado was fading. She didn't want to falsely accuse her friend outright of doing something shady. "It's just that, well . . ."

"Yes?"

"Was it you who made those calls last night when I was in the kitchen?"

"You believe that I . . . Really?" Anger flared in Roxanne's eyes, coupled with something else. Disappointment, maybe? "I wasn't the one who made those calls. How could you even think that?"

"Because it's a bit of a coincidence—both calls coming in when we were in different rooms."

"That's exactly what it was. A coincidence."

"It's not just the calls. You showed up yesterday and claimed the door was open. I know that wasn't true. I would never leave the door unlocked, let alone open. I set the alarm too. I remember doing it."

"I don't know what you want me to say. The door was open when I got here. I don't even know the code to get in."

"And what about last night? You heard someone in the house, but no one was there. And that framed newspaper page was back on the wall. Then you dragged me over to Cindy's on the pretense of proving she was never there. How did you know to look for the key under her back mat?"

"Holy crap, Tessa. You're acting crazy. I didn't put that framed article back up, and people leave keys under plant pots and doormats all the time here. I have a key under my own mat. This isn't the big city." She drew a faltering breath. "I'm your friend. I don't know what you think I'm trying to do, but you're wrong."

"Am I?" Tessa leaned forward. "Prove it. Show me your phone. Unlock it and let me see the call log."

"No." The anger in Roxanne's eyes was replaced by defiance. "I don't have to prove anything to you. You should trust me."

"I don't trust anyone. Ever." That wasn't entirely true. Tessa trusted Melissa explicitly. Her parents too. But that was different. She softened her tone. "Let me look at the phone. Just put my mind at rest."

"Wow. You really are paranoid, aren't you?" Roxanne pushed the toast away. "I'm not showing my phone to you. I shouldn't have to do that. You need to get a grip."

"Someone is messing with me, Roxanne. Scaring me. I have to know it wasn't you."

"It wasn't."

"Then prove it. Please, I can't do this anymore."

"Neither can I." Roxanne pushed her chair back and stood up. "I know you went through an awful ordeal in this house, but you won't get over it by accusing your friends of things they didn't do. I've been nothing but good to you. I spent the night here so that you could sleep. There was a noise. I swear on my life. And I don't know how that framed newspaper got back on the wall, but I didn't put it there. As for that house over the way . . . I'm not sure where to even begin. I'm not your enemy."

Tessa wiped a tear from her cheek. "Don't be like that."

"Like what? Hurt that you don't trust me?" Roxanne started toward the living room. "Screw this."

"Where are you going?" Tessa jumped up and followed her.

"Anywhere but here." Roxanne grabbed her coat and put it on. She picked up her car keys. "I have to be at work, anyway. When you come to your senses, I'll be waiting."

"Please don't go. Not like this. Just show me your phone so I can relax."

"Yeah. Not going to happen." Roxanne went to the front door and pulled it open. She stepped outside and slammed it behind her, leaving Tessa alone in the house and no closer to knowing the truth. Not only that, but she might have lost her only friend on the island.

62

After skulking around the house for most of the day feeling frustrated and isolated, Tessa finally pulled herself together and went into town. Because if she didn't, there would be nothing to eat for dinner except the frozen pizza that the terminally missing Cindy had brought over, which she couldn't bring herself to eat. When she passed the diner, she considered stopping and seeing if Roxanne was there. Trying to smooth things over. But her concerns were just as valid now as they had been earlier in the day, and while she understood Roxanne's stance on proving her innocence, Tessa would not be able to trust her until she had proof those calls the previous evening had not come from her friend's phone.

She continued to the grocery store, parked, and went inside. Walt was sitting behind the register. He gave her a welcoming nod as she took a cart and headed for the aisles. She went to the dairy section first before heading deeper into the store. In the cereal aisle, she encountered a familiar face coming toward her with a bottle of laundry detergent in one hand and a family-size bag of chips in the other. It was Roxanne's friend from a couple of nights earlier at the bar.

"Hey," Kyla said upon spotting her.

"Hello," Tessa replied, wondering if Kyla knew about her argument with Roxanne that morning.

If she did, Kyla said nothing. "You look exhausted. That house been getting you down?"

"Yes and no."

"I'm not surprised. I couldn't stay there." Kyla hesitated before speaking again in a voice barely above a whisper. "Look, I hope you won't be mad, but Roxanne told me who you are. She wasn't gossiping or anything. She just—"

"It's fine. Roxanne already admitted to telling you. Honestly, it's a relief that I don't have to pretend. Especially since . . ." Tessa was about to blurt out that she and Roxanne weren't speaking anymore, but she stopped herself.

"Since what?"

Tessa wavered back and forth, then decided Kyla would find out soon enough. "I kind of had a falling-out with Roxanne this morning. She came around last night to keep me company, and some weird stuff happened. Phone calls with no one on the other end of the line. Noises in the house. I thought maybe it was Roxanne doing it. She got mad at me when I asked to see her phone. I should probably go to the diner and apologize, but I can't bring myself to do it. Someone is trying to mess with my head and scare me. I'm sure of it. I hope it's not her but . . ."

Kyla was silent for a moment. "That sounds awful. Give Roxanne time. I'm sure the two of you will make up."

"I hope so. She's my only friend on the island."

"Not your only friend," Kyla said. "Although I won't be on the island for much longer."

"You're moving to the mainland?"

Kyla shook her head. "Just heading there for the winter. During the summer, I work in one of those art galleries on Main, but I can't survive from October through May with no income, so I close up the apartment and head down to Portland, where it's easier to find work. I have a friend who lets me crash in her spare bedroom."

"When are you leaving?" Tessa asked, disappointed.

"Tomorrow. On the five-o'clock ferry. It's lucky you ran into me. I wouldn't be here except that I ran out of laundry detergent, and I want to run a load before leaving. I hate coming back to dirty sheets in the spring."

"I was hoping we'd have more time to get to know each other," Tessa said, even though that wasn't entirely true, social interaction not being her strong point. Even the grocery store triggered low-level anxiety. She couldn't wait to get what she needed and return to the safety of her car.

"Me too." Kyla pulled a sympathetic face, then looked over Tessa's shoulder toward the cash register. "I hate to run, but I have a list of chores two miles long, and I haven't even started packing yet."

"Of course." Tessa pushed her cart aside to allow Kyla through.

Kyla lingered. "If it gets too much on the island, you should leave too. There's no point in putting yourself through hell."

"I know," Tessa said.

Kyla met her gaze as if she were about to say something else, but then appeared to change her mind. She turned and hurried toward the cash register.

Tessa continued down the aisle.

Noah was standing near an endcap with a hand truck of stacked boxes.

"Hello again." He looked at her as she approached. "Finding everything you need?"

"Yes, thank you." Tessa breezed past him, aware of his lingering gaze on her back as she turned the corner and headed down the next aisle. She hurried to fill her cart, then grabbed a couple more bottles of wine before heading to the register and paying for her purchases.

On her way out, she glanced down the aisle where Noah was placing items on a shelf. He looked back at her with guarded interest. A half smile played on his lips before he turned back to the shelves.

Tessa looked away quickly. She gripped the cart and wheeled it toward the door.

"Come back soon," Walt called after her.

Tessa mumbled a reply and pushed through the door into the parking lot. After loading her trunk, she wheeled the cart to a bay in front of the store, half expecting to see Noah lingering near the entrance watching her.

But he wasn't. Which was good because he gave her the creeps, even though she knew his awkwardness was probably because of social anxiety. She was hardly the poster child for extroverted confidence herself and sensed much of the same in him. Yet the feeling remained. Which was why she didn't relax until she was in the car with the door closed, heading back out of Seaview Point.

63

Tessa's phone rang at eight o'clock while she was in the kitchen slicing chicken to top a salad with and sipping a glass of wine. She put down the knife and answered, then put the call on speaker.

A familiar voice greeted her. It was Kyla.

"Hey, I hope you don't mind me calling. I had your number from the other night when I texted you those photos at the bar."

"You're good. I was making dinner, but it's just salad," Tessa told her. "What can I do for you?"

"Are you free this evening?" Kyla asked. "Like, in an hour?"

Tessa hadn't been expecting that. She didn't want to go out again so soon. "I'm not sure I'm ready for another evening at the Ship to Shore."

"It's nothing like that." Kyla sounded tense. "There's something I think you should know. Can I come over to your place?"

"Um, I guess, but you're leaving town tomorrow. Whatever it is, can't you tell me over the phone? You must be up to your ears getting ready."

"I am, but I can spare an hour. I'd prefer to tell you in person." Kyla went silent for a moment. "It's about Patrick Moyer."

Tessa was stunned into silence. She leaned against the counter and lowered the phone, overcome by a sudden wave of dizziness. What could Kyla possibly want to tell her about Patrick Moyer?

"Are you still with me?" Kyla asked, her voice thin and reedy through the phone's tiny speaker.

Tessa lifted the phone back to her ear. "Yes. Sorry."

"Look, I don't want to upset you, but this is important. It might explain what's been happening."

"Patrick Moyer is dead," Tessa said. "I don't see how—"

"I'll tell you when I get there, okay?"

Tessa was about to protest, but before she got the chance, Kyla ended the call. She looked down at the salad bowl and the half-sliced chicken lying on the cutting board, but her appetite was gone. Dropping the meat into the bowl without bothering to finish cutting it, Tessa put cling film over the top, then put it in the fridge.

She went to the living room and switched the porch lights on for Kyla before checking the front door. It was locked and secure. A green LED light blinking on the alarm box told her the system was in Home Mode. No one could enter the house without the alarm sounding. She turned around, her gaze lifting toward the dark second-floor landing. Unnerved, she went to the couch and sat down. Whatever could Kyla want to tell her about Patrick Moyer that was so important she needed to rush over the night before leaving for the mainland? Did it have something to do with his brother, Daniel?

Tessa's eyes dropped to the baseball bat leaning against the couch. She picked it up and cradled it in her arms—the cold, hard wood a small comfort. Then she waited.

64

Nine o'clock came and went. Tessa sat on the sofa with the TV on to drown out the silence and the baseball bat in her lap. At one point, she heard the rumble of an engine, saw the faint glow of headlights through the front window. She stood and went to the door, expecting Kyla to show up at any moment, but she didn't. When she peeked out the window, the road beyond was empty and dark. At half past nine, she went to the window again. Still no sign of Roxanne's friend. Maybe Kyla was running late? When ten o'clock came and there was still no sign of her, Tessa's conviction wavered. Wouldn't she have called or sent a text if she was running that far behind? After all, she had dropped a bombshell on Tessa by mentioning Patrick Moyer's name. The least she could do was show up.

Tessa took her phone out and called the last number on the log: Kyla's number.

It rang a few times and went to voicemail. Tessa hung up and tried again. Voicemail. Frustrated, she rattled off a short text message:

This is Tessa. Where are you?

Fifteen minutes passed. Kyla didn't reply.

Tessa called again and left a voicemail this time when Kyla didn't answer.

Another fifteen minutes went by, and the phone didn't ring. No one showed up at the door. Tessa was starting to get worried. She ran through scenarios in her head. Maybe Kyla had gotten busy preparing to leave the island and forgot the time. Maybe she decided that whatever she wanted to say was not important enough to drive out to the beach house at such a late hour. Or maybe she was just a flake. But none of that explained why she wasn't answering her phone.

Tessa didn't know what to do. Kyla had mentioned Patrick Moyer. She had to know why. The solution was simple. Drive to town and find Kyla. Go to her apartment. But that would mean stepping outside and going out to the car in the dark, then braving the lonely woodland road to town. Tessa shuddered at the thought of that. It just wasn't going to happen. She decided to give Kyla another half hour and then call again.

In the meantime, her hunger had returned. She put the baseball bat down and went to the kitchen, intending to retrieve the salad she had started earlier from the fridge. But as she entered, her gaze fell on the picture window overlooking Sunset Cove. The back-deck lights were off. Only the lighthouse on Snake Island was visible as its beam swept across the bay to warn ships of the treacherous rocky outcrops and protrusions that dotted the shallow waters.

The microwave light was on above the stove, bathing the room in a soft yellow glow. She reached for the overhead light switch just as the beam from the lighthouse made another pass toward shore. But this time, she saw something out of the corner of her eye—a shape standing at the window, looking in. It was just a fleeting glimpse, barely perceptible, before the beam slid away again.

Tessa staggered backward into the wall.

The lighthouse beam made another rotation. It flashed across the deck. The cove beyond.

This time, the figure was gone. All she saw was a shimmering reflection as the beam continued its sweep out across the water.

Her breathing slowed.

Maybe she imagined the shape. It was only the briefest of glimpses, and she was jumpy. On edge. Even so, she wanted the bat. It would help her feel safe. She dragged her eyes from the picture window and hurried into the living room. The fire was crackling. The room was lit by a lamp on the side table next to the sofa. More light spilled in through the front window from the porch lights she had turned on earlier. An image of the figure at the window played through her mind. Was it just shadows, or had someone really been there? Watching. Waiting.

Tessa snatched the baseball bat from the couch, then muted the TV and listened, her eyes darting from window to window for any aberrant movement.

The house lay still. Silent.

Tessa's grip relaxed on the baseball bat. Maybe it was all in her mind, after all. She thought about the salad in the fridge, took a step back toward the kitchen.

At that moment, the front-door handle rattled.

Tessa spun around.

The handle turned. The door shook in its frame but didn't open. The dead bolt was on . . . thankfully.

"Hello?" Tessa called out. "Kyla, is that you?"

There was no answer.

Tessa swallowed her fear and took a step forward. The living room curtains were still open. She hadn't drawn them because she wanted to keep a lookout for Kyla. But she was at the wrong angle to see who was standing on the porch. She had to know.

The door handle rattled again.

Tessa froze.

"Kyla, if that's you, please say something."

No response.

Tessa willed herself to move forward. The handle was still now. She crept across the room, never taking her eyes off the front door. She gripped the bat in both hands, ready to swing at anything that moved. When she reached the window, Tessa said a silent prayer and peered out.

The porch was empty except for a couple of moths fluttering around the light fixture, casting flitting shadows. So was the driveway in front of the house and the road beyond.

Tessa backed away from the window, overcome by a sudden conviction that whoever rattled the handle might be lurking beyond her field of vision with their back against the outside wall, biding their time and waiting.

A log moved in the fire, and she jumped, swiveling toward it. Images danced across the muted TV screen.

Then the wall phone in the kitchen rang, the sound shrill and menacing.

Tessa had to know who was calling, despite the terror that pressed in upon her from all sides. She raced to the phone, juggled the bat with one hand, and snatched the handset off the wall. Screamed into it.

"What do you want? Who are you?"

There was no answer except a faint intake of breath.

"Stop it!" she cried. "Why are you doing this to me? Leave me alone."

"Theresa." The voice was soft and sibilant among the hiss of dead air on the line. Barely audible. She couldn't tell if it was male or female.

Tessa dropped the handset as if it were red hot. It clattered to the floor. The back came off, spilling three AAA batteries, one of which rolled under the fridge. She pivoted toward the picture window opposite, terrified she would see a figure standing there again, looking back at her, but she didn't see anyone.

Yet the phone on the wall had rung.

A voice had spoken her name.

Her *old* name.

65

Tessa resisted the urge to scream. She turned and fled into the living room, snatched up her cell phone, and found Chief White's number. Her finger hovered over the call button, but she hesitated. He hadn't believed her the last time she called him. In fact, he'd made it out like she was seeing things. A hysterical woman spooked by her surroundings. But this was different. She hadn't imagined the rattling door handle or that awful voice hissing her name over the landline phone. Yet she had no proof and doubted he would believe her now any more than before.

But there was one other person on the island Tessa could call. Someone who could be at the house within minutes. She dialed Roxanne's number and waited for her to answer, praying she would pick up. But just like Kyla before her, Roxanne's phone went to voicemail. Tessa dialed again. Maybe Roxanne didn't want to answer because of their argument earlier in the day. Or maybe she was asleep and hadn't heard the phone ring. Tessa was about to leave a message, but she thought better of it and hung up. For all she knew, Roxanne might be a part of this somehow, which meant there could be a more chilling reason she was ignoring Tessa's phone call. Because she was outside the house right at that moment.

In desperation, Tessa phoned the only other person she could think of.

When Melissa answered, her voice was groggy, like she'd been asleep. "Hey, sis. I haven't heard from you in a few days."

"Melissa, thank God. I don't know what I would have done if you hadn't answered."

"What's wrong?" The sleep vanished from her sister's voice. "Has something happened?"

"Someone is outside the house. I think they're trying to get in." The words tumbled from Tessa's mouth as she told her sister about the figure at the window, the rattling doorknob, and the terrifying voice on the other end of the landline. As she talked, Tessa paced back and forth with the bat in her hand. She glanced nervously at the front window and the illuminated porch beyond.

"Call the police," Melissa said when Tessa finished. "Hang up and do it right now."

"I already called the chief of police out here last time something happened. He's the only cop in town. He didn't believe me then and won't believe me now."

"What do you mean, 'the last time something happened'? Never mind, we'll talk about that later. Call him right now, Tessa!"

"I don't want to hang up. I'm scared, Mel." Tessa was close to tears. "Stay with me on the phone. Please don't hang up."

"I won't hang up. But we have to call the police."

Melissa must have pulled the phone away from her mouth, because Tessa heard a mumbled conversation in the background. "Who are you talking to?" she asked.

"Josh. He's staying over. Do you have the police chief's number there?"

"It's in the kitchen, but I don't want to go back in there. I think someone's watching me." Tessa wished she had saved the number in her contacts.

"Are all the doors locked?"

"Yes. The alarm is set too."

"Good. Then you should be safe for now. Go into the kitchen and get that number. Do it quickly."

Tessa hurried into the kitchen, making sure not to look at the picture window. If someone was standing outside watching her, she did not want to see them. She went to the fridge and the dry-erase board, then read off Chief White's number to Melissa. She heard her sister relay it to Josh.

"He's making the call now," Melissa said.

"The chief isn't going to believe me. He thinks I'm crazy." Tessa fought back a sob. She considered grabbing her keys, running to the car, and putting as much distance between herself and the rental house as possible. But that would mean going outside, something Tessa was not willing to do. For all she knew, her tormentor was waiting to grab her the moment she tried.

"He'll believe you. Josh will make sure of it." There was another mumbled conversation before Melissa spoke to Tessa again. "Chief White is on his way right now. Just sit tight and don't open the door unless you know it's him."

"I won't." Tessa returned to the living room. She stood in the middle, near the sofa, which provided a good line of sight to most of the downstairs. "I'm so sorry about all this, Mel. I should never have come back to this island. I don't know what I was thinking."

"You were being stubborn, as usual," Melissa replied.

"You can say *I told you so.*"

"I'm not going to say that," Melissa said. "But if I thought it would do any good, I'd already be in my car, driving up there to bring you home."

"I know." Tessa's arm was growing tired from holding the bat up. She lowered it to her side. "You couldn't get onto the island, anyway. The next ferry isn't until tomorrow afternoon."

Melissa said something in reply, but Tessa wasn't listening anymore because she could see flashing lights through the front window. They painted the trees on the other side of the road a pale blue before a vehicle with a light bar on top came into view and stopped near the porch.

"Mel. The chief is here. I'm going to put the phone down, but I want you to stay on the line, okay?"

"I'm not going anywhere," Melissa replied.

Tessa put the phone on the table next to the couch and went to the window. She looked out to make sure it really was Chief White before disarming the alarm and opening the door to let him in. The chief lumbered up the porch steps, one palm resting on his holstered gun, the other adjusting his wide-brimmed hat. He wore a creased shirt. His trousers sat under the paunch of his belly, riding low because of his heavy utility belt.

He reached the door with a scowl on his face. "All right, little lady, why don't you tell me what happened this time?"

66

Chief White stood in the living room with his arms folded and listened without interrupting while Tessa explained what had happened. When she was finished, he rubbed his chin thoughtfully. "I can't imagine anyone from the island would do a thing like that. We're a tight-knit community, and honestly, there's barely any crime. I spend most of my days sitting in the office drinking coffee and reading the newspaper."

"I'm not making this up," Tessa pleaded, anger bubbling up through her anxiety. "Everything I've told you happened."

"Now, now. Don't get defensive. I'm just saying it's a mite unusual, is all. But we sometimes get folk who come to see this house because of its history. The place has a certain notoriety. Maybe someone thought it would be funny to scare you and got carried away. Could even have been a tourist."

"How would they know the phone number?"

"Phone's been here a long time." The chief sniffed and swallowed. "Probably not hard to find."

"And my name?" Tessa asked, without mentioning that it was her old name she'd heard. She still wasn't ready to reveal her true identity to the chief. That would only make him more convinced it was all in her head. "And anyway, there are no tourists on the island at the moment. All the hotels and guesthouses are closed for the season, and the ferry hasn't been here since last week, so where would they stay? It must have been a local. There's no other explanation."

"Well, be that as it may, they probably ran off once they saw me coming. I'll look around, but I doubt I'll find much." The chief studied Tessa for a moment. His gaze fell to the bat still clutched in her hand. "You have anywhere you can go tonight? A friend, maybe? It might be better if you didn't stay here."

"There's no one," Tessa replied, thinking of Roxanne and wishing that she trusted her enough to go there.

"Well now, that's a shame. I'd drive you into town myself, but like you said, all the hotels on the island are closed for the winter. I don't rightly know of anywhere else you can go."

"That's okay."

"Honestly, my money is still on a practical joke. Someone trying to spook you because of where you're staying." The chief turned toward the front door. "I'll do a turnaround outside to make sure nobody is lurking. Close the door after me and lock it. Don't open it again until I come back."

Tessa nodded and followed him to the door. When the chief stepped outside, she did as he told her and locked it behind him. She picked up her phone and told Melissa what he'd said, then went to the window and looked out with the phone still in her hand. The chief had left his light bar on. The strobes lit up the landscape. Tessa found it comforting. No one would try to get in with the police car parked out front. She wished it could stay there all night.

The chief returned fifteen minutes later and climbed the porch steps with the weary gait of a man who wished he was at home in his toasty bed rather than trudging around in the frigid night air.

Tessa rushed to the door and let him in. "Well?"

"All clear. Whoever was out there messing around is long gone." The chief removed his hat. "If you want my advice, you'll lock these doors tight as a button after I leave and find somewhere else to stay first thing in the morning. I don't know what's going on, but better safe than sorry."

"Why do you say that?" Tessa asked. "Did you find something?"

"There were some trampled bushes on the side of the house. A couple of faint footprints in one of the flower beds. Whoever it was tracked dirt up onto the back deck. I can't say for sure if it was an intruder. Could have been Lillian doing maintenance. But I can't tell you it wasn't an intruder either." When he saw the look on Tessa's face, he added, "Don't worry. You're perfectly safe as long as you stay inside and keep the doors locked. I'll drive back by here a couple more times during the night and cruise the area just to make sure."

"You don't mind doing that?" Tessa asked, relieved.

"I'd rather be snug in my warm bed, but since I don't have a deputy—and you can thank budget cuts for that—I'll do it."

"Thank you."

"And in the meantime, I'm a phone call away."

Tessa nodded. She felt safe with the chief inside the house. He had a gun and a badge. But she knew that once he left, the unease would return. She followed him to the door and let him out, wishing she could think of a reason to delay his departure, if only for a few more minutes.

The chief made his way back to the SUV with *Seaview Point Police Department* printed along the side. He climbed in and slammed the door, then waved through the window to her before reversing and swinging around toward town, turning off the light bar.

Tessa closed the door and locked it, then reset the alarm. She felt vulnerable again now that she was alone. But at least she had Melissa.

She lifted the phone to her ear. "Hey, you still there?"

"Always," came the reply. "I'll stay on the line as long as you need me."

That made Tessa feel better. She went to the sofa and sat down, laying the bat next to her. The TV was still muted, so she turned the sound back on at a low volume because she didn't like how quiet the house was.

"I'm not sure I can stay here anymore, Mel," she said at last.

"Then come home on the next ferry. You don't need to put yourself through this."

"Would you be disappointed in me?"

"Never. I didn't want you to go there in the first place."

"I know." Tessa almost cried with relief until she remembered the deal she'd made with Thomas Milner only a few weeks before. "What am I going to do about the book?"

"Phone that editor and tell him you can't write it from Cassadaga Island."

"I think that's the reason he wanted it," Tessa said. "He wasn't interested until I pitched the idea of writing about my experiences here. I can't just up and leave when I'm not even halfway through the month. I signed a contract."

"Call him in the morning and explain the situation. Tell him what's been going on. I'm sure he'll understand."

"You're right. I'll talk to him first thing tomorrow." Tessa could feel her eyelids drooping, but she was determined not to sleep. She didn't think she would sleep in the beach house ever again after tonight. The idea of leaving Cassadaga Island behind, getting on that five-o'clock ferry and never coming back, filled her with hope. Now all she had to do was get through the night.

67

Tessa spent the rest of the night on the sofa with the baseball bat next to her and the TV playing. Melissa had stayed on the phone, but after two uneventful hours, Tessa could tell she was wilting and convinced her to hang up with the promise that if anything else happened, Tessa would call her back.

After what felt like an eternity, the first rays of dawn pushed through the front window, sending a square of dappled light spilling across the cherry-colored planks of the living room floor. With the safety of a new day approaching, Tessa finally closed her weary eyes and soon fell into a fitful sleep. She awoke a couple of hours later, groggy and disoriented. She waited a moment for the world to click back into place, then rose and went to the kitchen, taking the baseball bat with her.

She propped it against a kitchen cabinet, made a pot of coffee, then poured herself a cup and stood at the counter because she didn't want to go near the table next to the picture window. Chief White had found dirt tracked onto the deck the previous night. She knew it wasn't her and didn't believe the caretaker, Lillian, did it either. Whoever had been skulking around outside the window had left an inadvertent calling card. She was sure of it. Even in daylight, she didn't want to see those footprints.

By the time Tessa finished a second mug of coffee, her brain fog had cleared, and she was feeling better. It was ten past nine and late enough to call her editor at the publishing house and tell him what happened.

A flutter of anxiety danced in her stomach, but it was nothing compared to the gut-wrenching fear she had endured the night before.

Tessa went back into the living room and retrieved her cell phone. She found Thomas Milner's number in her contacts and dialed. After two rings, his secretary answered and put her on hold. A couple of minutes later, Milner's baritone voice filled her ear.

"Miss Montgomery. I was going to call you today. The pages you've sent so far are excellent. Very promising."

Tessa couldn't have cared less about the pages. "That's not why I called."

"Oh?" Milner's tone changed to one of concern. "Is there a problem?"

"You could say that," Tessa said. "Weird stuff has been happening."

"What kind of weird stuff?"

"Frightening stuff." Tessa told him everything that had happened. The scream from Cindy's house. The footsteps when she was in the shower. Phone calls with no one on the other end. Finally, she relayed the events of the previous night. "Someone is trying to scare me, and it's working."

Milner took a moment to speak. When he did, it was not the response Tessa wanted to hear. "I think the police chief is right. Those screams could very well have been a bobcat. The other incidents are probably your overactive imagination, given why you went back there. And if he thought that what happened last night was just pranksters, well . . ."

"It wasn't pranksters."

"Look, I understand that you're spooked, but you can't let it get to you."

"I can't do this anymore," Tessa said. "Not here. I've decided to leave the island. I'm catching the ferry back to the mainland this evening."

There was another moment of silence on the other end of the line. She detected a sharp intake of breath.

When Milner spoke again, there was a hard edge to his voice. "Tessa, the book is about you returning to Cassadaga Island and facing your fears. No one is going to read a book about you giving up and running away."

"That isn't what I'm doing." Tessa clenched her jaw. "You're not listening. Someone has been breaking into the house. They've been lurking outside watching me. I haven't seen Cindy in days, and I'm sure she didn't go back to the mainland. I don't want to spend another night in this house. I'm terrified."

"Tessa, think about this. You signed a contract and took an advance based on writing that book. The contract states that you will spend a month in that house on Cassadaga Island and write about your experiences. I understand how you feel, but my hands are tied. It won't go well if I go back to my editorial director and tell him you're quitting. I'd rather not have to do that."

"Who cares if he doesn't like my decision?" Tessa replied. "I'm the one in the middle of this, not him. I'm the one writing the book."

"Look, I'm not trying to be mean. Quite the opposite. I want to save you from yourself. If you quit on this, the publisher will come after you for the advance. Do you still have it to give back?"

"No." Tessa sat down on the couch and stared into the embers of the fire. She had given Melissa the money to pay her credit card and then spent a good chunk of what remained to pay off her sister's car as a thank-you for the years Melissa had put up with her. Now that good deed was coming back to haunt her. "What happens if I don't have the money anymore?"

"I can't say for certain, but I know my boss. You'll probably end up in court."

"He'd sue me over this?" Tessa was dumbfounded. "How could he do that?"

"Because you have a binding contract."

"And what about unforeseen circumstances? You want me to put my life in danger just to write a book?"

"There's nothing in the contract about unforeseen circumstances. It isn't the kind of thing that is usually relevant. And you said yourself that the police chief doesn't think you're in any danger." Milner took a breath. "Look, you came to me desperate to sell your story. You're the one that came up with the idea of returning to the island. I did you a favor by taking it to the editorial meeting and fighting for this book. I convinced them it could be a bestseller even though what happened to you five years ago is old news."

"I'll write your book. I promise. Just not from here." Tessa was desperate. If the publisher came after the advance, it would ruin her. She had less than a quarter of the payment remaining in her bank account. And what if they came after Melissa and her house? Could they even do that? She didn't want to find out.

"The whole point of this book is the island," Milner said. "How about this? You stay on the island long enough to finish the first draft, even if that only takes another week. You write a happy ending where you overcome the ghosts of your past. I don't care if you make it up. That's not my problem. Write about this unknown person you think is harassing you. It will make the story more dramatic. Once you're done, I don't care where you go, and neither will my boss. Leave the island early if you want, but finish the manuscript first."

"I don't know."

"Look, if at any time the police chief actually thinks you're in danger, we'll get you off that island right away. If he tells us there really is someone trying to do you harm—to hurt you—of course you can leave. But in the meantime, don't let your fear of the past ruin the opportunity for a better future. Is that a fair compromise?"

Tessa didn't think it was fair at all. The danger was real, even if Chief White didn't believe it. But Thomas Milner was not going to budge more than he had already, and Tessa didn't want to drag her sister into this mess. After all, most of the money had gone to Melissa, one way or another, and even if the publisher couldn't go after her directly, she would feel obliged to return the money and bail Tessa out. Which would mean selling the car and racking up debt. Tessa couldn't allow that. "You promise I can leave when the book is done?"

"You have my word," Milner replied. "The moment you type *The End*."

"Okay." Tessa sighed. "I'll stay . . . for now."

"Excellent. Now get back to work. Those pages won't write themselves." Milner chuckled at his attempt to lighten the mood, but it sounded hollow.

She hung up without saying goodbye. A minor act of rebellion even if she had lost the war. Then, as she stood there staring at the phone in her hand, a thought occurred to her. Thomas Milner was all the way down in New York. There was nothing he could do—not physically—to keep her on the island. She considered calling him back, telling him that she was leaving regardless, telling him to go screw himself, then nixed that idea. After all, she hadn't told Melissa about using the credit card to book the beach house until *after* the deed was done, and that turned out fine . . . well, not fine, obviously, given her current predicament, but it had worked. She was here. Now the stakes were higher. The phone call, the whispered name—they were proof positive that someone on the island was out to get her, and she had no intention of sacrificing her sanity and safety over a dumb book. And she had barely unpacked. All she had to do was pick up her bag and laptop, put them in the trunk, and she was gone. She would give them a book as promised, but make it about whoever had her in their sights. Chief White wouldn't take her seriously, that much was obvious, but the cops on the mainland . . . They were a different matter. The book might even *be better*. And if Milner's company tried to sue, she would take her story wide. Settle it in the court of public opinion and see how long they pursued her then!

It was like a huge weight had been lifted from Tessa's shoulders. She only had eight hours before the ferry. By evening, she would be back on the mainland. The question was what to do in the meantime. She didn't want to be in the house any longer than necessary. Better to be out in the open air. Sit on the beach. Head into town. Go for a walk. All of that sounded better than the alternative. She settled on a walk. Tessa grabbed her jacket, pushed the phone into her pocket, and headed for the back door leading onto the deck and Sunset Cove beyond.

68

Tessa hurried across the back deck and down onto the pebble-strewn beach. It was low tide, and the water had receded beyond the rocks at the edge of the cove, leaving behind lines of stringy seaweed that wrapped around exposed boulders and trailed across the beach like the carcasses of elongated sea serpents. The sky was a featureless gray expanse interrupted only by the occasional seagull that wheeled overhead, its cry lonesome and heartbreaking. Her breath fogged the frozen air.

She crossed the beach and took a path rising over the rocks and through the woods toward the southern tip of the island. She had walked here with Roxanne the previous week, and they had climbed to the bluff overlooking Callaghan Bay and the string of smaller islands dotted all the way to the horizon.

This time, she didn't stop at the scenic overlook but continued into unknown territory. The farther she got from the beach house, the calmer she became. Out here, surrounded by a rich tapestry of trees and craggy overlooks that sported majestic views in all directions, and with the morning sun sitting high in a clear winter sky, it was hard to hold on to the anger. But the underlying unease that had been with her since she first sensed a malignant presence around the house remained. That wouldn't fade until she put Cassadaga Island in her rearview mirror.

Tessa came to a fork in the trail. One path led on toward the tip of the island, following the rise and fall of the land as it hugged the coast past a myriad of small inlets and coves. The other trail weaved through the woods, cutting across toward the narrow road Tessa knew would lead back to the house and then onward to Seaview Point because she remembered Roxanne saying it was the route she took on her morning walks.

She stopped and weighed her options.

The coastal path might run for miles and never loop back around. The woodland path was a better choice. She set off again, taking her time. Thirty minutes later, through a break in the trees, she saw a wide vein of asphalt up ahead. Fifteen minutes later, she emerged onto the road, which dead-ended at a turning circle surrounded by a wooden barrier meant to prevent inattentive drivers from ending up in the trees. The trail continued on the other side, snaking through the woods and into the unknown.

The house was over a mile and a half from her current location. It would take twenty minutes to walk back via the road. Retracing her steps on the trail would keep her out of the house for longer. That was good. The less time she spent in that place until it was time to pack up and leave, the better. Tessa turned to head back along the trail, but as she did so, she noticed something she hadn't seen before.

A car was sitting on the side of the road fifty feet away. It was parked at an angle with the front wheels off the pavement. At first, she wondered if someone had stopped there to hike the trail, but there was something odd about how it was parked. The car looked abandoned. As if it had been dumped rather than parked.

Tessa approached the vehicle slowly, her concern growing the closer she got.

The car was obviously empty. The driver-side door not quite closed. It moved a little with each gust of wind. The front wheels were turned at an angle. When she reached the car, Tessa stopped and opened the driver-side door wide enough to bend down and look inside. There was nothing to indicate who it belonged to or where they might have gone. She reached across and opened the glove compartment. It was stuffed with receipts, old car-repair bills, and assorted items like pens and even a couple of tampons in their wrappers.

Tessa rummaged through the items until she found what she was looking for. The registration document. A chill ran up her spine when she saw the name printed on it.

The car belonged to Kyla.

But why was it out here? Kyla was supposed to meet her the evening before but hadn't shown up. Had the car been sitting here all that time? It didn't make sense.

Tessa straightened up, leaned on the car's roof, and scanned the dense woodlands beyond. Why had Kyla driven out here? Was she out in the woods somewhere, hurt or lost?

Tessa shouted her name but received no answer.

All she heard was a flap of wings as birds in the trees above her took flight, disturbed by the sudden sound.

Tessa went to close the car door. Then she stopped. Kyla's phone was sitting in the center console. There was something else too. Underneath it, she saw what looked like the edge of a photograph.

She reached back inside and grabbed the phone, then picked up the photograph. It was a yellowed Polaroid like the ones she had seen on the corkboard at the Ship to Shore Tavern. There was even a pinhole at the top. Tessa wondered if this was where the picture had come from. But it was the contents of the photograph that left her gasping for breath.

Standing there, posing, arms wrapped around each other and goofy grins on their faces, were two people she recognized. One, because they had gotten drunk together at the beach house just two days before. And the other because he had tried to kill her five years ago in the upstairs bedroom of that same house.

69

Tessa stared at the photograph, unable to believe what she was seeing. Roxanne and Patrick Moyer were front and center, arm in arm, and obviously very much a couple. Behind them was a sea of faces, only one of which she recognized. Noah was standing in half profile, holding two pints of beer at the edge of the frame. He was paying no attention to the camera.

She could imagine how the photograph had come to be. The bartender at the Ship to Shore taking the camera down off the shelf behind the bar and snapping a memory for the corkboard. Just another random evening in Seaview Point's only watering hole. A moment caught on film that told Tessa everything she needed to know.

That was why Kyla phoned her after Tessa told her about the strange incidents at the house and her argument with Roxanne. She wanted to show Tessa this photograph. Let her know that Roxanne was keeping a secret. She must have remembered the picture was on the corkboard in the bar and went to get it before driving out to the house.

So how had her car ended up out here? Tessa looked at Kyla's phone. She pressed the side button. The screen lit up briefly to reveal the red outline of a drained battery, then went black again. The phone was dead.

There was one other person who hadn't answered her phone last night. Had Roxanne gotten wind of what her friend was going to do and followed her to make sure Tessa never learned the truth? If so, what had she done to Kyla?

Tessa stepped away from the car and closed the door. If something had happened to Kyla—and she prayed it hadn't—the car would be a crime scene, and Tessa had just contaminated it with her own fingerprints. But there was nothing she could do about that now. She slipped the photograph and Kyla's phone into her coat pocket, then walked back along the road, peering into the woods beyond. She called Kyla's name but wasn't surprised to receive no answer. She hoped she was wrong, but Tessa had a bad feeling. She glanced around nervously, wondering if Roxanne was somewhere close by, watching her.

It all made sense now. Roxanne had been in love with Patrick Moyer. Maybe she was even aware of the darkness inside him—the urge to kill. When Tessa identified Moyer as her attacker that night, it ended with the police chief shooting him dead after he resisted arrest. Did Roxanne blame her for that? It was the only logical conclusion. Roxanne had shown an interest in Tessa right from the start. She wasn't walking on the beach that first day just because it was her habit. She wanted to engage Tessa. Get close to her. Even the strange noises and footsteps in the house made sense now. The door and alarm codes, both of which were the same, were written on the magnetic dry-erase board on the fridge, which was located opposite the picture window in the kitchen. It hadn't occurred to Tessa before, but anyone standing on the other side of that window could read the code. What was the point of security if it was so easily breached? It was an oversight by Lillian, the caretaker. But on an island unused to crime—with one notable exception—where most people didn't even lock their doors, it was a forgivable one. Not that Roxanne needed to read the code from outside the kitchen window. Tessa had invited her in on more than one occasion. After that, Roxanne could come and go as she pleased, terrorizing Tessa at her leisure.

Tessa stopped and leaned over, gripping her knees for support, gulping the icy air. After the nausea passed, she straightened up. As she did so, a patch of red in the woods drew her attention.

It could have been anything. Trash left by some careless hiker. A discarded fisherman's buoy that had somehow found its way there. It might even be the remains of an old hunting stand. But she didn't believe it was any of those things. Not when Kyla's car was sitting abandoned at the edge of the road.

Tessa's hand went to her pocket. She pulled her phone out and almost called Chief White. But what did she have? An old photograph and a badly parked car. If the item in the woods turned out to be nothing, he wouldn't be pleased, especially since he was probably sleeping. Tessa had seen his SUV cruise past the house at least three times during the night. He'd done as promised, and she had felt safer because of it.

She put the phone back in her pocket and stepped off the road, pushing through undergrowth and weaving around rocks. The object she had spotted was lying in a space between two large granite boulders taller than she was. From any other angle, it wouldn't be visible, and maybe that was why someone—Roxanne?—had put it there.

She reached the boulders and looked down, then took an instinctive step backward.

Tessa's hand flew to her mouth. She stifled a scream.

Wedged in the space between two vertical granite walls and half-covered with leaves and twigs was a body wearing a red raincoat. A face peered up through the woodland detritus.

It was Kyla.

70

Kyla's head had been cleaved. Her scalp was nothing but a bloody mess of matted hair and bone. She lay with open eyes that stared lifelessly up through the canopy of trees into the forlorn sky above. Her skin had taken on a pallid, bluish hue.

Tessa's fingers found the photograph in her pocket. Kyla had died because she wanted to show her this. And at the hands of someone she thought was her friend. Tessa stumbled away, taking her phone out at the same time. She found Chief White's number, but it didn't ring. Instead, she heard a three-note chime and a monotone voice that told her the call could not connect. *Shit.* There was no service in the woods.

Tessa looked around. The killer was probably long gone and had no reason to return. Unless they were watching Tessa and had followed her when she left the beach house.

Something rustled in the bushes to Tessa's left. It might have been anything. A raccoon or a squirrel. Maybe even a fox drawn to the scent of death.

Tessa didn't want to find out.

What she *did want* was the safety of the beach house, where her phone would work and she could lock the door.

She turned and ran, fleeing back through the woods to the road. She continued on past Kyla's abandoned car, her footfalls heavy on the paved surface. Halfway back, she stopped to catch her breath, glancing around nervously at the dark trees on each side of the road. But then an image of Kyla lying in the woods flashed in front of her eyes, and she started up again, pushing herself forward despite the discomfort.

By the time she reached the house, her lungs screamed for oxygen and a stitch clamped down on her right side. But Tessa didn't care. She took the steps up onto the porch two at a time and fumbled to enter the door code. On the second attempt, the dead bolt drew back with a soft beep. Tessa yanked the door open and rushed into the house before slamming it shut behind her. She locked it and engaged the alarm system, then stood gasping for breath in the hallway.

She took her phone out and called Chief White again.

This time, it rang, and she sagged with relief.

When he answered, she didn't give him time to speak before blurting out what she had found in the woods. The words merged into a breathless torrent.

"Now, hang on there, little lady," the chief said. "Slow it down. You found a body, you say?"

"Yes. Her name is Kyla. She was supposed to meet me here last night but didn't show up. Someone killed her. I found her dead in the woods." As she spoke, Tessa hurried to the back door and made sure it was locked. She glanced out through the picture window toward the cove but saw no one there.

Then another thought occurred to her. What if the killer was already in the house? She rushed back to the living room and scooped up the baseball bat.

The chief was talking, but Tessa only half heard him. She was more concerned with her immediate situation.

"Tessa!" The chief raised his voice. "Calm down and pay attention to me. Where are you now?"

"I'm at the beach house. I tried to call from the woods, but there was no service." Tessa remembered the photograph in her pocket. "I know who the killer is. At least, I think I do."

"All right. How about you save it until I get there. I'm leaving right now."

"Please hurry," Tessa said.

"I'll be with you in less than ten minutes. You said there were no guns in the house, right? Just that baseball bat of yours."

"No guns."

"Understood. Keep your doors locked, and call me back if you see anyone approach the property. Anyone at all."

"I will." Tessa heard the breeze buffeting Chief White's phone on the other end of the line. He was outside. A car door slammed.

"I need to hang up now, Tessa," the chief said, then added, "It's going to be okay. We'll take care of this—I promise. Just keep calm and don't go outside for any reason."

"I won't." Like she was going back out there.

"Good girl," the chief replied. Then he hung up.

Tessa moved away from the door, then looked toward the stairs and the dark landing above. She remembered the footsteps. The voice that softly called her name. All those times she sensed unseen eyes. An icy dread enveloped her. The phone slipped from her hand and clattered to the floor. Despite what everyone said, she hadn't been alone in the house, after all. The person who killed Kyla had been there all along. Watching. Waiting. Toying with her. The question was, what did they want now?

71

Tessa was standing at the window, anxiously waiting, when the chief drove up to the house with his lights flashing silently fifteen minutes later, which was at least five minutes more than he'd told her on the phone. Five *long* minutes.

He climbed out from the vehicle, stood for a moment looking around at the forest that bordered the road, then reached into the cab and grabbed his hat before slamming the door and heading up onto the front porch.

She rushed to the door, turned the alarm off, and opened it to let him in.

The chief stepped across the threshold and nodded toward the baseball bat clutched in her hand. "I don't suppose you'd mind putting that away," he asked. "You look mighty jumpy, and I'd hate for there to be an accident."

Tessa hesitated, unwilling to let go of the only thing that made her feel safe.

"It's okay," the chief said. "I'm here now. You don't need to worry. How about you put it down?"

Tessa swallowed, then nodded and leaned the bat against the wall near the stairs. "Where's everyone else, all the other cops?" she asked. "Shouldn't you have called for backup or something?"

"All in good time, little lady." The chief rubbed his chin. "Why don't you tell me exactly what happened, and then I'll call the state police over on the mainland if I think it's necessary."

"I already told you what happened." Tessa couldn't keep the panic from her voice. She was shaking.

"Hey, calm down."

"I can't calm down. I just found a dead body." Tessa's legs started to buckle under her. She placed a hand on the wall to steady herself.

"You've had a mighty scare. Just take a moment."

Tessa waited while her strength returned. She let go of the wall.

"Better?"

Tessa nodded.

"Now, tell me what you found."

"Kyla. I found Kyla in the woods. She's dead."

"This would be Kyla McKenzie?" the chief asked.

"Yes. I came across her car abandoned on the side of the road and looked in the glove box to see who it belonged to. The registration was in there. Then I found Kyla. Someone had tried to hide the body. They covered it in twigs and leaves."

"I see." Chief White took a notepad and pen from his jacket pocket. "And you know who killed her?"

"Yes. This was in the car." Tessa pulled out the Polaroid and handed it to the chief.

He studied it for a moment, then looked up at her. "Patrick Moyer and Roxanne Trent."

"That's right. She's the killer. I'm sure of it. It's the only thing that makes sense."

"Because of an old photograph?"

"Look at the picture. They must have been dating. Kyla was going to show me this. Roxanne killed her to make sure that didn't happen."

The chief tucked the photograph into his jacket pocket. "Would you mind explaining that assumption?"

Tessa told him about her conversation in the grocery store and how Kyla had phoned her later that day to ask if she could come over because she had something to tell Tessa. "This is what she was going to tell me. That Roxanne is behind all the stuff that's been happening. She must be doing it as revenge for Patrick Moyer's death. She blames me."

"Why would she blame you?" The chief folded his arms and fixed Tessa with a deadpan stare.

Tessa realized she hadn't come clean about her true identity. Now she had no choice. "My name isn't Tessa Montgomery. At least, it wasn't five years ago."

"I know. It's Theresa Chamberlain. Recognized you the first time I came out here."

"You did?" Tessa had wondered if the chief knew who she was. Now she had her answer. "Why didn't you say anything?"

"Figured you wanted your privacy. Awful thing that happened to you in this house. Can't imagine why you wanted to come back here. Probably shouldn't have." The chief moved toward the door. "I've heard enough. I'm going to step out onto the porch and call the state police over on the mainland. Get them out here to deal with the body."

"You don't want me to take you there now?"

"You've been through enough. I'm not leaving you alone, and I'm certainly not taking you back out to some murder scene. Let's get the staties on the case, and then we'll deal with Kyla. If what you say is true, we'll have Roxanne in custody before you know it."

"Thank you." Tessa slumped with relief.

"You're welcome." Chief White turned toward the front door, taking out his cell phone at the same time, but when he went to step out, there was a dark figure blocking his path.

72

"What the hell are you doing here?" The chief backed up with an exclamation of surprise.

"What do you think I'm doing?" Noah pushed his way into the house and closed the front door. He looked at Tessa with a sneer. "I'm here to take care of business."

Tessa clamped her mouth shut against a whimper as the dreadful truth dawned on her. She had been wrong. Roxanne wasn't a murderer. It was Noah. He was responsible for everything that had happened since her arrival on the island. She took a faltering step backward, waited for the chief to draw his gun—to protect her—but the weapon remained firmly holstered.

"Dammit, boy." If the chief felt threatened by the sudden turn of events, he didn't show it. Instead, he just shook his head slowly. "I thought I told you not to come here. That I would handle this."

"You expect me to just sit at home and wait?" Noah sounded like a pouty child.

"That's exactly what I expected you to do. I'm the chief of police. It's my job."

"And it's my ass on the line." Noah pointed at Tessa. "She has to die."

"Yet another murder on top of the mess you've already made. Damn. You really are stupid, aren't you?" The chief glared at Noah. "Sometimes I wonder how you could be my son."

Son? Tessa could hardly believe what she was hearing. No wonder the chief had made no effort to keep her safe. He was protecting his offspring instead.

Noah glared at his father. "I'm not stupid. I was on the deck outside the kitchen window and heard every word of that phone call. Kyla knew about me. She was going to tell. I had to kill her. There was no other choice."

"There's always a choice. Just like you made a choice to come here right now instead of letting me take care of things the easy way."

"She knows what I did to that bitch, Kyla. You said so yourself."

"She didn't know anything, you goddamn fool. She thought that dim waitress from the diner killed Kyla."

"What?" Noah looked at Tessa. "Is that true?"

Tessa said nothing. Even if she had possessed the will to answer, she didn't trust herself to speak. Didn't want to let them hear the tremble in her voice, to let him feel her terror. Instead, she retreated another step and fought through the fear to sum up her situation. It was two against one. And both the chief and his son were stronger than she was. Fighting wasn't an option. That left flight—turning and fleeing for the back door before they realized what she was doing. She tensed, ready to bolt. But the chief anticipated what she was about to do.

"Don't even think of running, little lady." He slipped the gun from its holster and pointed it at her. "I'll drop you before you even make it five feet."

Tessa froze. She half raised her arms in submission.

"That's more like it," the chief said, then glanced sideways at Noah. "This could've been so easy. All we had to do was plant some evidence on that body, a couple of Roxanne's hairs to incriminate her, and you would have been home-free. But no. You couldn't wait on the sidelines like a normal person. There's even a photograph of Roxanne and Patrick Moyer together. They were dating. Did you know that?"

Noah shrugged. "He saw her a few times the summer before. So what?"

The chief swore under his breath. "It's motive. You understand what motive is?"

"You don't need to talk to me like I'm an idiot."

"Sometimes I think you must be." The chief kept one eye on Tessa. "How many times did I tell you not to piss in your own backyard? But you just had to do it anyway. You and Patrick both. If you had listened to me back then, none of this would be happening. I should've known you couldn't be trusted. Even when you were a kid, you weren't that smart."

"I don't know what you mean." Noah's voice raised a tone in pitch.

"Don't play dumb with me, son. I've covered for you too many times for the innocent routine."

"That's not true." Noah sounded more like a petulant child with each passing minute.

"Isn't it? How about the girl on School Street? You're lucky she couldn't identify you." The chief shook his head. "Or Bob Parker's daughter. You think that whole thing went away by magic? Shit. I should've taken care of you back then, put you out of your misery—but I was too soft."

"Don't say that." Noah's face creased into a glare. He jabbed a finger toward Tessa. "I didn't even touch her. It was Patrick. He's the one who saw them on the beach. He liked her."

"And you were more than willing to help him out. And now this. Christ. What a mess."

"I was just trying to fix things."

"No, you weren't. If you had just left it alone, she would never have been any the wiser. But you just couldn't stop yourself. Had to come sniffing around."

"I didn't know. When she came into the grocery store, I thought she must have recognized me from the house that night and—"

The chief cut his son off. "You didn't think. That's the problem."

A cold dread washed over Tessa. Patrick Moyer had not been alone in the house that awful night five years ago. It all made sense now.

There had been two of them. It had always bothered her that Moyer had subdued three girls all on his own. But he hadn't. Noah had been there too. That was why all this was happening. She had come back to the island, walked right into his life again, and he panicked.

Chief White rubbed his neck and grimaced. "What a royal mess. I already told you twice this week to stop skulking around this place and leave the damn gal alone. Instead, you came out here and did the exact opposite. Killed that Cindy woman."

Tessa glanced out the side window at Cindy's home beyond. She hadn't been wrong that night. Her only mistake was trusting Chief White. Now her kindly neighbor was dead. A tear rolled down Tessa's cheek.

"I had no choice but to kill her." Noah was busy defending himself. "She saw me watching the house. She would have said something."

"Holy crap, boy. Who do you think she would have reported it to?" The chief made a sound like something between a growl and a grunt. "Me. That's who. The chief of police. And I would have made it go away, just like always. Instead, I had to make excuses because you couldn't even kill the woman quietly."

"I did what I had to."

"Yeah. Well, too late now. We're in this mess together." Chief White sighed and rubbed his forehead.

"What are we going to do?"

"I don't know." The chief looked at Tessa. "But one way or another, she's not walking out of here. We don't have any choice, thanks to you."

"So just shoot her. Or give the gun to me, and I'll do it. I'd enjoy that."

"We're not shooting her. It'd be too hard to explain." The chief looked at Tessa. "Give me your phone."

Tessa didn't move. She didn't want to give up her only connection to the outside world. She might need it later.

"Give me the damn phone!" the chief boomed, his face contorting in anger.

Tessa flinched, surprised by the outburst despite all that had happened.

"Just give it to me," he said, lowering his voice back to a more even level. "Or I'll take it, anyway, and believe me, you don't want that."

Tessa extended her arm, hand shaking, and held it out.

The chief snatched it from her grip. "Smart girl."

"Now can we kill her?" Noah's eyes lit up. He looked between Tessa and his father before his gaze shifted to a kitchen knife lying on the counter near the stove. "I can do it real quiet. We don't need to use the gun. It'll be fun."

Tessa bit her lip. Willed herself not to make a sound. Not to show Noah the effect those few words had on her. She didn't want to give him the pleasure.

Chief White pocketed the phone. "I already told you. Not yet. Now, shut up and let me think."

A minute ticked away.

Tessa glanced toward the baseball bat leaning against the wall and summed up her chances of reaching it before Chief White or his son could react. It was too far away, and even though the chief had said he wasn't going to shoot her, Tessa still couldn't take that chance. Backed into a corner, he might very well put a bullet in her and worry about the consequences later.

The chief rubbed his chin with his free hand, then nodded. "All right. I have it. We're going to take her out to Kyla's car. Make it look like she went nuts and killed Kyla with the baseball bat, then took her own life."

"No one's going to believe that." Noah wrinkled his nose. "It's stupid."

"They'll believe whatever I tell them because I'm the chief of police. Just like everyone believed Patrick Moyer was trying to resist arrest." Chief White snorted. "Kid didn't even know I was there until I put a bullet in him."

"I still don't think—"

"Christ, boy. Have some faith in your old man." Chief White pulled the Polaroid from his pocket and showed it to Noah. Then he ripped it down the middle and crumpled the half containing Roxanne. He went to the fireplace and removed a lighter from his pocket, touched the flame to the ripped photo, then dropped it into the grate, where it curled and burned to black ash. Then he returned the half with Patrick in it to his pocket, along with the lighter, and walked back to his son's side. "As far as anyone is concerned, Kyla was seeing Patrick too. They were in love. She was the one creeping around here and doing all that weird shit out of spite because her boyfriend was dead. Theresa here found out, and they argued. She killed Kyla then took her own life in remorse."

"That just might work." Noah's face brightened.

"It will if you can keep your trap shut and do as you're told. And from now on, no more killings on the island. You hear me?"

"I was just trying to—"

"I don't want to hear it." The chief waved his gun at Tessa and motioned toward the front door. "All right, let's get this over with."

Tessa listened to this exchange with mounting horror. If she had been in a dire predicament before, now it had turned deadly. Her old reasoning—that the chief wouldn't shoot her so long as she did as she was told—didn't matter anymore. If she stepped out of that door, went with them, she would be dead for sure. Her only chance was to flee in the other direction. To get to the kitchen door and pray the chief wouldn't shoot her now that he had a plan. To hope that gunning down an unarmed woman in her own home would be too hard for him to explain. Which meant it just came down to who could run the fastest.

The chief was getting impatient. "Move."

Tessa did just that. She took a step forward, as if she were making for the front door, but then she pivoted at the last moment and bolted toward the back of the house.

The chief let out a howl of anger.

Tessa ran, terrified she was wrong and that a bullet would bury itself in her back. But it didn't. She reached the kitchen door and slammed it behind her.

She was halfway across the kitchen when the door crashed back open and Noah barreled through with the baseball bat in his hand. Chief White would not be far behind.

She raced for the back door, grabbed a kitchen chair, and tossed it in her wake.

The chair clattered across the floor and almost upended Noah, but he dodged sideways at the last moment.

She reached the door and tugged, then realized with horror that it was locked. Her hand flew to the dead bolt and turned it. The latch disengaged. This time, the door opened.

She fled onto the deck.

And there, crossing Sunset Cove, strolling on the beach, was her salvation. Roxanne, the person she had assumed was a killer just minutes before, taking a walk like she often did before her shift at the diner.

All Tessa had to do was shout and draw her friend's attention, but before she could take a breath, an arm snaked around her waist and a hand clamped down over her mouth to silence her.

Noah was faster than he looked.

Tessa bucked and squirmed, tried to bite his hand, but it was no use. He dragged her back into the house and kicked the kitchen door closed. Then he threw her onto the kitchen floor with such force that her head smacked against the hard tiles and bounced. Her jaw snapped shut. An electric bolt of pain shot down her spine. And then he was on top of her.

73

The impact of her head striking the kitchen tiles left Tessa momentarily stunned. She looked up at Noah straddling her, his face contorted with rage, and she was overcome by a sudden memory that surged out of her subconscious like a careening truck.

◆ ◆ ◆

Patrick Moyer sits astride her and looks down with all the insecurity of a cat that's caught a mouse and doesn't know what to do with it.

Everything hurts. After what he's just done to her, she will never be the same. Assuming she lives long enough to care.

She thinks of her friends.

Courtney, who had plans to be an actress in LA.

Shelby, who wanted to be an artist.

Madison, who was going into journalism, just like she was.

They are all dead, and soon she will join them—murdered by the man who now straddles her. But he is not trying to kill her. Not yet. And then she becomes aware of someone else. A figure standing in the doorway.

◆ ◆ ◆

A sharp and vicious slap to the face broke the spell, and the memory faded as quickly as it had come. Tessa's head snapped sideways. She fought to keep hold of the recollection. Felt like it contained a deeper truth. A truth she needed to finally understand.

◆ ◆ ◆

"Do it, man. I took care of the others. You take care of this one."

She turns her head. The figure steps into the room and approaches them. He has a bloody knife in his hand, which he hands to Patrick Moyer.

There isn't one killer in the house. There are two.

"Come on." The newcomer looks down at her gleefully. "Finish her."

Patrick Moyer takes the knife. He lowers it toward her face. She feels the blade bite into her flesh, releasing a sudden flow of blood. And then, ignoring her screams, he carves a line all the way from her jaw up to her ear . . .

◆ ◆ ◆

Another slap, harder this time, dislodged the memory for good.

Tessa blinked away tears, cheek stinging, and looked up at Noah—the man who had given Patrick Moyer that knife five years ago. It was Noah who had murdered her friends, then urged Patrick to kill her. That was why the others were stabbed while she had been strangled. Either Patrick hadn't had the guts to plunge the knife into her chest or he'd just wanted to choke the life out of her for fun. Feel her slip away. And it was no wonder Noah had never been caught; she hadn't remembered two killers, had only identified Patrick Moyer. She'd made it easy for Chief White to cover up his son's crime and pin the whole thing on Moyer. And just to make sure he didn't blab, the chief had shot him dead.

A sudden animalistic rage overcame Tessa. The emotion surged up from somewhere deep inside of her, raw and unbridled. *Noah had killed her friends.* She bucked and twisted, desperate to break free. The baseball bat lay on the floor several feet away, just out of reach. Noah must have discarded it there before he caught her on the deck. Kind of hard to tackle someone and drag them back inside with a baseball bat in your hands.

If only she could reach it . . . but Noah was still too strong.

"That's enough, son," the chief said, stepping forward. "You can't kill her here. We need it to look like suicide. She has to take the blame for what you did to Kyla."

"Screw that. Let's finish this." Noah's hands slipped around Tessa's throat and squeezed. She gasped for breath.

"I said no." The chief stepped forward, grabbed his son by the collar, and yanked him backward. The hands fell away from her throat.

Tessa coughed and sucked in air. She scrambled away, out of reach.

"Get up." The chief's gun was pointed at her again. "Try anything else, I'll shoot you dead and worry about the consequences later."

Tessa climbed to her feet, using the table to hold herself up. She was bruised and battered. The back of her head throbbed. She stood near the picture window with her arms at her sides. Any moment now, the chief would force her outside. He would take her to Kyla's car. She didn't know how he intended to stage her suicide, but it didn't matter. Dead was dead.

Then, from the corner of her eye, she caught a flicker of movement beyond the window. It was Roxanne. Tessa almost slumped with relief. She must have seen Noah on the deck, after all. Now she was standing with her back against the wall near the kitchen door. Neither Noah nor the chief could see her.

Tessa didn't dare turn to look. That would give her friend away. But at the same time, she wanted to cry out and tell Roxanne to run as fast as she could. Call the state police and tell them what was happening. It might not save Tessa, but it would finally bring justice to her friends. Noah and his father would pay for their crimes.

But her friend didn't run. She did the exact opposite.

The kitchen door flew open with a splintering crash. Roxanne stepped through it, looking as fearless as anyone Tessa had ever seen.

She held a compact black pistol in her hand, which she aimed at the chief with trembling hands. "Put your gun down."

If Chief White was surprised by the sudden intrusion, he didn't show it. "Roxanne, my dear, what do you think you're doing?"

"Put the damn gun down and step back." Roxanne waved her pistol between Noah and the chief.

"How about you put your gun down instead?" Chief White asked calmly. "This is police business. It doesn't concern you."

"I disagree."

"Tessa is not who you think. She killed your friend, Kyla. Caved her head in with a baseball bat. Nasty business. She's a sick individual. The body is out in the woods right now. I'm bringing her to justice."

"I know that's not true." Roxanne's hands were shaking more now. "I heard what you said."

The chief's gun was still trained on Tessa. Now he moved it to point at Roxanne. "You're not going to shoot. I bet that pistol of yours isn't even loaded."

"It is, and I will."

"I doubt it. Your hands are shaking. You're terrified. Have you ever even fired a gun before, little lady, let alone shot someone at close range?"

"There's a first time for everything," Roxanne said, but the bravado had vanished from her voice.

"That's what I thought."

Noah glared at Tessa. "You should've just let me kill her. Now we've got two of 'em to deal with. This is messed up."

The chief smiled. "Quite the opposite. It's a gift."

"I don't get it."

"That's because you're not as smart as you think." The chief glanced at Noah and then back to Roxanne. "I shoot this bitch; then we take her gun and shoot Tessa. It's a perfect setup. We don't even have to go out to the woods. Roxanne murders Kyla and shoots Tessa moments before I arrive. I'm left with no choice but to kill her. After all, she's armed and dangerous. A cold-blooded killer who won't be taken alive. And all because she wanted revenge for Patrick Moyer."

"That's crazy," Roxanne said. "You won't get away with it."

"Yes, I will." The chief's finger tensed on the trigger. "Goodbye, Roxanne."

74

Another second and Roxanne would be dead. Tessa had done nothing to help Courtney, Shelby, and Madison. She had let them die while she cowered under a bed. She wasn't going to let another friend die. Not this time.

The baseball bat was still lying near the door where Noah had tossed it when he chased her outside. This time, she knew she could make it. Tessa sprinted forward, grabbing for the bat in a desperate attempt to save her friend.

Noah realized what she was trying to do. He lunged forward to stop her.

Chief White's gun went off just as Tessa's hands closed around the bat, and Noah passed in front of Roxanne, blocking his father's shot.

The bullet smacked into his arm above the elbow, eliciting a grunt of pain. He pivoted like a ballerina amid a spurt of blood and dropped to the floor with a grunt.

"Dammit." Chief White was already aiming for a second shot, and this time, Roxanne might not be so lucky.

Tessa swung the bat. It arched down and slammed into his outstretched arms before he could pull the trigger. He howled in pain and dropped the gun.

She pulled back to swing again, determined to put Chief White down for good, but Noah was on his feet despite the blood coursing down his arm, apparently not as badly injured as he appeared earlier.

He lunged at Tessa and slammed into her with a snarl of rage, driving her backward.

Her feet snagged the chair she had thrown in his path earlier, and she went down, but this time she kept her head up so it wouldn't slam into the tile. Noah wrenched the bat from her grip and flung it aside, then went for her throat. His fingers closed over her windpipe. He squeezed. Pinpricks of light danced before her bulging eyes. She twisted and bucked, but he was too strong. Tessa was going to die with a pair of hands clamped around her throat, after all, except that instead of Patrick Moyer, it was Noah.

A wild anger surged through her. An untamed rage fueled by thoughts of Shelby, Courtney, and Madison. By thoughts of her neighbor Cindy and Roxanne's friend Kyla, who had done nothing to deserve death except show Tessa kindness. And in that moment, she decided: this was *not* how she was going to die. Not if she could help it. But she had to act fast, because if not, the darkness closing in at the edge of her vision would swallow her, and then it would be over.

With a gargantuan effort, Tessa marshaled a reserve of strength she hadn't realized she possessed. She lifted her arms, went for Noah's face. Pushed her thumbs into his eye sockets as hard as she could. It was a self-defense trick she had learned on the internet in the dark days after she left the hospital. And it worked. Noah screamed and fell sideways. He clawed at his face and writhed on the floor.

Tessa jumped to her feet.

The chief had pinned Roxanne against the wall. He was struggling to wrest the pistol from her grip. He looked sideways at Noah, who was only now regaining his composure.

"Dammit, boy. Get my gun."

Noah pushed himself up and crawled toward the chief's discarded service weapon. If he got his hands on it, she and Roxanne were both dead. There would be no more second chances. Tessa drew her foot back and kicked him with all the force she could muster. The blow caught

Noah under the chin. His head snapped back, and he twisted, dropping to the floor in a crumpled heap. This time, he didn't get up.

Now it was Tessa's turn to go for the gun.

The chief had wrestled Roxanne's pistol away from her. He sensed what Tessa was trying to do. Restraining Roxanne with one hand, he brought her gun to bear with the other and pulled the trigger.

A bullet whizzed past Tessa's head as she made a frantic dive for the chief's dropped weapon.

Her hand closed around the grip, and she pulled it toward her, rolling sideways as a second bullet flew past the spot that she had occupied a split second before and smacked into the floor, sending shards of tile flying. Without thinking, Tessa flipped over onto her back, lifted the chief's gun, and pulled the trigger.

75

Tessa had never fired a gun before. She wasn't expecting the recoil, and her elbow hit the floor, sending a fresh jolt of pain up into her shoulder. She lost her grip on the weapon, and it clattered on the ground somewhere behind her, out of reach.

But there was no time to retrieve it.

Because her wild and flailing shot had done something else. It had forced Chief White to release Roxanne and dive aside in the split second before she fired. Now her friend was slumped against the wall, trying to catch her breath even as the chief regained his senses after the narrow miss.

It only took Tessa a split second to decide. They weren't going to overpower Seaview Point's dangerous police chief and his crazy son. That much was obvious. There was only one remaining option. They had to flee before it was too late.

She pushed herself up and half stumbled, half ran toward Roxanne, then grabbed her hand before pulling her forcibly toward the back door.

As she flung it open, the chief made his move. He lumbered toward them with a speed that belied his flabby gut and sagging jowls. But he was still too slow, reaching the door a fraction of a second after they were already through it and racing across the back deck toward Sunset Cove. Tessa braced for the pop of the gun, to feel a bullet bury itself between her shoulders. But that didn't happen, perhaps because the chief was worried that gunshots in the open would draw too much attention, even out on the lonely southern tip of the island. Gunshots could be heard for a couple of miles and would surely raise eyebrows in a sleepy place like Cassadaga Island. Some curious individual might come looking for the origin of those gunshots. Or they might call the local police, which in this case was the chief himself, and make it harder for him to cover up the events at the beach house in a way that didn't implicate himself and his son.

They were on the beach now. A wall of fog was moving across the ocean in their direction, obliterating the horizon. It was freezing. Goose bumps rose on Tessa's skin. She risked a glance back over her shoulder. She expected to see Chief White still giving chase and was surprised to find the back deck empty and the kitchen door standing open.

But it was a brief respite.

A moment later, the chief appeared again, and he wasn't alone. Noah was back on his feet and looking just as dangerous as ever.

Roxanne had seen them too. "We have to get out of sight. It's our only chance."

"There," Tessa said, pointing to the trail that led up and over the bluff.

"Are you serious? We'll never make it all the way to town on foot."

"Have you got a better idea?"

"What about your car?" Roxanne's breath was coming in short, heavy gasps. "It's parked in front of the house."

"And the keys are on a hook next to the front door," Tessa said. She had already thought about the car and dismissed the idea.

"Then we just circle around to the front, let ourselves in, and get them."

"It won't work." They had reached the trail now and were starting up. "They aren't that far behind us. The chief would realize what we were up to, and then we'd be trapped back in the house . . . or worse."

"Then what are we going to do? We can't outrun them forever."

"I don't know." They had reached the top of the trail now. Tessa stopped to catch her breath. But they couldn't linger. The chief and his son were surely making their way up the trail, and even though Chief White was obviously out of shape, they wouldn't have long. She glanced to her left and saw Cindy's house a couple of hundred feet away, and then she had an idea. "Follow me."

"You want to hide in Cindy's house?" Roxanne said, hurrying beside her as Tessa sprinted toward the building.

"Not inside it." Tessa led her around the side of the home toward the cellar's bulkhead entrance she had seen days before when searching for Cindy outside the house. "Under it. We can wait it out until the chief and Noah are looking for us deeper in the woods, then circle back to the house and get the car keys."

"You think that will work?"

"It has to." Tessa reached down and gripped the handles, flinging the doors open, grateful they weren't padlocked. "Come on."

Roxanne stared down into the cobweb-filled darkness. "I'm not going down there."

"We don't have a choice. We have to hide. It's our only chance." Tessa stepped down onto a rickety set of steep stairs that descended into the gloom. She reached back up and held her hand out to Roxanne. "Get down here," she hissed. "Quickly. Before they see you."

Roxanne hesitated a moment more, then followed Tessa into the musty darkness. When she was mostly down, she reached out and grabbed the bulkhead doors, then swung them shut.

They were plunged into darkness.

Tessa felt Roxanne's hand touch her shoulder. "You still have your phone?"

"No." Tessa felt around with her foot for the next step. "Chief White took it."

"I still have mine."

There was rustling in the darkness. When Roxanne spoke again, she sounded dismayed. "It's gone. It must've fallen out of my pocket while I was struggling with the chief."

"Perfect." Tessa could hardly believe their bad luck. Under any other circumstances, she would have suggested climbing back out of the cellar, but that wasn't an option. "We'll just have to keep moving."

"How are we going to see anything?"

"I don't know." Tessa reached out and touched the wall next to the steps. She felt something sticky and fibrous under her fingers. A cobweb. She drew her hand quickly away when something scuttled across it. No doubt the spider whose home she had just invaded. She shuddered and felt for the next step, moving lower.

Roxanne pressed close as they descended. Tessa risked reaching out for the wall again and was relieved not to encounter any more arachnids. Near the bottom, her hand brushed something else. This time it was hard and smooth with a recognizable blocky protrusion in the middle. A light switch.

She flicked it on with relief.

The cellar was instantly bathed in dim yellow light from a single bare bulb attached to a joist holding up the floor above. The walls were made of rough stone. Water had seeped down through the foundation, leaving the stones slick and wet in places. The dirt floor was hard-packed and frozen. A large oil tank sat near the steps, its surface pitted and black. Farther away was a boiler. On the other side of the cellar was another set of stairs that ended at a white-painted door leading to the interior of the house. But it was an object lying in the center of the cellar that drew Tessa's attention. A heavy canvas tarpaulin, which might at one time have been used to cover a wood stack. Except now it was covering something much worse, judging by the dark crimson stain that had soaked through the tan-colored material.

Tessa took a faltering step forward. Her heart hammered against her ribs. The lump under the tarpaulin looked almost—she hardly dared to think it—human-shaped. She remembered the scream from a few nights before. Tessa was afraid that beneath the tarp would be the source.

"I don't like this," Roxanne said from somewhere over her shoulder.

"Me either." Tessa didn't want to look, but she had to know if it was Cindy.

She reached out tentatively, avoiding the dark stain, and took a corner of the tarp. With a shaking hand, she pulled the grimy canvas sideways and off, resisting the urge to turn her head away in fear of what the tarpaulin concealed. She was right to be afraid. Because what lay beneath was so much worse than she could ever have imagined.

76

There wasn't one body under the tarp. There were two. Cindy lay on her back, face frozen in a rictus mask of fear. Her throat had been cut, and she had endured several stab wounds to her chest and abdomen. Next to her, reclined in an almost serene position with her legs straight and arms folded over her chest as if she had simply lain down and expired willingly, was the caretaker, Lillian. The only clue to the violence of her demise was the way her head lolled to the side at an unnatural angle. A broken neck.

Tessa recoiled and took a quick step back, bile rising into her mouth. She swallowed, fighting the urge to throw up. Managed to contain it . . . barely. Behind her, Roxanne gave a strangled cry that sounded like something between a moan and a scream.

It was too loud.

Tessa spun to face her. "Be quiet," she whispered. "They'll hear us."

"Sorry," Roxanne said in a croaky voice. She chewed her bottom lip. "I guess you were right about Cindy all along."

Tessa didn't bother to say *I told you so*. There was no point. She looked down at the two dead women, mouthed a silent apology. It was cut short by a sound from up above, on the other side of the bulkhead doors. A voice.

It was Noah.

He was calling out to his father. "Dad. Over here. Quick."

Tessa exchanged a look with Roxanne. Father and son must have split up to cover more ground. Had Roxanne's cry alerted him to their hiding place? She was tempted to climb back up to the bulkhead. To peek out and see. But that would be foolhardy, not to mention dangerous. If Noah really was zeroing in on them, if he really did suspect they were in the cellar, revealing herself would just confirm it. But she didn't want to wait around idly and find out either.

Luckily, there was a third option. The door at the top of the stairs. The one they had been on the verge of opening in order to check the cellar on their nocturnal trip a couple of nights before. It wasn't lost on her that if they had gone into the cellar, they might have discovered its gruesome secret earlier. But before they could do so, Chief White had shown up, cruising along the road in the middle of the night. Afterward, she had attributed it to him doing his job and making routine passes by the house so she would feel safe. Now she realized it was probably the opposite. Chief White wasn't trying to ease her fears. If anything, he was out looking for Noah, trying to curb his insane son's worst urges. But it wouldn't have made a difference, anyway. Dialing 911 would have brought Chief White to their doorstep. She shuddered to think where it would have gone from there.

Noah's voice was getting louder. He was still calling for his father. Tessa had no doubt they would soon be discovered if they stayed where they were.

"We have to go," she said, heading toward the stairs leading up into the house.

This time, Roxanne didn't protest. She followed along quietly and climbed the stairs so hard on Tessa's heels that she could feel her friend shaking.

When they reached the top, Tessa gripped the door handle and turned it, expecting the door to open. Instead, her shoulder ran into it, and the door remained stubbornly closed. "Shit."

"What's wrong?" Roxanne pushed beside Tessa on the narrow ledge at the top of the stairs.

"It won't open. It's locked from the other side."

"It can't be. We were about to come down here a couple of nights ago."

"Did you actually check the door before Chief White showed up?"

There was a moment of silence. Roxanne drew in a quivering breath. "No. I never got that far. I was reaching for the handle when we saw his lights." Her voice faltered when she spoke. "This is bad. So bad."

"Take it easy." They weren't done yet. For all they knew, Noah had moved on without bothering to check the bulkhead. "We'll go back down into the cellar and hide. We'll wait it out."

"Hide where?" A look of horror passed across Roxanne's face. "I'm not getting under that tarp."

"Neither am I." Tessa turned around and started back down the stairs. "We'll find somewhere. Behind the oil tank, maybe."

"Okay." Roxanne didn't sound too sure. "Let's do it." She hesitated. "I'm sorry I didn't believe it when you said something happened to Cindy. I really am."

"I know." Now was not the time. Tessa was halfway down the stairs. She could see the oil tank on the far side of the cellar, near the bulkhead steps. Maybe, just maybe, they could slip behind that and stay out of sight long enough to survive. It all depended on how much space there was between the tank and the wall. And also, whether Noah really had heard Roxanne's scream.

She got her answer a couple of seconds later, when the bulkhead doors crashed back on their hinges and a pair of legs appeared on the steps, climbing down into the cellar.

77

A sharp spear of daylight lanced through the darkness and lit the bulkhead steps in an almost ethereal glow. But the animal coming down those steps was anything but angelic. Noah White looked more like he was descending into the depths of hell, which was, Tessa thought, exactly where he belonged.

"Well, lookee here." Noah was almost at the bottom of the steps. His left arm hung limp at his side. Blood had soaked through his shirtsleeve where Chief White's bullet had struck him during the struggle in the kitchen. But he wasn't any less dangerous for it. He held the kitchen knife that had been lying on the counter near the stove in his other hand. The leering grin on his face—he looked almost wild with anticipation—left little doubt about what he wanted to do with it.

"Don't come any closer," Tessa said, realizing how futile her words were, considering they were trapped halfway down the stairs leading back into the house.

"Aw. That's exactly what Lillian said when she stopped by the other morning to lock the attic door and found me waiting for you in there." His gaze dropped from the stairs to the pair of corpses. "I see the four of you have been getting reacquainted."

"You were hiding in my attic?" Tessa had already guessed as much, but confirmation from Noah's lips sent the hairs on the back of her neck standing up.

"Not all the time. But it was a great place to go if I couldn't get out the front door quick enough. The attic window didn't even have an alarm sensor on it. Pretty sloppy, if you ask me. All I had to do was climb out onto the front-porch roof and jump down. I got inside that way a couple of times too." Noah was halfway across the cellar floor now. He was moving slowly, taking his time. Relishing their fear. He knew they had nowhere to go. "And to think I went to the trouble of disabling the sensor in the upstairs bedroom before I discovered it."

"If you thought I recognized you that day in the grocery store, why didn't you just kill me?" Tessa wasn't sure she wanted to know the answer, but the longer he was talking, the longer they would stay alive. She took a slow step back up the stairs, then another, waiting for her moment. With any luck, she could keep him engaged long enough to reach the top. The door might be locked, but it couldn't be that sturdy. Maybe she could bust it open before he reached them. "You had plenty of chances."

"I know. Crazy, huh?" He chuckled, the sound anachronistic, given the wicked-looking blade in his hand. "I almost did a couple of times, but I wasn't quite sure about you. And honestly, I was kind of enjoying myself. The anticipation—watching you squirm and panic—it was exquisite. But then I heard you talking to Kyla on the phone. Heard her talking about Patrick. Figured she knew about me. Guess I jumped to conclusions there."

"Kyla." A sob escaped Roxanne's lips.

"You thought she was going to tell me about you and Patrick, not Roxanne dating him." Tessa was almost at the top of the stairs now. Just two more steps. The bad news was that Noah had reached the bottom.

"We all make mistakes." He shrugged. "But it's all good. Now I get to kill both of you. Double the fun."

"Your mother must be so proud," Tessa said, hoping that invoking the memory of his dead mother would give him pause. Instead, it had the opposite effect.

"Ah, dear Mommy. Tumbled down the stairs. Went head over heels all the way to the bottom. With a little help, of course." Noah placed a foot on the bottom step. It groaned under his weight. A visible shudder ran through him, but not of remorse. It was more like pleasure. "You never forget your first."

Tessa had heard enough. She was back at the door with Roxanne at her side. It was now or never. She set her shoulder and drove it into the door near the frame above the handle.

It shifted in the frame but held fast.

"I don't think so." Noah picked up the pace, taking the stairs two at a time.

Tessa squared her shoulder and leaned back to try again. If the door didn't open this time, she wouldn't get another chance. But as she steeled herself to do it, gathering the strength required to break free, Roxanne stumbled into her with a terrified scream.

Tessa almost pitched forward down the stairs, grabbing the handrail at the last moment to save herself. But not before she glimpsed Noah's knife arcing down toward her.

78

Tessa twisted sideways and raised her arm, blocking Noah's attack and deflecting the knife sideways. She felt a rush of air before the point buried itself into the door inches from her head.

Noah grunted and pulled the blade free, but before he could mount a second assault, Roxanne grabbed his wrist and twisted, trying to pry the knife from his grip. He howled with rage and brought his knee up into her gut, then wrenched free as she doubled over, gasping for breath.

He slashed wildly.

The blade sliced across Roxanne's arm near her wrist and opened the skin, drawing blood. She recoiled with a cry of pain and lifted her free arm to stop him from burying the knife into her chest.

Tessa took the opportunity to strike.

She gripped Noah's other arm, the injured one, and squeezed. Her thumb pressed down into the wound. She felt the skin give under the pressure, felt the bullet hole open up. His blood was hot and slick.

Noah yelped and tried to pull away.

"Bitch." He spat the word as if it had the power to hurt her. A string of spittle flew from his lips and landed on her face. He gave up on Roxanne and brought the knife around, quicker than Tessa had anticipated.

There wasn't time to avoid it. Instead, she tried to bat it away with her free arm, felt the blade slip across the back of her hand. The touch of steel was cold and familiar. The pain even more so. The faces of her dead friends swam in front of her eyes. Madison, who wanted to be a journalist. Shelby, who loved to draw and paint. The effervescent Courtney. She could sense their spirits right beside her, holding her up, giving her the strength not to die.

And she needed all the strength she could get, because Noah was bringing the knife down again, the blade aimed straight for her chest. There was no way she would be able to deflect it. Not this time. Instead, she let go of his arm, balled her hand into a fist, and brought it up under his chin as hard as she could in a quick uppercut.

His head snapped back.

Roxanne saw her chance. She lunged forward.

Noah was standing with one foot on the top stair and the other a step below. Roxanne's full body weight slammed into his chest. The blow to his chin had left him momentarily off-balance, and he teetered on the edge of falling. He tried to steady himself, reached out for the railing with his injured arm, but Tessa swatted his hand away before his fingers could close on it.

For a second, Noah appeared to hang motionless, as if frozen in place. Then he pitched backward. His foot slipped from the top stair. He tumbled, arms flailing, fingers grasping at empty air. The knife fell from his grip. A scream welled in his throat, even as he cartwheeled, bouncing from one stair to another until the cellar floor below broke his fall and silenced him.

79

Noah had barely hit the ground before Tessa was on the move. "We have to get out of here. Right now."

"You don't need to tell me twice." Roxanne hurried behind, descending the stairs with a hand pressed against the open wound on her arm. Blood seeped through her fingers. When they reached the bottom, she stopped and looked at Noah. "Is he dead?"

"God, I hope so." Tessa skirted around his prone and motionless body without bothering to check. But somehow, even though she had no proof, she knew he was gone. That he had died in the same manner as his mother wasn't lost on her.

"Poetic justice," Roxanne murmured, obviously thinking the same thing.

"Yeah." Strangely, Tessa felt no satisfaction at Noah's death. In fact, she felt nothing at all. It was like she was an empty vessel, devoid of emotion. She almost reached for the knife to scoop it up, but then thought better of it. The chief had a gun. He'd shoot them before they ever got close enough to use it. Besides, she'd had enough knives for a lifetime.

A patch of light still shone down on the bulkhead steps leading out of the basement. Tessa wanted nothing more than to climb those steps and get away from the gruesome scene under Cindy's house, but when she got halfway there, she realized she was alone.

Roxanne was still standing over Noah, staring down at him, wide-eyed. She was probably in shock, Tessa thought, but they didn't have time for that. "What are you doing? We can't stay here."

Tessa's voice jolted Roxanne from her daze. She cast Noah one last glance, then hurried toward the bulkhead steps.

At that moment, a shadow fell over the bulkhead, and the sunlight was blocked out.

"Noah? You down there, boy?"

Tessa scurried away from the steps.

Roxanne grabbed her arm, mouthed silent words to her. "It's the chief. He's found us."

Tessa didn't bother replying. She steered Roxanne sideways toward the oil tank.

The bulkhead steps creaked as Chief White stepped onto them.

The gap between the oil tank and the wall was narrow. Tessa wondered if there was enough space to hide there, but there was nowhere else. And they were out of time. She could hear the chief coming down the steps, grunting under his breath with each footfall. Maybe he'd once been in shape, but he had let himself go to the point where even descending into the cellar left him winded.

Still, another few seconds and he would see them.

She flattened herself against the wall and slid sideways behind the tank. It really was tight. She sucked in her stomach, but the real problem was her breasts. Tessa wasn't exactly well endowed, but they were big enough to make wriggling into the tiny gap almost impossible. She gritted her teeth and kept going, fighting the urge to cry out as the tank pressed painfully into her chest. She could barely breathe.

Roxanne had an easier time with it. She was thinner than Tessa, although not by much. Fear was a pretty good motivator too. She wiggled into the tight space the moment there was room to do so.

The chief had reached the bottom of the steps. His gun was holstered, but his hand rested on the butt. Tessa could just about see him from her vantage point, which meant that he would also be able to see her if he looked sideways. That was the last place he would look now, though, because he had just spotted Noah.

"Son?" He rushed forward with a desperate wail and dropped to his knees beside his unmoving offspring. He reached down with two fingers extended, pressed them to Noah's neck. The wail turned into a shriek.

Despite all that had happened, a ball of sorrow rose in Tessa's throat. But then she reminded herself exactly why they were in this situation and what the chief and his son had wanted to do to them. Her empathy evaporated like dew on a hot summer morning. She nudged Roxanne, nodded toward the steps.

Roxanne shook her head.

Tessa nudged her again. The chief was distracted by his own grief. They wouldn't get another chance. All he had to do was look over his shoulder and he would see their legs beneath the tank. They would be trapped, unable to fight back when he took out his gun and shot them.

The same thought must have occurred to Roxanne. She finally moved, sliding back out without making a sound. Tessa inched along behind her, grimacing as her chest scraped against hard, unyielding metal. For the second time since entering the cellar, her hand brushed something soft and leggy on the side of the tank near the bottom that tried to crawl up her arm. She clamped her mouth shut over an involuntary whimper, managing to stifle the sound as she flicked it away with a shudder and kept going.

She slid free, finally able to fill her lungs.

The chief was still kneeling over his son. He had been oblivious to their presence so far, but now he turned his head in their direction, perhaps hearing Tessa's barely audible intake of breath. Or maybe he just sensed a stirring of the air behind him. There were tears on his cheeks. His mouth was a thin pressed line, barely visible on his meaty face.

His hand fell to the gun at his side.

Roxanne screamed.

"Go." Tessa shoved her friend toward the steps. From the corner of her eye, she saw the chief draw his weapon from its holster.

Roxanne scrambled up toward the daylight.

Tessa barely waited until there was room before clambering up behind her.

"You killed my boy." The chief's voice sounded different. Tight. Reedy.

Tessa ignored the urge to look back and kept climbing.

The silence in the cellar was interrupted by a deafening boom. The stair an inch to the right of Tessa's head disintegrated in a shower of flying splinters.

Roxanne was at the top. She launched herself through the open bulkhead doors and vanished into daylight.

Tessa scrabbled up the last few steps, tumbling out into the open a split second before a second boom shattered the silence.

She landed hard on the frozen ground, ears ringing, eyes squinted half-shut against the sudden brightness. But there was no time to gather her wits. If Chief White had been cool and calculating before, he wasn't now. He was blinded by rage and grief.

Tessa sprang to her feet and reached for the bulkhead doors just as the chief appeared below. He raised his gun, finger curled around the trigger. Tessa let the doors slam down. Then she turned to Roxanne, a single word on her lips. "Run."

80

Tessa sprinted toward the trail without bothering to see if Roxanne was following, because she could hear her ragged breath and pounding footfalls as she raced a few steps behind. They weaved through the trees and up over a small rise of granite, then half slid down the other side.

The ocean came into view—or rather, the white expanse where it should have been. The fog had rolled in thick and fast beyond the bluff, giving the appearance that they were standing on the precipice of a vast and featureless void. Sunset Cove was gone, replaced by a blanket of shifting, impenetrable vapor that sat low over the land. Not even the beach house was visible.

Tessa reached the trail and turned toward Sunset Cove.

"Where are you going?" Roxanne faltered and stopped. "That's the wrong way for town."

"We talked about this. We'll never make it there on foot." Tessa came to a skidding halt on the trail and turned back toward her friend. "My car keys are in the house. It's the only way we're getting out of this alive."

Roxanne wavered, glancing in the direction of Seaview Point.

Behind them, the bulkhead doors crashed open.

The chief's voice filtered through the trees. "There's nowhere you can run."

He sounded deranged. Running on raw emotion.

"Roxanne. For heaven's sake." Tessa held an arm out toward her and noticed that the back of her hand was slick with blood. It was only then that she remembered Noah's knife slicing into her flesh as she struggled with him. In her terror, she had put it out of her mind. She had needed every ounce of concentration just to stay alive.

Now it stung.

When Roxanne started toward her, she dropped her arm with relief. They followed the path down into Sunset Cove and the welcoming, concealing fog.

Their feet crunched on shingle as they crossed the beach. It sounded too loud, but there was nothing they could do about that. Their only saving grace was the muted rumble of waves crashing ashore somewhere beyond the depth of their vision.

Tessa guessed that visibility was less than fifty feet. There were no landmarks with which to orient themselves. She listened to the waves, trying to decide if she was walking toward them or away from them. In the end, she decided they were moving parallel to the shore. Which meant that the beach house would be to their right. A few moments later she got confirmation of her hunch when the spectral outline of an upturned rowboat appeared out of the mist.

She almost cried with relief.

"We have to go up the beach, to the right," she said, touching Roxanne's shoulder.

The words were barely out of her mouth when the sharp crack of a gunshot drowned out the waves.

The ground near Tessa's feet kicked up in a hail of rock and sand as a bullet slammed into it. She pivoted to see a figure emerging from the fog, faint at first but soon coming into sharper focus.

Roxanne screamed. "He's found us."

That much was obvious, although Tessa was surprised that he had made it onto the beach and located them so easily in the swirling fog.

The chief held his gun at arm's length in a double-handed grip. His hat was gone, and his shirt was partly untucked and flapping in the wind.

Tessa did the only thing she could think of. She turned and grabbed Roxanne around the waist, pulling her toward the upturned rowboat as the chief took another wild shot that whistled off somewhere into the fog.

Tessa lunged across the rowboat's keel, dragging Roxanne along with her. They landed hard on the other side and stayed low. It was meager protection, but it was better than nothing.

"What are we going to do now?" Roxanne asked in a throaty voice.

Tessa didn't answer. They were in an impossible situation. Any moment now, the chief would stride up to the boat, point the muzzle of his service weapon down at them, and that would be it.

So much for serve and protect. The absurd thought flashed through her mind like a bad joke. She hadn't been safe on the island from the moment she arrived. Chief White hadn't possessed the fortitude to stop his son now any more than he had five years ago. That task had been left to Tessa, and she was glad to have done it. One less monster in the world.

But that didn't help them with the very much still-alive monster. She could hear the chief's footsteps, hear the shingle grinding and compressing under his boots. A moment later, he came into view, looming over the boat, gun in hand.

And in that moment, Tessa knew what they had to do. She dropped her arms and gripped the edge of the boat, ignoring the pain in her injured hand. At the same time, she glanced sideways and locked eyes with Roxanne.

A silent understanding passed between them.

Now Roxanne reached down and curled her fingers under the rim of the boat.

The chief took one hand away from the gun—just for an instant—to wipe a tear from his eye.

They wouldn't get another chance.

"Now!" Tessa screamed the word at the same time as she stood up, lifting the boat along with her.

Roxanne did the same, and together they heaved the boat up onto its side and pushed with an almighty grunt, sending it toppling onto its keel and landing right way up.

The chief was too close.

It knocked him off his feet, and he landed on his back with a pained grunt. But to Tessa's dismay, he kept hold of the gun.

Without giving herself time to think, she leaped over the boat and landed astride him, then reached for the weapon to pry it from his grip.

But he was too big and strong.

He bucked her off, and now he was on top, fighting to turn the gun on her. She gripped his wrist with both hands, pushing his arm up and away, but even so, the muzzle inched down. Another few seconds, and it would be pointing directly at her face. That would be all he needed.

Then, out of nowhere, a raging banshee appeared, wielding an oar. It was Roxanne, her face twisted into raging adrenaline-fueled anger.

She swung the oar.

The blade impacted the chief's head near his right ear, spinning him sideways off Tessa and leaving him sprawled onto the beach.

And now he lost the gun. It flew from his hand and landed harmlessly a few feet away.

Tessa lunged.

Even through his daze, Chief White realized what she was doing. He tried to stand just as Roxanne's oar found its mark again and sent him staggering backward.

Tessa's hand closed over the gun. Her fingers curled around the grip just as the chief regained his balance. He flew toward her, arms outstretched, lips curled back into a maniacal snarl.

Tessa pulled the trigger for the second time that day.

This time, she didn't miss.

The bullet hit Chief White square in the chest and stopped his forward momentum. But unlike in the movies, it didn't throw him from his feet. Instead, he stumbled, looking down in surprise. He lifted a hand and touched his shirt where the bullet had entered.

Then he dropped to his knees, swayed, and pitched forward onto the beach.

81

Roxanne dropped the oar and raced to Tessa's side. She helped her up, gently placing a palm over Tessa's hand and the gun. "You can let that go now. It's over."

Tessa nodded but didn't release the gun. Instead, she gripped it tight enough to drain the blood from her knuckles and looked at the Seaview Point chief of police as if she expected him to rear back up like the bad guy in some B slasher movie.

"He's dead." Roxanne and Tessa started up the beach and toward the rental house. Soon, the back deck appeared out of the fog, and behind it, the beach house.

They stumbled up the steps and entered through the back door, locking it behind them.

Only now that she was safely inside was Tessa willing to let go of the gun. She placed it on the kitchen table and righted an upturned chair before sitting down. She looked up at Roxanne. "I just shot the Seaview Point chief of police, and we have no proof of anything that happened here."

"That's not entirely true." Roxanne glanced around, then crossed the kitchen. Her phone was lying on the floor near the door. She picked it up and went back to Tessa. "There's this."

She unlocked the screen. A moment later, the chief's voice came out of the speaker. It was muffled but clear enough to hear what he was saying. Then Noah chimed in. It was as good as a signed confession.

"You turned on the voice-recorder app when you were outside the back door earlier." Tessa almost fainted with relief.

"I caught everything they said." Roxanne turned the recording off and put the phone in her pocket. "Should be good enough, don't you think?"

"More than enough." Tessa was exhausted. Her whole body ached.

"Good." Roxanne sank into a chair on the other side of the table.

Tessa looked at her. "I'm sorry about Kyla. I know the two of you were close."

Roxanne nodded. "I can't believe Noah killed her. And all over a stupid photograph." She sniffed. "I'm sorry I didn't tell you I dated Patrick. We only saw each other for a few months during the summer before everything happened. But when I got close to him, I realized there was something wrong. He said all the right things. Played a good part. But it was like he was dead inside. There was no real emotion. That's why it never developed into anything more than a casual fling."

"It's okay. I understand why you didn't say anything. It can't have been an easy subject to bring up under the circumstances." Tessa reached across the table and took her friend's hand in hers. She squeezed. "I wasn't truthful either. I didn't tell you who I was until that night at your house after we went to the bar. We're good."

"That's different," Roxanne said. "I should have told you. I struggled with it. Went back and forth. I was worried you'd somehow blame me for what happened."

"I wouldn't have."

"I'm glad. I'm not trying to take anything away from what you went through. I know it was so much worse, but Patrick Moyer left me broken. I didn't sleep at night for months. Eventually, I went and bought a gun. I kept it under my pillow when I went to bed for over a year. Even now, I carry it when I go walking." Roxanne lifted her shirt to reveal a concealed-carry bellyband holster.

"I understand." Tessa forced a smile. She was actually glad Roxanne hadn't told her earlier. It would only have increased her suspicions, which had turned out to be unfounded. She nodded toward the cell phone in Roxanne's hand. "How about you call the police? I think it's time to end this."

82

Three Months Later

Tessa ran packing tape across the top of a box that contained books, mementos from her childhood, and knickknacks she had gathered over the years. She picked up a marker and wrote on the box so she would know what was inside, then added it to the growing pile that would soon be on its way across town to a brand-new apartment near the waterfront.

Her manuscript was done and with the publisher.

Thomas Milner and his boss had been happy for her to finish it from the mainland. The explosive ending was more than they could have ever hoped for. What had started as a journal about rediscovery and healing would now be the true crime sensation of the year. She had written it in record time, determined to get everything down before the details faded. And because Thomas Milner had urged her to have it in his hands as soon as possible. They were fast-tracking the publication to take advantage of the renewed publicity Tessa's ordeal on Cassadaga Island had generated. She was in the news again. The reporters were back. But this time, she didn't run and hide. She dealt with their attention and simply refused to comment. And with good reason. Even if Tessa had wanted to give interviews, Thomas Milner wouldn't allow it. He wanted to keep the details of her ordeal a secret until the book was published.

"Hey, you," a voice said from the bedroom doorway. "Looks like you're almost done here."

"Just a couple more boxes to go," Tessa said, turning toward her sister and Josh, who lingered a few steps back in the hallway. Her trip to Cassadaga Island had been the cathartic experience Tessa hoped it would be, although not for the reason she originally thought. Surviving Noah's obsession with terrorizing her, and finally learning the truth about what happened on that dreadful night five years before—that she could have done nothing to prevent the deaths of her friends—had given Tessa closure. After all, she could never have fought off both Noah and Patrick to save her friends. One assailant would have been possible . . . maybe . . . but not two of them. She wasn't completely healed and probably never would be, but she could now face her demons head-on. And that started with being comfortable around the opposite sex again. Especially Josh, who loved her sister and had endured so much over the last few years just to accommodate Tessa.

"Did you see the news yet today?"

Tessa shook her head. "No. Why?"

"The FBI are investigating Noah White in relation to a string of unsolved murders across New England over the past eight years. They've placed him in the vicinity of three killings so far. One in Bangor, another in Portland, and one in Boston. They think there may be more. Into the double digits, they said. All young women."

"I'm not surprised." Tessa remembered what Chief White had said to his son. *How many times did I tell you not to piss in your own backyard?* The FBI had already asked her about the other victims Chief White had mentioned: Bob Parker's daughter and the girl on School Street. Noah might not have killed them, but they were the first in a series of escalating incidents that created what she was sure would turn out to be a prolific serial killer. And it all started with his mother. His first kill. Tessa put the packing tape down. "Who knows how many women Noah murdered? And his father, Chief White, knew what he was doing. Shielded him. Protected him all these years, ever since he was a kid."

"It really is unbelievable," Melissa said. "Honestly, I was hesitant to even mention those news reports and ruin all the progress you've made. But you would have seen them anyway."

"I'm sure it will be the first thing a reporter asks me. There's no hiding away this time, not with Noah's crimes getting found out and the book coming out soon."

"Can you handle it?" Melissa looked concerned.

"Yeah." Tessa nodded. "No need to treat me with kid gloves. Not anymore."

"I'm so proud of you." Melissa stepped into the room. "I thought going back to that place was a terrible idea, but you were right."

"It almost got me killed." Tessa thought of Kyla, murdered by Noah for trying do the right thing. Cindy, who showed her nothing but kindness. Lillian, who was in the wrong place at the wrong time. Her throat closed up. For a moment, she couldn't talk.

"You all right, there?" Melissa placed a hand on Tessa's shoulder.

"Yes. Just memories." Tessa forced a smile through the tears. "I'm okay. Really, I am."

"Good." Melissa looked at the pile of moving boxes. "I never thought I'd see the day when you got your own place and went out into the world. Before I know it, you'll be holding down a job."

"I already have a job," Tessa said. "I'm an author. The publishing house expects the book to be a smash hit. I've already signed the contract for a follow-up—not that I have any idea what I'm going to write yet."

"I'm sure you'll think of something."

"Me too. And it's perfect. I get to work on my own all day. Sit in solitude and type. What better job for a girl who spent five years afraid of the outside world?"

"Just don't fall back into that pit," Melissa said. "You've made remarkable progress over the last few months. More than I ever expected. I'd hate to see you relapse."

"Don't worry," Tessa said. "That won't happen. But I doubt I'll ever be an extrovert. Not in this life."

"Good enough for me." Melissa pulled Tessa into a tight hug. She only released her when the phone rang.

Tessa picked it up and looked at the screen. "It's Roxanne."

"Then we'll leave you to it." Melissa retreated and followed Josh back toward the living room.

Tessa closed the bedroom door and answered. "Hey. I was thinking about you this morning."

"Great minds think alike. I was thinking about you too." Roxanne sounded upbeat. "Are you still up for a visit this week?"

"Looking forward to it," Tessa said. "I'm taking the last of my belongings over to the apartment right now. I've already set up the spare bedroom. It's waiting for you."

"Awesome. Can't wait to get there."

"Me either." Tessa and Roxanne had been talking on the phone almost every day, but it would be good to see her friend in person. Especially since Roxanne was considering a move off the island. Tessa hadn't broached the subject yet, but she was thinking about offering the spare bedroom to Roxanne permanently, if she wanted it. Not because she was afraid of being alone anymore, but because she hadn't had a friend in so long. But that conversation could wait until Roxanne arrived the following Wednesday.

"Hey. Still there?"

Tessa realized Roxanne was still talking and she had zoned out. "Yes. I was miles away. Sorry."

"You do that a lot. Must be a real three-ring circus inside your head."

"You have no idea." Tessa didn't mention that the ringmasters were Patrick and Noah. They still haunted her weakest moments. Those times when the old terrified and paranoid Tessa tried to reassert control. She wondered if they always would. But thankfully, those lapses were few and far between—and getting rarer. She really was changed, even if the journey to get there had been hard and almost deadly. For the first time in years, she saw a bright future for herself. She was even toying with the idea of going back to college part-time, finishing her degree. If not for herself, then for her friends who weren't lucky enough to escape Cassadaga Island alive. But not yet. She would go slow, enjoy the journey. There was time enough for that. Right now, Tessa was content to live in the moment, revel in her newfound freedom, and enjoy the life she thought had been taken from her forever.

ACKNOWLEDGMENTS

This novel started life in Los Angeles, where my wife (who is also my writing partner) and I were renting a West Hollywood garage-conversion guest suite for our honeymoon after tying the knot in Las Vegas. Sonya decided to take a shower one morning before we went out for the day and foolishly left me alone with my laptop. While I was sitting there, an idea popped into my head. A chapter about a young woman hiding under a bed while her friends were being murdered downstairs. I had no idea what the rest of the story would be, or even if there would ever be a story beyond those few pages.

When Sonya returned, I read the chapter to her, and she promptly asked if it was too soon for a divorce. Thankfully, we didn't get divorced. Instead, what became the prologue for this book sat on my hard drive for five more years while we talked about and rejected many story ideas. Then, finally, we hit upon what we thought was a winner, and that solitary chapter written in LA was an orphan no more.

But this book might still be languishing on our laptops if it wasn't for our wonderful agent, Liza Fleissig, who went the extra mile and found it the perfect home. Thank you, Liza. We are forever grateful for your enthusiasm, support, and advice.

A big thank you also to our acquiring editor, Alison Dasho, at Thomas & Mercer, who saw the potential in Tessa Montgomery's journey to Cassadaga Island and gave it wings.

Thanks also to Charlotte Herscher, our fantastic developmental editor, who made the story so much better with her insightful suggestions and observations. We feel truly lucky to have such talent on our team.

Thanks to our copyeditor, Amanda, and proofreader, Jill, who both did a stellar job.

Thank you to everyone at Thomas & Mercer, who have worked tirelessly on cover design, layout, marketing, and production.

We would also like to thank our good friends Lisa Herrington and Cat Blyth, who read early drafts of this novel and gave their candid advice.

Finally, we would like to thank our readers, without whom none of this would have been possible!

ABOUT THE AUTHORS

A.M. Strong is a British-born writer living and working in the United States. He has worked as a graphic designer, newspaper journalist, artist, and actor. He currently resides most of the year on Florida's Space Coast, where he can watch rockets launch from his bedroom balcony, and part of the year on an island in Maine, along with his wife and two furry bosses, Izzie and Hayden. A.M. Strong also writes under the pen name Anthony M. Strong.

Sonya Sargent has a degree in design; a passion for anything dogs, travel, and the arts; and a love for reading and cooking. She is from Vermont, but now splits her time between the coast of Florida and an island in Maine, along with her husband and two adorable rescue mutts.

For more information, visit amstrongauthor.com.